Knight's End

ANN DENTON

Le Rue
Publishing

Le Rue Publishing
320 South Boston Avenue, Suite 1030
Tulsa, OK 74103
www.LeRuePublishing.com

ISBN: 978-1-951714-00-0

To magical laughter and happily-ever-afters...

Gitmore

Sedara

Isles of Peth

the
KE

CHAPTER ONE

e stood on the hill outside the cave, in a sea of dead Raslen soldiers, and stared at one another silently as a gentle pink dawn swept over us. But the light did nothing to combat the dark reality we faced.

Connor, my best friend since childhood, swallowed hard when his worried blue eyes met mine. I longed to brush back his tangled brown curls and tell him that everything would be okay. But that would be a lie.

Blue's words echoed in my head. Human. My knights were human.

I looked at Declan, my Sedarian knight. His face was pale and drawn. All his life, his magic had been sought after, prized, treasured. He'd been sent to our kingdom to help protect my sister, to help seal the alliance between Evaness and Sedara via marriage. And now, my sweet, magical scholar was facing the possibility that he might be human.

How the hell could we end a magical war without magic?

The sea crashed into the rocks behind us, reminding me of the dangers lurking beneath its waters. We had already been outnumbered. We had two countries on either border targeting us. Queen Isla and Sultan Raj were bound and determined to remove Sedara's control of the sea and wipe out my country, Evaness, in the process. The sea witch they'd recruited had stolen my only sister and now, the three of them were on a warpath.

With three different types of magic—wishes, the giants' strength, and sea magic—against us, our half-human country was outnumbered and outmagicked.

I looked at my general. Ryan stood ramrod straight, his head and shoulders rising above my other men. He was part-giant, a true warrior full of grace and brutal strength. His proud soldier's posture contrasted his face, which was dark, his brow furrowed as he chewed on his thick lips. Even he must have been thinking how desperate our situation was.

My heart sank. What little hope we had was lost.

Sard. Even as I had that thought, I quashed it. I smoothed my features and scanned my men's faces; they were devastated enough. I couldn't let them see any disappointment. I couldn't add to their misery. And they were clearly miserable.

Quinn hadn't sent me a single thought, not a joke, not a quip, since Blue had made his declaration. That alone told me that my quiet spy master was brooding. He ran a hand through his jet-black hair, tucking it behind his slightly pointed half-elf ears. He paced near me, like a trapped animal.

The only one of my knights who didn't appear quite as upset was Blue. I turned to stare at my newest knight, a half-djinn I'd once thought was my enemy. His dark brown hair and skin were smooth, his forehead unwrinkled.

"You seem to be taking this discovery well," I said.

Blue shrugged and the Raslen soldier's shirt he'd donned slipped down, revealing several of the tattoos on his chest. "I've always known I only had three wishes. That once they were gone, I'd be basically human."

I nodded. He'd had to mentally prepare for this reality all his life. Whereas my other husbands hadn't. My eyes roamed again.

Declan pursed his lips and looked down at his hands, hiding his ice blue eyes. But my blond knight flexed his fingers as if he were testing them, trying to get them to emit a magical light and prove Blue's statement wrong. Ryan rubbed the back of his neck as he stared, unblinking, at the dead bodies around us. Quinn just kept pacing. Connor gazed out at the sea, avoiding eye contact.

My knights, my poor knights … I had spent so many years avoiding my magic, repressing it. But they'd used theirs on a daily basis to strengthen Evaness and protect it. Without it … I wasn't sure what we would do. I was torn. Comforting them would show pity instead of confidence in them.

Should I go to them or not? I wondered.

Desperately, I turned to Cerena. My castle mage stood slightly off to the side, giving us a respectful amount of space as we mourned the loss of their magic. Her silver hair was a frizzed, matted mess from the flight we'd taken on our way to this deathly cave, but she gave me a thin smile as I approached her.

I asked, "When will Donaloo be back? Do you know of any spells to restore power? Did he say anything?"

The old woman just wrinkled her brow and shook her head. "I don't know exactly when he'll be back. He took off with the dragon and that boy. He didn't say where he was going." Her hand flew up and gestured toward my knights. "I've never heard of this happening. The only place I can think to look it up is in the mage's books back at the castle."

The castle. Shite. It was still frozen. And likely, under further attack.

As the sea started to thrash more violently against the rocks behind us, I turned to my husbands. "We need to do what we can back at the castle. We'll figure this out." I tried to keep my voice strong, confident. I tried to channel mother's courtier voice.

My job was to hold us together. My job was to find a way through. My job was to lead them through the blackness into light. I had no idea how the sarding hell I was gonna do that. But I'd find a way. I had to find a way.

My expression hardened and I said, "Look at me." They each turned reluctantly, and I waited until every set of eyes was boring into mine. Then I said, "You swore an oath to protect Evaness. My fathers were human. And they did a damned good job of it. So, don't go thinking you're off the hook."

Connor at least made an effort to smile for me—but the others still held devastation in their faces. I knew magic was an integral part of them. This loss would be hard, like the loss of a limb. I tried a different approach and eased my tone. "It could be worse. The magic could have brought you back without dicks."

That did earn a reluctant chuckle. I jerked my head toward Evaness. "Without the wizard, I suppose we'll have to walk, unless we can confiscate any mounts from the dead soldiers."

Ryan shook his head. "They all ran off. I think the walking trees might have been a bit much for them."

I smiled in relief, if he was up for mockery, that was a good sign. I had no doubt that we had a long, dark road ahead of us, both literally with the war, and within each of their minds … but humor gave me hope.

We set off walking through the trees, our pace steady but not quite fast. We were all worn down. I flitted from knight to knight, trying to keep their spirits up—or, at least, keep them from sinking too far down—distracting them with discussions of what we might do when we returned to the castle, about how we needed to send messages to each of the provinces, how we needed to send militias to the borders. I tried to keep them talking, keep their minds focused on anything but the loss of their magic. I couldn't tell how successful I was, because each time I would turn to another knight, the last one I'd spoken with grew quiet and somber again.

Clouds roamed overhead like fat white cows, grazing on blue sky, eating it up until their swollen bellies covered the sun. The wind picked up, and a storm seemed imminent. Dammit.

Rain fell in fat, round drops and within an hour, we were trudging through muddy roads, without a single shelter in sight.

Quinn gave a huge, exaggerated sigh. *We should never have trusted the wizard to bring us here.* He sent us all mental pictures of Donaloo and the dragon, holed up in a nice warm cave, the dragon sending a thin stream of fire toward a rabbit Donaloo had speared on a stick. Donaloo held the stick up and he and the dragon then alternated bites, and behind them—out of nowhere, a string quartet appeared and started playing a romantic waltz. Donaloo's unpatched eye fluttered flirtatiously.

I laughed, but my laugh turned into a cough and Quinn cut off his mental entertainment. Connor came over and checked on me, because what I'd thought was a mere cough started to hurt when I couldn't stop it. Ryan came over and pressed his hands on me, forgetting for a moment he didn't have power. When his pink light didn't show, he cursed.

"Sarding hell!" His hands fisted and he stomped off, smacking a tree branch out of his way. His arm was so strong that the branch cracked and fell, nearly braining Blue.

Blue yelped and jumped back, but when Ryan turned to apologize, Blue said, "I'm okay!"

My coughing eased after another minute, but Ryan's face stayed angry, even when I came and slipped my hand into his.

Tensions were high as we continued our journey.

Declan slipped in a puddle a few minutes later and landed with a splash. Mud splattered his face, painting him like an Appaloosa horse.

This is shite, Quinn thought, as he yanked on Declan's arm to help his fellow knight out of the mud. Quinn sent us all a mental image of a squadron of gargoyles. *Wouldn't it be nice if a whole fleet of gargoyles just appeared? It would be like your mother sarding had in the last Fire War.*

"I wish," Ryan muttered.

Me too, I wish we—

Quinn's thought cut off as the sky went black. At first, I thought the storm clouds had grown thicker. But then trees broke around us, branches cracking and falling; the ground vibrated as a hundred different obsidian stones hurtled toward the ground and landed in the mud. We ran, trying to avoid them—were Isla or Raj using a catapult? Had they discovered us? Were they launching stones with spells?

We ran, going this way and that—down hills, through streams—but we couldn't get away. No matter how deep into the forest we fled, the rocks kept chasing. A spell, then. No catapult had such range. Perhaps the sultan had come for us. Was he angry that I'd freed Blue?

My chest and calves burned as I tried to suck in enough air to keep pushing.

There was no escape. Once the stones began to land in front of us and cut us off, Ryan held out a hand and halted our progress. We ended up in a huddle in a bit of meadow, and all around us stones as tall as my giant, pelted the land, creating huge divots.

My heart beat frantically in my chest as we formed a small circle. I latched onto Declan's arm and Blue's, the knights on either side of me. We clung to one another, no one bothered to hide their fear. Goodbyes formed in our eyes and leaked down our cheeks, even as I struggled to find some way to get us out of this impossible situation. I was the only one left with innate magic. But peace didn't work on stones. Cerena's hedgewitchery was no use. Her potions couldn't stop boulders from falling from the sky.

I moved my eyes from knight to knight as another stone fell two feet in front of us. Sard. Was this it? The end? This soon? We hadn't even had a chance—

The boulder in front of us rolled closer, and an awful screech filled the air. Suddenly, massive wings erupted from either side of the stone. A face formed in the side of the rock; it resembled an etching with two glowing yellow eyes. The face erupted from the rock slowly, a rasping, scraping noise filling my ears as the etching became three-dimensional. The monstrous face pushed itself into existence and then stretched its neck. Two twisted horns crowned its head, and the glowing amber eyes blinked, lighting up a wide nose and a mouth with two tusks shooting upward, grazing its cheeks. A gargoyle stared at me as its arms and legs erupted beneath it.

"Holy sarding hell," Connor whispered.

I glanced at my knights, but barely had time to look at them before the awful screeching surrounded us and wings popped out of every stone that had fallen from the sky. My hands flew to protect my ears. We all stood and stared, with our hands as muffs, while gargoyles sprang into existence all around us.

The fear that had churned in my stomach lifted, and awe took its place.

"What the sard is happening?" Ryan asked.

It was Blue who reached over and squeezed my arm to get my attention. I turned away from the sight of a hundred gargoyles growing legs to see what he wanted. Blue's hand

9

went to Quinn's shoulder and he turned the other knight to face us.

Quinn's face was pale. His eyes were wide. And unlike the rest of us, who wore a mixture of confusion, relief, and astonishment in our expressions, Quinn's face was terrified. His grey eyes met mine and his lips opened and closed.

"Quinn?" I reached for him. He grabbed my shoulders and stared at me desperately. His eyes squinted and his face scrunched, but he didn't say anything. Didn't send me any silly images. "Quinn?" I asked again.

He shoved my hands up to his forehead and put his face closer to mine. The desperation in his eyes started to scare me.

"Quinn, what is it?" I whispered.

His only response was to throw his head back and scream at the sky; a wretched, broken sound erupted from his unused vocal chords.

I leaned to the side to stare at my other knights. Ryan looked horrified. Declan had tears in his eyes and he clasped his hands in front of his chest—as though Quinn's sadness was too heartbreaking for him to bear. Connor looked pensive. I turned to Blue, the first knight to somehow notice Quinn's behavior.

"What's going on?" I asked, as I pulled Quinn into me for a hug. His cold, wet arms enveloped me. My poor silent knight clutched at me desperately and I tried to reassure him by running my hand up and down his spine.

Blue's deep brown eyes were solemn as he gazed down on me. "I think I may have been wrong. At least about some things. I think Quinn somehow came back with djinni powers. I think what he and Ryan wished for came true."

My mind felt as though it had been dropped like one of the black boulders that had transformed in front of me. My brain felt as though it had smashed into the ground at high speed. Everything I'd thought was true … wasn't. The new reality I'd started to accept, that my knights had no powers … was that wrong?

I stared beyond Quinn's shoulders at the massive gargoyles. They blinked, but otherwise stood still and silent, as though they were awaiting orders. But whose? Were they waiting to attack? Or was Blue right?

Cerena cleared her throat. "Might as well test that theory, no?"

Ryan was the first to act, his military training sending him out of our huddle to stand in front of the foremost gargoyle. "By order of the General of her Majesty, Queen Bloss of Evaness, you will stand at attention."

The gargoyles' wings snapped into his sides and he straightened. But he must have been standing off balance, because that tipped the beast forward and he face-planted in the mud. Ryan barely jumped out of the way in time. The gargoyle scrambled back up to standing.

Sard it all. My jaw dropped. My eyes scanned the stone beasts. There had to be at least a hundred of them. A hundred stone giants who could repel most spells, fly without getting tired, who could use their bodies to break down castle walls.

We'd gone from hopeless to fierce in a single instant. Evaness had a chance. We had a chance. I gave a sigh that was half disbelief and half relief. Tears filled my eyes and I hugged Quinn tighter to me. But he didn't share my joy. In my arms, Quinn still shuddered, his face buried in my neck. I stroked his hair and glanced back at Blue.

"His price is a living nightmare," my new knight reminded me.

Horror flashed like lightning through me.

I put my hands on either side of Quinn's face and pulled him up to meet my gaze. His red-rimmed eyes stared at me.

Quinn? I asked in my mind.

He didn't answer.

I imagined a little squirrel on his shoulder, shaking its tail in his face.

He didn't respond.

I gave a sob and smashed Quinn back into my chest, wrapping myself around him.

My knight. My poor silent knight.

He'd given us a chance in this war. But he'd lost the only means of communication he'd ever had. Even the magic beads from Donaloo couldn't overcome the price of wish magic.

Quinn was stuck inside his own head. Alone.

CHAPTER TWO

*C*onnor was the first of my knights to come
forward and embrace Quinn. One by one my
other husbands did the same, even Blue.

I was touched to see them show their support, their solidarity. But at the same time, I was sick to my stomach
for him.

Once my knights had hugged him, I made my way over. I
stared into his eyes for a long moment, then rose up on
my tiptoes and said, "I love you, husband." I pressed a soft
kiss against his lips. Slowly, that kiss turned into more
and my hands sneaked up to wrap around Quinn's neck.
Quinn put his hands on my waist.

Behind us, someone started up a whispered chant. "Dip
her. Dip her." Soon enough, all of my idiots had joined in.

I could feel Quinn's smile grow as we kissed and suddenly
my head was falling backward. He dipped me so low my

hair brushed the mud. Then he pulled me up and released me.

Quinn nodded to the group in thanks, but I could still see the devastation swimming in his eyes. He'd never told me much about his childhood or the years before Donaloo had gifted him with the beads, but I knew he adored the wizard, and that the beads had changed his life significantly. By the way he stared off in the distance, ignoring the gargoyles, I knew this living nightmare tugged at his soul. And that made my heart ache. I couldn't imagine what it would be like to feel like you were trapped in your body, unable to reach out or voice your pain.

I looked to Cerena, but she shook her head. "I know no way to counter it."

I slid my hand through Quinn's. "We'll find a solution," I told him softly.

He nodded, but his eyes wouldn't meet mine. He didn't seem to believe me.

Blue stepped forward, wringing his hands. "I'm sorry, Quinn. For what happened. I don't know how it did. But the nightmare, it's not forever. It's temporary, just like any nightmare."

My heart swelled. I whirled to stare at my newest knight. "How long?"

He shrugged. "It depends. The bigger the wish, the longer the nightmare."

Declan asked, "How large would you rate this wish?"

Blue's deep brown eyes flicked over the gargoyles that surrounded us. "It's not the largest wish I've seen come true, but it's pretty massive. I'd guess the nightmare might last several days. A week even."

Quinn's shoulders sunk.

We all stared out at the gargoyles for a minute, their eyes unblinking. How did Quinn get wish magic? How did these gargoyles come to be? I was utterly thankful he'd wished for gargoyles, because any other winged animals would have been chaos. These stone giants simply sat awaiting orders.

Declan cleared his throat, drawing everyone's attention. "Does anyone else think … that it's possible that our powers didn't completely go away?"

His words were a punch to the gut and a bird taking flight in the same moment—shock and hope. My mind reeled and wistfulness fluttered in my stomach. Was that possible? Could some remnant of power still surround my men?

Blue responded first, with a shake of his head. "A wish won't let you bring someone back the same—"

"I know that. But Quinn's magic isn't the same. He's never had djinn power before. How did Quinn get wishing powers? I think the magic transposed our powers. I think *that* was the change it wrought. I suspect *he* has *your* powers." Declan's words were sunlight piercing a cloudy sky.

17

Yes, please, my mind whispered. Let him be right. Let it be true.

I had never wished for anything as much as I wished for this.

Quinn's gaze turned from the distance; he focused on Declan's pale face. Then Quinn and Blue exchanged a startled glance.

Declan tapped his lips in thought and then said, "Quinn, see how fast you can run."

My knight released my hand and stepped back, staring down at his feet and lifting them, as though testing his own weight. Quinn started off at a normal jog through the mud, the splatter coating his calves. But then, suddenly, out of nowhere, he disappeared—leaving nothing but a spray of mud behind him.

My heart leapt. Yes! Hope, happiness, relief swept through me like a flood, nearly taking my feet out from under me.

Seconds later, my spy master returned, a triumphant smile on his face as he stopped right in front of Declan. My blond knight was hit by a jet of mud that reached all the way to his nose.

Declan grinned, and immediately started choking on mud. He wiped his mouth and spat. But he didn't mention the mud. His relief was evident as his hand went over his heart. "Thank goodness. There's still magic."

Quinn clapped Declan on the shoulder, a grin on my silent knight's face.

Blue said, "Check your pockets for a ring. If you're a part-djinni, you'll have a ring."

Quinn patted his pockets and removed a simple black ring with a small diamond on it. He stared at it and blinked for a moment, then handed it to me.

"Why don't you keep—" I said.

But Quinn shook his head and closed my fingers around the ring. I slid it on my thumb, surprised when it fit perfectly.

"Be careful with that. If someone else gets ahold of it, they can make wishes and he'll have to grant them," Blue warned.

"Can anyone just take it?" I closed my fingers into a fist, alarmed.

Blue wavered his hand in the air. "Physically, yes. They could take it from you. Magically, the ring is tied to you. So, if you mean—can it be wished away? The answer to that is no."

Ryan took a step forward and his deep baritone was hushed as he asked, "Does that mean that the rest of us have powers?"

Everyone glanced around the circle.

Connor ran a hand through his very messy dark curls. "I haven't felt anything since we've been brought back, but in all honesty, I don't know what any of your powers feel like. I've always been so overwhelmed with emotion that everything now feels … empty. As if I were completely alone."

Blue jumped in. "I can't tell if anything is different, because everything is different for me. With these beads, I'm constantly hearing everyone's thoughts and it's just a constant barrage of military formations and worries about the castle, and which spells to use—"

"Which spells to use? Who's been thinking about what spells to use?" I interrupted, scanning faces.

Cerena slowly raised her wrinkled hand. Her eyes darted from me to Blue. "I was trying to think of a spell that might help any of them." My castle mage shrugged, her sagging eyes keen. "I haven't come up with anything, though."

My eyes scanned the rest of my knights. "Can anyone else hear Cerena's thoughts?"

Everyone else shook their heads.

Quinn gestured to get our attention. He put his hand to his throat and drew it upward, like his hand was spilling out his mouth.

"Talk," Declan muttered. "That's true. How can you still talk?" He tilted his head and studied Blue.

Blue shrugged. "Am I not supposed to be able to?"

Ryan said, "Quinn has never been able to talk."

Declan's eyes narrowed. "I wonder … Blue, focus on Cerena's thoughts. Cerena, focus on a spell. Blue, try to recite it."

Blue turned and stared at Cerena as though she were a test that a tutor had set. His eyes widened; I could tell the moment he got the gist of her thoughts. And his mouth opened, but nothing came out. He opened wider. He beat at his chest, tried to clear his throat. He visually yelled, but not a drop of noise spilled from his lips.

Declan walked over to stand in front of Cerena, blocking Blue's view. "Stop reading her mind."

Blue squinted hard, but eventually, he straightened. He opened his mouth and at first, only the tiniest sound could be heard. But eventually, he was able to talk again. "What was all that?" he asked.

Quinn strode back over to Declan and threw his arms wide, his gesture shouting, "How is this possible?"

Declan glanced between the two men, thinking. I could almost see his mind whirling as he ran through the options. He held up a hand, as if telling both men to stay calm. "Now, this is just a theory. But, I wonder, because your power isn't innate for Blue, he wasn't born with it, if it takes effort for him to use it. And when he's not using it, it seems like he can speak. I mean, my power—my *old* power—didn't require constant reductions. I only had to reduce when I multiplied." He shook his head. "I'm not sure why I never thought of this before. I just always assumed some powers were absorbent versus creative and the absorbent powers were constant. No study has ever shown they could be turned off—"

Ryan interrupted, "But no one's ever switched powers before, have they?"

Declan shook his head. "No. Not that I've read. Perhaps the absorbent powers were only constant for you and Connor because you were born with them. And you didn't know that you could turn them off."

We all stood as we realized what that meant. But my heart gave a leap when I realized what that meant for Quinn. I rushed over to him and said, "This means you can speak!" I grabbed his hand and pressed it to my chest.

Quinn's jaw dropped.

Connor came over and put a hand on my shoulders. "It means he can learn to use his vocal chords, Bloss. But it will take practice. He's never spoken before."

Quinn opened his mouth and emitted what sounded like a moan. He was so surprised by the noise that he jumped.

But I jumped after him and threw my hands around his waist. I hugged him hard.

Connor just smiled. "I'm certain he'll get the hang of it and be insulting us all in no time."

Ryan piped up. "Yes. Connor's an expert at useless talking, Quinn can learn from the best."

Connor rolled his eyes but grinned at Quinn when my silent knight threw his arm around my best friend's shoulder.

Declan interjected. "Before we get off track onto subjects like talking … Blue has Quinn's powers and it seems that Quinn has Blue's."

If two of them had swapped, could my other knights have switched powers as well? "Someone else describe what your powers feel like, so we can see if they've transferred to someone else." I ordered.

"If anyone's feeling particularly emotional … I know today has been a trying day for all of us, but if you're feeling random bits of emotion, like you're being tugged in a thousand different directions at once … if your tongue tastes a bit funny—that's the mix of emotions, and when there are so many, it can be a bit like mud—"

Declan's hand immediately shot into the air.

Ryan tried to push Declan's hand down. "Quinn just made you eat mud."

Declan pulled his hand away and pushed it back up. "I know. But I tasted it even before it started raining. Emotionally, I just thought I was having a panic attack. I thought I was finally going off the deep end, or that my system was on the fritz from having died and come back. Thank the gods I'm not crazy." Declan threw his head back and laughed. "I don't know how you stand this all the time, Connor. It's sarding awful."

ANN DENTON

Connor shrugged. "I didn't have a choice."

"Did you ever get used to it?"

Connor wavered his hand side to side. "Sort of."

"Ever like it?"

They shared a long look, and I felt awful as I realized how much Connor had truly hated his own power. He'd never outright said it to me. I hadn't ever asked.

He said, "Sorry. In time, you get used to it. You start to sort out whose emotions are whose, and eventually, even kind of decide which emotions are actually yours."

Declan shook his head. "Does it always taste bad?"

Connor shrugged. "I think spite has kind of a black licorice tinge."

"What about joy?"

"Being around Bloss always tasted like raspberries to me. So, if you like raspberries ..."

Declan waggled his brows. "I definitely like raspberries." Then he pitched his head back and laughed. "This is the worst power in the history of the universe. And I have it." He declared between bouts of laughter that grew steadily louder until he was doubled over and gasping, clutching his ribs.

I stepped forward and grabbed his arm. "Dec?"

He started to cough again. But he didn't stop laughing. He laughed and coughed in fits, until Ryan started smacking his back. "Are you choking?"

Declan tittered, "I think … it tastes … like powdered … sugar."

I turned to Connor, filled with alarm. "Is he okay?" Connor had never reacted this way, ever.

Connor nodded. "I think the giddiness we are all feeling—the hope that we might actually still have some sort of power, some sort of usefulness—might be getting to him."

Connor's prediction turned out to be true. Only seconds later, Declan started to jump up and down in the mud, splashing all of us until we backed away. "I feel so happy!" he crowed.

"Well, you look like a nutter," Ryan scolded, but he was smiling. My giant clapped his hands together. "So, Declan got Connor's powers. If there were three powers left, the three of us couldn't do a one-for-one swap like Quinn and Blue. So that would mean, if the wish switched our powers. Aw, shite. I have Declan's powers."

"Hey! My powers were amazing!" Declan called from his jumping spot.

"It took you years to learn how to master your powers," Ryan shot back, covering his face with his hand. "Do you all remember how many rolls of parchment Declan went through making his lists of opposites?"

I bit my lip. As a teenager Declan had always been scribbling something on parchment. Always. We hadn't spoken much back then. I hadn't known what he'd been doing. But that made sense. He knew which rocks to switch, which crops to rotate, he had it all dialed down to a very precise sort of science.

He rolled his eyes. "Dec, what's the opposite of coriander?"

"Cilantro," Declan's jumping slowed. "But you cannot switch coriander to cilantro, you can only do the other way around."

"See—what the hell is that? How am I supposed to figure out the opposite of every stinking thing?"

"Ask me," Declan answered.

Ryan sighed. "Can I reduce this mud and get us some dry dirt?"

"Carefully. Keep your focus," Declan stated.

But Ryan had already stretched out his palm. Yellow light radiated from it.

Suddenly, my mouth felt dry as a bone. Because Ryan hadn't just taken the water out of the dirt, he'd taken it out of the very air around us. I was so parched that I started wheezing and coughing. Around me, everyone did the same.

"Shite!" Ryan tried to reverse the spell, which created a giant, suspended ball of water that slowly descended on us, choking us in an entirely different fashion. I sputtered as the water fell past my shoulders toward the ground, cupping my hands as it passed and bringing as much as I could to my lips to drink. My knights and Cerena did the same.

"Sard it all, sorry," my giant knight apologized. I think he blushed, but it was hard to tell, we were all so flush from the near drowning.

Connor looked at Ryan. "If you have Declan's powers, and he has mine, then I must have healing."

The scratch on my arm—the one I'd made to test Ryan's healing outside the cave—wasn't deep, but I shoved back my sleeve and held it out toward my best friend.

Connor stared at it pensively, then looked at Ryan.

"How do you—"

"I'd feel safer if you tested it on me," Ryan said, grabbing a small dagger and slicing his palm. "Think of this kind of shallow wound healing as a delicate process like sewing. It's about precision. You need the tiniest thread of magic, gather it in your palm and—"

Pink magic blasted out of Connor's hands, into all of us. My scratch instantly mended, but I was left dizzy and my tongue felt heavy.

"Whass happening?" I asked, my words slurred. I nearly lost my balance and had to grab onto Quinn to stay upright. My stomach churned.

Around me, no one looked much better. Cerena muttered under her breath, but my knights were all holding their heads.

"Too much," Ryan gritted out. "Too much healing is like an overdose of medicine. It can make you—"

Next to him, Declan doubled over and threw up. That made Ryan start to dry heave. Then Blue.

Quinn and I turned away before we were drawn into the cycle.

The gargoyles sat there still as stones, as unaffected by our puke as they'd been by our blasts of magic.

Cerena's muttering grew louder and she finished a spell, flicking her fingers as she walked and spitting at each of our feet.

As soon as she passed, I felt better. My head cleared and my stomach stopped roiling.

"Thank you," I mumbled. She nodded and moved to the next person.

Once she'd restored us all to normal, we walked a bit, leaving the puddle of sick, and going closer to our gargoyles. I leaned up against one's stiff back as my knights all caught their breath, recovering from Connor's accidental overdose.

"So, we all have new powers. And we're all shite at them. Promising," Connor murmured.

I tried to be encouraging. "It's better than what we thought an hour ago. That you had no powers at all."

Connor simply raised a brow as Ryan choked back another round of dry heaving. Cerena's spell must not have completely settled his huge body.

"Is it? Or is it just giving us false hope?"

I swallowed hard and pressed my lips together. I hoped what Connor said wasn't right. I hoped that my knights could learn their new powers quickly and adjust. That magic that had taken each of them years to master could somehow—magically—take only hours or days. Ugh. I was wishing for the impossible.

A roar interrupted my thoughts, and I glanced sharply to the side, eyeing the gargoyles. They stood as still and unmoving as ever, even the one I leaned against.

The bellow sounded again, and I glanced behind us through the trees. But nothing was there. It was only when Blue tapped my shoulder and pointed straight up that I realized where the sound was coming from. Isla's flying bears shot overhead. They were in perfect triangular wedge formation, an attack formation I'd studied many times with my mother. And the bears were headed straight toward our capital.

I stumbled through the mud toward the nearest gargoyle. I scrambled onto its back, scratching my hands in the process. "Fly." I commanded. "Take them down."

The creature flapped its wings and I rose into the sky. But not a single other gargoyle rose up with me. My own flying gargoyle didn't heed my second command. I pointed desperately toward the bears that were now receding in the distance, "Attack!"

My gargoyle did not spring forward. He continued to hover just above the tree line, letting me watch as the bears formed a diving formation and swooped downward into the Cerulean forest. Was that just at the border? I could only imagine the terror of my poor villagers.

Another gargoyle finally rose next to me, Ryan perched on its back. "They haven't been trained," he said.

I groaned in frustration. I had no idea how to train a gargoyle. My mother had only given orders. The training had been left to our beast master and our generals.

"What do we do?" I asked frantically. The bears were on their way. Our castle would be next, I was certain.

Ryan shook his head and struggled with his own mount for a moment. His gargoyle tended to list to the right, and he had to verbally correct it and then yank on its neck in order to get it to straighten out and hover at the same height as mine. "Most of our fleet of gargoyles were destroyed when I was a teen. Other than our two old gargoyles, who were already trained, I've never worked with them before. I never trained on gargoyle formations or battle techniques because it was always thought that wizards created the old gargoyles. We thought no one else had enough power to recreate them."

Sard. Ignorance was a blow I didn't need. My knights had powers they didn't know how to use, and now we had these beasts, these aerial stones that could act as both attack animals and turn back into boulders to act as huge projectiles. They were fire resistant, resistant to most magics, a boon. Quinn had suffered to give us one of the greatest aerial weapons possible. But not one of us knew how to use them.

I wanted to scream in frustration.

I have a kingdom to protect. How the sarding hell am I going to do that? I wondered.

My heart fell to the earth, as heavy as the stones that had made our gargoyles. Sarding magic. For all the good it did, I once again felt helpless.

CHAPTER THREE

e finally figured out how to fly. It took nearly three hours and it wasn't pretty. It also wasn't in any sort of combat formation. Isla's bears could have flown to the edge of Evaness by then. We had no hope of catching them. No hope of stopping them. We could only focus on what we could do at that moment—learn to fly. As Ryan pointed out, you could only win the battle at hand. You couldn't worry about things beyond your reach.

"The castle's frozen. The militias have been mobilized," he told me. "We need to do what we can to make the most of this opportunity. We need to get these gargoyles to fly."

Each of my knights straddled a beast and took turns taking off and falling off the stubborn creatures, most of whom refused to touch back down to the ground to let us dismount. We had to slide off and try not to face-plant in the slippery mud.

Connor did his best to heal whatever bruises he could under Ryan's coaching, but more often than not he created too much new skin, until we had raised, itchy, patchy sections of flesh. Cerena ended up with a raised patch on her chin that looked as thick as a mole. Declan started refusing healing altogether, stating that the bruises were preferable.

We coaxed the beasts like they were stubborn toddlers. They required constant direction, threats, and entice-ments. We pooled our knowledge of Evaness' old gargoyles, Shire and Hazilla. We had all ridden on them before, Declan sparingly, but those gargoyles had been trained extensively, ridden for nearly fifty years. Those gargoyles were like the best trained horses. They only needed a nudge to head in the right direction.

These new gargoyles had to constantly be reminded of their purpose, their mission, even which direction to head. Gestures alone didn't work to control them. We were all constantly muttering commands: "Forward, up, lean left." They were often distracted by things like clouds.

On a practice circle over the forest, my stupid shite of a gargoyle spotted a creek and attempted to barrel roll through it. With me on its back.

"Up!" I screeched, as soon as we surfaced, half-drowned by some shallow rapids. The water was ice-cold, even at midday, because winter was rapidly making its way toward the seven kingdoms.

After the creek incident, I decided newborn gargoyles were quite exhausting and exasperating.

Declan seemed to have the worst trouble with his mount. It appeared his gargoyle was lazy and didn't like to fly high. It was constantly skimming the trees with its wings.

Ryan wouldn't let anyone ride with me for security reasons. "Better if more of us can block and protect you," he said. So, I rode alone, though some of my knights doubled up. Quinn, since he had just discovered he could speak and couldn't yell himself raw commanding an idiot gargoyle, rode with Cerena. Blue, since his speech could be impaired by his new power at any moment if he listened to a thought, rode with Ryan.

Our five beasts put us through a battle of wills that made me swear I never wanted children the next time we took a break and sat.

I sat on a stump and wailed, "Magical infants are the worst. I'm never having any. Hear me now. None!"

My knights had only laughed at that.

Blue had said, "We can just give the kids away. Maybe as tournament prizes. 'Congratulations. Your skill with the sword has earned you a year of swaddling.'"

"No one would ever enter a tournament again," Ryan said.

"Good, then I'd never have to sit through another one," Declan contributed.

Connor said, "That's what nannies are for."

Declan added, "Or we can give the kids to foreign nations. Send them off for some treaty when they start throwing fits. That'll teach them." He joked, but there was a bitter undertone of reality to his words. He hadn't been a toddler throwing fits, but he'd been sent away by his mother, an embarrassing bastard child the Sedarians hadn't wanted to see. Of course, they'd sent him to protect Avia, too. But he hadn't known that. He'd only known he'd been sent off like some poor pig to slaughter.

My Declan had been hurt by that. It still hurt him. It ripped me to pieces to know that it still ate at him. I couldn't stand that. He was worth so much more. And knowing how he used to hurt himself, how much self-loathing he used to carry because of it—my hands curled into fists.

I clambered off my beast, fought sliding into a split in the mud pit, and went to him on his gargoyle. I held up my hands. He had to pull me up, because his gargoyle was a bit too tall for me to mount on my own.

Once I was seated behind him, I wrapped my arms around his waist, leaned my cheek against his back. I tried to picture our lovemaking in my mind, and how utterly and intensely adored he was. I tried to pull those emotions up so he could feel the truth of my words.

His hand settled around mine and squeezed when I said, "Nope. Never sending our kids off. That would be a very foolish thing to do. Our kid would probably be a genius. And grow to love that other kingdom so much that he felt like it was home instead. And he might just become a national treasure there, with his own holiday, and—"

"Excuse me, getting jealous over here," Blue called out. "How come I'm not a national treasure? And what's this holiday business? How do you get your own holiday? Do you all have holidays? I've got a shite parent, too." He sent us all a mental image of Sultan Raj and then opened his mouth to complain again, but nothing came out.

I laughed and sent him a mental image of himself wearing a jester's hat and saying, *Duh-oh, I forgot I can't talk.* His jester-self started dancing a jig, his long hair bouncing up and down on his shoulders.

He lifted his hand from his gargoyle's neck to shake a fist at me but laughed.

I gave Declan a quick squeeze and a kiss, before sliding down and going to sit in front of my new husband, who'd moved his gargoyle close.

I hated the thought of any of them feeling left out. Or jealous. Not when we needed to bond and work together— not when so much was at stake. I also got the added benefit that Blue was much better than I was at controlling his gargoyle during our practice flights. Or he had been before I climbed on with him, anyway.

When we took off for another round of flying, his movements were far more jerky.

I wondered if he was nervous. I was. Sitting in front of him made my stomach swoop with jitters just as much as

37

the rise and fall of his gargoyle did. I knew him, but I didn't. I knew his bird-self, a silly companion I'd grown fond of. But I didn't really know Blue—the man. Not compared to the knights that I'd known for years.

I think he felt nervous too, because though I felt his excitement as he grew against me, he carefully backed his hips away, like he was embarrassed.

I sent him a mental image of us kissing. Of his hand sliding into my shirt and cupping my breast.

He sent me one back of him yanking my shirt down to my waist, freeing my breasts, placing his mouth on my nipples.

A rush of heat went through me.

"Whoa!" Connor yelled from his gargoyle beside us. "Do you want us all to crash? Don't be sending those thoughts midair!"

I giggled, "Guess you thought-projected that to the whole group."

Dammit, Blue thought at me. *I wish I had a handle on this thought-talk thing. It's difficult.*

You'll get there.

Our naughty thought exchange ended, but I tried to get to know him a little, by asking questions as he tried to steer his stubborn gargoyle in a circle.

What is your favorite childhood memory?

Blue pictured the day he arrived at the barracks on the border, far from his father. I watched him look at his own youthful expression in the mirror when he arrived and placed his few belongings under a window. He'd been skinny then. He hadn't had much muscle tone or any tattoos—those clearly came from his time in the military. But his young face was still handsome with his thick black brows, straight nose, and thick lips. I had never pictured him without his beard, but his jawline was strong, with just a hint of stubble.

How old were you?

Sixteen.

Blue's thoughts from that memory rolled through both of us as his commanding officer arrived and he stood at attention. He was a disgraced prince, not powerful enough to inherit. He watched the judgement in the officer's eyes, tensing.

"Well, you're a skinny mite, we're gonna need to change that. But, no worries, you'll be prime pickings for the brothel ladies in no time. Just lay off Halea, she's mine. She tells you different, she's just trying to piss me off."

Blue's shock had been complete. But his memory of the hope and immediate fondness for his commanding officer shone through the memory.

"I'm here to work hard, sir," Blue had said.

"Good. You can go for a run, then meet me in the practice ring."

The memory faded.

I squeezed Blue's hand. *Thank you for sharing.*

Will ... would you mind sharing something? Blue's thoughts lacked the confident bravado of his words. His joking persona was gone, and inside, in his thoughts, I felt like I might be getting a hint of the real him, the insecure man beneath the mask of happiness.

I thought for a minute, deciding between memories. But ultimately I picked the first memory I had of Avia playing with me. I'd hovered over her cradle, trying yet another round of peekaboo. Her little brown hair had still had tiny baby curls at the end. Her little double chin had been adorable. And that day, that random day, I'd snuck into her nursery and away from my studies. I tried peekaboo for the millionth time— she'd been disinterested, or napping, or crying, every other time. But that day was the first time she giggled. My sweet little sister had laughed at me, and it had been a soul-stealing sound—that sweet, hiccup-sounding baby laughter.

Anyone who could hear that giggle and not fall immediately in love is a gargoyle, I thought at Blue.

You and your sister got along then?

I nodded. *I used to joke that Avia was my better half. The good sister. She's always been sweet and perfect. I was always a bit pig-headed. But she was so thoughtful. She used to give all the servants flowers on their birthday.*

I brought up a memory of that and showed Blue an eight-year-old version of my sister, skipping down the hall and giving a daffodil to a maid who was up on a stepstool, dusting a painting. The simple flower had brought tears to the woman's eyes.

I ... don't really know anyone like that, Blue admitted.

She's one of a kind, I thought longingly. My chest ached a bit for her. And while Blue couldn't feel my sadness, I guess I still projected my thoughts. My mind shifted to the last moment I'd seen her, when she'd been snatched by Blue's shapeshifting dragon brother, before being carried off into the sky.

His hands tightened on my waist.

Our conversation had made Blue lose a bit of concentration concerning his gargoyle, and we found ourselves floating high in the air above the rest. He turned his attention to our willful beast, and I turned my thoughts back to the impending war. We didn't speak again, but he did scoot a bit closer. And he didn't try to hide from me when the friction of riding and pressing against one another naturally made him hard.

When we took a break, he helped me off the gargoyle with a shy smile. "Thank you."

I leaned forward and pecked him on the cheek, a tingle running through my toes. "No, thank you."

We'd joined the others and sat on a fallen tree trunk, debating what we should do next.

"Clearly, these beasts aren't what we hoped," Declan was brutally honest. "I don't think we can defend the castle in any meaningful way with them yet. Not until they're trained."

"Would anyone know how to train them?" I asked.

"Jace might," Ryan responded. Our castle's beast master was an old grizzled man. And he had been around since childhood, so perhaps he did know.

"Someone should go for him," Connor said. "Bring him here."

"You want to split up?" Cerena asked.

"I don't want Bloss exposed to whatever attack is going on there. If we bumble in on five of these monsters," Connor gestured at our mounts, "we aren't going to be effective at protecting her."

"Agreed," Ryan said. "I'll go."

Blue piped up. "Actually, I've been thinking. The sea witch, fairy woman ..."

"Sea sprite," Cerena piped up. "That monster, by the sound of it, is a sea sprite. Nasty creatures. At least they have the decency to be rare." She grumbled as she hauled over a flat rock and set it on the tree trunk. She grabbed a pouch at her hip, opened it, pulling out a small tin jar the size of her palm. She yanked at the tiny handle on the lid to open it, and sprinkled a powder from inside onto the stone. She muttered a spell over it. We paused our conversation to watch. Soon, she'd magicked up six small, dense loaves of bread.

Blue grabbed his too soon, burning his fingers. "Ah!"

Cerena chided, "You couldn't wait another minute?"

"This is the first food I've had in human form in weeks!" he protested.

"Ah, well then," she waved him on. "Go on."

Blue took a bite and sighed like he'd gone to heaven. "Amazing."

Everyone chuckled as they took their own loaf. Even Quinn.

His chuckle was a soft, breathy matter. Hearing it made me scoot closer and bump him with my shoulder. I leaned up and whispered in his ear. "I can't wait until you learn to say my name."

His eyes shone back down at me, full of everything he would say if he could.

I pecked his cheek and then took another bite of bread.

Connor leaned forward in his spot and asked Blue, "What did you want to say about that sea sprite?"

"Well, she thinks she killed Bloss, right? Because Declan looked like her at the time. So … if she's told her allies, then my father and Rasle's queen—"

"Isla," I supplied the old vulture's name.

Blue turned his clever gaze on me. "They all think you're dead. I just wonder … how can we use that to our advantage?"

Quinn leaned forward, his first attempt to participate in the group conversation. His eyes were alight as he drew a slow, steady finger across his neck.

Watching that made my heart pound faster in my chest.

"Exactly," said Blue. His tone grew more excited as he and Quinn stared at one another. "If Ryan goes and gets the beast master ... can the rest of us come up with a target and a plan?"

A wicked, naughty grin spread across Quinn's face. And for the first time since we'd thought he was human, the first time since his living nightmare had hit him, I felt like I had my spy master back.

"Well, we are in Rasle," Declan contributed. "Isla would be the easiest natural target."

Quinn gave a sharp nod.

Connor argued. "She's going to have herself well-protected."

"From what?" asked Blue.

"Sedara's still a force to be reckoned with," Declan contributed. "If they didn't think my mother was a threat, they wouldn't have united."

Blue reclined against a fallen log. "That's true. But we haven't seen any sign of Sedara. No ships. No elves. They have some gargoyles of their own. Why haven't they come? And then, the three rulers leading this—how united are they? How much do they trust one another?"

I watched my newest knight as he considered the possibilities. His eyes were sharp and calculating. "My father trusts no one. Even those who owe him wishes, whose families he could devastate with that wish."

I'd long heard of how twisted Sultan Raj was. But Cerena hadn't. Growing up in the Cerulean Forest, away from politics, she didn't know just how heartless the monarchs around us could be.

"Come again?" she asked.

I leaned forward to explain, but Blue beat me to it. "My father loves when peasants can't pay their taxes. He accepts a wish in place of payment. And his favorite punishment—should anyone in that family upset him, is to call in that wish. He forces the family member who gave him the wish to wish evil things upon the others."

Cerena sucked in a breath. "Like what?"

"Can't wish death on someone. But lost limbs is a favorite. Barrenness."

Cerena stared down at her bread and shook her head. "Awful."

Declan said, "I think we need to get our focus back on Isla. As awful as Raj is, he's not the closest possibility, if we're going to try what I think you're suggesting."

"Agreed. Focus on Isla. But how can we figure out where she is?" I asked. Quinn couldn't talk to his spy network, which he thought had been compromised anyway. What could we do?

"I could see her if I had a scrying stone," Cerena shook her head regretfully.

Connor held up a hand. "Hold on. I studied our maps extensively for her recent visit. And we've flown past Rasle's lone river—" He stood up and glanced around us at the hills to our north, then he pointed inland. "If I'm not mistaken, I think there used to be a hedgewitch lodge just east of here."

"Used to be?" I asked.

"Supposedly, it hasn't been used since the last Fire War," he responded.

Cerena nodded. "Many of us have refused to gather since then. Too dangerous. Too tempting for someone to erase the local magic in one fell swoop."

I looked over to her. "Will they have what you need?"

She shrugged. "It's likely been ransacked, but scrying stones are heavy. Maybe."

I eyed my husbands. "Worth a try."

Ryan was the only one who looked uncomfortable with the arrangement. He walked over to me and extended his hand. I stood and he led me away, weaving through some pine trees, so that we had a little bit of privacy.

The smell of dry pine wrapped around me as Ryan's deep eyes seemed to drink me in. "I don't like the idea of being separated," his voice was a low rumble.

His words pinched my heart. But emotion and reality were two separate things. We both knew it.

He took my hand and his giant fingers stroked my palm.

I enjoyed the sensation, and let his fingers circle my wrists, then trap them, push them to my right side as he stepped in and leaned down for a kiss. His lips pressed hard on mine. His tongue plundered my mouth and desire surged through me. Ryan always had the ability to make my body melt in pleasure at the slightest touch.

But Ryan didn't press further. He ended our kiss with a rough nip and pressed his forehead down to mine.

I sighed. "I don't like the idea of separation either," I admitted. "But we need to act quickly. Those gargoyles … if we could control them easily, think what we could do. Right now, Evaness is too vulnerable."

He straightened and nodded. "I know. We have to. I don't like it, though. I don't like the idea of you being in danger."

I shrugged. "We're in a war now. We're all in danger." Even so, the idea of Ryan flying alone made me cringe. "If anyone attacks you, suck the water right out of the air like you did earlier—they won't be able to see clearly, much less think."

He laughed gruffly. "Neither will I."

"Declan," I called out.

My blond scholar trotted toward us dutifully. Out of all my men, he wore soldier's garb the worst. Used to soft boots and pants, he was already limping from the rough, poorly made boots. And I had no doubt he hated the dark blue leather armor that Isla had her cavalry wear. My own outfit was hot and sticky, even with the chill of winter and the hint of sea wind in the air.

"Can you help Ryan learn enough about your power in ten minutes to kill a few people?"

"Ten minutes?" Declan's eyes nearly bulged out of his face.

"Yes. Because the sooner he gets Jace, the sooner the gargoyles get trained, the sooner we can beat down these sarding shites attacking us."

Declan walked over to Ryan.

"Ten minutes. The rest of us need to head to that lodge."

Declan swallowed hard and nodded. "We're going after Isla, then?"

I smiled, the old queen's sharp features coming to mind as I thought of ending her. "We're sure as hell gonna try."

And I left my knights to it as I walked back to the rest of the group.

We had a murder to plan.

CHAPTER FOUR

*R*yan wouldn't agree to take Connor with him, though I tried to insist.

"You're headed into battle," I argued.

"You're headed into the unknown. To attempt assassination."

"You don't have healing anymore. You need the healer. You can't just—"

"Declan's taught me enough."

I raised a brow.

He simply raised his as he stared down at me. And that attraction between us grew. It flickered like fireflies. And then like a candle's flame. Ryan took a step toward me, and the draw between us heated, like a fire newly stoked. Hot coals turned over inside me. He roughly grabbed my hair and pulled back slightly, hurting just the tiniest bit. His dark chocolate eyes were molten as he stared down at me, radiating command and confidence. "You're *my* queen. And you'll do what I say."

My knees went to jelly at those words.

I swallowed hard against my attraction and my tears. "Yes, sir."

He leaned down and scooped me up, giving me a harsh kiss. His tongue dove into my mouth, owning it, ensuring my submission. Once he felt me grow soft and compliant, once my arms looped over his broad shoulders and sought to bring his body tighter against mine, he abruptly dropped me into Quinn's arms.

He stared down at my spy master and used the tone of voice he used on his soldiers. "Use that speed. Scout ahead. Keep her safe."

Quinn nodded.

And with that, my giant mounted up, cursed his stone beast, and took to the sky.

We left the majority of the gargoyles behind. I ordered those that remained to return to rock formation until Evaness soldiers could return to ride them. They'd surprisingly obeyed that order without hesitation or difficulty. Perhaps they were naturally inclined to laziness. Or … naptime? In any case, the beasts dutifully rolled themselves back up into balls, like little stone pill bugs, their etched features fading back into ebony boulders. I could only hope that the gargoyles had a better attention span for sleeping than they seemed to have for flying.

Ryan had flown southeast, toward our capital, Marscha. The rest of us flew due east, along the hills that separated Cheryn and Rasle, the two countries warring against us.

Fear pricked at my neck the entire journey. I was on high alert for bears, giants, djinn. There weren't many creeks or large waterways in these parts, so I was less worried about the sea witch. When Connor, who took the lead, started cursing and kicking his gargoyle into a descent, I was relieved. I realized that I'd feared an aerial fight. Our toddler-level flying skills would be no match for any creature—even a pegasus—in battle.

We flew down toward a stone lodge that was set in a dead meadow. The flowers and grasses looked as withered and stooped as old women. Clearly, the area had been through a drought. Everything was a pale tan. We fought to get our gargoyles to land. Mine did so reluctantly, and I slid into the crunchy, dead grass.

Blue's gargoyle tipped him sideways, rather than touch down in a field. Instead, the beast tilted until Blue slid off, cursing. He accidentally sent us all thoughts of taking a sledgehammer to his gargoyle.

He's just a baby, I scolded, teasingly.

He's a magic sarding rock. In Cheryn, he wouldn't last half a second before someone wished his will away. Blue brushed dust and dead grass out of his hair.

They can do that? Wish away someone's will?

Why do you think we all became animals? Under threat, it's better than becoming mindless zombies. We let that wizard transform us rather than let my father wish some worse fate upon us.

An image of his father popped up in Blue's mind. I saw Sultan Raj, sitting on a jeweled throne, laughing viciously as he made four poor old men dance as if they were nubile young girls. One man's hip went out and he fell to the floor. The crack echoed throughout Blue's thoughts. But the old man climbed back to his feet and continued to dance, favoring his good leg.

Blue scrubbed at his face as though he wanted to erase the memory.

I walked over and slid my hand through his. I gave a little squeeze. "Royal parents can be … unkind." I tried to be diplomatic.

He stared down sadly at me and shook his head. *Your mother was kinder than most.*

Images flooded my mind. A whip. A chain. A dish of food set on the floor just out of reach. The harsh voice of the sultan as he said, *"Transform, boy! No heir of mine—"*

Blue squeezed my fingers and tried to stop projecting his thoughts. *Sorry. I didn't mean to send that.*

No, don't be sorry. I want to know you. I want to know—

No one wants to know that.

And with that, my newest knight turned and pulled me toward the rest of the group, effectively ending our conversation.

But I wouldn't let go of his hand. I held onto Blue, twining my fingers tightly with his as we walked toward the low-roofed stone structure where hedgewitches used to meet.

Quinn ran around and then inside it, a blur so fast that I had to blink to be sure it was him. He gave us an all-clear signal before we headed inside.

When we walked into the lodge, it was clear it had been abandoned for a long time. Pieces of thatch were missing from the roof, allowing weaker shafts of winter sunlight to drift down and make the floor a patchwork of light. The rushes on the floor were dark and covered in dust and mouse droppings.

Declan recoiled. "Ugh. Try not to touch anything."

"Not a problem." I responded. I was glad for my thick leather boots as we trudged through the mess. There was a long table at one end of the room, and Cerena immediately headed that way. The chairs that surrounded the table were mostly overturned or broken. She shoved aside the pieces looking for a scrying stone.

"What color and what size would it be?" I asked.

"It would be a flat black rock. About the size of a plate."

We all bent to search around the table and on the home-made shelves built into the wall, but it looked as though everything had been scavenged from the building long ago.

Until Blue nearly tripped and fell on his face. "Ow! Sarding rock!" He grabbed for his boot but pulled his hand back when he saw how covered in droppings it was. He left his sore foot alone then.

Cerena hurried over. Her knees creaked as she used the table for support and slowly bent to dust off the rock on the floor. It was black and flat, though the edges were far more jagged than any scrying stone I'd ever seen at the palace. "It's broken. But it'll do."

Connor went over and picked up the stone for Cerena. She gestured, and he laid it on the table for her.

Declan found the sole unbroken chair. He took off his blue Raslen vest and dusted it off for her.

Cerena nodded her thanks. She took her pouch of potions and set them on the table, pushing them aside so they'd be out of her way. We all crowded near and I ended up peering over her right shoulder at the stone. She spit onto the top of the rock, scratched it with what smelled like a cinnamon stick, and muttered under her breath. Instantly, the rock turned glassy, as though a miniature lake floated on top of it.

We all stood silently as Cerena chanted under her breath and watched as she pulled a hair from her head and dropped it onto the stone. Instantly, the water seemed to ripple, and the hair was sucked under, disappearing into the depths.

A scene started to emerge, a very familiar scene. Isla stood at a poker table, a war map spread out on the green felt and held down by steins full of ale. Several blue-clad generals surrounded her, and one pointed at a location on the map. Her keen eyes studied it for a moment before nodding sharply.

A door opened to the side of the room and Kylee stumbled in.

My skin prickled with goosebumps.

No, I thought. No.

The tavern keeper who'd been fool enough to hire me, take me in and keep me while I'd been a selfish teen on the run from her fate, was now a prisoner.

One of Rasle's soldiers stood at Kylee's back, a dagger glittering between them. Kylee wore the same green vest he'd always worn when I'd worked for him. Only now, it was stained with dark patches. I couldn't decipher if they were dirt or blood.

I fidgeted with my skirt as I watched, hoping Kylee wouldn't be hurt, but knowing there was absolutely nothing I could do about it if he was.

My old boss stumbled toward Isla. The soldier behind him forced him into a rough bow.

"Respect your queen," the soldier hissed.

Kylee's face grew dark. My throat tightened.

Don't say anything rash, I silently urged.

Luckily, the tavern owner had always been more adept than me at holding his tongue. "My apologies," he said.

I noted he didn't add 'your majesty.' So, there was still some small bit of rebellion in him.

"I was told you would decide upon the dinner for your soldiers. We have one cow, typically used for milk. Two pigs—"

Isla tilted her head. The smile she gave to Kylee was bone-chilling. "The soldiers I have coming here are pure giant."

Kylee's face paled. "There are horses as well."

"Oh, no. That won't do at all," Isla shook her head. "That won't be nearly enough. I did hear you have ten guests?"

Kylee swallowed hard and straightened. His eyes glittered with rage. He opened his mouth—

My hand clamped down on Cerena's shoulder. It was an unbidden response to the anxiety in my stomach. But I distracted her. We lost the image in the stone. It rippled and went dark. The water-like surface disappeared, and the stone became nothing more than a flat black slab once more.

Blue shook his head. "That doesn't give us much to go on. Could be nearly anywhere—"

"I know where it is," Cerena and I spoke at the same time.

We glanced at each other, tension radiating from each of our bodies until it felt like we were tangled in strands of it —awful, choking ropes of anxiety.

Declan was the first to break away toward the door. "We'd best get going. How far is this place?"

"The Cerulean Forest," my voice was breathier than I liked. But Kylee had been the closest thing I'd had to family back then. I knew exactly what his response to Isla's request would be. And I knew his fate. I blew out a breath.

Connor squeezed my hand and pulled me toward the door as Blue helped Cerena up from her chair.

I glanced back at my castle mage and tripped, falling over a chair leg.

Connor caught me just before I hit the floor. I smacked into him and he tumbled onto his ass, yelping. "Ow!"

I pushed myself off him and stood quickly. "I'm sorry!" I hadn't meant for him to catch me.

"No, it's not you. I fell on something," Connor pulled himself up and dusted off the rushes. He rubbed at his hip and studied the floor. He kicked aside a broken chair seat and a pile of rotted straw. "Umm… I think I might've found something."

I peered around him as he kicked aside more rushes, revealing a trapdoor with a rusted metallic ring for a handle.

"I fell on that," he pointed at the ring.

Something about the trapdoor and the ring made me think of dungeons. Why would hedgewitches have

57

dungeons? Who would they keep down there? What would they do? I'd worked with many hedgewitches while I'd been on my own. But always individually. Never in a group. They'd always been sweet, helpful. I'd always thought of them more as healers than anything else. But dungeons ... A shiver crept up my spine. I glanced up at Cerena, who still held Blue's elbow. "Is it common to have trapdoors in hedgewitch lodges?"

Her eyes grew narrow. Backlit by a ray of sun, with her face in shadow, the whites of her eyes seemed to gleam in an ominous manner as she said, "Only if this place was active after the last Fire War. As a place to hide, perhaps. Or if ..." she trailed off and then glanced around the room. She walked toward one of the bookshelves and traced her fingers over it. Beneath the dust, there were a few magical runes. She traced a few of the symbols. "Or if this place was used for death magic."

I sucked in a breath. Death magic was possibly rarer than wizards. It was as dark and dangerous as the name implied. Death magic's goal was to weave a spell and imbue power into an amulet that could reduce anything to dust, or so the old castle mage, Wyle, had told me. The danger was that the legendary amulets most often reduced their makers to dust upon creation. Like alchemy, death magic had always been more of a fairy tale than a reality.

I asked Cerena. "People actually ..."

"There's always someone willing to try." Cerena's response was brusque as she eyed the group. "If we go down there, don't touch anything." She wagged her finger at Quinn. "I know you're the most ornery. Maybe you should stay up here."

Quinn crossed his arms and shook his head.

"Promise me," Cerena said.

Quinn made an X over his heart.

My castle mage sighed. "Let me go first. You all only follow if need be."

Cerena nodded. And she jerked her head at Connor and gestured for him to pull open the door.

He yanked it open and revealed a ladder descending into the earth. The musty scent of dirt drifted up toward us from the black maw of the secret room.

I held up a hand and pushed out, using a bit of peace magic to light the space in a dull, peridot green light.

Declan immediately started to protest. "Peace, don't hurt yourself."

I held up my hand to silence him. "I'm the only one of us right now who knows how to steadily control their power and make a little stream of light. I know what I'm doing."

His lips thinned and he grumbled, "Ryan's gonna kill me."

I smirked. "No. He'll spank me."

That just made Declan's look go dark for another reason. "Don't distract me."

I rolled my eyes and went over to help Blue lower Cerena onto the ladder.

She looked up at me as she clung to the top rung. "Just in case, I left my pouch on the table. There's a little more food magic. One disguise spell. And a love potion."

"A love potion?"

She rolled her eyes. "The wizard insisted on it. It was an old one I had lying around. He said I might need it to strengthen my old heart."

"I thought love potions made people fall in love."

"Well, they do. But how do you think they do it? They make your heart stronger than your head."

That was something the castle mage had never taught me in my lessons. I was beginning to think Wyle had been a bit of an imbecile. Of course, I thought of Donaloo's skipping—maybe all those who sought magic were a bit mad.

I shook my head in companionable annoyance. "Donaloo is a bit of an oddity."

She barked out a laugh. "He's downright mad, that one. Then, most geniuses are. Now, shine your light a bit to the left so I can see the side railings," she instructed.

I moved my hand and let the light shine as she'd requested. I tried to ignore the constant scratching feeling as the skin of my wrists slowly shredded.

Cerena climbed down at a snail's pace.

Blue knelt on the floor and supported her for as long as he could. Once she was below his reach, he crouched next to me and put an arm around my waist, helping hold me firm as I leaned forward and tried to provide light for the woman.

Blood dripped down my sleeve and droplets splattered onto the ladder.

"Connor, I think she might need help," Blue murmured, nodding toward me.

Connor came to my other side and sandwiched me between them. He tried hard only to push a little magic into my arms. But he had no control, and a bright pink burst of light flared from his hands.

My scars healed over instantly, and I grew dizzy and sick to my stomach, pitching forward. My knights both pulled me back from the hole in the floor, but I wasn't focused on them. I was focused on the dungeon room, which his power lit up like a wildfire lit a forest. The room was little more than a square carved from the dirt, with a floor roughly covered in rotted planks. Somehow, despite the darkness, or maybe because of the magic, a single pink flower clung to existence between a crack in the floorboards. But the flower wasn't what made my jaw drop. Dangling from hooks shoved into the hard-packed earthen walls were hundreds of black amulets.

Cerena's feet reached the floor and she turned. When she caught sight of the amulets, she gasped.

"How … how is this possible?" I whispered down at her.

She shook her head. "I don't know."

She padded closer to one of the walls and studied the black stones, threaded on leather strings. Her face was full of awe. "Whoever created them had incredible magic. The stamina. The knowledge to create all this. Look at the amazing little runes." Her eyes started to glow, and not with the light of my green power or Connor's new pink power. Her eyes glowed white. "Perfectly carved. I wonder—" she breathed, as her hand reached out.

"Don't!" I cried.

But I was too late.

My castle mage exploded into a fine, black, powdery dust.

CHAPTER FIVE

"*S*hite!" Blue's exclamation was an understatement.

I met Connor's eyes, and saw my own devastation and frustration reflected there. His blue-green eyes were troubled as he ran a hand through his curls. He exhaled harshly.

"Why did she touch it? Shouldn't she have known better than to touch it?" I whispered.

Connor shook his head. "She was enamored by it. For all we know, it could have an attraction spell on it, drawing people to it."

Declan immediately jumped to the practicalities. "We need to make sure no one else can find this place. We need to destroy that room and knock down this building."

Blue released me and stood, leaving Connor to hold me. He turned to Declan and crossed his arms. "Shouldn't we find a way to use these amulets? They're an amazing weapon," my newest knight argued.

"If we can't touch them without dying ourselves, they're not much of a weapon." Declan's sarcasm was not subtle. His lips thinned and he shook his head as he stared at Blue.

"What if we tried to wrap our sleeve around our hands? Picked them up through clothing? "

"Go ahead. Be my guest." Declan gestured toward the ladder.

Blue wrinkled his nose in frustration. "There has to be a way to use these. Someone made them without dying."

"That someone was a wizard, most likely. An insane wizard. And who says they didn't die? What if they made those as a batch? What if there is an attraction spell like Connor proposed?" Declan said.

"If only we could levitate them or something…" Blue gazed down at the pit, which had gone black again as Connor and I had slowly dimmed our powers. "We could wish for the ability to carry them without their magic working on us."

Quinn took a step backward, toward the door.

I stood, going toward my silent knight, but my arguing husbands blocked my path as they stepped toward one another, in a heated, testosterone-filled face off.

Declan lifted a hand and raised a finger. "First, while that's creative, we only have two wishes left. We can't use them willy-nilly on every thing that comes up." He raised another finger. "Secondly, Quinn hasn't even recovered from the first nightmare, which you claimed was temporary." He leaned forward and got into Blue's face. "Third, if wish magic was enough to control amulets, don't you think your nightmare of a father would be using them all over the place?"

Blue accidentally shot us all a thought of him grabbing Declan by the throat and strangling him.

"Try it, I might like it," My blond knight just grinned.

Blue's next thought was punching Dec's balls and Declan's hands moved to protect himself.

This was getting out of hand. "Stop," I put my hand up between them and walked forward, forcing them both to take a step backward. "Or I'll blast you both with peace."

They glared at one another.

"Let's think this through," I said. "It's fine to talk it through. Fine to have different opinions, but let's not get so off-track that we lose sight of our purpose. We came here to find Isla's location."

"Yes, and we found the perfect weapon to get rid of her!" Blue exclaimed.

Declan turned to me, instead of continuing his face off with Blue. "I think our best bet is to close this place up. We can put the table over the trapdoor, throw broken chair

ANN DENTON

pieces down there so that no one else gets in. Then we can use the gargoyles to take out the house." He gestured at the secret room. "I think we walk away. We're already dealing with magic that's out of control at every step. Eventually, after it's all said and done, we should come back and try to bury or destroy all those amulets. Because no one should have that level of destructive power."

Blue grabbed my hand and turned me to face him. "I think you might be missing an opportunity here."

I glanced back and forth between them. My knights were my advisors, but I had to make the final call. What Blue was saying was true. We needed every bit of help we could get. But Declan was right; we already had a fleet of uncontrollable stone animals and I had five knights with powers they didn't know how to use.

Blue clenched his fists in frustration. "You don't under-stand what you're up against. My father is a full djinn. He has endless wishes. He can't grant his own wishes. But he can tell anyone else exactly what to say to him so that he can grant that wish. And he doesn't have the side effects of a half-djinn. He suffers no nightmares." His thoughts flew rapid-fire through different memories, but they were so quick that I couldn't decipher them.

"How does he get others to wish for what he wants?" Declan asked.

Blue shook his head. "He doesn't typically even use his own wishes. My father thinks it's beneath him. He makes

66

others use theirs and suffer the nightmare. He writes out what he wants them to say. Once, he tried to force my mother to wish that an entire town lose their legs from the knee down."

"Why?" I asked.

"Because several of their sons refused to join his army."

Declan tilted his head. "He can write down whatever he wants. But can you force someone to make a wish?"

Blue shook his head. "You know why my father first took a harem? So he could turn those women against each other. They're so caught up in status and jealousy and fear that most of them will do anything. My mother happened to refuse that particular wish. She wouldn't cripple a village for the sins of a few."

"So, he doesn't always get his way."

Blue's laugh was bitter. "Oh, he does. One of his other wives wished it for him. And then a third wife wished for my mother's hand to necrotize. Her hand rotted off before her eyes. She was forced to stand there and watch. I was forced to stand there and watch."

His story alone made my stomach necrotize. I nearly puked at the mental images he sent of his mother screaming and collapsing in pain as her fingers shriveled and blackened.

Blue's voice grew thick, even though his face stayed harsh. "These amulets are merciful. *Death* is merciful compared to what happens when you're under the control of the monster."

The rest of us were frozen in shock. We knew the sultan was bad. I had an ambassador that lived in Cheryn's palace. The reports back had never included dark dealings between the royal family—perhaps because my ambassador was worried about what might happen if his scrolls were intercepted. A sultan who'd destroy an entire town wouldn't have much consideration for a lone ambassador.

I turned to ask Quinn what his spies knew about the sultan and I realized I'd never gone to him.

I stepped past the others and went to my spy master, taking his hand. "Did your people ever see—"

Quinn ran a hand through my hair and caressed the back of my neck as he nodded solemnly. His eyes tried to speak, but no thoughts followed. He gave a frustrated grunt before turning and striding out the door.

I almost followed, but just then Blue moved, and my attention was drawn to him. My knight from Cheryn strode over to the dining table. He yanked Cerena's pouch off the top, opened it, and dumped its contents out. He grabbed the tin jar immediately. "Anyone know how to make that spelled bread?"

We all shook our heads.

"Then this stuff is useless." He dumped out the powder inside the tin onto the tabletop. Then he marched over to the ladder and started climbing down.

No! He doesn't mean to—my thoughts were a panicked wail.

I took a few steps toward him. "Wait," I called out. He couldn't do this. What if he … what if what happened to Cerena happened to him?

I didn't really know him. I hardly knew him as a man. But I knew that fierce little bird that had tried to stop Abbas from choking me. I knew that fierce little bird who refused to let me go to a cave in another country to rescue Declan alone. I knew that we were bonded, even if I didn't know his favorite things, even if I didn't know how to make him laugh, even if my mind couldn't fully under-stand how or why—he was mine.

Didn't he feel it too? How could he throw it away?

Blue looked up at me. And I couldn't read his expression in the shadows. It made me ache.

His tone was harsh, even though his words were polite. "Give me a little light, please."

He was going to do this! No! I refused to let him. "You can't!"

He just took another step down the ladder.

My feet were automatically drawn closer to him. Shouldn't he listen to me? Shouldn't he stop? He was being a fool. I was his queen. He should listen to my orders. He should know we're bonded. But … we'd just gotten married. My hold on him wasn't going to be strong enough.

I thought of his father, a man who'd ordered about and abused him endlessly. I briefly wondered if Blue had ever gotten to do anything he'd wanted in life. I highly doubted it. And that's when it hit me. I couldn't order him to stop. He was making a choice. Even if it was one of his final choices. I had to respect it. But I couldn't help the sad words that poured out of my mouth. "But what if you …" I trailed off. I didn't want to say it. But I was already crying … already anticipating what was about to happen.

Blue's words were a harsh whisper. "Then at least I tried to help you."

Our eyes argued. But he shoved more memories of his father at me. Memories of being thrown across the throne room. Memories of his father forcing his brothers to transform and hunt him through the halls of the palace, when speed was Blue's only weapon against his brothers' shape-shifted teeth and claws. He shoved memories at me of finding his mother hanging from the ceiling of her room after she took her own life to escape the sultan.

He needed to do this. I could feel the desperation in his thoughts. He'd rather use this weapon on himself than let his father ever get ahold of him again.

I extended my hand and let my arms rip open as I lit the room slowly for Blue.

Next to me, Connor shook his head, his dark curls falling across his face. But he didn't say no. He wouldn't. Not after I allowed it. My best friend simply came up beside me and put his arm around my waist, supporting me as I used my power and tears streamed from my eyes.

Blue reached the bottom rung and hopped down onto the dusty floor. He walked slowly toward the wall, studying the hanging amulets, tilting his head this way and that. He leaned close to them, so close that I clutched Connor's arm in alarm.

"Stay back!" I called out. "If there's an attraction spell, resist!" I shot a little peace at Blue. I had no idea if it would counteract the attraction, but maybe it would slow him a bit. Dull him a bit. Let him sink into lethargy. His eyes didn't turn white as Cerena's had. I hoped that was a good sign.

But the peace magic didn't only affect Blue.

The little pink flower turned its head toward my magic and unfurled its leaves.

"More," a squeaky voice said. "I need more!"

I started, and Connor had to yank me back from the edge of the hole.

Blue turned around and stared at the flower, whose stem started growing rapidly, until it looked like a vine nearly as tall as his waist.

"Pluck me, pull me out!" the flower cried, its five pink petals curling and unfurling rapidly.

Blue turned and looked up at us, his face crumpled in confusion. "Do flowers talk in Rasle?"

71

Connor and I shook our heads.

"Please!" the flower begged. "I'll owe you a favor. I've been stuck in here for nearly a century!"

Connor and I exchanged a look.

Behind me, Declan shuffled forward. Even his insistence that this was an awful idea couldn't overcome his curiosity.

"A flower sprite," my scholar whispered.

"Help me, sir!" the flower begged.

Blue looked up at me, questioning. "Think it's a trick?"

I shrugged. "I don't know."

"Why didn't you ask for help from the old woman?" Blue gazed down at the flower.

"Magic makers," the flower's high-pitched voice spit vitriol. "They can't see past their own desire for power."

"Why do you think I came down here if not for power?" Blue asked.

"To grab a weapon. That's different."

"Killing someone is just death." The flower shrugged. "All things have to die. But magic makers are lying, betraying tufts of monkey grass!"

We all stared at one another, weighing the flower's offer.

"You know what a favor from a sprite is worth?" the flower asked. "I can—"

"Swear it," I stopped the sprite before she could go any further. "Swear allegiance to the country of Evaness for one hundred years." I glanced up at Dec, for reassurance that sprites did live more than a hundred years. I thought I remembered that from tutoring.

His nod reassured me.

I glanced back down at the flower; whose leaves stroked its yellow face in thought. "You want allegiance to your country?"

"To the land and citizens of Evaness and the throne, yes."

"Not to you?"

"To myself while I'm on the throne, but to my heirs and their heirs, however many are within that hundred-year span."

"That's quite the favor."

"You're in quite the hole," I replied. I wasn't exactly certain of all the powers a flower sprite might have. But I didn't want a single one used against me.

The flower stretched its face toward me, stem growing even taller until her yellow stamens fluttered in front of my face as she studied me. Or I assumed she studied me anyway, from the tilt of her petals. She didn't actually have a face.

"You have a deal if you offer to carry me to your kingdom and protection during the interim of the deal."

I nodded. "Done."

ANN DENTON

The flower shrunk back down and turned to Blue. "Pluck me carefully. And then, if you want one of those nasty things, be careful not to touch any part of it."

Blue nodded and knelt down. He set down the tin jar and grabbed the flower by her stem.

She giggled. "Ooh, not there, you dirty man! Higher!"

Blue moved his hand slightly upward and pulled. The flower squeaked. He pulled again.

She squeaked again.

He wiggled her back and forth, and finally her roots came loose, out of the ground, wriggling as he pulled her up.

"Hurry," she gasped as Blue went up the ladder one-handed.

Blue gave me the poor flower, who looked as if she was wilting already, though she'd somehow survived down in a black pit for so long.

I clutched her close to me and asked, "What do I do?" But her roots sank into my forearm. I screamed. It burned.

Connor and Declan moved to bat her away, but I stopped them. "We have a deal," I told them, as the roots wiggled under my skin.

The flower sighed, and as soon as she sucked up a bit of my blood, her petals regained their color. "Much better," she whispered.

I just watched her, chest heaving, as she settled in on my arm, lengthening her stem and looping it several times around me until she had a good grip. When she was done, she turned to me. "I'm Dini, by the way." Her voice appeared to come from nowhere, because she had no face or lips.

"Bloss," I replied, questioning my sanity a bit.

Dini dipped her petals. Then she turned and faced Blue.

"Well, aren't you going to grab a weapon?" she squeaked.

Blue looked at me.

I pressed my lips together but gave a single nod.

Beside me, Declan threw up his arms in frustration and stomped off to the other side of the room.

Blue went back down the ladder, grabbed the tin, and went over to the dirt wall. He took a deep breath as he pulled the tin apart and edged closer to an amulet that hung on a hook by itself, a dangling black drop of death.

My throat tightened and I couldn't breathe.

The flower said, "Calm now."

Blue slowly raised the tin until the black stone clanked against the inside of the jar.

I bit the inside of my cheek, drawing blood, as the amulet stone clunked down on the bottom of the tin.

That noise was sweet relief.

Blue let out his own breath when the amulet settled into the bottom of the tin and he remained standing. But he held it again as he used the lid to slowly edge the leather string off the hook.

His thoughts were clear. He imagined himself exploding in a puff of dust. *It won't hurt,* he told himself. *If it happens, it won't hurt.*

Eventually, Blue succeeded. He used the lid to lift the leather cord and slowly drop it into the tin jar.

He clamped the lid down.

My heart unclenched.

Declan called out from behind me. "Well done. We have a massive weapon in a jar. A weapon we can't touch without dying. What are you planning on doing with that thing now? Are you gonna sling it at the first enemy you see? Open the jar and drop it onto their head? How are you gonna pick it up again? How are you gonna stop it from hurting someone else?"

Blue kept his eyes on the tin in his hand. "I don't know."

Declan said. "Bloss, for the record, I'm still against this. If you don't know how to use a weapon, then you shouldn't have it."

"If you don't have a weapon strong enough to defeat evil, it will win." Blue looked up at us, his eyes lit by my green magic. They glowed as he said, "Make no mistake. We are fighting evil."

"Ooh, we are?" Dini asked, her petals fluttering like she was excited.

Unlike Dini, I felt no excitement. The truth of Blue's words sunk into my bones like a shipwreck sinks into the sea. The truth swirled and twisted and grew as ugly and jagged as a broken vessel, until it drifted down and landed in my heart. He was right. Hadn't we just seen it? Isla was planning to feed people to her giants. The sultan tortured his own children, his wives, destroyed entire towns for the offenses of a few.

Desperate times … but did we have to use such dangerous measures?

Blue's eyes looked a little manic as he climbed back up the ladder. When he reached the top, he knelt before me and offered me the tin.

I took it with steady hands, but inside, I felt shaken.

"With this, we'll find a way to get him," Blue whispered to me as he stood.

Maybe I shouldn't have scrutinized his words. But his thoughts didn't picture Isla or the sea witch. His thoughts leaked out, and I don't even know if he was aware of that fact. But his mind shoved a picture of the sultan's face into all our heads. Blue didn't seem nearly as concerned with the war as he did with revenge. His father was evil. But we had larger goals. More important goals.

Raj was only one part of the puzzle.

Avia was still out there. But even I knew getting to my sister couldn't come before stopping this horror.

Blue gazed longingly down at the tin. I handed it back to him, testing his thoughts.

"Can you carry it? Perhaps in Cerena's pouch?"

He grabbed it back quickly and nodded.

I watched him as he put the tin carefully in the pouch and secured it to his person, in easy reach.

None of his thoughts moved toward betrayal. Nothing in him spoke of ill-intent or dishonesty.

He simply had a fixation. But that alone could be the destruction of all of us.

He strode out the door and I watched his back as it was swallowed up by afternoon sunlight.

And part of me started to wonder just how much I could trust my newest knight.

CHAPTER SIX

*O*ur flight to the Cerulean Forest wasn't nearly long enough.

Quinn rode with me this time, and having his arms wrapped around me was the most comforting thing I could imagine. Several times, I forgot I couldn't send him thoughts and I tried to think funny observations at him. It cut my heart to pieces that I couldn't have a thought conversation with him. So, I ended up wrapping one arm backward and down, so that my hand held onto his hip. It meant I spent a good part of our jolting flight in a very uncomfortable position. But when his lips brushed against the back of my neck, reaffirming our connection with soft kisses, it was worth it.

No matter what happened, I had him and he had me. I used that thought to reassure myself as we descended.

But when we landed, I wasn't ready to face what I was certain we would find. I didn't want to see my old friends

—Jenna, Marcus, Abel, or the other people who worked at the tavern—in the aftermath of what I was certain Isla had done.

I clutched Quinn's hand as we dismounted in a forest clearing a bit away from the buildings and then crept toward the edge of the dirt road to peer at the scene.

The tavern faced the trees, the only building on that side of the road; the front doors faced us. They were closed, but two blue-clad guards stood sentry. To the left of the tavern were some stables—where Abel and Marcus worked. Then there was a blacksmith's forge. All the buildings down the road were dark, though it was midday. No children ran down the street. No people were out, other than two more soldiers in blue who walked back toward the tavern, swords sheathed like they hadn't a care in the world. Their voices were the only sound the wind carried back to us. Either everyone was in hiding. Or …

One of the soldiers kicked a stick in the road.

"Damn giants leave such a mess," he muttered.

My eyes zeroed in on the stick—which wasn't a stick but a bone. I studied the road again. What I'd mistaken for fallen twigs were suddenly gruesome reminders of a giant's strength. The dirt in front of the tavern was already littered with blood and bits of bone. My stomach churned.

A distant scream sounded, and goosebumps formed along my arms. Isla was encouraging the giants to let their bloodlust run wild. They had been living in peace with us for the past two centuries. Taming them had been part of Isla's grandmother's ascension to power. The giants had been encouraged to interbreed so that there were very few purebloods left. But a head popped up behind a roof farther down the road. The head was the size of a carriage. Shirtless, with a mouth streaked in blood, the giant appeared to be thirty feet tall.

My skin crawled as if a swarm of insects had landed on me. Apparently, Isla had scrounged up a few of the purebloods left. I scratched at my arms and Dini's leaves smacked my hands. "Stop, that tickles!" she scolded.

"Don't you see the giants?" I asked her.

She turned to look, and her petals wavered. "We should hide underground. They don't go underground."

"We can't." We'd come here to find Isla. Not to hide.

Dini shook her head. "If I'd known you were this crazy, I wouldn't have made a deal with you."

"Yes, you would have," I said. "You wanted out of that blackness. Do flower sprites have magic that can be used against giants?" I asked hopefully.

Dini turned her face toward me. "You made a deal for my loyalty. Not my magic."

I clenched my fists. I wanted to rip her petals right off. But she was right.

Idiot, Bloss, I scolded myself.

"Let's hope I can outrun them then," I snarled.

Dini just turned her face away from me and wiggled on my arm, the micro hairs on her stem scratching me just enough to itch like mad.

Ugh. I'd made a very poor choice. Why'd I gone and made a deal with a flower sprite? The sea witch's face sprang to mind. Still, I wanted to take back my word and end the deal. But the stupid flower was sucking the blood from my veins. I didn't know how to detach her. Could I just rip her out and forget the roots? Or would she grow right back?

"Connected like this, I can tell what you're thinking. Try it."

She could definitely grow back then. I wanted to scream in frustration. But I couldn't. Not without attracting the giants. I decided to ignore Dini. I'd figure out how to rid myself of her later.

As we watched them through the trees, I was incredibly grateful for Blue's insistence that we take that amulet. In fact, I wished we had three or four so we could just catapult them at the giants from the distance. Because right now, the odds of us killing Isla and escaping seemed quite slim. Particularly, with this useless shite of a flower wrapped on my arm.

Dini tightened her hold.

I took a deep breath to steady myself. I closed my eyes.

Remember, Bloss, you're here for Isla. It would be best if we could slip in and out without the giants noticing.

That meant we needed some form of distraction. Ryan had left with Declan's former power, reduction and multi-plication, so that option was out. I was disappointed but glad that Ryan wasn't here to see this.

"At least we're dressed like Raslen soldiers," Connor said. "Maybe that will at least get us in the front door?"

Declan glanced at me. "You need to take that disguise spell from Cerena's bag. You're too recognizable."

"Me? Connor's the diplomat! The rest of you have all been active at court the last four years. I would think I would be the least recognizable. Except for Blue." Only Isla's little entourage had seen me. But Connor's face was familiar. He'd gone on diplomatic visits to the surrounding nations each year.

I turned to Quinn, forgetting that he couldn't think his opinion at us. His face scrunched in frustration. But then he raised a finger and pointed right at me, indicating he thought I should drink the potion. I rolled my eyes but complied.

I dug through my pockets and pulled out both Cerena's spells and held them up to the light so I could tell which was which. The purple potion I set back in my pocket. I downed the disguise spell and let the familiar change wash over me. Dini let out a little howl as she got swept up in the change and turned into a misshapen lump of bark-like skin on my arm.

I ignored her and focused on the rest of my body. I tried not to change in size too much, so that my uniform would still fit. That meant I ended up looking like a very short, very skinny man. I wasn't certain about the rest of my features, but my two front teeth were so large that it was hard to close my lips completely.

"Had to choose a rabbit face? Couldn't you have gone with something more discreet? You're pretty memorably ugly right now." Blue shook his head.

I bit my thumb at him. "Sard off."

He grinned. "It's fine. I'm used to playing with a deck stacked against me."

Dini groaned on my arm. But she didn't speak.

Good, maybe she'll reconsider living on me, I thought. I'd get back to the castle and find more of these spells, downing one after the other until she fled my skin.

She just moaned again, and the lump on my arm shifted uncomfortably, like some moving tunneling growth. I shoved down my sleeve so I wouldn't have to look at it.

Quinn grabbed my hand and pulled me to the ground. Then he started to write in the dirt with his finger: *I'll run ahead. I'll take out any guards.*

Before I could protest, Quinn took off. It was like he disappeared before my very eyes.

We waited with bated breath. But when I saw the two guards in front of the door fall without a sound, the anxiety in my chest eased a bit.

Quinn can do this, I told myself.

Still, I searched out Connor's hand and clutched it while we waited. My toes flexed in anticipation, ready to run.

The guards in the road were next. They went from gossiping and laughing to falling face first into the dirt. And all I could see near them was a blur. Quinn was so fast that he looked like nothing more than a strong breeze, a trick of the eyes, a quick flash of color.

It seemed like only a minute had passed when Quinn was back in front of us, breathing hard and sweating. His sword was out, and it was bloodied. His black hair was plastered to his forehead. He gestured for us to move forward. He jogged in the front, going just fast enough that I could still see him. He circled and tried to protect our flanks as the rest of us moved forward toward the tavern.

I led us to a side door, a worker's entrance. We piled into a back stairwell. It was narrow, so narrow that we needed to walk single file. My knights would not let me walk in front.

"I know where I'm going!" I seethed in a whisper.

"No. First, you're our queen. Second, I can use the amulet if need be." Blue argued.

"Whoa! What if you drop that thing and it falls down the stairs to hit the rest of us? You should be in back," Declan whisper-yelled.

"Shut it! Everyone!" Connor said. "Get the hell up the stairs before we're trapped here."

We headed up, single file, Blue leading us. He held the tin in front of him, one hand on the lid, in case he needed to remove it and toss the thing at someone. I pictured him fumbling with it and dropping it on his shoe.

Hey! Blue protested. *I got it off the sarding hook just fine.*

Sorry, I mentally apologized. *It was just a random thought.* But I agreed with Declan on one thing—we needed to figure out a better way to wield it, that was certain.

When we got to a small platform that opened onto the guest chambers on the second floor, where I suspected Isla and her generals would be staying when they weren't planning in the poker room, I whispered to Blue. "See if you can listen to Isla's thoughts. When you think you found her mind, share her thoughts with us through the beads."

He nodded and closed his eyes in concentration. His head moved as he broke through the thoughts of the people inside the room down the hall. After a minute, he pushed his thoughts toward all of us. *She sounds happy. They're talking about the attack upon the capital. Details of stuff. Something to do with Raj.*

Which capital? Ours? Sedara's? A winter chill settled in my chest and my face went ashen. Ryan had headed for our capital. I closed my eyes as a cold sweat came over me. *Send us her thoughts directly.*

I'm trying! I don't know how to do that!

Sarding hell! I thought, my eyes opening and searching out Quinn. But the only knight who might be able to help Blue, to instruct him, was muted.

I almost asked Blue to stop what he was doing and check on Ryan. But the rest of them would be in danger if I did that. And even if I knew what was happening to my poor Ryan, there was nothing I could do. My mother's lessons echoed in my ears. I saw her face, bending over me in the war room during one of the practice sessions from when I was fourteen. "Focus on what you can control, Bloss. On what you can change. Losses are inevitable. Defeat is not."

So, I resisted asking about Ryan, even though it tore at my heart to do so. I pushed against the piece of my soul that pulled me to go to him.

I turned on my step and looked up at Declan, who was still taller than me, even though I was a step above him. I leaned up on my toes and whispered in his ear, "Dec, can you sense what her emotions are?"

He nodded and closed his eyes, trying to feel out how to use his new power. But my Declan didn't know how to go small. He'd always struggled with small reductions and multiplications. He'd always been more comfortable switching entire fields than single bowls of grain. I felt the ripple of his power as he sucked away a little bit of each of our emotions. Out of habit, he turned and spread his hands like he would have if he were using his old powers. His fingers stretched in the direction of the guest bedrooms.

A physical pulse shook the air and Declan took a step back, like he'd been hit with an arrow. I reached my hands toward him, concerned—

Blue's excited thoughts interjected before I could ask if Declan was okay. *Isla's thoughts are turning dark!* He exclaimed. *She stopped thinking about battle. She's thinking of her daughter ... of saying goodbye to her daughter—*

Next to me, Declan started to shake.

"Sard it all," Connor whispered, his tone awed. "Dec's sucking out all her joy."

"Can he do that? Could you do that?" I asked, shocked.

Connor shrugged. "I never tried. I only ever sipped."

Keep doing it! Blue shouted in all our heads.

I cringed.

She's thinking about climbing out the window, ending it all!

My hand flew to my mouth. "No!" It couldn't be this easy.

I turned to Declan, who was leaning back against the wall, shaking his head from side to side and fanning himself. He was sweating profusely. His face went through a rapid series of emotions, bliss, maniacal silent laughter, pain, and ultimately sadness. He doubled over.

I grabbed his knife and yanked on it when he reached for it.

But I wasn't strong enough. He pushed me back and set the knife on his wrist—

Connor yanked the blade away from him. Then Connor put a hand over his sword and his face near Declan's. "These aren't your emotions. These aren't your emotions."

Declan started to tremble.

Helplessness choked me. I didn't know what to do. I came forward and hugged Declan. I could feel him trembling. I sent a little stream of peace into him, hoping that might help. "Just another minute Dec. Just a little longer," I whispered.

She's opening the window— Blue reported before turning silent again.

Gods, can Declan do this? Can he kill her? I wondered.

His face was in shadows as he slumped into me and Connor.

Quinn tugged on Connor's sleeve, desperate to find out what was going on. Connor leaned down a bit and whispered to Quinn, updating him as I poured even more peace into Declan, whose back arched as if he were in physical—not just emotional—pain. I shoved both hands on either side of his face, ignoring the blood that dripped from my wrists onto both of us. I pulsed peace into my blond knight.

On my arm, Dini stirred, my power or my blood seemed to rouse her. She stretched on my arm.

My eyes met Declan's in the green glow of my power. I held his gaze as he struggled with emotional overload. Dec's mouth opened. And then he fell forward in a dead faint.

I caught him, but if Connor and Quinn hadn't moved to catch me, I'd have tumbled headfirst down the stairs. My two knights helped me and eventually shifted Declan over so that Quinn could sling the scholar over his shoulder.

Shite! Blue cursed. *She didn't jump. And now she knows we're here. She thinks Quinn planted thoughts of suicide in her head.*

Connor ignored him as he used a little bit of pink light to partially heal my cuts.

Quinn used his fingers to mime running, and we nodded. Having lost the advantage of surprise, we needed to get away and regroup. And heal Declan somehow.

Quinn disappeared with Declan. Carrying the other knight didn't seem to hamper his speed at all. The rest of us were silently picking our way down the stairs when, suddenly, the thatched roof was ripped off the building.

Two giants peered down into the darkness. Their breath washed over us, and it smelled of death. Blood and rot. They gnashed their teeth as they peered down inside. Each one of their teeth was as large as my hand. Luckily, they'd been in bright sunlight, so the darkness of the back stairwell was a bit harder for them to see.

We all froze for a second in horror. And then we forgot that we were in Raslen uniforms. That we might have simply walked down the stairs and made our way out. Prey instinct made us run.

It was the running that tipped them off.

A giant hand reached toward me.

Behind me, Blue screeched. I heard the sound of the tin squeaking as he opened it. I didn't look back. I kept running, heart pounding as I ducked the huge fingers. I heard Blue's grunt as he launched the tin and amulet at the huge giant. The creature's fingers snatched my disguised hair and I felt a sharp, tight tug that sent red ribbons of pain darting across my vision. I was lifted a foot—only to come crashing down on the stairs as dust fell like rain, filling the stairwell.

Blue snatched me up as I coughed and darted toward the open servant's door.

The footsteps of the other giant, who must have been on the other side of the tavern, shook the earth as it ran around the building toward us. In front of me, Connor suddenly blurred and disappeared in a whip of wind. I hoped that meant that Quinn had grabbed him. But I didn't have time to think, because just then, a huge, bare, calloused foot stepped around the corner, and a shadow fell over me and Blue.

The second giant snarled down at us and my eyes flew up to meet its furious gaze.

It stomped forward.

But instead of running toward the forest, Blue backed up with me in his arms.

What are you doing? I thought furiously.

Look at the ground.

My eyes scanned the ground and spotted the black stone. Blue must have hit the first giant with his throw, and the stone must have fallen with the dust pile.

Dini reformed on my arm. She turned and saw the giant, letting out a terrified squeak just before the giant's foot smashed down onto the amulet.

I barely had time to close my eyes before a second cloud of dust washed over us.

That's when Blue ran for the forest with me in his arms. I leaned over his shoulder to look back at the road. I couldn't be sure but I thought I saw a little pile of black dust amongst the rest. It looked to me like the giant had destroyed the death amulet.

Connor had Declan already mounted onto the gargoyle in front of him, his arms around the other knight to ensure he wouldn't fall.

Quinn helped Blue and me mount up and then he slid onto Declan's former gargoyle.

"But—" I started to protest. Quinn couldn't nag the beast to get him moving.

Connor cut me off. "He's been practicing. He'll be fine."

And my stupid shite of a gargoyle took off before I could hear my silent knight say his first word. He took off so fast that my bloody wrist scraped against his neck and my wound reopened. The blood soaked into the stone.

We flew over the tavern, watching as Isla and her generals burst outside to see what had happened.

Isla's howl of rage was music to my ears.

We hadn't cut the head off the snake.

But we'd certainly wounded her.

I made my gargoyle dip low. I had no way to kill her, not without the amulet—not with her soldiers and generals still surrounding her. Not yet. But I could add salt to the wound. I made certain she could see my blue uniform as I called out, "Your Majesty, it's been a pleasure betraying you!"

I yanked at my gargoyle and, for once, the damned thing obeyed easily. We swerved and gained speed as we flew off.

Dini laughed into the wind. "That was the best adventure I've had in nearly two centuries!"

I ignored her. As Isla disappeared below the clouds, my thoughts turned to my capital, Marscha, because that's where Ryan had gone.

Isla's thoughts about the battle there had been happy thoughts.

Fear lit like a torch in my heart.

I selfishly prayed to the gods Ryan hadn't been hurt. That he was safe. That he'd arrived after any attack that had occurred.

I urged my stone beast to hurry, but I knew, whatever had happened, I was already too late.

CHAPTER SEVEN

$\mathcal{W}$e arrived back at the capital an hour before dusk only to see utter devastation. Marscha was flattened. Not a building remained standing.

From my place on the back of my gargoyle, I surveyed the damage. Searing pain filled my body at the thought of what had happened to all those poor souls. The pitched rooves of the houses were still intact, but the walls were gone, blown out and collapsed. On every single building. This was too much to have been the work of giants.

My eyes searched the wreckage for a gargoyle—they could withstand most things. But I didn't spot one. I didn't know if that was good or bad. I didn't know if that meant Ryan had gotten sidetracked on his way here or …

Blue pulled his mount up beside me, to hover next to mine. "It's wish magic," he said.

"You're sure?" I asked. Even growing up during the last Fire War, I hadn't seen such devastation. I'd seen towns

half-burnt. I'd seen fields set ablaze. But even a dragon
hadn't been able to raze an entire capital city so that no
building remained standing. Could it be wish magic? I'd
never seen it, not during the last war. Of course, mother
had had an alliance with the sultan, so perhaps that
was why.

Blue scrunched his face in concentration. A minute later,
he sent me a mental image of a town that was nestled into
a sand dune in the middle of the desert. His memory
played out as though he watched from his camel, the
beast's neck occasionally coming into view. A line of half-
djinn soldiers each whispered a wish. Then, on the
sultan's signal, they all said, "Granted," at the same time.
The soldiers all writhed as their nightmares set in—tentacles sprouting from their arms, eyeballs going missing.
The brick buildings with their turrets and towers capped
by red onion domes, collapsed in upon themselves in one
fell swoop. The onion domes had been the only items to
survive, rolling across the hot sand like toys, like children's tops that had been abandoned. The sight was
haunting. And it clearly reflected the scene in front of us.

Horror churned in my stomach. *How's that possible?*

*He calls it stringing wishes. Every wish can only have one
objective or target. But he decides ahead of time on each target
—the mill, the granary, and so on. Then he has each soldier
make a wish to blow out the walls of one building. When they
all grant them at the same time ... It's how he ended the town of
Qaleh,* Blue thought sadly. *He made my brothers and I watch.*

I'm sorry. I imagined giving Blue a hug.

96

He returned the hug in my head, holding me close and swaying back and forth, letting me pat his back as he buried his face in my neck.

I'm sorry, he replied. *I never thought I'd have to see it again. I'm sorry he did this. If I could wish for him to lose his throne, if I could wish for his death, I would.*

Blue ... I wanted to tell him that everything would be okay. But one look at the scene in front of me made those words a lie.

How could everything be okay? How could this possibly end well? I wondered.

I pulled out of our mental conversation and waved my hand at the crushed city in front of me. "Wouldn't the nightmare for collapsing an entire building be too much?"

Blue sighed and scrubbed a hand over his face. It was a minute before he could speak aloud again. A minute in which the guilt ate at me, growing like a pit in my stomach at the thought of all the people who'd died. People who'd been my responsibility.

Blue finally spoke, "My father, though wishes cost him nothing, thinks wishing is below him. He'd rather watch others suffer. He doesn't care if the nightmare's too much."

"Why would anyone accept that? Be part of it?"

"My country isn't like Evaness. Those who refuse are ostracized, tortured, wishes are turned against them."

My other knights flew closer to hear Blue's words. Declan had come to, but he looked horrid. He was pale and wan, as though he'd been in his sickbed for a year.

I motioned for us to land. We touched down at the edge of town on the side farthest from the castle. My gargoyle knelt so I could slide off unassisted. I patted its head, glad it was maturing, hoping that meant that maybe Ryan would be able to get our flying fighters moving. I tried to force myself to believe he was unhurt and here some-where, helping. I tried to convince myself that he was alright. I reminded myself that four of my knights were bound to one another. If Ryan had been killed, they would have fallen down dead.

But death and injuries were different. He could still be hurt and bleeding. His legs could be crushed under a wall. I cut off my thoughts. They were wandering too far into frantic speculation. I reined them in, but my fingers wouldn't stop shaking.

Dini said, "Well, you've turned out to be a rather unstable ride." She wriggled on me, tugging uncomfortably at my skin in her bark-like form. I scratched at her until she cooed and settled back, "That's the spot. A bit lower. A bit lower."

When I scratched a bit harder, she made a moaning noise.

I stopped. "Dini? Did I hurt you?"

"Why'd you stop?" she protested. "I was almost there."

Shock and disgust flooded me as I realized the implication of her words.

No, she can't mean that, I thought. I'm projecting.

I cleared my throat awkwardly and turned to my gargoyle.

"Stay," I murmured to my beast. He sunk to his stomach. The other gargoyles seemed to follow his lead, which was good for us. I didn't want to lead them through town. They'd be more likely to cause even further destruction than be a help.

I walked over to Declan to check on him. He sighed and waved me away. "I'll be fine, Bloss. You don't have time to worry about me. We need to find Ryan."

I nodded, crossing my arms over my chest as if to brace myself for impact. I wanted to ask Blue to search for Ryan's thoughts. But at the same time, I was terrified of what he would find. Or wouldn't find. My chin trembled despite my efforts to clamp my jaw closed. I had to swallow down the bile that rose in my throat as I turned toward Marscha.

The castle still rose in the distance, battered from the attack before Donaloo had put the freezing spell on it. The mage's tower was the only bright spark of blooming life amongst the wreckage that stretched for miles. The unnatural flowers on the tower contrasted the devastation with little pinpoints of orange, yellow, and purple blooms.

I closed my eyes and allowed myself a moment to take one long, bracing breath before I started forward.

I was determined to walk through town, not only to honor those who had passed, but to see if anyone survived in the wreckage. I was certain it was impossible. But I'd seen the impossible happen before. And if I could save even one of my citizens, it was my duty.

I walked first, down the middle of the road. My knights walked two by two behind me. We moved toward the first building slowly, my ears and eyes on high alert for any movement or sign of distress.

Suddenly, my vision blurred. Flattened buildings seemed to pop up and regain their shape. Walls restored themselves. And what had looked like a crumbled ruin became a home. I glanced back; my knights' faces were still dark with sadness and guilt.

"Come here," I whispered urgently. They lined up beside me and I watched their startled faces as they took in what I saw.

"Is the house back?" Declan asked.

Quinn nodded. He pointed at his eye and at his head and then put his fingers in an X.

I nodded. "Yes. It's kind of like the illusions you make."

We took another step forward. The silence of a dead city was suddenly replaced by the laughing, shouting rumble of a town that was alive and well. Townspeople filled the street, looking alive and well, if a bit odd. They were all out, crawling around on their hands and knees—children, the elderly, everyone. One man's face popped up over a roof ledge, "I'm searching the thatch."

Our people were safe. But they'd gone mad.

My knights' faces were confused, disoriented by this double reality. But it hit me. "Donaloo. He's back."

A third step revealed guards, lined up, protecting the town. When they saw us in our Raslen garb, their spears lowered to point right at our chests.

*I*t was Quinn who stopped them. Even without words, my silent spy master's name and face were known throughout the kingdom. He side-stepped a spear point and tossed his blue vest on the ground. He tugged at his hair and fingered the bead there.

The eyes on the soldier nearest him widened. "Knight Quinn? Quinn Hale?"

Quinn gave the man a small smile.

The soldier turned to one of his comrades. "Get the general!"

My heart nearly collapsed in relief. If they were saying that, Ryan was okay.

A soldier scampered off and their commanding officer was soon tromping over. He was a thick, burly man whose hair was mostly grey. Luckily, this man recognized Connor as well as Quinn.

Connor used his normal charm on the soldier. "Is there somewhere we can wait for Ryan? We've been on a confidential mission and will need to discuss it with him."

"Of course, sir," the commander clicked his heels together and escorted us away from the road toward a small barracks that had been built to guard the edge of the capital. He left us in a plain wooden room with a long table and several benches. Another soldier brought a pitcher of water and several cups and set them out for us.

Dini started to screech for some sugar water, but Declan had a very convenient coughing fit that covered it up for us. I scratched at her bark to shut her mouth.

Her little moan wasn't much better.

"Do you need anything else?" the commander asked, looking at us oddly.

Connor came forward and shook the man's hand. "No, thank you, that's wonderful, Commander—"

"Lawton, sir."

"Commander Lawton. We'll be fine here. I'm so happy to see that everyone is okay. When we flew up, we had quite a fright."

"Yes, that wizard. He's an odd duck, but glad he's on our side. When the sultan and his horde flew overhead and circled the city, I thought we were goners—"

The man's thoughts must have projected clearly to Blue, and I think he might have sent them through to all of us without meaning to, because suddenly we saw the sultan and his entourage floating in midair, their midsections dissolving into colorful twists of smoke as they hovered above my capital like vengeful ghosts. It seemed like the sultan had brought his harem with him, for he was surrounded by beautiful women who wore no armor, simply embroidered silk, with gold bands adorning their wrists, gold cuffs along their ears, gold rings piercing their bottom lips. They flew slowly over the town, almost like a parade of terror. The sultan smiled and waved at those who came out and screamed and pointed at him. He didn't stop his slow flight until he was right over the center of the town, his twist of navy smoke swirling around as the wind picked up.

My stomach dropped even though what I watched was a memory. I knew what came next.

The djinn women linked hands and closed their eyes as Sultan Raj wove his hands through the air.

The captain hadn't been able to hear the sultan's words, but the intent was clear. They were going to attack. A golden haze formed in the women's hands, as if the wish was so strong, it had to manifest in physical form. Raj reared back his muscular arm and pointed. The women launched a gold jet of magic—

Shouts and screams sounded off in the memory, and I cringed because they were so loud inside my head as Blue sent us the captain's thoughts.

The ball of magic spread out as it flew through the air, flattening like dough, spreading out until the sunlight filtered through the dark gold fog and turned all the faces around the captain a sickly orange color.

But then a single phrase had blasted through the streets, as if spoken through a bullhorn. "Wishes were made to grant happy ever afters, not cause sad disasters." Donaloo had *tsk*ed. "A djinni who makes others wish mean things, loses his rings."

Sultan Raj had roared when one of the women in his harem had gasped, reaching for her hand.

But the ring fell, glinting in the afternoon sunlight.

Raj opened his hands and pushed out his wish, diving at the same time to try to recover his ring.

But Donaloo's voice spoke again. "Mirror mirror oh, so fair, reflect only what the sultan wants to see—everywhere." A giant bubble, shimmering with rainbow color, appeared to encase Marscha. The golden wish magic hit the bubble and was absorbed by it; the bubble wobbled as it ate the magical attack.

An evil smile spread over Raj's face when he saw what he wanted—when he saw what we'd seen—a flattened capital. Then his hand reached the bubble and closed around something.

A little ping and a wobble of the bubble were the only things I could tell happened. Did the ring hit the bubble? Did it get out? Or bounce back?

Another ping confirmed the ring had fallen back down and rolled on some cobblestones somewhere.

But Sultan Raj glanced at his own hand, satisfied. A tiny bubble shimmered on his hand. So … the enchantment was making him see his ring, making him see what he wanted, even though it wasn't there—

My thoughts were interrupted as Donaloo's words blared through the captain's memory once more. "If any citizen finds the sultan's ring and brings it to the palace so I can destroy that sarding djinni, I'd be much obliged. Oh, and I'll grant you a spell."

I put a hand to my forehead and laughed as I rubbed away the tension. Sarding Donaloo. Thank the gods he was helping Evaness.

The captain looked at all of us, not realizing we'd just watched his memories. "Sorry about that, just—been a bit of a day, you know?"

"Oh, yes, I do." I nodded, forgetting I was still a rabbit-faced man. "Thank you, Commander. We'll make sure your service is noted."

He gave me a bit of an odd look but nodded before marching briskly out of the room.

Blue sat down and put his head on the table, worn out after projecting all those thoughts. I poured him a glass of water and knelt beside him.

"How could Donaloo wish for a ring? I thought you said they no one could wish for a ring—"

"Loopholes," he grumbled. "Donaloo … I'm guessing he just wished that the ring was lost or something."

"What about us? Could we wish that the ring was found?"

Blue bit his lip. "Not by us. And we ultimately want the ring to wish him ill. Rings are … not alive, but magical enough to sense intent. We want the ring to destroy Raj, thereby destroying the ring."

"Can we wish Raj was just suddenly an idiot? Or didn't have any more magic? Or couldn't make more wishes?" I brainstormed.

Blue shook his head. "He made wishes years ago to protect himself from all those sorts of attacks. Don't you think they've been tried over the centuries?"

"Can you help me find a loophole?"

He sighed. "I've been trying to figure out a way to destroy him since I was eight. Haven't yet. But I'll try."

I kissed his forehead and rumpled his hair before going to check on Declan.

Connor and Quinn had set Declan up between them on the bench. I squatted down so I could get a good look at him. There were shadows under his eyes. "How do you feel?"

He shrugged. "Nothing a little whipping wouldn't cure."

I narrowed my eyes. "You look awful to me. Worse than that."

"Gee, thanks."

"Connor," I barked.

Connor glanced up from his seat next to Declan. He also looked a bit worse for the wear. Given the fact that we hadn't slept, it wasn't surprising. "Yes?"

"See if Dec has any injuries from taking in all that emotion."

Declan rolled his eyes, "I don't have any physical injuries—"

Connor's pink healing magic cut him off. It sunk into his skin and his eyes closed. His expression relaxed.

Hmmm.... My mind whirled. It seemed like it might be working. Could healing work for more than just injuries?

"Connor, see if you can heal his mind, his emotions…" I ordered.

Declan's eyes flew open. "That's not possible!"

I shrugged. "You were able to suck all the emotions out of Isla. Nearly killed her. We didn't know Connor's former power could do that. So, who's to say Ryan's old power can't heal emotional wounds as well as physical ones?"

Connor moved his hands to turn Declan's face toward him. He placed a palm on each of Declan's cheeks and the pale skin of my scholar lit with a rosy, pink glow. After only a few seconds, Connor removed his hands.

"Is it not working?" I worried.

But Declan turned back to me, a gentle smile on his face.

"No, it worked, Peace," he said softly. "Thank you."

And then, Connor yanked him up off the bench and punched him in the gut.

Blue ran to pull my best friend off Declan, but I waved him back. "It's a side effect of healing," I said. "I'd thought he had a handle on it, since he hasn't had an issue before now." I lifted my hands and shot a jet of peace power at Connor, not stopping until he went limp. Quinn caught Connor before his face smashed into the table and laid him out on the floor.

Blue shook his head dolefully. *At least with wish magic, I had a limited number of wishes. This magic seems to be an endless seesaw of up and down. Good and awful.*

I shrugged. *You get used to it.*

He opened his mouth, but nothing came out. He exhaled hard in frustration. *No. I don't know if I will. I'm gonna go stand by the other mute and write in the dirt or something.*

He walked over to Quinn and pointed at his throat, rolling his eyes. Quinn gave him a half grin.

Then Blue pulled Quinn over to a dirty corner of the room—the soldiers had tracked plenty of mud in here— and started writing in the dirt. Quinn's head bent to read what the other had written. Watching them bond, knowing Quinn finally had someone who knew what he went through, tugged at my heart strings. It made me want to walk over and kiss them both.

But I didn't want to interrupt them. And I was still a man. So, I just poured myself a glass of water and took a drink.

I spilt water on myself when Ryan and Donaloo walked in. Because the first thing out of Donaloo's mouth was, "Do you prefer being a man, Bloss?"

CHAPTER EIGHT

I ignored the rude shite of a wizard and ran to
Ryan. I embraced him, throwing my arms
about his waist and burying my face in his well-defined
abs. The hug came with a myriad of emotions that I hadn't
been expecting. Anxiety, fear, and relief all made me
clutch him closer. I'd been repressing how terrified for
him I'd been.

Ryan patted me gently on the back but didn't really hug
me in return. I leaned back and stared up at him. His eyes
weren't on me. He was studying Donaloo's face. "Is this
really Bloss? You're not just trying to embarrass me
again?"

I pulled away from Ryan. I took a step back and looked up
at him. "What are you talking about?"

"You're the third man today that Donaloo has tried to
convince me is my wife."

"WHAT?" I roared in outrage. My manly bellow filled the room.

Ryan crossed his arms as he glared at the wizard. "I nearly kissed the first."

Snickers erupted around the room. My other knights found it hilarious.

I didn't. I turned to Donaloo and the urge to smack him across the face was tempting. But I resisted. Instead, I told him what I thought of him. "You bespawler."

Donaloo shook his head, his purple eye patch flapping. "And here I was going to do a kindness and turn you back. But you had to make a comment so foul and black."

Dini popped out of my sleeve at that moment, her red flower back in full force. "You nearly crushed me, you dunderhead!" she squealed.

At the same moment Donaloo yelled, "Dini!"

The flower swiveled to look at my wizard. "YOU!"

She dropped her hold on my arm and somehow was across the room before I could blink. Donaloo's hands lifted in a spell but she was on him in less than a second. Her roots dug in near his ankle and she wrapped her vine around his entire body until he tilted where he stood. He would have fallen face first into the floor if Ryan hadn't reached out a hand to steady him.

"You pompous, prattling pansy! As awful a sight as the taste of tansy!" Donaloo said.

"Take that back!" Dini used one of her leaves to dig into Donaloo's ear and tickle it.

He shook his head, trying to get away. "Never! No matter how you nettle, you can't defeat my mettle!"

My knights and I exchanged a look.

"What is going on?" I asked.

Dini answered as she grew thorns. "This saggy sack of skin and I used to court."

It took me a minute to register that statement. "Court. As in you had a courtship?" A flower? Donaloo had courted a flower?

"That's not what it was, you crazy bud, I watered you once, but you were a dud!"

"Oooh!" Dini squealed and started stabbing with her thorns.

"Is watered a metaphor?" Ryan leaned over and asked me.

"No. No, it's completely literal. Because I cannot stand the thought of it being anything else," I responded.

I watched as Donaloo hopped in place, squealing as Dini poked at his most tender bits. As amusing as it was, she looked intent on actually hurting my wizard. And he, unlike she, had used his magic countless times to help me.

"Dini!" I called out. "You are being disloyal. Donaloo has proven he's a friend of Evaness. And you promised to be loyal to my country."

"Is he your heir?" Dini asked. "A citizen?"

"Well, no—"

Dini blew a puff of pollen in Donaloo's face that made my wizard wheeze. "I promised loyalty to your land, your heirs, and your citizens."

Connor quickly interjected. "Donaloo, we formally invite you to become a citizen of Evaness."

"I accept!" Donaloo shouted, his eyes watering.

Dini *harumph*ed. She unwound herself from Donaloo's body and her flower settled around his ankle. I thought that was the end of it, but then her flower disappeared under his trouser leg. Donaloo kicked and shouted as the flower wriggled her way up his body.

"Rain down, wash away, this blight that—" he yowled and couldn't finish his spell. I didn't even want to know what Dini'd done to cause that yell.

The flower wriggled across his belly, his chest. He smacked at himself, trying to crush her. She wriggled up his neck and her roots traveled over his face, jutting underneath his skin like spider veins. She stopped when she reached his forehead. She clung to his face, her flower bouncing up and down on the side of his head like a feather in the cap of some ostentatious courtier.

Donaloo swung at her again, but she merely wiggled away so that he punched himself in the face.

My hand flew to my mouth, and I couldn't help the snort of laughter that escaped.

Dini preened, her leaves smoothing her feathers down. "Yes, I think this is an excellent spot."

"I'll rip you stem from limb," Donaloo threatened.

"Try it," she shot back. "I buried my rootball in your nuts."

Behind me, Quinn and Blue erupted in laughter. I turned to watch for a moment as my silent knight laughed with sound for the first time since I'd met him. It made a little smile form on my face.

But then I turned back to Donaloo. "Can you please transform me?"

Donaloo muttered one last curse at the pink flower bobbing on his forehead but then he complied. He muttered some words and threw a pinch of something on the ground in front of me. Seconds later, my body changed shape and my boobs returned. I clutched at them.

Thank heavens! I'm myself again, I thought.

I'd spent enough years in disguise spells; I never wanted to do so again.

I turned around in relief, ready to hug Ryan once more and get a proper kiss in return. I turned too soon; however, because my rabbit face hadn't fully restored itself. All of my knights give me an odd look when they saw my massive smile. Only Blue's thoughts about the disjointed man's face on my body clued me into what they saw. I nearly shuddered myself as I saw Blue's view of my face. My skin slid around like bread dough. Watching someone transform after a disguise spell was equivalent to watching a doctor set a broken bone. It made one cringe automatically in sympathy.

Most of my knights looked away. Only Blue maintained eye contact with me the entire time.

I've seen worse, he thought at me.

Well, don't think about it right now, I told him quickly in my mind. *I'm trying not to puke over how my face looks as it bubbles and reforms. In fact, maybe you should stop looking at me.*

Fair enough, he thought. But then Quinn tugged on his sleeve and wrote something in the dirt. Blue leaned over to read it. He laughed. Then he immediately put my transformation on replay, sending it to me. Only, he modified it, so that my head changed to a lion's, then a crow's, then a squirrel's. I walked over and smacked Quinn across the back of the head. "That's not nice."

Quinn grinned up at me, his devilish smirk erasing my irritation. I rolled my eyes. "You're lucky you're adorable."

Ryan came up behind me and lifted me up in the air. He gave me a giant bear hug from behind. Then he twisted me around in his arms and wrapped his hands under my thighs. He kissed my nose. "I'm so glad it's finally you."

I traced his giant biceps and the veins that popped along his arms.

Ryan grinned when I squeezed his arm, but my hand didn't even fit a quarter of the way around his massive muscles. I smiled back at him and resisted pressing closer. If I pressed against Ryan, I'd want to do naughty things. And we didn't have time for that now. Plus, we had an audience.

Ryan's eyes grew hooded, as if he could read my thoughts via my expression. He gently set me down and said, "The wizard did think to bring you a dress, so that you wouldn't have to walk up to the castle like this."

"That was thoughtful of him," I turned surprised eyes over to Donaloo. The wizard seemed to enjoy torturing me, so this bit of thoughtfulness seemed a bit off for his odd personality.

"The people of Evaness need to see their queen is alive and well. They need their spirits strengthened before we rebel." Donaloo's wise words were undermined by the fact that Dini had decided to form a flower crown on his forehead.

I walked over to the wizard and took his hand, ignoring the fact that his shirt was untucked, and his green vest was misbuttoned. I definitely ignored Dini, who fluttered her petals at me. She needed to see what Donaloo meant to Evaness. "Thank you, Donaloo. From the bottom of my heart. Thank you for helping my people." We exchanged a long look.

And I wondered if employing him might further strengthen Dini's inability to pester him.

"Don't even think of asking that. I'd rather transform into a rat," Donaloo said, yanking his hand away and turning sharply. He strode toward the door.

"Asking what?" Ryan asked. "You didn't say anything."

"I was thinking about asking him to be our new castle mage."

"Your castle mages have a tendency to get themselves blown up," Donaloo gave me a flat look, not bothering to rhyme.

"Yes, I saw the last one," Dini squeaked. "Might be just the right job for you!"

I ignored the sniping flower and looked at Donaloo. "How—"

"I had him scry you," Ryan admitted. "You all spoke about it as you flew here."

I turned to Donaloo. "One of those was not under my reign, so that one's technically not my fault."

"Cerena also touched a death amulet when we specifically told her not to," Connor joined in.

"Death amulet?" Donaloo turned around, his one eye wide, the other brow arched high above his eye patch in a questioning manner. He bit his lip in a tiny tell of desire, or so I thought.

Dini's lip curled in disgust. "See what I said about magic makers? Can't resist power."

Donaloo reached up and flicked one of her petals.

"Ouch!"

"I don't want power, I want peace. Happy endings—a war to cease."

"Lies!" Dini grumbled. "You magic makers are all obsessed with proving yourself the cleverest."

Donaloo shook his head fiercely, causing Dini to squeal and flail her leaves. "A buzzing brain is but dung and flies. The heart is where humanity lies."

Between the two of them, the wizard had proven himself to me. And despite the concerns Dini's words created, I trusted my instincts, the way my father had taught me to do as a girl, when we'd run through the forest to hide from dragons. He'd tried to take me up a hill, but I'd insisted we go down. We'd found a small stone overhang at the base of the craggy hill and taken shelter. We'd shivered together and he'd pulled me close. The dragons had rained down flames around us, but we had survived that day. My instincts told me I could trust Donaloo, but that it might be better not to reveal the location of the amulets.

I'd need to move and destroy those as soon as possible. I gave Donaloo a very practiced apologetic look, one that had served me well during coin collection when I worked at a brothel. "I hope that death amulet wasn't your creation," I said. "Cerena was drawn to it like a moth to a flame. Then a giant stomped it to pieces."

Donaloo shook his head in sadness and disappointment. His lips thinned and his eye pierced me like a knife before he shrugged and threw out a hand as if he were scoffing at me. "I've never wanted to touch death. Too dark and grim that loss of breath."

I exaggerated the eye roll I gave to the ceiling. "Well, someone was dumb enough to try it. And they stuck Dini down there for some reason. Probably because she's more annoying than you!"

"Hey!" Dini shot a jet of pollen my way.

I dodged it and returned to my conversation with Donaloo. "But now, we better move. Isla will be furious she's lost a pair of giants. At some point, Raj will realize he's been deceived. And has anyone seen a sign of that sea sprite?"

"Sea sprite?" Dini tilted her petals.

Both Donaloo and Ryan shook their heads.

I sighed. "Then she's planning something."

"Agreed," Declan said. "Donaloo, I'd like to speak with you about the properties of magic, for a moment, if I could." My blond knight escorted Donaloo out of the room, peppering the old man with questions about the qualities of mixed magic, whether he knew of any cases of transference, of the likelihood of new capabilities forming … Declan got into full scholar mode.

Donaloo didn't rhyme once when he answered, which was annoying. But perhaps the fact that the flower on his head disagreed with every other answer he gave annoyed him.

Ryan stopped me from following them when he handed me a bundle I hadn't noticed before. I went into one of the bunk rooms and changed into a dress while Ryan stood guard at the door. I ended up in a black silk gown that was conservative in front but showcased my back.

Ryan couldn't help but caress the exposed skin and whisper, "Soon." His touch lit me up and his words had me desperate to turn the soldier's bunkhouse into a bit of debauchery. But we couldn't. Not yet. Another attack was imminent. We'd gotten lucky. But we needed to prepare.

I roughly tugged my hair up and twisted it behind me. I didn't have pins, and so I knotted it roughly. Ryan gently slipped a small tiara onto my head. It was nothing compared to the elaborate crowns my mother had worn. But my people needed hope, not a gaudy display of wealth.

Our procession riding on the gargoyles—which Connor insisted upon—was both nerve-wracking and exalting. I worried at every moment that my beast would dive off into the crowd, disobeying my commands and hurting someone. To my shock, my gargoyle was perfectly docile. And since I led the procession, perhaps that was why the others behaved as well.

The people of Marscha cheered. And not the way they'd cheered my coronation—polite duty.

The shopkeepers raised their fists with rousing calls of "Hoo-ra!"

A butcher held his cleaver in the air and shouted, "Long live Queen Bloss!"

"Destroy those djinn!" a woman cried.

Two little girls ran up to me with homemade crowns. I stopped the procession and had my gargoyle kneel so that I could climb down and speak to them. One placed her crown of woven blue leaves over my tiara. The other one refused and said, "This one's for your pony." So, I'd lifted her and allowed her to crown my gargoyle, who I decided deserved a name.

When I mounted, I leaned forward and said, "Come on, Pony." And Pony rose and continued along through town, as if he'd been trained for years and knew exactly what to do.

When we reached the drawbridge, I turned back to face the town one last time. And a massive cheer rose up—a call to action for me. I had to do better. I had to do more. These people had survived because of Donaloo. Not me. Not their queen. I needed to do whatever was required to save them. I fingered my leaf crown. Those giggling little girls were a reminder of everything that was at stake.

As we crossed the relatively empty moat, I asked, "Have we had any soldiers or messengers from Sedara?"

Ryan didn't respond immediately, but from the very fact that he was quiet, I knew. My heart fell. The most powerful kingdom had not sent help. Declan's mother had not sent help.

Behind me I could hear Declan say bitterly, "Bastard sons don't matter. She won't lift a finger to help us."

"Have we sent a messenger?" I asked.

Ryan did respond to that. "Yes. I sent one out on one of the gargoyles just after the sultan left. He should be back sometime tonight with her reply."

"We could certainly use at least some Elven weapons. I've heard they cleave through wish magic."

I turned to look up at him. Ryan was eyeing our gargoyles rather than crossing the moat. I walked a few steps back toward him. "My gargoyle has become more complacent. Has yours?"

Ryan shook his head. "Not at all. I cursed the bugger halfway here. Did you do something specific?"

I shrugged and shook my head. "No."

"Can you make them sit?"

"Maybe Pony. But I don't know about the rest of them," I responded.

"Pony?"

"That's what the little girl who gave him the crown called him. My pony. Thought it was cute." I leaned around Ryan and said. "Pony, sit."

Pony sat. And so did each of the remaining gargoyles.

ANN DENTON

Ryan came and scooped me up. He didn't kiss me, but he dipped me so that my head nearly swept the ground. "Whatever you did, it's brilliant. Hopefully, when Jace gets back with the rest of them, they'll follow Pony's lead."

I tapped his arm. "About to pass out from head rush here."

"Sorry," he set me back on my feet and scooped up my tiara and leaf crown. He set both back onto my head. "I need to research formations."

I nodded. "Yes. That sounds good. We also need to go through our royal documents for strategies regarding ancient sea sprites. Weaknesses, etcetera." I turned to Declan. "Do you think you might be able to look into that?"

Declan gave a quick nod. "Of course." He stepped around a massive crater in the courtyard, left from the attack yesterday. Ryan strode after him, calling out, "There are still people frozen in some of the rooms!" Declan nodded but I couldn't hear his response, they were too far. The pair of them disappeared up a stairwell.

Unbidden, a yawn rose on my lips as we entered the great hall. We wove around frozen citizens who stood like statues. They still had two days left until they unfroze and went on their way. A small part of me envied them. But envy wouldn't win any wars. I couldn't rest. Speaking of … I turned to Donaloo, where he and Dini were having a whispered argument.

"Is there anything you can do to ward off exhaustion?" I asked.

"Magic is a start but true solutions lie within the heart. When done with love, a sacrifice can turn the tide and end the strife," the mage winked at me.

Dini growled. "Stop the rhyming! It's obnoxious."

The little flower was right about that. But I smiled when the wizard gave a jaunty little heel click that made her squeal and headed toward the stairwell that led to the mage's tower.

"So, that's a no?" I asked.

He hummed as he left, a nonsense song about a jester's jokes killing his audience with laughter. I stared after him, trying to decide if his words were nonsense or something else. "You trust him, Connor?"

Connor came and stood next to me, staring at Donaloo as the old man hummed. My best friend cleared his throat. "It would be easier to give you an answer if I could still read his emotions. But, let's say I trust him for now. I'll trust him until he gives me reason not to."

"And the flower?"

"She's a big unknown. But Donaloo seems to enjoy her company."

"What?" I turned to stare at him. "Are you crazy?"

"I was back beside them during the procession. They nag each other like an old married couple."

I nodded. If Connor said it, then I believed him. He was far better at reading people than I was.

Quinn led us to the yellow parlor to sit and talk strategy. I found myself on a small couch and Quinn slid over to sit beside me. He wrapped an arm around my shoulders and gently pulled my head onto his chest. My eyelids grew heavy, and even though I fought, I knew I was fighting a losing battle.

"Close your eyes, Bloss Boss," Connor ordered. "When Donaloo gets back here with the potion, we'll wake you up so you can drink it."

"Are you sure he's making a potion?" I yawned.

"Yes. Now sleep," Connor said.

Quinn smacked his hand over my eyes, forcing me into darkness. I laughed and squirmed, but he held tight. Eventually, I gave up fighting. The moment he loosened his grip, I shot up and away from him. I scurried across the room and stuck my tongue out at him, in a very queenly fashion.

Blue laughed.

I turned to Connor. "What about your powers?" I asked. "What if sleep is like an injury? What if fatigue is just my body's poor response to something, what if it's a need to repair itself—"

"You're reaching," Connor said. "I don't know what Donaloo's done but annoy you."

"Nothing," I shrugged.

Connor shook his head when I clasped my hands together to beg him to try. "No! I punched Declan out the last time I used these new powers. I don't want to do that again. I was out of control."

I walked over to him and grabbed his hand. I did our secret handshake from childhood. "Please?" I jutted out my lower lip.

Connor groaned and rolled his eyes to the heavens. "You're not fair."

"Queens aren't fair," I winked. "It's in that royal indoctrination document we have to sign."

Connor smiled with amusement as he set his hands on my waist and slowly allowed pink light to flow from his hands into me.

I started to feel more alert almost instantly. My back stopped aching from the gargoyle ride over. I grew giggly, and it took a minute before I realized I might be overdosing on healing. I pulled his hands down but said, "Quinn! Blue, come try this!"

Quinn stood next to me and Connor moved his pink light from my waist to Quinn's shoulders. I watched as Quinn visibly perked up. His sagging shoulders straightened, and his eyes regained their naughty gleam.

But seconds later, before he got to Blue, Connor cut the magic off. "I can't!" he roared. His lip curled up in a snarl and his hands clenched into fists. He pushed past us and stomped out of the room. He slammed the door behind him yelling into the hall, "I need to punch someone. Anyone volunteer?"

I bit my lip and turned to Quinn. "I hope he doesn't punch one of the frozen people."

And while Quinn gave me a half smile, it was more sad than laughing. We both knew that Connor prided himself on controlling his emotions, on feeling out the emotions of others and putting them at ease. Ryan's power countered everything he'd ever used to define himself.

I went out, determined to find Connor and give him some peace. But I underestimated just how out of control he was.

CHAPTER NINE

*I*t took me awhile to find him. I should have asked Blue, but I knew that Connor wouldn't want any of the other knights around. He saw his anger as a weakness, as a lack of control—not as what it truly was, the price of his magic. For him, I could only imagine what a nightmare his uncontrolled rage was. He was a diplomat. Anger was counter to everything he'd ever tried to achieve.

I searched our normal haunts but couldn't find him in any of them. He wasn't in the stables or near the bell tower. He wasn't in any of the secret passageways he'd loved to use to spy on the nobles. He wasn't in my old room. I'd nearly given up my search when I found him beating his hands bloody against a satyr statue in the hallway near my bed chamber.

"Connor!" I cried, bolting toward him. I extended my hands and shot green magic at him until his hands sunk to his sides and his eyes were glazed with the dullness of peace. I reached up to caress his face, but he jerked away from my touch.

That movement felt like a slap. Connor had never pulled away from me. Not growing up, at least. He'd been slower to warm upon my return to the castle, but that was understandable. He'd thought I'd left him. But, now? Just when all had become good between us again?

"Connor?" I asked.

My knight hung his head, ashamed that I'd seen him acting so wild and crazed. "I'm sorry, Bloss Boss. I just can't contain it."

"Sweetheart, I know. Don't worry."

"I'm a danger."

"No. You never thought Ryan was a danger, did you?"

"He had years to perfect his control. And military training to—nothing—you don't understand what it's like. I can't see straight."

"Blind with rage, huh?"

"Yes. I want to hit the first person I see. And you're too close—so often, you're too close."

I stroked his arm and shot a little more peace over his clenched fists. This time he didn't pull away. I considered it progress. I opted for a soothing tone. "But think what you can do, who you can help."

"What good is it to heal someone if I want to rip them apart seconds later?" Connor laughed bitterly.

"Have you asked Ryan about it?"

Connor bit his lip, and I knew he hadn't asked. I didn't lecture him, since, honestly, there'd been no time to ask.

I grabbed him by the wrist, his knuckles were too bloodied for me to take his hand, and I led him into my chambers. Gennifer was frozen mid-step near my bed, one of my petticoats held aloft in her hands as she carried it toward my dressing room to hang it.

I led Connor to the bathing room. My tub was full. Gennifer had probably filled it last night.

I grabbed a washcloth and a bar of soap. We were both filthy from the cave and the gargoyles. I stripped down and ordered Connor to do the same. I washed myself quickly and efficiently because the water was horribly cold. Connor did the same and the cold and accompanying shivers seemed to cool him down. I couldn't help but admire his body as he bent and washed his calves. His ass had dimples just above it, and the way his waist tapered made me itch to put my hands on him. But I resisted, letting him get clean and calm first.

"Well, we have one potential solution," I smiled at him as we walked back to my bedroom in the nude. "We can have Ryan learn to multiply snow and dump a bucket of it over your head when you're angry."

Connor laughed. "I might actually take you up on that."

I leaned over and reached up to caress his cheek. "The anger that you're feeling is unnatural. Try to hold onto that. It's part of the magic. Your price. You used to pay in depression. One might think this is better. It's at least easier. It's a bit more temporary."

"True, I never realized I could stop drinking in emotions." Connor sighed. He pulled me in for a hug. "Thank you, Bloss Boss."

My hardened nipples pressed into his stomach, and the feel of the flat planes of his abdomen and the muscle of his pecs turned me on. My eyes traveled up the strong lines of Connor's neck, to the curly mess of hair that I so loved.

Connor's sea blue eyes stared down at me. "I'm supposed to be the logical, level-headed one out of the pair of us."

"You can still be if you want."

My hands slid to his pecs and I let my fingertips gently glide over his nipples. I smiled at his sharp intake of breath and rubbed my own hard nipples against him, stimulating them, too. I leaned forward and placed a kiss on his left pec, near his heart. And then I let my tongue trace a naughty trail around his chest and stomach as my fingers continued to tease his nipples. I made sure to keep my own rubbing against him too, so that he'd know exactly how hot he made me.

When I saw his arm start to reach for me, I took a quick step back, abandoning my teasing. "You said you're supposed to be the practical one, right?" I asked, as I played with my nipples.

Connor nodded; his eyes drawn inevitably toward my breasts.

"Well, you could tell me that it would be utterly impractical for us to make love right now. You could be practical and tell me not to go climb up on my bed naked and spread my legs for you. You could be practical and ignore me while I do this." My hand traveled south.

He bit his lip as he watched me play with myself. "You could be practical and say we have no time for sex. You could say we need to plan for a war instead." I leaned forward and caressed his neck. His pulse beat rapidly. Knowing how excited he was made my own desire grow.

Anticipation crept up my spine and heated my core.

I raised my hand to push back my hair, and realized my wrists still bled a little, from the peace I'd shot at Connor.

He seemed to realize it at the same moment. His hand shot forward and closed around my wrist.

"Only a tiny bit," I said, as pink magic pulsed along my skin.

He nodded and cut it off quickly. My new skin was still pink and tender, not perfect the way Ryan might have healed it. But it would do.

Healing me had distracted Connor. I decided I needed to get him back on track. So, I grabbed his finger and sucked it into my mouth, swirling my tongue around the tip. Then I controlled his hand as I traced a lazy, swirling pattern down my chest and abdomen, until his finger touched my wetness.

His finger started to enter me.

And again, I stepped back.

But this time, after using his power, there was more fire in Connor's gaze. His nostrils flared.

And something inside me liked it.

"Are you gonna be practical, Connor?"

Connor cleared his throat and gazed up and down my figure. But then he glanced to the foot of the bed, where Gennifer still stood, frozen like a figurine.

"What about ... what about your maid? Is she frozen but sentient? Does this spell still let her see?"

I leaned forward and pressed my breasts together so that my nipples were close. I spread my legs and put my hands on my thighs, posing for him as I raised a brow. "You'd like that, wouldn't you? To think she's watching us?"

Connor swallowed hard and nodded. "But would you?"

I walked over toward Gennifer and climbed onto the bed right in front of her line of sight. I scooted backward on the coverlet, my eyes steadily on Connor's. I slowly spread my legs. "So, we'll let her watch." I let my hand drift down to my mound. I dipped my fingers inside to gather some wetness and rub it up over myself.

Connor groaned.

"Come closer to your queen," I ordered. I pulled my pussy lips apart so he could see how wet I was.

I leaned back on my elbows and realized my flower crown and tiara were still set in my hair. I left them there as my hands gestured for Connor to join me on the bed.

Connor's chest heaved like he had run a foot race. But I knew he was just trying to control himself, like he always did. He was trying to hold back, despite the tension I saw in his body, despite the hard dick in his hands. He stroked himself slowly, getting his voyeuristic fill.

"I'm still on edge, Bloss," he whispered, as his hand slid up and teased the head of his shaft. "I don't want to hurt you."

I needed him. I needed him on top of me. I realized I'd need to go further to tempt him. "Connor," I whispered. "I want it rough." I rolled over and let him see my ass. I looked back over my shoulder as I said, "I want you to spank me. Use that anger. And I want you to hold me down as you suck me from behind and yank my hair, then I want you to rut me hard."

"Gah!" He strode to the edge of the bed, stroking himself. "Get up on your knees. I want to watch you play with yourself," he ordered.

I rose up and arched my back so he could see my slit. I used my middle finger to circle my clit. And then I started moving in figure-eight. Pleasure mounted inside me and I laid my head down on the mattress so that I could use my other hand to pinch a nipple.

"No," Connor's hands latched onto my ankles and pulled me roughly toward the edge of the bed. He flipped me so that my back fell to the mattress. Then he leaned forward, so his body covered mine. "Your nipples are mine." His lips latched onto the left one and he rubbed his lips against my swollen bud in gentle circles, teasing me. His lips barely touched my flesh. It was maddening. So good and yet not enough. I rubbed my gash harder and tried to arch my breast up into his mouth. But he used his other hand to hold me down.

"You said you wanted me to be mean." He pinched my nipple and then lightly smacked my breasts before reaching down and yanking my hand away from my sopping slit. "Turn over," he growled.

My mind lit up in a lust-filled haze. Connor had never given me orders. Our entire life, our entire friendship, had been based on me being a brat and him being the good-natured peacemaker who smoothed things over. I didn't know if dealing with this magical anger brought out a new side in him, but I knew I liked it.

I turned over beneath him. He held his body suspended over mine as I did. But once my ass was back up, Connor shuffled off the side of the bed and stood. He pulled on my waist so that my ass was up and facing him. Then he spanked me. He smacked my ass three times, just enough for me to yelp. Just enough for it to sting. Then he pulled my ass cheeks apart and his face dove down into my pussy from behind. He lapped at me, flattening his tongue and using long, slow strokes.

I moaned as I heated up like an inferno. I longed to grind myself into his face, but he held my hips and ass too tightly.

"Connor, I need you," I moaned as I teetered on the brink of orgasm.

He stopped and I wanted to cry. My orgasm receded.

"Beg more," Connor smacked my ass one more time and then flipped me so that I star fished on the mattress.

My chest heaved and I begged, "Please. Oh please."

His fingers slid inside me and curled, and he held down my stomach as he gave me lip service. He was a sarding mouth artist. My legs writhed on the mattress and I nearly kicked him when I finally exploded. My vision went black, the sensory overload too much. I died a little death and my head floated in the clouds.

And even as my orgasm tapered off, every part of me still ached for him to press his cock inside and just ream me. My mind was overcome with primal urges. I whimpered, "Connor, I've never wanted anything more in my entire life than you."

His arm came up around my neck, squeezing lightly as his dick slammed into me, owning every inch of my pussy. He rutted me hard and fast until he was close to completion. Then he stopped, pulled out, and sank his teeth into one on my breasts, biting me as he forced his cock to calm down. He ran his dick back and forth over my clit, soaking it with my own hot lubrication. Then he went down on me once again, sucking my clit into his mouth with so much force that I came instantly, rocking my pelvis against him and screaming.

He gave me no time to recover before he slammed back into me and rode me again. This time, he threw one of my legs up over his shoulder. "Take it," he cried, as his dick hit my cervix.

"Yes, Connor," I breathed, mindless with my afterglow even as he pummeled me. He got so deep that it hurt. I tried to hide my whimper. But he wouldn't let me get away with that.

He put a hand on my stomach and pink light permeated my skin, easing the pain. And then he pushed even harder. He grabbed my other leg and bent both legs toward me so he could hump deeper. After his pink healing magic, the pain was only a sliver of sensation that heightened my senses. And I moaned, clutching the sheets, as an orgasm deeper than any I'd ever felt before took me.

Connor dropped my leg and smacked my hip, pulling out. "Ride me," he commanded. He lay back on the mattress and stroked his dick as I struggled to recover enough to get up and do what he wanted.

When I sank down on him, he grabbed my breasts, pushing them together. I used my knees to pump myself up and down on top of him and he leaned forward, his tongue flicking from nipple to nipple. Impossibly, my pleasure started to grow again. Sparks flitted across my vision. And I reached the high point of pleasure, clenching around him as he groaned and pumped up hard into me.

Afterward, we lay across my bed, sated. Connor's hand traced up and down my spine as he stared at the bed canopy.

"That was amazing," I told him. "Everything I never knew I wanted."

He chuckled.

"I'm definitely making you use your magic a lot during sex," I promised. "That was sarding hot."

He gave me a satisfied smirk. "It was, wasn't it?"

I grabbed his hand and squeezed it tight. "I'm so lucky."

He started to laugh but post-sex emotions took over, and I said softly, "I'm serious, Connor. Not just because your magic is hot. I'm lucky to have you. You've always been my best friend. Even when I left, you were my best friend. I know you never got my letters … but I've always loved you. And I feel lucky to get to love you as you evolve."

He squeezed my hand and his eyes misted. But he swallowed hard and tried to joke, "Devolve, more like. These powers make me a brute."

"Hey, angry sex with you is hot, so if you ever need to burn off some magically-induced rage …"

He chuckled. "I have a feeling I'm gonna be angry in a lot of places, Bloss. We're gonna need healing magic for a lot of things. Battlefields, for one."

"Good thing you like the idea of people watching then," I jested.

He laughed but gathered me up and cradled my head on his arm. "Thank you, Bloss Boss. I needed this."

I rolled on my side to stare at him. "Connor, I'm here for you. I'll always be here for you."

"And I, you."

"Secret friends forever?" I asked, raising my right hand for our secret handshake.

Connor lifted his hand, too. And there, in bed, after the most amazing sex, we did our secret shake. And my heart felt certain that everything would be alright.

My heart was shite at predictions.

After Connor and I dressed, and he helped me comb and plait my hair, we went in search of the other knights.

We stopped short in the great hall. A gargoyle had entered the palace. Not one of our newly created young rocks— one of the two ancient gargoyles that had served my mother and grandmother. The gargoyle saw me and immediately bowed. Then it knelt on the ground, its old body creaking as stone rubbed stone when it bent.

I walked toward it and realized something was lashed to its back.

It was our messenger. And his throat had been cut.

CHAPTER TEN

I smashed open the door to the private royal library. It was a room kept separate from the literature and histories provided to the courtiers. This room had been solely for my mother and fathers' research.

The library rose three stories in front of me. The bottom floor was lined with windows on the left and two additional floors could be accessed by ladders. Those floors were lined with marble balustrades and narrow aisles with plush red carpet to muffle footsteps as courtiers looked for books. When we were younger, Connor and I had once used the carpet to our advantage to sneak to the edge of the balcony and pour an ink pot down on Lady Agatha.

I rushed past books and scrolls, maps and ledgers. I ignored the scent of aged parchment. Normally, when I came to this room, I could appreciate the beauty and the knowledge that it held. But my heart was beating furiously, and I was so enraged I saw red. Declan looked up from the scroll he was studying.

"What is it?"

"Your mother's responded." I seethed.

"She killed our messenger," Connor said softly behind me.

Declan closed his eyes and shook his head. "I'm sorry," he breathed.

Ryan appeared at the balcony of the second floor, a book in his hand. He gripped the railing hard with his free hand and said, "Too bad all of her ambassadors have turned into such cowards. We could have responded in kind."

I walked over to Declan's table and slammed my hands down on the tabletop. "Sedara is the reason for this mess. This war is against them and Queen Diamoni's unfair trade practices. But Evaness is the only country suffering."

Connor took a seat next to Declan, rubbing my scholar's shoulder in solidarity. Ryan descended the ladder to come stand behind me. My giant knight wrapped his arms around my waist and pulled me back into him. His fingers traced circles on my hips. "It'll be alright, Little Dearling."

I sank back against him, drinking in the comfort of his hold. I tried to let go of my anger. But urgency still gnawed at me. I stared down at Connor and Declan. "What can we do?"

Connor rubbed his forehead thoughtfully. "We can send messengers south to Lored. But they haven't the battle power. Neither does Macedon to the north of Cheryn. At best that country could be a distraction." He trailed off chewing on his lower lip as he sank deeper into thought.

Declan's contributions didn't help the matter. "Everything I've read said that the sea creatures we're likely to face are sirens, who can lure you to drown yourself, and ashrays— which are worse."

"What are those?" I asked.

Declan grabbed an open book next to him and pushed it toward me. I leaned forward to look. The page showed an illustration of several murky blurs with glowing green eyes floating in the water. They looked almost like the sea jellies I'd seen washed ashore, but for the eyes, which were hauntingly human.

Declan's finger traced the outline of one of the ashrays. "They are sea ghosts. Humans tempted to die by sea crea- tures. Their souls become trapped under the sea. They spread terror. But, more importantly for us—they spread cold. They can take a sixty-degree patch of ocean and turn it into one that's just above freezing. Our soldiers wouldn't have time to drown before they died of hypothermia or fear."

A shiver ran down my spine at the thought of falling over- board and being surrounded by these creatures. I tried to combat my fear by returning to my anger. My frustration. "Hell!" I cried. "Why can't our enemies be sarding human?"

Declan cleared his throat. "I've been thinking about this. I've only ever manipulated physical things. But temperature is technically physical. I wonder if Ryan—"

The clank of armor interrupted Declan's train of thought. We turned to see one of Ryan's soldiers standing in the doorway.

"Sir," the man had clearly come straight from his horse. He still wore his cape and his riding boots, though he'd pushed the cape back to reveal his balding head. He saluted and waited for Ryan to address him.

Ryan turned away from the rest of us, but stayed next to us, so we could overhear the conversation. "Commander Blythe. Proceed."

"Duchess Agatha's province is overrun with djinn."

My heart drummed so quickly that I couldn't separate the beats. "We had mostly evacuated the province due to the dragon threat, hadn't we?" I hated how tight my voice came out. It was not confident or calm at all. I took a slow breath, hoping to ease the tension that had me wound so tight.

Sard it, Bloss, I scolded myself. Hold it together for this man. Who knows if he's got family there? I couldn't tell by the look in the soldier's eyes, but Ryan tried to station soldiers within a two hour walk of their home village.

Ryan looked at me as if he knew what I was thinking. He frowned as he said, "Evacuations were in progress."

My heart fell. That wasn't a good sign. I resisted clasping my hands together. I looked back at the commander. His eyes were lined with crow's feet from years of smiles. But he didn't smile at me now.

"They've taken the Duchess Agatha's estate, sir," the soldier reported.

"Were any of her husbands there?"

Commander Blythe nodded and his lips thinned. "Yes, Your Majesty."

"Deceased?" It killed me that I had to ask it nonchalantly.

"Yes, Your Majesty."

Another noble family smashed apart. My thoughts flew to Agatha and Willard. I realized that I didn't even know if the pair had survived the attack on the castle.

Ryan took over after that—asking about what few Elven weapons we had on hand. "Get a contingent together. Take those Elven weapons with you; they'll cleave through wish-created creatures," Ryan advised. "Send any citizens here."

The commander saluted again before leaving the room.

Shite, shite, shite.

"They think I'm dead and that they've destroyed our capital, but Raj is still sending people after our provinces?" I raged.

ANN DENTON

I didn't hear Blue and Quinn enter the room until Blue walked up behind me. "I'm sorry," he said. "My father's a locust. He won't stop until everything here is a wasteland."

To my surprise, and his, my hand reached out and automatically clamped around his. But I needed someone to hold onto or I was going to lose it. I was going blind with panic and fury. I needed the warm, dry feel of his palm covering mine to anchor me. I turned and stared into his eyes, which reflected back my own agony. Was my country about to be lost? Were we completely without the hope of any ally? "We need help," I ground out.

"The only other possibility is Gitmore," Declan said.

I froze and stared at him. "What on earth can we possibly give Gitmore to convince them to ally with us? My mother always said their queen was beyond unreasonable—"

A throat cleared behind me. But when I turned, I didn't see another soldier. One of my least favorite people appeared. It looked like Jorad had survived the attack on the castle after all. I briefly wondered if Donaloo had unfrozen him or if the steward had fled the castle. He was so attached to these stone walls; I didn't think it likely he would have left.

I turned to look at him, abandoning our current conversation. I might not have cared for Willard, but he was one of my nobles. The portly man had done me a good turn recently. He'd just lost at least one of his fathers to the djinn. And Jorad cared for Willard. "Did he make it?" I asked.

Jorad's lips thinned and he gave a brief shake of his head.

Willard had been killed by the explosives in the noble's wing then. Surprisingly, the thought that he was gone made my heart ache. I reached my free hand for Jorad, but he stepped back, staying formal and inclining his head.

"Did any of the nobles in the wing make it?" I asked.

"Fer, Orunta. The pixie Sunya. Duchess Kycee and her entourage left early so Connor's family wasn't even here during the attack."

I felt like he'd hit me over the head with a log. "That's it?"

Malia had been a traitor. Agatha was gone. Duke Aiden and his wife were also dead. Nearly half my noble families had been wiped out in a night.

"What's the death count?" I couldn't dwell on emotions. I needed to deal in numbers until the shock wore off. Then I'd figure out what to do next.

"One-hundred-ninety-three, Your Majesty."

I nodded. "You'll take care of funeral arrangements at the crown's expense—"

Jorad nodded. "Already begun."

I pressed my lips together and took a moment to regain my composure. "How many frozen?"

"Six-hundred-eighty two, including the entire kitchen staff."

My hand started to fly to my neck, but I stopped it halfway. I had to maintain control of myself. "We'll need to get food brought in for whomever shelters—"

"It's been done."

As much as I didn't really enjoy him as a person, Jorad was efficient.

"How is it you weren't frozen?" Declan called out.

I wanted to smack my scholar. Sometimes, tact was not his forte.

Jorad looked at the ground. "I'd received some disturbing news—"

I recalled how Jorad had found out Willard had cheated. I quickly interjected, "He had leave to take a few hours." I could hardly imagine Jorad drowning his sorrows at a tavern, but wherever he'd wandered, his heartbreak deserved a bit of privacy.

Jorad nodded at me in thanks. Then he spoke. "When I came in, you were discussing Gitmore and the difficulty of creating an alliance with them," he said. "There were very personal reasons for the hatred between your mother and Queen Shenna."

"What? What do you mean? Our reports say Shenna's unbalanced. She's filled that desert of hers with undead soldiers—"

"She created a barrier between herself and the sea. Now, you know why." Jorad inclined his head. "Other nations didn't agree with certain methods, didn't believe in the same forms of protection as your mother."

My eyebrows raised. I had never heard Jorad blaspheme my mother like this. Me, yes. Absolutely. But he'd always been one of her lapdogs. Did he disagree with how she kidnapped Avia? I opened my mouth to ask when he dropped another bombshell on me.

"Besides, your mother was always a bit biased. And I don't know that she ever told you the truth." His tone was carefully court appropriate. The disdain that normally dripped from his lips when he spoke to me was absent. I froze. That meant the truth he was referencing was about to cut me to the bone.

I didn't have the time or energy or the emotional capacity for any further surprises. But it didn't seem to matter with my capacity was. Fate kept prodding me down the path anyway. War and destiny took without mercy. "What truth?" I asked.

Jorad looked a bit smug when he said, "Your mother married the Queen's brother."

"And?" I didn't understand. My thoughts raced to my four fathers. None of them had had the blue hair typical of Gitmore. But, in the past, when wizards had been more plentiful, some royal families had taken to having their appearance permanently altered. I'd never asked my fathers... my thoughts started to pull me in different directions.

Jorad shook his head. "Your mother married him in a private ceremony. When she was just eighteen. She married him and him alone."

"That's not possible. Her marriage was arranged—"

"He was a sailor. Self-proclaimed bachelor in love with the sea. Then they met. Once. She ran off, defiant. Hotheaded. Much like her daughter." The disapproval was back in Jorad's tone and in the slight curl of his lip. But I hardly noticed.

I was so astonished I took a step back, reeling from this new information. How could I not know something so important in my own mother's history? A woman who had determined the ins and outs of nearly every single day of my existence up to the age of eighteen. The woman who seemed to know everything about me. But it felt like the mother I thought I knew—the Queen I thought I resented—was actually a stranger.

It felt like a punch to the gut. Tears filled my eyes—from shock and betrayal. Ryan wrapped his arms around me from behind. Connor reached up from where he sat and took my hand. Fortified by their touch, I swallowed and tried to push back the little girl inside who wanted to scream. I blew out a slow, steady breath.

Connor rubbed my hand with soothing circles. "She had a life before the one you knew. I doubt she wanted to talk about an old husband with her new knights around."

"She should have told you she ran away. You probably wouldn't have repeated that move if you'd known she'd done it," Declan teased.

His joking helped take the edge off my hurt. I glared at him teasingly for a moment before I turned back to Jorad. "Who was he? What happened?"

"They were attacked on their flight back to Evaness. By a dragon. The squadron of our flyers had been chasing it. Prince Andersen's pegasus burned. He fell into the sea. Your birth father was amongst the soldiers. His peace power was the only thing that kept your mother from the same fate. It was how they met."

It felt like a tree branch had just fallen on my head. I was hurt and shocked, even heartbroken for mother. It was too much. I moved from Ryan's arms and dropped Connor's hand. He pulled out a chair for me and I sat. I couldn't believe it. I imagined my poor mother … married maybe a day before her husband was torn away from her. I stared listlessly at the tabletop and traced the wood grain with my finger now. "My father always said he met my mother rescuing her from a dragon. I thought he was joking."

Jorad shook his head. "Gitmore called the attack deliberate. They called it an assassination. Since then, the Queen has maintained quite a propaganda campaign against your mother. The locals there might be hard to convince."

My head sunk into my hands. The entire world was against us. Dragons, I could fight. Beasts, I could tame.

But hatred? Disdain? How could I fight that? "How can I convince any of these other countries to put their people at risk for mine? What could I possibly offer?"

Ryan's voice was a dark, scary scratch, like a claw on your windowpane in the middle of the night. "I don't think we should offer anything. I think we need to ensure that they know it's in their best interest to fight."

"How do we do that?"

"We bring the fight to them."

"But our provinces … how can we bring the fight to Rasle or Sedara? How can we do that and stop them from taking over more of our provinces? We don't have the manpower—"

Connor's hand slid over mine. "You're gonna have to choose, Bloss Boss."

Everything inside me tightened, though I knew he was right. Lose a province? Or eventually lose a kingdom? My mother's face appeared in my mind. One of the many lessons she'd forced me to endure as a teenager unfurled. Queen Gela's gaze had been calm when she'd told me exactly what I'd gotten wrong in that day's disastrous lesson. "Sometimes a queen must choose who to save and who to let go."

I'd told her that was a shite excuse for lazy people.

She'd simply smiled and tilted her head. "It's the sad reality we face. One day, you'll see."

I took a deep slow breath as every eye in the room fell on me. Tension and anticipation filled the room like mist, making the air heavy and hard to breathe. I let the sharp words fall from my lips like an executioner's axe. "We need our allies. Sedara in particular. But how can we convince them?"

Ryan's grin reminded me of why he'd become my general. "I have a few ideas."

CHAPTER ELEVEN

*R*yan's ideas all included our new fleet of nearly indestructible gargoyles. He stated that if they weren't able to fly in formations yet—which was my argument—they would be able to protect me, surround villages, trap marching armies.

"But they only listen to me!" I argued. "Or Pony does, anyway, and the rest seem to just follow along. I can't be everywhere we need." We needed to divide and attack from multiple directions at the very least. Even better if we could send some of the gargoyles against Isla and use some to guard Evaness.

Ryan rubbed my arm softly. I yanked it back, thinking he was patronizing me, but when he grabbed my hair and pulled it, then bent down and gave me a searing kiss, I stopped protesting. I stopped thinking and become a puddle of heat in his arms. Damn him. When he dominated me, there was no argument, no reason. My body just surrendered completely. My mind gave up and just awaited his orders. The thought of what he might do to my body filled me with longing. The places he might touch. The way his tongue felt on mine. There, in the middle of the library, as all my other knights watched, I rubbed myself against him like a cat in heat.

Jorad took the moment to excuse himself. "I'll see what might be in the cellar for dinner." And he shuffled away, muttering.

I hardly noticed, because Ryan's lips nipped at mine.

Ryan pulled out of our kiss with a grin. "Tomorrow, you're going to work with Jace to train those gargoyles. And you're going to figure out how to make them into the fleet I want, aren't you?"

I pressed my chest into him, nipples tightening. "Yes, sir."

Every one of my knights moaned at the sight.

"I think it's time to play pass the princess," Blue said, pushing back his seat at the library table and holding out his arms.

I had no idea what he meant, but his comment brought a round of cheers from my knights. Ryan laughed, scooped me up and set me on Blue's lap.

Blue was hard beneath his trousers and his hands went to my hips. He slanted his head and started to plant a row of kisses on the side of my neck.

His thoughts accidentally projected. —*So beautiful. I hope she likes this.*

I love it, I thought at him. *Right there*, I groaned as he hit a pulse point.

Would she mind if I grinded up into her? he wondered to himself, not realizing he sent the thought to me.

I didn't get a chance to tell him I didn't mind at all. I was scooped out of Blue's arms and deposited in Declan's lap before my newest knight could do anything further. Declan yanked my wrists behind my back. His mouth wandered down my collarbone and then he pulled my wrists hard, making my back arch. He bit my nipple through my dress.

Lightning flickered through my veins. "More," I begged. "Please."

Declan had just shoved my dress underneath my tits when Donaloo walked in, Dini still bobbing on his forehead.

"Settled in for an evening snack instead of preparing for an attack?" The old wizard danced a jig as Ryan moved protectively in front of me to block the view as Declan yanked my dress back up.

Shite! I thought.

My face flushed red.

Donaloo waved his hand, letting a pouch fall from his sleeve and dangle by a leather cord. "I have magicked up eternal day, but I'm here to warn you all away."

Connor stood and went forward, my polite counterpart. I was still burning with embarrassment. "Thank you,

Donaloo. Your help means the world to us. Without you, Evaness would be lost."

Donaloo shook his head. "Lost things can be found, but things destroyed cannot rebound. I am here to play my part, for those who forget to feel with their heart."

Dini smacked Donaloo's forehead with a leaf. "Enough with the rhymes already. Unless you're going to compose sonnets for me."

I leaned around Ryan's legs to glare at the wizard. "Dini's right. You only tend to rhyme around me. If I walked out of the room right now, you'd speak to the rest of them normally, wouldn't you?"

Donaloo just booped his nose and said, "Hatred closes men's ears and fills their hearts with fears."

Ugh. He was as annoying as he was helpful. I didn't even mind when Dini grew and wrapped her stem over his mouth. As he pried her off, I stood and mocked, "I can only speak in annoying rhyme because I love to waste Queen Bloss's time." Then I waggled my tongue and crossed my eyes, parodying the old man. I couldn't help but laugh at myself. I felt ridiculous.

Donaloo wasn't offended a whit. He came forward and grabbed my hand. His one eye whirled in a circle and he waggled his tongue back at me before saying, "There are so many reasons for sorrow that we must always seek joy."

Something in his tone hinted that he'd seen many sorrows in his three centuries. Even Dini didn't do more than sigh after he said that.

I put my hand on top of his. "That's true. Today has proven it. Has anyone found the sultan's ring?"

Donaloo shook his head. "We always search longest for the thing we treasure most. The people still look, though they search for a ghost."

"You think whoever finds it will turn it in?"

Donaloo winks. "Whenever you're told something is cursed, death to touch, you fear the worst."

I laughed. "Fair enough. Most likely they'll turn it in then."

He winked at me and I smiled, giving a relieved sigh. But then I tasted something awful in the air. I looked around and realized that I'd smelled whatever was in the pouch he was holding. "Ew! What is that?"

"Staying up has a price for the tongue and the price is dung!" Donaloo tossed the foul bag at me with a laugh. It smelled like the worst dog turds. I tossed the bag on the table.

Declan, ever curious, opened it and pulled out a small white tablet. "Smells so much worse than it looks."

"Just like you," Ryan quipped.

I glanced over at Quinn, who was sitting at the end of the table, watching the merriment from afar. My sweet naughty knight would normally be interjecting with thoughts and images at every turn. But there he sat, alone, outside the conversation, just an observer, not a participant.

I went over to him and sank onto his lap. I pressed a gentle kiss to his forehead. Then I wrapped my arms around him, saying nothing, because he could say nothing. Instead, I showed him I loved him by wrapping him up in my arms as hard as I could and refusing to let go, even when Declan pitched one of the foul white tablets at us.

"You shite!" I turned my back so that the tablet bounced off of it and back onto the table.

"Stop playing favorites then!"

That just caused Quinn to hold me tighter and shove his tongue out at Declan.

The little bit of playfulness from my silent knight had me relieved. He was so quiet. I stroked his cheek while talk resumed around me—talk of weapons and inventories, of troops and refugees. Talk filled my ears until my eyes drifted shut and I fell asleep in Quinn's arms, most definitely avoiding Donaloo's tablets.

The next morning, Jace arrived back at the castle with our unruly gargoyles in tow. He'd had to chain them together to fly them home. And his haggard look told me they hadn't cooperated.

The beast master and I spent a day training with them while my knights went off to different spots, all working on perfecting their new powers.

Quinn and Blue went off to spy on people in Marscha before the sun or I awoke. Quinn insisted—via the parchment note he left on my pillow in the morning—that Blue needed to get used to hearing strangers' thoughts en masse. His note said: "If we're going to take him into battle, Dove, he'll need to get used to the din." He'd also written that he'd come back with a list of wishes for me, ones he thought might help us. I'd crumpled the parchment on reading that. I wouldn't use another wish. Not when I'd seen what wishes cost Blue and Quinn.

Ryan and Declan had snuck out of bed after I'd yawned and stretched. They had taken turns kissing my cheek as I'd begged them to sleep next to me just a few more minutes.

"Can't, Peace," Declan whispered as he stroked my hair. "See, this whole power switch has gotten me thinking. Your magic allows an exchange of an intangible for a tangible. I'd always believed my magic only dealt with tangible items. My entire list of opposites is built on that. But what if Ryan could multiply heat and decrease cold? What if he could decrease the volume of a siren's call and multiply our battle cries? Or another possibility—"

I'd chucked a pillow at my scholar. "It's too early to be excited."

Next to me Connor had groaned and agreed. "Shut it."

161

He'd been up half the night, reviewing the seven king-doms—their strengths and weaknesses, the sizes of their armies. I'd woken in the middle of the night to see him hunched over the desk near the bed—candle flickering as he scratched away at a piece of parchment. I'd gotten up and kissed him.

"Any revelations?" I'd whispered.

"Just that we need Sedara and probably Gitmore."

I had nodded and snuffed his candlelight with my fingers, dragging him into bed with the rest of us. I'd fallen back asleep dreaming about the reclusive country, its vast desert and its mysterious black castle. Gitmore had once rivaled Sedara; it was the only country with a magical military big enough to take on our foes.

Ryan and Declan had yanked the covers off of Connor and me.

"Get up, you lazy ducks," Ryan said. "I need those gargoyles trained toot suite."

I bit my thumb at him as he and Declan laughed and headed out.

Connor dragged himself up beside me. He went over to the basin and splashed some water on his face. "I'm headed out today with a small group of soldiers to the Cerulean Forest."

That made me wake right the sard up. "What?"

"I just want to see if there's anywhere I can help. I need to practice my healing."

My throat closed a little, though I realized the necessity of his actions. "You be careful. I don't need a hero. I need a healer."

He nodded. I got out of bed and wrapped my arms around his middle. "Don't get close to Isla—if she's still out there."

"Ryan's soldiers report she's moved north to meet up with Raj's forces. More of them are setting sail."

I leaned up on my tiptoes and muttered in his ear, "Save some of that rage for later for me."

He smiled wide as he pulled back. "Anything you want, Bloss Boss." Then he left.

Jorad came in with a tray, but I ignored it since my knights were gone. My mind turned to the day ahead—a day full of torture with stubborn, infantile rocks.

As I'd predicted, the gargoyles listened to me. And only me. If I wasn't directly commanding them, the stupid beasts milled about the courtyard, knocking over frozen residents like a game of bowls or skittles. Jorad ending up asking several soldiers to spend the day clearing the courtyard of frozen citizens. I watched as Ryan's men passed, carrying courtiers frozen mid-run by their heads and feet, hefting them over their shoulders like sacks of wheat, even dragging them on boards. The guards filled two ballrooms with frozen people.

That was another nightmare I'd have to deal with—when they finally unfroze and found themselves staring at a different world. But that was tomorrow's problem. I had to solve today's. Unfortunately, the gargoyles were just like other young animals. If I wasn't giving them direct orders, or Jace and his unfrozen staff members weren't struggling to get them to line up in formations, the stupid things liked to wrestle. Seven-foot boulders with wings wrestling was a bad idea. One of the more playful gargoyles fell into a crater left by the explosion and couldn't get out. He snuffled and snorted and even whined piteously when I looked down on his stone face. But what he thought was pouting, was actually a horrific display of his tusks. We left him there. One less roaming, quisby stone to worry about.

Donaloo didn't help a whit. He danced around the court-yard like a jester tempting bulls to gore him. If others hadn't been watching, I might have let the gargoyles nip at him a bit. The fact that the man took so little seriously—when my people were dying—made me grind my teeth. He'd already done so much. But was there more he could do? Could he be creating a mirror spell or a shield for my entire kingdom? Was it fair for me to want him to stretch himself so thin—Donaloo attempted to frog-hop over a gargoyle who'd splayed out on the ground. It was a poor decision, because his old legs didn't have the strength to clear it. He flopped backward and landed on his ass. And laughed.

Dini was not nearly as amused. "You could have crushed me if you'd fallen forward, you old fool!"

"Get out of my head, then," he'd told her.

I was working so hard. I was so focused. So much was at stake—and they were playing children's games. And causing a racket. I wanted to shake him. I wanted to pull off one of Dini's petals. If we'd been at the tavern … a fantasy of all the spit that would drip down Donaloo's face filled my mind.

That's not nice, Dove, a familiar voice said in my head.

I twisted in my seat on top of Pony. Then I slid down his back. I ran across the courtyard, dodging the dumb beasts. "Sit!" I screamed—my feet bouncing and the cobblestones shaking as the tonnage-total of their asses hit the ground at the same moment. But I ignored that. Two of my knights stood under the archway at the entrance to the courtyard. I threw my arms around Quinn. "You're back!" I squealed in his ear. "The nightmare's over!"

He hugged me close and spun me around. He sent me a mental image of him whirling me in a field of flowers. It didn't have the illusory power of his old magic, but I understood the sentiment.

"I'm so happy to have you back," I whispered. I kissed his neck lightly, then his lips. I caressed his cheek and had to hold back tears. But, as always, Quinn wanted to get playful. He smacked my ass and bit my lip. So, I bit back. I bit a little too hard. His lower lip started to bleed. He dabbed at it with his shirt sleeve.

"Oh, Quinn! I'm sorry!"

"Are you playing favorites again?" Declan called as he and Ryan walked up.

I turned to protest as Blue started laughing.

"She is! Completely ignored me."

Quinn held his hands up, pretending he was intimidated by Declan. *It wasn't me. It was all her,* he thought at all of us.

Stop that! I swung out to smack him and he jumped away.

Quinn brushed against a gargoyle, his stained shirtsleeve touching the beast just as he thought, *You'd better kiss them all and even the score. Come on now, give out the kisses.*

The gargoyle next to us shifted and stood. It stuck its face between Quinn and I, nudging us apart with its nostrils. And then the beast gave Quinn's mouth a long, lingering lick.

Quinn's face contorted in horror. Mine scrunched in mirth.

Behind us, Declan gave a whoop of joy. "Sarding hell! Finally!"

I turned and looked at him. "You've been waiting for a gargoyle to kiss Quinn?"

Declan grinned. "Nope. That's just a bonus. I've been trying to figure out how you control the beasts. And now we know."

He scratched his own palm and walked a few steps toward the lazing gargoyle that Donaloo had failed to hurtle. Declan swiped a line of red over the beast. The gargoyle launched straight up into the air, circled, and then landed back in place, right next to Declan.

My blond knight turned to Quinn and I; his excitement palpable. "Gargoyles form blood bonds."

CHAPTER TWELVE

*W*e hovered in the clouds as a new day dawned. We peered down on the kingdom that had given birth to my Declan, on the kingdom that was supposed to be our greatest ally. A kingdom that was building a giant seawall out of magical crystal that stretched as far as the eye could see. It looked as though the inside of a geode had been planted on the beach and then enchanted to grow eighty feet tall. The wall was slightly purple in color, and the sun's gentle rays bounced off it and made me squint.

The sight of the monstrosity made my stomach sink down to the sea below. "They're preparing for a siege from the sea."

Declan hugged my middle. He'd ridden over with me on Pony, since Sedara only knew of two mounted gargoyles in Evaness' possession. "Typical mother. Honor means less to her than her personal preservation."

Ryan pointed at some shadows at the base of the wall. "Look at those. Do they look like shipwrecks to you?"

I tried to see below the water, but I couldn't tell what the shadows were. "Perhaps."

"I think Raj and Isla might not have left her as untouched as you'd thought."

"Still not enough."

"Of course not," Ryan agreed. "But every loss makes them a little weaker. Down there are several hundred soldiers we don't have to fight."

That was true. But truth and vengeance aren't always brothers. And my need to drag Diamoni into this, my need to make her feel as ripped apart as I was feeling, was stronger than any logic. I turned and simply stared at Ryan.

Ryan grinned back at me. "Diamoni is a fool. And like any fool, her own actions are her downfall. She's putting a lot of trust in us to fight that war for her."

I nodded. "Too bad my mother always told me to trust my allies only slightly more than my enemies."

The war still raged on our borders. Reports had come in last night that Lady Agatha's northern province was completely lost to Raj. Malia's province looked like it was next on their list. If I didn't get my enemies to focus on other locations … if I didn't get Raj and Isla to divert their attention from Evaness … if I didn't get Sedara and the other kingdoms of Kenmare involved, I had no chance.

Evaness couldn't win this war alone. If we had to plunge other countries into this bloodbath, so be it. All the better if it was Sedara.

"Speaking of enemies, I'm going to go get our enemy forces ready." Ryan flew in front of me with his gargoyle. He gave me a cocky nod that had my core tightening with anticipation. Then he flew off toward the remaining gargoyles, which were hovering in place a mile back, each one blood bonded to one of Ryan's commanders.

We had a fleet of gargoyles. And we finally knew how to use them.

I grinned over my shoulder at Declan, whom I'd fussed over before dawn, dressing him in a vest and cape that showcased Evaness' burning rose. I wanted to walk into Queen Diamoni's castle and have Declan's attire be a punch in the face to that old hag of a queen. Her son wasn't hers anymore. He was mine.

He'd laughed when I'd said that, pulling my hand down from where I was straightening his cape. "Of course, I'm yours."

I'd stared at him long and hard. "First of all, she thinks I'm dead. Which means she'll think I'm weak."

"You're not."

"Which means she's going to accuse you and the other knights of failing to protect me. Which means she's going to try to undermine your confidence and ultimately convince you that she'd be better off protecting all of us.

She'll try and convince you to stay there and keep me there so she can control us more easily, and she'll want to use you for your old powers—"

Declan had laughed. "Bloss, that's ridiculous."

I'd shaken my head. "No. If she thinks she can annex us— take credit for protecting Evaness and take it over like she did the Isles of Peth, that's what she'll do. She'd enslave us like she enslaved the elves. I stayed up most the night, thinking about it, talking with Connor. We think that's what my mother would have done."

Declan's face had paled, and he hadn't said a word after that, just let me fuss over his clothes and then helped me with my own black gown. The gown was layered to look like rose petals, and the under layers were orange and red. Declan and I were dressed to match. And though Gennifer was still frozen and my hair was only in a simple plait, I knew our solidarity was going to be important.

I turned on my gargoyle and stared at Declan. He looked a little ill, but I chose to believe that was from riding— which he hated—rather than what we were about to face. "Almost time," I told him.

Declan nodded.

I faced forward again and looked down at the palace, "I can't wait to hear her every thought."

Connor interjected, "You might not like them."

I gave a vicious grin. "I just hope they're useful. But she doesn't know about Blue."

Satisfied smirks went around the group.

My thoughts went to Quinn. He'd stayed behind with Donaloo to guard the palace.

Yes, Dove. I'm safe. Just playing chess with Donaloo in our undergarments.

He sent me a silly image to accompany his thoughts. Donaloo's undergarments were—of course—pink.

Then he offered, *If you need a wish—*

No. I'm not doing that to you again.

If you need it, though. Don't hesitate.

I gave him a nod of thanks. I'd make sure I didn't need it.

I turned to Connor and Blue—who shared another gargoyle—next. "You two follow behind and see what gossip you might pick up. Connor, if you can wander off and steal any documents or information about this sea sprite … or any of our enemies …"

He nodded.

I'll read thoughts; Blue offered.

I rolled my eyes and teased, *Yes, I'd rather hoped you'd volunteer for that, seeing as you're the only one who can.*

Quinn chipped at Blue and Blue accidentally projected Quinn's words to the group. *You sure you're qualified for that? You're better at projecting thoughts than reading them.*

Immediately, my mind went to the mental image Blue had accidentally projected that morning, when he'd been having his morning constitutional. He apparently needed more leafy greens in his diet.

I cringed. "No! Don't make us relive that!" I waved my hands at both of them.

Pony wavered a bit as we got caught in an updraft. Never a fan of riding, the sudden change made Declan say, "I think I might puke." And then he leaned over to the side and did—effectively cutting off one of the most uncomfortable thoughts I'd ever accidentally experienced.

§◆

When we flew down below the clouds, my jaw dropped. I had visited Sedara as a child, but my memories were mostly of the carriage flown by a team of pegasi and the candy that had been at our welcoming ball.

I didn't have much memory of the capital, but the layouts were burned into my brain after last night's discussions.

Lotis city was inland, but Sedara was known for its ships and so a century ago, they'd hired a wizard to create canals. Over gleaming sidewalks and gracefully arching marble bridges, the city appeared to be floating, even though the buildings were firmly set on land. The entire city was made of crystal towers that jutted up into the sky. Depending on the district, the crystals were colored light yellow, orange, or pink. It gave Lotis the impression of existing in a permanent sunset.

The towers would've been indistinguishable from a dying sky were it not for the winking reflections on the corners of the walls. Constructed by Elven magic, even the humblest homes looks like castle towers. We were descending upon a city of jewels. The site was so impressive, so awe-inspiring; it left little doubt in my mind as to how Sedara was able to maintain its place as first among the seven kingdoms.

While I was caught up in the beauty of Sedara's capital, Declan eventually recovered enough to peer down behind me.

"Where the canal boats?" he asked. "The trading ships?"

I looked down and realized that he was right. I'd been so caught up in looking at the wall and the buildings, that I hadn't noticed that the walkways and the canals were vacant. The water was rapidly draining out of them.

"They don't want to give the sea witch any inroad," Connor said. "They're going to remove all water."

Fury smoked inside me. She scratched her claws and flexed her wings, begging me to unleash her like a dragon. She spent all this time on a wall. On draining her canals. Not a single thought spared for the country across the sea who'd taken on the risk of raising the sea witch's child. Not a single thought for my country, where people were dying by the minute.

Ryan was right.

She deserved to have the war brought to her. She deserved to see what it was like to have to choose between letting a province burn or letting the crown fall entirely.

Sard her.

Connor and Blue hovered in front of me, their gazes solemn as they measured my reaction. My fingers clenched the reins hard to force myself not to yank back on them and send Pony pelting through the sky like an arrow, aimed right at Queen Diamoni.

Connor twisted on their shared gargoyle to look at me. He knew just by glancing at my face what was going on. He may have lost his ability to read emotions, but he had not lost his ability to read me. "The Queen will say that her treaty was with your mother, that her alliance was with your mother and that their agreement died with your mother."

"I know." My voice was edged with violence. "Let's make this quick. I don't know how long I can hold myself back."

"Ryan will lead the attack. But you have to give him time—"

I took a deep breath and let it out. "I know."

Then I steered Pony into a dive. I didn't head straight for the castle. I deliberately landed in the pink district of the nobles. Blue and Connor followed. I commanded Pony to lead the other gargoyle behind as we made our way toward the castle.

Most nobles merely peered out of their windows at us, curious. But one or two came out on their stoop to wave. I spoke to those.

"Evaness has been attacked," I told them, letting my face show just the tiniest bit of concern. "We came to warn you that Rasle has somehow come up with an entire fleet of gargoyles. And they're flying this way."

"Gargoyles!" one elderly man, dressed entirely in white, declared. His 'a' sound dragged with a typical Sedarian lilt. "We were told a sea sprite was attacking."

I shook my head. "She's gotten herself some allies. A wall won't stop flying gargoyles. Nor will it stop Cheryn's djinn. They can wish your wall gone in an instant."

The man's eyes widened, and he quickly bustled inside, shutting his door behind him.

"What are you doing?" Declan whispered.

"Ensuring Diamoni doesn't control the story," Connor grinned and waved at a little girl peeking through a window. When her mother scooped her up, he made a concerned face and pointed behind them. "Take cover!" he called loudly.

Three or four more nobles came out onto their stoops after that, and I gave each of them the same spiel before royal guards came tromping down the street toward us.

The commander of the guard stopped when he saw Declan and me. I adjusted my tiara and gave him a small nod when he said, "Queen Bloss?"

177

"We've come to warn you of an impending attack from Rasle, sir."

His eyes widened and he nodded, his guards immediately forming an escort to the palace.

I kept my head tall and my back straight as we went through the gleaming courtyard paved with blue crystal, up the steps, into the castle, which was made of white crystal.

My knees trembled and I was grateful for my thick skirts. Because I was about to attempt to goad the most powerful woman into war. And I was about to lie to her face about it.

Trumpets and a herald announced us at the top steps of the throne room.

I stared across the crystal hall.

Declan's mother was tall, elegant, and ice cold—she was everything you would expect the queen to be. She stood to greet us as my knights and I made our way toward her throne. The dais and her chair were the only color in the room, a warm, opulent gold that gave the illusion of sunlight solidified. The Queen stood in front of her golden seat, her golden hair in a braid that circled her head, a long, silver gown flowing past her feet and trailing elegantly over the steps. Beside her stood each of her knights. They were all dark, solemn, and imposing. Each had a black beard so thick that it was hard for me to distinguish one from the other.

Our footsteps echoed as we walked toward them.

The few courtiers who mingled in the palace today were brought to dead silence by our arrival. Their stares dug into me like ploughs cut through soil. They tried to plant doubt and insecurity and sow discord.

But I kept my eyes on Diamoni. I watched the tiny tightening around her mouth as she realized her spies had fed her false information about my death. False, or unverified.

I let a grin spread across my face, with a hint of sarcasm in it, just enough to make her question whether I'd purposely faked my death. Or purposely fed her spy bad information. Or bribed him. I let my grin grow wider.

She'd never trust that informant again.

I stopped halfway through the throne room and waited for her to come to greet me.

She hesitated when her husband reached for her arm. And then she refused him. The queen did not descend the stairs to shake my hand as an equal. She nodded at me, and then sat on her throne as though I were some peasant, come to beg a boon.

My blood boiled and my cheeks flushed. But clenching my fists would only show her that she had gotten to me. I couldn't lose composure so quickly. It would undermine my ability to negotiate. It would let her know that her first move had put me off balance.

Since she did not descend the stairs, I did not bow. I simply stopped halfway through the throne room and stared. I let the silence draw out to a long, uncomfortable pause full of tension, thinking mother would be proud. Then I said, "I was unaware that Sedara had changed the custom of greeting foreign allies."

"My alliance was with the queen now dead. From what I hear, your capital and your country no longer exist."

My smile widened. "Ah ... but didn't you hear that I was dead? I fear you've gotten a good deal of misinformation recently."

Diamoni's eyes didn't narrow but her gaze did flicker from me to Declan, who stepped up beside me.

"Mother, I'm disappointed," he scolded her. "Your disrespect for my wife shows poor manners."

That did make her grow pale. One did not chastise a queen in public and live.

Even my eyes grew wide at Declan's declaration.

Diamoni was quick with her retort. "Your wife's reign has been a disaster. Isla and Raj have both sent me word about their disastrous visits. And she's lost the one thing that restrained the monster of the seas. Your wife's ignorance has put us all at risk."

"Her ignorance or your arrogance?" Declan stepped in front of me.

Diamoni's knights took a step down from the stairs. Sailors, with the power to create wind, though it cost them their breath. Still, when they combined their efforts and alternated, they were able to push entire ships quickly through the sea. A fierce wind blasted us, whipping my hair straight back, nearly unseating my tiara. Declan reached back a hand to keep me upright as my skirts billowed and twisted around my legs.

The courtiers—who'd remained silent since our arrival— quietly took a few steps back, retreating behind pillars. This was more than they'd bargained for when they'd come to the palace today.

I hoped that our arrival, Diamoni's arrogant display, and the impending attack would sway public opinion in our favor.

I stepped forward until I was side by side with Declan. I held up a hand and waited until Diamoni called off her shite husbands with a flick of her wrist.

"Despite your lack of hospitality, and utter arrogance, we came with important news for you. Isla isn't only after us. She wished for an entire fleet of gargoyles from Raj. She wants Sedara."

Diamoni's stillness was her only reaction. I had surprised her. My arrival had surprised her, which Connor and I had expected. We hoped it was enough to make her question the quality of her informants, hoped it was enough to make her believe my claims.

We hadn't anticipated her hostile welcome though, so I was uncertain what her next move would be. She surprised me by standing, descending from her dais, and

ANN DENTON

coming to greet me with her hand outstretched. "I may
have spoken in haste."

"We all do upon occasion, no need to apologize," I
inclined my head to hide my smile.

Oooh, she hates that you said that, Blue told me.

I know. It's why I said it.

Diamoni flicked her gaze from me to Declan, shifting
gears and her tone. "My son," her lips lifted slightly, as if
that were as close as she could get to a smile.

His hand clenched around mine, fingers squeezing tight.

I called out to Blue. *Tell Dec not to read her emotions.* The
woman was a living snake.

But ... from the look on Declan's face, it was too late.

CHAPTER THIRTEEN

Queen Diamoni descended with open arms and gave my knight an awkward hug. Then she took Declan's arm, and urged her entourage to follow her. Her husbands trailed after her, leaving us awkwardly behind.

Once again, she broke royal protocol by not inviting one of her husbands to be my escort. She was snubbing me at every turn. That made everything we were about to do all the more justified in my mind. The bitch had evil coming to her.

She took us to what she called her receiving parlor, a small round room furnished in wood. But at least the echoing crystal was covered by tapestries. They muffled sound, which meant she expected some degree of privacy for the remainder of our conversation. I almost smiled to think that she'd get no privacy inside her own head.

Blue, what's she thinking?

I don't know that you want to know, Blue's tone was dark. I looked over at him and though he kept his face controlled, like any experienced prince, his fingers were clenched into fists. I slid my arm through the crook of his elbow and pretended to be the doting bride. I smiled at him and batted my eyelashes.

Tell me.

She's wondering how she can weasel Declan away from us and lock him up so she can use him.

Blue's eyes flickered to mine in surprise. *She wants him? She sent him away.*

She wants his power. I suppose your father would've been the same, I raised an eyebrow.

Blue's face was calm as he accepted a cup of tea from a maid, but internally he gave a harsh bitter laugh. *At least Declan is useful to his mother. My father wouldn't have minded if all of my brothers killed me.*

Yes, royal parents have a tendency to be greedy-gut shites. How's Declan holding up?

He's trying to close off his power, but he's having a bit of a hard time.

Donaloo's annoying face popped into my head and I thought, *If the wizard was here, he'd say some dense thing like hope is the pill that makes you swallow poison again and again.*

You didn't rhyme.

I shrugged as I took my teacup. I stared down at the golden-edged white china. *Tell Connor to be ready to heal us if this tea is poisoned.*

You're joking.

Sadly, I'm not.

I thought other courts were better than my father's.

Some are worse.

Yours isn't.

The stupid wizard's one-eyed face showed up again. I wondered if he was scrying me or something. He giggled as he danced a jig in my head. *The answer to any question depends on who you ask. Ask only the one most suited for your task.*

Go away! I shouted at him. Then I realized something. Something similar had happened to me before. When Quinn had sent me images, and I hadn't known he could talk. I narrowed my eyes as I stared up at Blue. *Did Quinn give him a bead?*

No. Blue responded.

Then how am I ...? Quinn had a habit of sending me annoying, inappropriate thoughts. *Is Quinn sending these?* I demanded.

Blue's eyes widened and he quickly took a sip of tea, turning from me to engage in small talk with one of Sedara's legitimate princes.

185

Dammit, Quinn! I thought-yelled as I tried to keep a pleasant smile on my face.

His chuckles sounded in my head. That nigmenog!

I'm gonna— I didn't get any further in my threat before the crown princess arrived and greeted me. Unlike her mother, Princess Amabel curtseyed and smiled at me. Her curly black hair was shorn short, and a subtle tiara perched on her head. She wore a pale-yellow gown embroidered with soft green vines. I couldn't help but think Dini would like it.

I smiled blandly back at Amabel, biting my tongue. I had to resist the urge to ask if the shadows Ryan had seen were sunken ships.

But then she had to ask, "And how is everything in Evaness?"

My court-face faltered. "Do you mean how does my capital look after the djinn attack? Or my forest after Isla ran two giants through it? Or did you mean the northern province Raj has seen fit to invade?"

Connor grabbed my arm and steered me away from the shocked princess. I'd broken protocol just as much as her mother had. "Excuse us, Her Majesty is a bit tired from her trip." Connor deposited me in a chair and shoved a tiny slice of cake at me. "Eat some cake and let me do the talking."

I pretended to take a sip of my tea and set my cake plate on my lap as I watched Declan's ass of a mother usher him over to a settee and perched next to him, turning her back to us and putting her arm around him, giving all the appearances of an intimate, loving mother-son conversation. No one in the room was fooled.

Part of me was sickened by her ploy—by the fact that all of Connor's predictions about her were right—the other part of me was happy that Declan could read her emotions and wouldn't mistake her gestures for real.

The crown princess had drifted over to the cake table, as far away from me as she could get.

Next to me, Connor turned on his charm. He engaged two of Sedara's princes in conversation. "Must say, I was impressed by those new ships you all sent over the last fall. Cut through the water like champions."

Both men smiled, eager to move from our tension filled conversations into more normal territory. "Yes, we've been perfecting that design for years."

"You all have a dangerous job. The sea is not a friendly place," Connor commented.

"Especially now," one of the princes muttered.

"True. That's why we came by air. I heard that sea witch is a bit of a beast."

"That's an understatement. Mayi cracks boats like twigs," the one with more grey in his beard muttered.

We have a name, Blue thought excitedly.

Yes, I responded. Mayi. Our monster had a name. But did she have a weakness?

I took another sip of my tea, trying not to hide my awe at how quickly Connor had moved the conversation in a direction that was useful for us.

"She's that powerful?" Connor asked, running a hand through his curls as if he couldn't quite fathom that. "I thought she could merely control the undertows."

I hadn't ever noticed before, but Connor often played ignorant, allowing the other party to be the expert and fill in all the details he needed. Realizing that just made him twice as attractive to me. I had to fight to keep my gaze on my teacup. I didn't want to interfere with his conversation in any manner. Especially not when I'd nearly lost my temper five minutes ago and ruined our shot at information all together.

"Undertows," one of the men scoffed. "No! She can control any sea water—causes horrid waves. I've seen her create a thirty-foot swell once. Seen her make a whirlpool, too."

"That's awful. Can't we stop her?"

The men laughed and shook their heads.

"It's why we did. Until she got back the girl."

"You have to steal something that the sea sprite loves most."

Connor leaned back on his heels and tilted his head as if he was digesting this new bit of information. "But why?"

The prince shrugged and started to walk toward the cake table. "Not sure. My grandmother was a wizard's paramour once. And that's what he told her."

I'd thought the princes had simply succumbed to Connor's natural charm, and that I'd been ignored, but once the first had wandered off to the cake table, the second man sat down beside me. Connor gave me a warning glance. I widened my eyes slightly and he read my look.

"Prince Dane, how have your sugar fields done this year?" Connor asked the Queen's husband. Just as my knights were not named kings, Sedara had long called the Queen's husbands mere princes.

I smiled politely, like I was interested, but really, I was just sarding relieved Connor had given me a name so I didn't embarrass myself.

"Quite a few storms we've had lately," Dane replied vaguely.

I nodded. "It's a pity that we can't have fair weather when we want it."

Blue's voice shot through my head. *Quinn says this prince sometimes feeds him information. But he's very—Quinn said Donalooish—is that a word? So, watch out.*

Dane tapped the side of his teacup thoughtfully as he gazed at me. "True. True. We'd all like our way all the time." He chuckled. "Life and weather don't seem to cooperate like that. But storms lead to new growth, often allow young shoots to unfurl their leaves."

I couldn't help but think he wasn't speaking about the weather. I felt sure of it when he glanced over at his daughter. But damn him for being like Donaloo! My smile was thin as I said, "I have a friend you might get along with. He likes metaphor, too. Drives me mad with it, actually."

The prince smiled over the edge of his cup. "Sounds like a clever fellow. The unfortunate thing about driving people mad is that eventually the madness takes over." His eyes flickered to the window and he stared at the wall.

Was he against it? Was he for it? Was the prince criticizing his wife for building it or was he saying that Raj and Isla had gone insane?

I'm about to throw my tea in his face, I warned.

Blue came hurrying over. He bent in front of me with a warning look as he said politely, "Let me take your plate—"

WHAM!

A teeth-rattling, chandelier shaking clap of thunder smacked my ears.

All eyes turned to look outside, where a group of soldiers on gargoyles, wearing Raslen blue garb gathered from a mountain near the sea, fluttered at the top of Sedara's wall.

WHAM!

We watched a second gargoyle slam into the wall.

Diamoni shrieked, "Call out the elves! Repair the wall!"

One of her husbands hurried to do her bidding. But Dane stayed seated beside me.

Was it in protest or in shock? I wasn't sure.

Again and again and again, the stone bodies clanged against the crystal. My ears rang but the gargoyles didn't let up. They slammed one after another in a vertical line up and down the wall.

Warnings sirens went up throughout the capital—soldiers blowing through long conch shells.

People spilled out onto the narrow sidewalks like ants. The city had been dead when we'd arrived. Now it swarmed with panic as citizens realized they were being attacked.

I watched horror crease Princess Amabel's face, and anger color Queen Diamoni's.

My thoughts echoed Quinn's whispers inside my head.

Good. We need them invested.

We needed Sedara in this fight. Needed their trained soldiers. Their ships. Their magic. And all the anger they could give.

A crack formed in the wall before Sedara's elven slaves could climb up to repair it.

Princess Amabel appeared at my shoulder. "If they're attacking us, you should leave."

Queen Diamoni whipped around, eyes flashing. "How do we know you didn't lead them? Invite them? Tempt them?"

"What incentive would I have to do that?" I asked. I was proud of how calm and emotionless the words came out. "I came here with the belief that we were allies."

The crack spread and widened.

Diamoni turned to Declan and grabbed his arm. "Repair it. Use your power and repair it."

Declan's eyes flickered to mine. I held his gaze.

I tried to tell him I loved him with my eyes, tried to project my love across the room. I wasn't certain if he was still blocking his ability to taste emotions.

But then a small smile crossed his face and he stepped out of Diamoni's hold.

"I can't," he shrugged, looking her right in the face.

And I was proud of him, because I knew how hard that must have been for him to say.

Diamoni gestured and another of her husbands walked closer. Again, Dane stayed in his seat.

The queen took her husband's arm. I noticed the move put his hand close to his scabbard, within quick reach of his knife.

Blue! I warned. *They might hurt him!*

Connor and Blue immediately stepped up behind the queen and cleared their throats.

Her husband turned.

That's right you pig rutter, can't kill all three of us, can you? Blue taunted mentally.

Diamoni appeared unphased by my husbands as she murmured, "Declan, this is your country, think of your sister—"

"I can't," Declan repeated, "because I don't have that power anymore. I was killed and brought back without that power."

Diamoni's eyes flickered to her husbands. "That's not possible."

Beside me, Dane tilted his head. "Isn't it? I had heard the mad wizard is in Evaness."

Diamoni scoffed. "That fool—"

"That fool is loyal and good-hearted," I interjected. "He's gone out of his way to save more of my people than you ever have."

"Call our castle mage!" Diamoni commanded. "Have him tested." She jerked her head toward Declan, who took a step away from her.

But two guards detached themselves from the wall and approached.

I stood. "He's no longer your citizen. You have no authority over him. Declan, come on, love. We're leaving."

"He's standing on my soil. That means his life is mine if I want it."

Her soldiers drew their swords.

Amabel stiffened but made no move to counter her mother. Neither did Dane.

I had no such qualms. She'd threatened my knight.

I shot peace at both her soldiers, aiming for their necks and faces. The room lit with green light as my wrists tore open. The soldiers' eyes dulled, and their swords sagged.

Diamoni screamed at her husbands.

A blast of wind threw me into the wall. Connor and Blue ended up pinned against the tapestries as well. The force of the wind held my torso in place. I couldn't escape it, though I tried. I was pinned.

The door opened and Diamoni's mage walked in. He didn't bat an eye at us, though Amabel had the decency to look a bit flushed, Dane a bit regretful even as he pinned us on his queen's orders.

Diamoni gestured for the mage to join her and Declan. They whispered quietly.

That's when the gargoyles stopped.

The pause turned every head in the room, including mine. The attack of air ceased and my knights and I were released. Every eye went toward the window.

The gargoyles flew up out of sight into the clouds. The attack had stopped. But why?

Quinn's yell sounded in my head. *Dove, Ryan says get out of there. Now!*

A rumbling started in the distance. An ominous sound like thunder, unending thunder.

What is it? I asked Quinn. But he didn't respond.

Connor and I exchanged a glance. His face remained calm, but his sea-colored eyes shot a warning at me. He gave me one of our childhood hand-signals. The one for escape.

I marched over and grabbed Declan's hand. Queen Diamoni turned to tell me to stop, but that's when the screaming started.

Tsunami!

Quinn's yell roared in my head, just as I saw the wild white foam smash into the wall. The cracks made by the gargoyles crackled and spread. A trickle of water burst through in one spot.

I grabbed my knights and ignored Diamoni—who started shouting orders.

Her husbands poured out onto the balcony of the room. Wind raced toward the wall and over it, shoving back the crest of the tsunami.

We left them to the fight. We ran through the palace, Declan leading us through the halls, whipping past pastel-colored nobles who were whispering frantically to one another. We ran through the courtyard, which was rapidly emptying of soldiers marching toward the wall.

We got outside the castle walls.

"Pony!" I yelled, as Sedarian merchants streamed past us, fleeing the city with their wagons.

My gargoyle and the other we'd traveled on, swooped down. I didn't know if he'd heard me or if blood-bonded gargoyles could read thoughts. I didn't really care as I mounted up and yanked on Declan to mount behind me.

We rose into the air. The wind from the princes at the palace shoved us toward the sea and our beasts had to fight to gain height.

Sedara's army stationed themselves on rooftops and balconies, calmly awaiting their orders.

I heard a siren start to sing and I urged Pony higher, so we'd get out of range.

The first row of soldiers on balconies shot out spears. They flew through the air and hit the water. I saw at least one lifeless siren float to the surface.

Then I saw Mayi. She was slightly behind the crest of the tsunami. Her white hair whipped back in the wind caused by the princes. Her white wings fluttering inside the column of water she floated on. The silver-white scales on her arms reflected the mid-morning sun as she shoved her hands forward and sent another wave crashing into the seawall of Sedara.

I glanced back. The elves of Peth had topped the seawall. They responded by sending crackling lightning dancing across the waves.

Ally or not, it didn't look like Queen Diamoni would escape this war.

Good.

I hoped Sedara would keep our enemies busy enough to divide their attention.

Because if they were looking away from Evaness, they wouldn't see me creep up behind them.

They wouldn't see my sword until they looked down and saw the tip protruding from their stomach.

Isla. Raj. And the witch who now had a name.

They thought they were going to end Sedara.

But I was going to end them.

CHAPTER FOURTEEN

*a*s we flew, I noticed several ships with Cheryn's flags in the distance. Their human soldiers must have been aboard, sent to fight in a distant land.

I hoped Raj was aboard one of those ships, and that he and the sea sprite would concentrate their attacks on Sedara for the time being. That would give me another shot at Isla.

We shot up through a wet patch of clouds to meet up with Ryan and our fleet of fake Raslen soldiers. I gave them all a wide smile.

"Well done," I praised, before going to the head of the formation. "Let's go home."

My men cheered and whooped, and I spent a moment reveling in their success before I realized Declan was still and silent behind me. Trusting Pony to keep us safe, I turned slightly so I could look at his face.

It was pinched and tight.

"Dec?" I asked carefully. In my head, I requested that Pony make the ride smoother. I knew my blond knight had a sensitive stomach.

Dec's eyes stared at me, but his gaze was distant. He was trapped inside his own head. I grabbed his hand and drew it around my waist. "Hey," I told him. "I'm sure your family will be okay. They have elves and magic and a huge army at their disposal."

He didn't acknowledge me.

Quinn? I asked. *Is Dec okay?*

Quinn answered. *Give him time to process, Dove.*

But process what? What part?

He's never had Connor's power before. He knew his mother didn't love him. But there's a difference between knowing it and feeling it ...

Quinn's words chopped me open. I yanked both Declan's arms around me and started to pull up every good memory I had of him. I thought of the first day we'd greeted him at the ship when he'd disembarked. We'd both been awkward teenagers, but his hair had fallen near his eyes and he'd had to brush it back. I remembered thinking he was adorable. I thought of the first time I heard him give a detailed answer in class, once he'd gotten control of his accent. I remembered how impressed he'd made me. I thought about the number of times I'd watched his ass as he walked up the stairs in front of me. I thought about the secret thrill that had raced through me one time when we hadn't debated but had actually agreed in class. He'd smiled at me that day. And his smiles had been so rare that it felt like I'd gotten something more precious than gold. His smile had liquified my insides, in a way that had utterly terrified me. Because that had been shortly after I'd made my decision to leave.

Declan didn't respond to my memories, or the emotions they dragged up for me, so I couldn't tell if he had shut down his power, or if it just wasn't enough to overcome his melancholy.

When we landed, Declan immediately strode off into the castle.

I went over to Ryan, who was giving orders to troops as Jace came to collect the gargoyles. I waited until his men had all been sent off, and then I grabbed his arm.

"I think we need to talk to Declan," I said.

"Quinn told me what happened. He might need time."

I wanted to pull my hair out. "He had hours on the ride back."

"Two more. Give him space and then I'll go with you." Ryan said as Jorad approached him.

"But—" I cut myself off and sighed. "Fine." I didn't like it. I felt like I needed to be there. But I knew that some things were easier to process alone. Maybe this was one of them.

I counted down those two hours as a useless mess while Connor dragged me to the library with Donaloo and Quinn, intent on researching Mayi and her powers. "There's a list of known sprites somewhere," Connor had muttered. "A huge gathering was held during your grand-mother's reign …"

I tuned out his muttering and thought of Declan. My scholar had taken the brunt of the attack at the palace. I could only imagine how it hurt for him to realize that Diamoni saw him as a pawn. I paced while I waited. I waited until I couldn't stand it anymore. When I saw Ryan pass by the door, I hurried after him.

"Ryan," I called. "I can't wait anymore. I'm going to find him."

Ryan sighed and nodded. He gestured for his soldiers to carry on without him.

"Bloss—"

"You know as well as I do where he is," I snarled. "I've given him a bit of time, but I'm not letting him lash himself to death."

We went down to the practice yard and into the weapons room. I couldn't tell exactly what Declan had taken, but I felt certain he'd been here. Ryan sighed as he walked past me. "He's not gonna want to see you yet."

"I don't care. I need to see him." Ryan was wrong. Dec needed someone. I'd given him space, but he needed to know that he was loved. He needed to wash away whatever his mother felt and feel what I felt about him instead.

Ryan shook his head but opened a secret passageway. He led me through the tunnels and stairwells until we arrived at Declan's old room, the one he'd stayed in when he apprenticed under my fathers. When we pushed open the entrance in the wall, I could hear the smack of the whip.

The scent of blood hit my nostrils almost immediately.

Declan was hunched over his bed, clutching the bedpost. He was shirtless and his back was striped with blood. He held a cat o' nine tails limply in one hand.

Horror and sadness swirled in my gut as I rushed toward him.

"Dec!"

Ryan stayed back, but I wrenched the cat out of Dec's hand.

"Bloss—" he protested when he saw me, but I pushed him back against the pole. I swung the cat so that the straps lashed his ass through his trousers.

"Ow!" he exclaimed.

A tear rolled down my cheek. But I lashed him again. Then I threw aside the cat. "You told me you'd come to me if you needed this. I told you I'd help—" I choked on an angry sob. Seeing Dec like this was a smack to the heart. "She's not worth this."

ANN DENTON

Dec was quiet for a moment as he processed my words. "Bloss, without my powers–"

"Sard your old powers. You still have a mind. You still have a heart."

"Not to her."

"Well, they mean something to me." I grabbed his arm and pulled him around. I leaned up on my toes and shoved my face right in his. "I'm your queen now. Not her. What she wants does not matter."

Declan's breathing grew shallow. His eyes didn't reach mine. He stared at the floor.

"Did you hear me? You're mine. I want you. I sarding love you. And that bitch doesn't matter," I yanked at his hair until his blue eyes rose to meet mine.

"You are so hot right now," he whispered.

I slammed my lips onto Declan's. I slammed my mouth into his like it was a weapon. I tried to cut through his damned ignorance about his own self-worth. I tried to carve my initials into his soul. My hands squeezed his shoulders, my fingers reached into his back. But I was done with gentleness. Declan didn't need gentleness, he needed to be claimed.

I pulled back and looked at the other man in the room, "Ryan," I called, "come here."

My dark giant pulled away from the wall and walked toward us.

I turned back to Declan. "Ryan and I love you. And we're gonna show you how much. I want you to use your power."

I took a step away from Declan and he reached for me. I shook my head. "Feel me. Do you feel what I'm feeling?"

Declan's pale blue eyes swam with emotion. "Yes," he breathed.

I reached forward and undid the ties that held Declan's trousers closed. I knelt as I pulled them down and unlaced his boots. Ryan slowly traced the smaller man's side and triceps.

Declan's eyes flashed to mine. "I'm not —"

I grinned up at him. "Ryan's gonna spank you while you ride me. We're gonna give you what you need."

Declan's ice blue eyes lit up at the very thought. The expression on his face made me grow wet.

Ryan reached down and helped me up. He slid the top of my dress down. My nippled hardened immediately at his touch and he tugged them, one after the other as Declan watched.

Declan's breathing grew shallow.

Ryan put his lips to my neck as he shoved down my skirt and bared me to Declan's gaze. Ryan's huge hands stroked the inside of my thighs, making me spread them open. But then he stopped his kisses and caresses. He held his right hand out toward Declan. "Suck my fingers," he commanded.

Declan stepped forward and slid Ryan's fingers into his mouth. The sight of him fellating my giant's hand got me hot. Excitement ran through me. When Ryan started to pump his fingers into Declan's mouth, I couldn't help but swivel my hips and moan at the sight.

"I think our queen likes it," Ryan said. "Suck her tits while I use these fingers on her."

Declan released Ryan's fingers and leaned forward, capturing my nipple in his mouth. He rolled his tongue in circles, stimulating the tip and Ryan used his lubricated fingers to rub up and down my slit, teasing me. The dual stimulation had me clutching at both of them. "Yes," I moaned.

Ryan plunged two thick fingers inside me and scissored them. Declan kissed my breast and then blew on my stomach as his face traveled south. He sucked my clit into his mouth as Ryan fingered me. My nails dug into Declan's shoulders as I screamed.

The orgasm was so intense that I saw red at the edges of my vision. Ryan had to carry my limp form to the bed after. My eyelids fluttered.

Declan said, "Maybe she needs a minute—"

"No," Ryan cut him off and his fingers wrapped around Declan's dick. He pumped my shocked knight a few times before saying, "Ride her, now." Then he smacked Declan's ass.

I watched through fluttering eyelashes as Declan climbed on top of me.

"Tease her first," Ryan ordered, smacking Declan's ass again and then caressing it. I watched him stroke his own length through his riding breeches.

Declan slid the hot head of his dick over my opening, back and forth. The heat and friction had me writhing.

"Yes, I need you Dec. Do you feel it?" I whimpered. "I. Need. You."

"Ugh, I'm gonna—" Dec moaned.

Whack!

"Don't you dare come yet!" Ryan ordered.

"But—"

Whack!

Declan moaned and shoved inside me, pumping roughly. He yanked my hips and pulled them up toward him. He was frantic, mindless. He shoved into me with grunts and groans. And every time Ryan smacked him, he shuddered as if it nearly made him come. I loved seeing him this out of control, knowing that he could feel everything and that it drove him into this rutting beast mode.

I wanted to see if I could drive him further.

"Dec, stop," I commanded.

My sweet sub froze on command, staring down at me with eyes that pleaded for release.

"Not yet," I said. "I want Ryan to take my pussy while you take me from behind."

Both men moaned in pleasure at that.

Declan climbed off me and pulled me to standing. Ryan shucked his clothes faster than I'd ever seen and laid down on the mattress seconds later.

"Come here, Little Dearling," he called.

I climbed onto the bed and crawled on top of him. He was so wide that my hips were spread just trying to straddle him.

I grinned down at him and then glanced over my shoulder at Declan. "No one gets to come before I do."

Ryan's hand spanked my ass. "You don't give me orders."

I turned back to my giant and raised a brow. "You don't want to be the weak link, do you? You don't want to be the first one to come."

Ryan groaned. "Get on my dick. I'll show you weak link."

I slid down on Ryan's huge length slowly. Declan had stretched me, but Ryan was so large that the sensation rode the edge of pain.

"Do you feel that Dec?" I asked.

"Gods, yes," my blond knight whispered. "Thank you."

"Don't thank me, defile me," I ordered.

When I'd seated myself, Declan climbed up behind me and leaned me forward until my breasts brushed Ryan's muscles.

Ryan's hand slid between us and he played with my clit as Declan spit on my backside and his dick, lubricating them.

When he lined himself up, I tensed, nervous. But Declan soothed me. "It's okay, Peace. I'm not gonna hurt you." He rubbed his hand over my back gently, and only sunk one finger into my ass, loosening it up.

Ryan's mouth sank onto one of my breasts and he flicked his tongue over my nipple. He played with me until I was arching up and pumping back down. Then he pinched my clit and stroked up into me. Declan's hands snuck up between Ryan and I and pinched my nipples. It was like someone had lit a torch from my breasts to my pussy. I was on fire. In all the right ways. I plunged into a hot, core melting orgasm.

Declan yanked out his finger and plunged inside me and I screamed from the intensity of it all. But then I felt a heady bliss. I had two of my loves in me at once. Four hands roamed my body, tweaking my nipples, digging into my hip bones, sliding back and forth over my clit.

The men worked me, only thrusting slightly so they could focus on my pleasure. They teased and tickled and heated me up to the boiling point until tears streamed down my face from the intensity of it all. And when their fingers worked together to bring me to another orgasm, it was so intense that I blacked out.

I came to and both my knights were waiting for me, grinning.

"You're evil," I told them.

"No, Bloss," Ryan grabbed Declan's ass and lifted his hips until the other man was squatting on the bed. Then my giant started to rut up into both of us, holding Dec firmly so we couldn't get away.

Each stroke had his thick dick pressing past my g-spot, but I was so hungover from orgasms that I teetered on the brink of oblivion as I watched Ryan use my body to chase his own fulfillment.

Declan cried, "God, I can feel you sliding up and down inside her. It's sarding amazing."

And then Ryan stroked harder. "We. Are. So. Damned. Good!" he roared as he came.

I felt his hot cum spurt into me and his thick dick flexed in a way that tapped my g-spot in rapid succession. A final orgasm exploded through my body like a cannonball. My mind was full of sparks and smoke in a forceful powerful I couldn't deny as I clenched and moaned.

Declan groaned when he felt me tighten around him. He pumped into me a few more times and then shuddered on top of me as he finished.

I sunk down on top of Ryan, and Declan sunk down on top of me. Ryan's arms wrapped around us both, careful not to hurt Declan's back.

After a minute of serious afterglow, Ryan said, "Dec, I'm sorry. But if we get to shake the sheets like that every time you see your mom, I'm making you visit her at least once a week."

Declan's laughter shook my entire body. He rolled off me and pulled me off Ryan, snuggling me between the two of them.

I could hardly open my eyes. My bones had turned to water and I felt like I was soaking into the sheets. "We are never visiting that bitch again."

Declan chuckled and nuzzled me.

I leaned into him. "I love you Dec."

"What am I, chopped liver?" Ryan said. "I thought Blue was just being ridiculous, but—"

I kicked his calf. "Of course, I love you too, you big baby."

Ryan grinned. "Baby? Baby?" He leaned forward and tickled my ribs. "Hold her down, Dec! She can't get away with that!"

And Dec held me down while my general tickle-tortured me into submission.

"I love you too! I love you too!" I wheezed between laughs.

When they finally relented, we all got cleaned up. Ryan and I took special care wiping Declan's back and helping him bandage it.

I leaned over him where he sat on the bed as I put the last bandage in place. Then kissed his head and said. "Remember, next time, call us. We're here for you, Dec. However you need."

Declan grabbed my hand and pulled my wrist to his face. He gave it a soft kiss. "I know, Bloss. I mean, I knew it. But now, I really know."

I traced his cheek. "Love you."

"Love you more."

I shook my head as we walked toward the door that Ryan held open for us. "You can feel how much I love you, so you know that's not possible."

⁂

The three of us returned to the library to find everyone there, still researching. Connor, Blue, and even Quinn were shooting annoyed looks over at Donaloo as they pored over document after document. I could see a discarded pile of items at their feet. Donaloo was no help, of course, he'd worn borrowed trousers today and they kept slipping down as he danced around chanting, "A child is a mother's heart, she is broken when they're apart." He slid on a discarded scroll and nearly lost his balance.

Dini tried to grow her petals large enough to cover his face. "Can I please just smother him?" she squeaked as she pressed the petals down. She squealed when Donaloo nearly ripped one of her petals as he freed his mouth. She shrunk back to her normal size with a grunt.

I stared over at her with a sarcastic raise of the brow. Donaloo might be a fool, but he'd proven useful. Which was more than she'd done thus far. "You going to create a mirror spell to protect the capital from djinn?" I asked her.

Her petals had fluttered. "You're fighting djinn?"

Declan muttered, "And giants and sea sprites," as he tossed aside another book. It landed with a *thunk*.

"Sea sprites!" Dini squeaked. "Those are my cousins!"

"Yes, what do you know about a sprite named Mayi?" I asked.

"There's no such sprite," Dini responded, her petals slowly twisting back and forth like she was shaking her head. "My kind are rare. Sea sprites even more so."

"Well, you're wrong. There is such a sprite. We've seen her," I argued.

"Not possible. The last sea sprite died in an underwater earthquake seventeen years ago. And his name wasn't Mayi. It was Losho," Dini crossed her leaves.

"How do you know that?"

Dini rolled her petals in an exaggerated fashion, like she was rolling her head and eyes at me. "Because sprites can communicate with one another, obviously."

My stomach dropped. To my mind, there was nothing obvious about a flower communicating with anyone. But Dini was right about sprites being rare. I turned to stare at Donaloo, "Is that true?"

The wizard bobbed his head from side to side, causing Dini to smack him with a leaf. "Truth is … what you believe you know that you believe. Those cobbled facts that you perceive."

"Do you know what a sea sprite looks like? Have you ever met one? Is Mayi one?" My questions tumbled out and stacked one on top of the other.

Donaloo just shrugged and turned his hands palm up.

I gritted my teeth. "Never mind. Quinn can Dini use your last bead for just a moment?"

Quinn took a bead out of his own hair and walked toward Dini, who cringed backward. "What are you doing?"

"This bead will let him transfer a mental image to you, so you can see who we see. If this isn't a sea sprite we're dealing with, we're planning our attacks for her all wrong," I clicked my fingernails together impatiently as Dini grew a small shoot so that Quinn could slide the bead onto it. If Mayi wasn't a damned sea sprite, we needed to know what the hell she was. The witch was fighting Sedara now, but we needed to know how she could be defeated.

I could tell the moment Quinn sent Dini the mental images of Mayi that we'd picked up at the tavern. A shiver ran up her stem. "Oooh, you're close! That thing is certainly *not* a full sea sprite. But she is a halfling. Oh, Losho must have gotten busy under the sea ... but really? A human?" She made a *tsk*ing sound.

Donaloo scolded her. "You scoff, but you fed at the same trough."

Quinn and I shared a horrified glance at the thought of some sea version of Dini getting busy with a human. What would that mean? A human and a strand of seaweed? A sea urchin? I was tamping down on my gag reflex out of official royal politeness. Until Connor changed the direction of my thoughts.

"If Mayi's half-human, then there's a price for her magic."

Those words rushed like a waterfall down my spine. A thrill raced through me. All of us turned to stare at him.

Connor stared solemnly at me, his dark blue eyes burning into mine. "If she pays a price and we figure out what it is ... we can end her."

I looked at Quinn. "Tell Ryan to send men back to observe the fight between Sedara and Mayi. Set any spy you still trust to follow her where he can. We need to see exactly where she goes and how she uses her powers."

Quinn nodded.

I glanced around the room, and I couldn't stop the smile that spread over my face.

"Dini, thank you. I think you've been an incredible help."

The flower preened and two new blossoms popped out of the shoot she'd grown for Quinn. Donaloo batted at them since they blocked his good eye.

"Blinding me, binding me! Get those out of my face, I need to see!"

I turned and left the room, a skip in my step. We had a lead on the sea witch—she had a weakness, we just had to find it.

CHAPTER FIFTEEN

*T*he next four days passed in a blur. There was so much to do. I started taking Donaloo's disgusting tablets, because there weren't enough hours in the day. The wretched things made me gag, but so did all the reports that I got. The one time I tried to eat, I puked all over Jorad's shoes as he stood there holding a plate of pastries. I was trying to eat and read reports about my provinces at the same time—and that particular report describe the gruesome way two of our soldiers had been caught and executed.

I hardly saw my knights—other than Connor. Declan and Ryan disappeared so that Ryan could practice multiplying different kinds of metals to make weapons for our side and diminishing weapons with their opposites to hand-icap the other side. Apparently, it was incredibly hard for him to avoid just diminishing all weapons on the battle-field at once. Declan reported an incident where they'd flown over a skirmish on our borders between Raslen soldiers and ours. Ryan had ended up turning every sword in the entire battle into a feather. The battle had degraded to a barroom brawl of fisticuffs until Ryan had called out several gargoyles.

Declan had been wheezing with mirth when he'd drunk my amusement. "Tastes like honey," he'd gasped. And written it down, because of course, Declan was categorizing and codifying each emotion's taste.

Quinn and Blue decided they didn't trust Quinn's former spy network, so they were out on gargoyles at all hours, scouring the country for troop movement, treasonous thoughts, and attack plans. The two became as thick as thieves. Their mental conversations were hilarious to watch because Blue was so expressive. He often started forming words with his lips, forgetting he couldn't talk. And his facials were something we all started to copy when the nights grew long, and we grew a bit loopy from staring at the war maps for hours on end.

Connor and I tried to help the displaced people of Evaness and reach out to the other kingdoms of Kenmare. My diplomatic knight sent missives to Macedon, who offered some minor assistance—they agreed to sanction the two warring nations. Lored didn't respond at all to our request for assistance.

At first, I was furious, until I heard the queen there had suffered from a stroke. We were still debating the best way to approach requesting help from Gitmore. Connor thought we needed to go in person to show our sincerity and commitment. It would also allow us to bring gifts.

But I wasn't willing to leave Evaness again, not after Sedara's queen had tried to take my Declan.

Since we reached an impasse regarding Gitmore, we turned our attention to attacking Isla. Of the kingdoms warring against us, hers had the most resources. Raj depended too heavily on wish magic. He wouldn't have grain stored for winter or extra armor we could use. We needed to defeat her first.

But she must have known, after our botched assassination attempt, that we were after her. Isla seemed to have disappeared. I didn't know how she—with her giants—could disappear. She didn't have a system of mines and dwarves, like they had up north in Macedon. I wondered if Raj had made her invisible.

But when I'd brought this theory to Blue, he'd said, "My father wouldn't do that. He'd know that Isla is the weakest link of the three. He's lived through thirty wars. He'd know that you'd gun for her—and that while you did, it would keep you off his back. He'd leave her exposed."

So that theory went up in smoke.

I asked Donaloo and Dini one day if they knew how Isla might be hiding. The wizard had been just outside the walls of the castle, waving his hands in the direction of Marscha and finishing up a chant, when I happened upon him and the flower sprite who was still embedded in his forehead, her pointed, pink petals jabbing in time to his words. He was busy restoring the mirror spell. It took three hours of maintenance each day for him to keep the spell active. I didn't fully understand what he did, other than it required a lot of cumin imported from Lored and fourteen dozen eggs from the chicken coop. Ryan's youngest recruits had not been happy to see their breakfast diminish.

Donaloo completed his chants and I repeated my question.

"Do you have any idea where I might find Isla?"

The wizard simply shrugged his shoulders at me multiple times. "Is she who you really seek? You can't end a war by killing the weak."

My nostrils flared. "Well, we still haven't found the gods-damned ring for Raj! And we still have no idea what weakness the sea sprite—"

"Eh-hem, half-sprite," Dini chimed in.

I resisted rolling my eyes. "Any ideas on their weaknesses?"

"Djinn's weakness are wishes," said Donaloo.

"Wishes are their weapons," I countered.

Dini shook her little flower head. "No. He's right."

"That makes no sense. Gah!" I pulled at my hair. I should have known better than to come ask Donaloo myself. But Connor was having lunch with Fer, the fairy duchess who oversaw the Cerulean Forest, and I hadn't wanted to disrupt him. My crass mouth wasn't helpful when he had to talk frantic nobles down.

I was about to ask how wishes were a weakness when Jorad emerged from around the corner of the castle. The manservant gave me a stiff bow.

"Jorad, everything alright?"

He gazed down on me, arrogant as ever, as he replied. "As well as could be hoped with half the castle out of commission, but an entire battalion of soldiers to feed and house. Why hasn't everyone unfrozen?"

I turned to Donaloo, the same question in my eyes.

"To the gates of hell and back, you must go to get them back."

"Thanks for clearing that up," I pressed my lips together and fought the urge to smack him. He was full of useless answers today.

Jorad just grumbled as he walked off.

Dini's petals turned to watch him leave. "I don't like him. You want me to eat him?"

I laughed. What a sweet, silly offer. "I don't like him much either, but he's very good at organization." Then I turned back to Donaloo. Despite his idiotic method of answering, his jumbled rhymes had helped me before, with Blue. I needed his help again. I needed to know what I could do to defeat his enemy. "How do I use wishes against the djinn?" I asked.

"You have a half-djinn," Dini said.

Horror washed over me. She meant I should use Quinn? I stared back and forth from flower to wizard. "Are you mad? I can't do that to Quinn!" I couldn't force him to be silent again. "Any wish that would take down Raj would be on such a huge scale—Connor just read to me about a nightmare that lasted three years for one djinni. Three years!"

The flower just curled and uncurled the tips of her petals, and I rather got a feeling from her that if she were a person, she'd be arrogantly studying her nails. "You're just not thinking cleverly then. There are ways—"

"Tell me!"

Donaloo shook his head. "I can't win all your battles or fight all your wars. At best, I can unlock your mental doors, help you to see beyond your nose, to possibilities where magic flows."

"What?" I asked. "What does that even mean? You're helping me fight my battles right now!" I waved my hands at the giant mirror spell above our heads. "What do you call this spell? Why do you help Evaness so much when I haven't asked, but then when I do ask for advice, say things like that?"

Dini sighed. "He hasn't told you about our daughter, has he?"

Shock and a series of very disturbing images flitted through my head. *No!*

Quinn popped into my head, noticing the unusual thoughts. I must have projected them.

Flower sex, Dove?

I didn't answer him. I was too busy gaping at Donaloo, who had a slight blush on my cheeks.

What tumbled out my mouth was a completely unqueenly, "WHAT?"

Dini's petals drooped. "Our sweet little Posey, she'll be one-hundred-eight this year."

I glanced back and forth between them. "This isn't some joke that Quinn's coordinated with the two of you, is it?" I asked. I mean, Quinn's timing jumping into my head was suspicious. Had he been waiting for me to think about flowers? Had he been waiting for me to imagine how a human/flower mating might be physically possible?

I glanced around, searching for my knights. My eyes scanned the parapets along the edge of the castle. I didn't see anyone there. If this was a joke, wouldn't they be hiding, wanting to see my every reaction?

Quinn, did you tell Donaloo to trick me? Not funny!

Dove? Hold on a sec—

Where are you?

Local tavern, getting some info. Seems like something' odd has been seen down south.

He nearly distracted me. But Quinn loved practical jokes. I narrowed my eyes as I listened to him and studied Donaloo and his lady-flower friend suspiciously.

Dini's leaves folded over one another and she held them close to her stem, like a woman might hold her hands close to her heart. "Posey's the sweetest girl. But she got caught up in politics in Gitmore."

Donaloo shook his head sadly. And for once, the silly facade faded from his face. I could see the lines etched from a father's worry on his forehead. "Try as you might to teach them right, your child's day could be your night."

Dini shook her petals. "She wanted to be a warrior. Nothing we could say could talk her out of it. Do I look like I passed on a warrior gene? I'm a flower sprite, for goodness sake! But off she went, got caught up …" her voice sank from its normal squeak to a melancholy pitch. "She ended up in the undead army."

Donaloo reached up a hand and gently stroked Dini's petals.

My heart constricted as I watched them. They looked heartbroken. But shouldn't they be proud? Their daughter got what she wanted, the life she wanted, even if it wasn't the life they'd wanted for her. The undead army. The thought of that didn't appeal to me at all. But maybe it was someone else's dream. My mother had fought so hard to restrict my own freedom, that a bit of my old resentment reared its head. And my stupid tavern-wench mouth had to spout off my opinion. "Why is that a bad thing?"

The wizard said, "Sometimes we choose our path without knowing the price we'll pay—"

Dini pulled away from Donaloo and interrupted what was sure to be a long-winding rhyming monologue. "She was tricked into it; that's why we're devastated. Didn't know what she signed when she signed it—the queen and that old bastard wizard, Raster, had no scruples. About twenty, twenty-five years ago, they recruited a lot of young kids, runaways, the like. Promised them they'd see the world, travel as soldiers, get all the glory—only to kill the kids and wake them back up, undead. Posey wasn't a kid, but she was always trying to find a way to fight more, do better. They fed her a line of fertilizer—"

My cheeks heated. "I'm sorry."

"Don't be sorry. You're destined to fix it!" Dini twirled her petals.

I took a step back. "What?"

"Donaloo went to another wizard—one who specialized in fortune telling—when Posey first got wrapped up in that mess years ago. And she told him only the queen who refused her crown could give the undead army peace." Dini's petals swirled unnaturally, spinning on her stem. "And look at your very power!"

Did someone just toss a boulder on my chest? I thought.

Because, suddenly, it felt like a huge weight was pressing down on me. Pressure. I had to save their daughter? An entire undead army? I couldn't even save my own godsdamned sister! What they said made me want to hurl. So, I word-vomited on them. "Oh, well, that's not intimidating *at all*—in addition to the war that I'm stumbling around in, and the three lunatics I'm already trying to kill. Tossing an army on there is—"

"They aren't that bad. They'll be a cinch compared to everything else." Dini waved a leaf. "Oh, I know! Scry them, Donny. Let Bloss see our Posey."

That sounded like a horrible idea. I swallowed hard and tried to think of a good excuse so I could leave. I did not want to try to pretend their undead daughter was adorable. But, Donaloo was keeping up the mirror spell over Marscha. He'd frozen my castle to stop the bombs. I knew that Ryan's knights had been able to remove at least one explosive and catapult it so that it exploded midair over a field rather than hurt anyone inside my castle.

How could I refuse him? I wondered.

I couldn't. Now when what he wanted was simply to help his family.

And Dini, if she hadn't helped us yet, at least she hadn't harmed us … and sprites were powerful. Mayi's attacks were only those of a half-sea sprite. It made me think that Dini, as a full sprite, held even more power in her tiny petals.

I needed them. And they needed me. The least I could do was try to help them after all they'd done for my country.

I nodded at Donaloo. "I'd love to see Posey." I tried to discreetly take a deep breath and brace myself. Everything my tutor had told me about the undead army of Gitmore was that it was a horrific nightmare. The country had lost the last Fire War and been stripped of weapons—they'd created the army as a result. The army roamed the desert, a breathing barrier that Gitmore used to protect itself— because the undead didn't quit. They'd follow soldiers and hunt them down after a battle. There was no escaping them, because they had all the time in the world.

Donaloo pulled a pebble off the ground and spit on it. Unlike Cerena, it didn't seem like he needed a scrying stone. I watched as he went through essentially the same motions that Cerena had, but then he added a strange little circling wrist flick at the end, which expanded his pebble to the size of a small plate. We stared at it as the image rippled and undead faces came into view.

The pupils of their eyes were blown out, the iris void of all color. Undead eyes were a black circle floating in whiteness. Their skin was a dusky green white, scarred and whipped by the sandstorms in the desert. Some of them, those who had been undead the longest, were missing skin in places: the edges of their mouth, their eyelids, their fingertips. The places that were used most. The undead army marched, patrolling the beaches of Gitmore, keeping intruders from invading the shore. Their stiff bodies moved north as the waves crashed to shore behind them. Row after row after row, it seemed like all of Gitmore had joined the army of the undead.

Donaloo and Dini both gave a little squeal when they spotted Posey, emerging from underneath the water, walking calmly toward the shore and joining the undead in their march, unaffected by the seaweed that clung to her shoulder and the water that dripped down her soaked clothes.

"She's made captain!" Dini's leaves went to her stamens. "Our little girl made captain."

Donaloo's voice got husky. "Always bright as the sun, our sweet little shining one."

Their daughter was taller than most of the other soldiers. As she shook her head to remove some of the seawater, I realized she had petals instead of hair, a collection of wide purple petals that framed the top half of her face as they dried. The back of her head was green as a stem. Instead of fingers on her hands, she seemed to have curling green shoots. Her face was human, and more horrific than most of the other undead soldiers, her lips were half-gone and her teeth were exposed. Her eyes were the same inhuman white and black as all the undead. But she marched proudly at the front of a column. Her back was straight, and she called out an order as her eyes scanned the churning sea for ships. On her chest, pinned to a ragged yellow band embroidered with Gitmore's griffon, a captain's star gleamed.

"I'm happy for her. Congratulations to the two of you," I commended, uncertain what else to say. Dammit all. I needed Connor in situations like this.

I forced my polite court smile to stay in place as Donaloo moved the picture closer to her.

Posey turned to a fellow captain and her skeletal mouth opened. "The sea is awake. We need to let the queen know."

Dini sighed. "She always was so aware of her surroundings. It really did make her an excellent soldier. Well, now you'll know her when you see her."

The image on the scrying stone started to go black but I held up a hand.

My stomach fluttered as I asked, "May I see Avia?" I held my breath, hoping.

Dini and Donaloo both turned their faces toward me.

"I want to know what she looks like now. I don't want to accidentally attack her. When she was here, she always looked human," I rushed to explain.

The memory we'd seen from the maid who'd be present at Avia's "birth" had explicitly said that Avia would appear human. If Avia was truly part sprite, she wouldn't appear fully human. Not if she was anything like Posey. I needed to know what she looked like. All the practical reasons I gave Donaloo were true. But I also just missed her. We'd hardly reconnected when she'd been taken from me. I needed to know she was safe. I wanted to know that Avia was okay. And if I figured out her location and could send some troops to bust her out and save her, all the better.

Dini nodded furiously. "That's a very good idea."

Donaloo chanted and swirled his hand over the scrying stone again; slowly Posey's image faded. An underwater cave appeared. A shaft of blue sunlight filtered down from an opening in the rock above. And a beautiful, ethereal creature —who looked more like a fairy than anything else—fluttered in the water. She had a human body, but her sides were lined in multicolored fish scales. Her hair was no longer brown but golden. Avia's smiling brown eyes had turned lavender. And they were sad and mournful as she floated in the water. Her wings stretched behind her; they were translucent with streaks of orange and purple, and they reflected the weak sunlight. They looked almost like beta fish fins as she floated in the sea. Avia wore a short dress that was purple on top and faded to burnt orange. She shuddered as an ashray swam past, its glowing eyes lighting up the cave.

"They're guarding her with sea ghosts," Dini clucked her tongue. "Idiots. They need to keep them back or that water will get too cold."

My eyes glanced up at her flower face, concerned. "What do you mean?"

"Even sprites need warmth." Her petals drooped. "Maybe they're keeping her cold to keep her compliant."

Fury made my insides as hot as a blacksmith's anvil. I pressed my lips together. I wanted to forget everything else and go yank Avia out of there. "Mayi is her mother! She's treating her own daughter like a prisoner?"

Donaloo let the scrying stone fade to black as Dini said, "Well, now. Her daughter was raised by strangers. Mayi happens to be in a war against the kingdom that raised her daughter. I can see how she might not know where Avia's loyalties lie."

My nostrils flared. "If the bitch had come to me and told me what my mother had done, this war could have been preven—"

"Be careful of could haves, should haves, too. They can wrap you up in wondering, when there are things to do."

I could have punched Donaloo—that snoutband. My fingers were curling into fists when shouts came in from some of the guards on the parapet behind us. I looked up.

"Messenger on a pegasus, Your Majesty," one called down to me.

I made my way to the drawbridge to greet the messenger. Donaloo and Dini trailed behind. I hoped it wasn't bad news, but my stomach sank when I saw Connor come out onto the drawbridge as well. He'd abandoned his meeting with Fer.

"They spotted one of my fathers through the looking glass," Connor stated, watching the winged horse gently come to a landing in the field in front of the castle.

My eyes widened when I recognized the man dismounting. "Michael!" I ran forward and embraced one of Connor's fathers. My best friend hugged his father as soon as I let go.

Their hug was long and spoke volumes. Bad things were afoot.

Michael let go first and turned to me. "Your Majesty," he started to bow but I hit him in the shoulder.

"You aren't allowed to kneel for me."

He smiled, but it was a thin, wan smile. It didn't meet his eyes, which were lined with worry. It was the kind of smile one gave to a dying person, a lie that said everything would be okay, when it most definitely would not.

"What happened?"

"Your Majesty, we are under attack."

I nodded and tried to keep my face neutral. Dammit all! Quinn and Blue hadn't noted any attacks going on near Connor's family! I would have yanked them all back to the castle if we'd heard hide or hair of this sort of attack.

I hated that I had to ask, "Which country is attacking you?"

Michael shook his head and ran his hand through his grey hair. "That's the thing. I'm not certain. We're under attack from a rainbow."

CHAPTER SIXTEEN

I yelled to Quinn in my head. *Tell Ryan there's an attack in Kycee's province. We'll need gargoyles. I'm not sure what else.*

What kind of attack? Quinn asked me.

Magic.

I turned to look at Donaloo and Dini. "Any ideas what it could be?" I asked the pair.

Dini bobbed her flower head. "Water fairies."

I rubbed my brow. "Has every magical creature in the damned universe suddenly decided to fight us?"

Dini responded, "At least now you know where Isla was. She was probably under the river, meeting with them."

Fury surged in me. Gods, I hoped that Dini was right, and Isla was with them. We needed to take her out.

Declan and Ryan must've been nearby, because they landed on their gargoyle just minutes later. Blue and Quinn said they'd meet us in the air.

We took to the sky together, following Michael. I didn't even take the time to change out of my ruby red dress. I just shoved my skirts aside as I straddled Pony and took to the sky.

Ryan had a group of soldiers fly with us on gargoyles. My knights wanted me to stay behind with Dini and Donaloo, but I refused.

"I can use my peace magic to stun some soldiers into lethargy. And I need to see if Isla is there." I didn't say it aloud, but I wanted to be the one to end her. It was a selfish desire. A foolish one, probably. But the woman had walked into my castle, intending to betray me. She'd turned some of my own nobles against me. And now she'd attacked Connor's family. She more than deserved death at my hand.

The cold winter air stung our eyes as we flew quickly to the south. There was a river there and an inlet, that Kycee and her husbands used for trading. I assumed that the water fairies had come from the river. Typically, the tiny fairies completely hid themselves from humans. I was surprised that Isla had gotten them to meet with her. But perhaps having a sea-sprite on her side had swayed them.

When we got close to Connor's childhood home, a manor house that was not far from the harbor, I saw exactly what Michael meant.

A rainbow stretched across the sky. But unlike a natural rainbow, this one wasn't a thin arch. This rainbow was like a blanket that spread across the sky and hung down over the little port town. From above, I watched as patches of the rainbow suddenly dropped out of view. Entire legions of tiny fairies dove to the earth to attack my people.

One would think that tiny fairies could have no effect. One would be wrong. The fairies didn't even have to touch my soldiers. They simply stopped midair in front of my soldier's faces. The fairies used the bubble of water that surrounded them to encompass my soldiers' noses and mouths. The wicked creatures drowned my men where they stood. They drowned my men as sunlight glinted off their water bubbles in a beautiful array of colors.

Death had never been more gorgeous and horrific.

How the sarding hell do you kill a water fairy? I asked Quinn.

His answer made my insides as cold as my surroundings. *I don't know. Fire?*

Ryan didn't have the same question I did. Or perhaps he and Declan had already talked about the fairies on the flight over.

"Blue and Declan—watch my back," he yelled.

Then my giant knight flew in front of us, raised his hands, and sent a blast of yellow power through the sky.

I gasped and choked and clutched onto my gargoyle. The sky was suddenly parched. Air wheezed through my lungs. It was so dry that it felt like the sky was scratching my throat. My eyes squinted against the desiccation. But I didn't blink. I watched as the rainbow below me rippled and faded, and the water fairies shrieked and dropped from the sky like a swarm of dead insects.

Ryan struggled to restore a bit of water to the sky around us as I glanced around.

"It can't be that easy, can it?" I wheezed; my throat still dry as a bone.

That's when the first winged bear barreled into us. It smashed into Declan from the side and he was nearly knocked off his gargoyle. I dove on Pony to rescue him and shove him back upright.

"It was a lure," Declan coughed when I'd righted him on his mount. "Get out of here."

But it was too late.

Winged bears surrounded our force and clawed at us from every angle. Above, below, behind. My gargoyles were nearly indestructible. But my soldiers were not. And Isla's warriors knew just how to attack. Their bears swooped and latched onto my soldiers' backs, lifting them from their mounts and throwing them aside—their screams were horrid, piercing shrieks as they fell to their deaths.

I blasted peace at the nearest bear and his rider—blood-lust surging through me as I saw the pair drop like stones. I turned to blast another.

Declan's face screwed up in concentration beside me and I watched one of the bear-riding soldiers deliberately nosedive his bear into the trees below. A sickening *thunk* made its way back up to our ears moments later.

Ryan blasted the air again, but I think he was disoriented by the two bears swooping with claws aimed for his head. His yellow blast of power soaked us all with water but did little more than make the battle become filled with shivers as we sought to destroy one another.

To my right, I saw a twist of navy smoke appear and Sultan Raj appeared in midair, behind several bears.

Blue saw him too.

Ryan lifted his arms and shot out another jet of yellow light—just as Blue let out a war cry and dove at his father.

His father disappeared in a puff of navy smoke just as double the number of bears and riders appeared.

Sarding wish magic! I thought-yelled.

One of the new bears had a clear shot at Ryan's side, the spot Blue had abandoned now open.

It swiped at him, raking his side and leg.

My giant cried out in pain.

Terror filled me. I trembled where I sat. The world turned slow as my hand reached out. I blasted everyone and everything around me with peace magic. My arms shredded. Two bears flying at me were slit down the middle, their blood hovered in midair a moment, a sacrifice for my magic, before bear and rider tumbled to the earth below.

Everyone within twenty feet of me appeared dazed. Everyone but Connor, who was used to dealing with emotions that weren't his own. Used to fighting them off. Connor shook off the lethargy of my power and made his gargoyle dive toward Ryan. He extended his hands and pink healing light erupted from them.

Ryan moaned, "Slower."

Connor tried, but the bears and Raslen soldiers were shaking off their daze. The rest of our force moved to protect them, and as they did, I saw an odd-looking soldier in the back.

He was a non-descript, bland-faced soldier. I might never have noticed him, except for the fact that the rest of them seemed so practiced. This rider's bear just moved slightly to the side, in a way that seemed unpracticed and unintentional.

I shot a jet of peace in that direction, and immediately, two soldiers sprang up in front of the bland soldier, blocking my magic.

"It's Isla!" I cried. "In a disguise spell!"

My eyes flew to Ryan's but he shouted, "After her!" and waved his arm.

I didn't second-guess him. I shot forward, urging Pony to bowl over the bears in front of us.

The bland-faced soldier turned his mount and shot off through the sky.

Fighting erupted behind us, but I ignored it. I urged Pony to go faster and faster. We gained slowly on the bear, which had more training. I heard shouts behind me but didn't turn to see what was happening. Every piece of me was focused on the queen in front of me.

The chase seemed endless. There was no way to trap her in the sky. There were no barriers. No roadblocks.

But I had one thing in my favor that she didn't. Gargoyles didn't tire.

Eventually, her bear started to huff. I saw its wings drag as it struggled to stay airborne. Isla kicked at the beast, but there was nothing she could do.

I could taste victory on my tongue. It had a raw, metallic taste, like blood. A harsh smile curved my lips.

I raised my arms, ready to blast Isla and her bear. It wasn't the death I wanted to give her, but it would have to do.

But then, an entire legion of soldiers on flying bears rose out of the trees.

And I realized we'd flown right to Isla's castle.

Shite! I screamed in my head, as the bitch turned to smirk at me. She knew I wanted her. My fingers flexed on Pony. I started to shake, not out of fear for my own situation— which was dire—but out of pure fury.

Don't move, Bloss! Quinn commanded in my thoughts.

I froze.

And then suddenly, the entire line of soldiers dive-bombed at once, suiciding themselves.

Isla's smiling expression turned to frightened shock.

And a dark piece of my heart lit with black fire. *That's right. You think you know what magic we have. But we have more than you'll ever know.*

Tell Declan excellent work, I thought.

Then Pony and I shot forward toward the bitch queen.

"Bloss, wait!" I heard Connor shout behind me. So, my knights had followed.

But I was too attuned to the hunt, my prey just beyond my jaws, her scared scent in my nostrils.

Isla's bear dove onto a balcony on the third floor of her palace. She yanked at the doors as I grew close. They were locked.

I chuckled, easing Pony down. I debated whether she deserved to be doused with peace before I shoved her off the balcony or if I wanted Pony to rip her limb from limb the way her bears had tried to kill my Ryan.

I got close enough that I could see the whites of her terrified eyes.

And fate be damned, someone unlocked the door for her just as I swooped down.

"Arrrgh!" I growled in disappointment as Pony and I rose back up in the air, out of the reach of Isla's bear. It was too exhausted to fly after us, but not too exhausted to swipe at us and defend itself.

I took a moment to evaluate her palace.

The palace was huge. It was three times the size of mine. That wasn't because Rasle was wealthier. The palace was larger because it was necessary, so giants and part-giants could fit. Each stone block that made up the walls was as tall as I was, and probably twice as wide. They were a dull blue grey.

I scanned the palace. There didn't seem to be many sentries about, but perhaps the line of soldiers that Declan had killed were the ones set to guard the palace just then.

As I circled, I felt a change in the air beside me. I looked over to see my knights and several riderless gargoyles.

My eyes flew to Ryan. "Are you alright?"

Ryan gave a stiff nod.

Declan spoke before I could question Ryan any further. He leaned toward my giant. "Remember our practice on stones?"

Ryan nodded and raised his hands. Yellow reduction magic lit the front wall. The blue stones turned a dull green.

Declan's recent training with Ryan seem to have worked, because the wall started to disintegrate into air before our eyes, turning the castle into a life-sized dollhouse.

Courtiers screamed and came streaming out of the front of the palace like ants. A woman in an orange dress went mindless with panic when the wall disappeared. She toppled from the third floor and became a screaming blur before she turned into a puddle of silk and blood on the ground.

Someone rang the alarm bell that signaled attack. Archers appeared on the trip of the castle and arrows whizzed through the air below us. I could see their purple streaks, laced with poisonous magic. We were out of range.

I ordered our gargoyles to dive bomb. Resistant to the arrows, they could take out the archers while we searched the open-faced rooms for Isla.

"Another wall," I ordered.

Ryan's face was strained and sweaty, but he only nodded.

Connor hovered beside him, feeding him tiny bits of pink healing magic as he strained himself to take out another side of the palace.

This time, we spotted Isla, and her daughter Corinna, trying to escape into an inner stairwell. I shot peace at both of them. It glinted off some of Isla's armor, off the quiver of purple arrows at her back, but Corinna was dressed as a princess. My magic soaked through her long blue dress until she stood like a dumb rag doll.

Pony and I flew lower, even as my men protested.

Bloss, dont! Just wish that she walk herself to the edge of the palace! It's a tiny wish! I can do that! Quinn yelled in my head. *Declan can get her to jump this time!*

But bloodlust rose inside me. It was a beast with glowing red eyes. A beast who growled with the desire to avenge Kylie and all the others. That beast wanted to rip Isla apart.

I landed as Isla struggled to yank her comatose daughter into the stairwell.

"Corinna! Come on!" she grunted, her disguise-spelled voice that of a weak man. It was thin and stringy.

Her daughter was too stunned to move.

Pony walked forward, guarding me. Two more gargoyles landed with thuds beside us and stomped forward. This close, I could aim my peace magic better and I hit Isla in the throat, so she couldn't run.

Using my power so much left me light-headed. Unlike in the air, the gargoyles had no blood to lend me. The price was all my own. My thighs were soaked in sticky, wet blood as I strode toward the queen of Rasle.

I let my gargoyles surround them.

Isla stared at me with dull defiance.

243

I waited, letting my power wash away. I didn't want her to die peacefully. The vengeful part of me wanted her to scream as my gargoyle ripped her apart.

I watched Isla and Corinna until their eyes started to clear.

I ignored Quinn and Blue shouting for me to let the gargoyles kill the pair out so we could leave.

I ignored my knights until Blue mentally shouted, *Watch out! The princess is mad!*

That's when Corinna grabbed an arrow from Isla's quiver and shoved it right into her mother's jugular.

CHAPTER SEVENTEEN

I had Pony knock out Princess Corinna by smacking her across the face with a closed paw.

I considered that merciful.

Shiter thought differently. The little lavender rabbit launched himself at me from underneath a chair. I hadn't noticed him hiding there, but I did notice when Pony's wings suddenly unfurled and I heard a *thunk*. Shiter had smacked to the ground but he bared his naughty little bunny teeth at me before leaving a pile of pellets on the floor.

"Hello to you, too," I told the enchanted bunny as he hopped forward to check on his mistress. I noted he didn't shite on her. That rump-faced hopper!

I grabbed Shiter by the ears and had one of the gargoyles take Corinna carefully in his claws.

Then we flew the princess and her loyal, shitey little bunny back to Evaness.

Connor helped me dismount and immediately encompassed me in pink light as I sagged against him. I hadn't realized how much I'd been running on a combination of Donaloo's tablets and adrenaline. But my head lolled against his chest and my knees nearly buckled once it was all over.

I dropped Shiter, who scrambled to get away from us. I assume the overdose of healing magic made him feel sick. Blue snatched up his enchanted brother by the ears. "Harsh," he greeted him.

I didn't even have the energy to laugh when Shiter shited in response.

I looked around for Ryan and Declan, but they were still mounted, discussing things. Quinn took Princess Corinna from the gargoyle that had carried her. He shouldered her and dragged her inside. She moaned dully and put her hand to the goose egg that had formed on her forehead.

I tapped on Connor. "Follow," I ordered, because I didn't have the strength yet to walk on my own. He half-carried me to the green parlor, the pink light of his magic offsetting my blood loss. By the time Connor helped me into a chair, I was feeling a bit better. Less light-headed. He brought me water, and a soldier tossed over an apple he'd been about to eat on his watch. After I ate, I felt much better.

Connor spent a few minutes healing Corinna while I ate. That's when I noticed a frozen courtier in the corner of the room. I pointed and asked Quinn to take the frozen woman over to the ballroom with the others.

He gave a sigh of discontent but complied. *We're really going to need to figure out how to unfreeze these people.*

Add it to the endless list of things to do, I replied.

I turned back to Rasle's princess. "What the hell were you thinking?" I asked the freckle-faced, raven-haired Corinna. She was nearly six years older than me, in her mid-twenties—and already married to some schmucks her mother had chosen. Corinna, out of all the crown princesses in the kingdom of Kenmare, was the one I'd least expect to commit matricide. It threw everything I thought I knew about her into question. Sickly, shy, a pawn and simply a mouthpiece for her four husbands— that was the reputation that followed her like a shadow.

"I thought it would be more merciful to kill her myself than let you torture her first," Corinna's voice was calm and collected. She held eye contact with me.

"And you were willing to do that?"

"If anyone else had done it, it would be treason. It would've been unfair to ask them."

I leaned back in my chair and studied Corinna. She was thin and her eyes were over-sized for her face. But she didn't look as weak as the rumors made her out to be. "I think the reports of your illness may have been overstated," I told her.

"I think the reports of your death may have been overstated," she replied.

Behind me, Connor chuckled. "It's so hard to get good information these days."

Admiration lit inside me. A mercy killing for her own mother. I couldn't begin to imagine how hard such a thing might be. Of course, my mother hadn't been Isla. Still, I didn't think I could do something like that. She was right though. Her mother's end had been much kinder than I'd planned.

I smiled thinly at her. "You guessed correctly."

"I suppose I have a trip to the dungeons in order?" Corinna asked, folding her hands on her lap. She was quite calm about it.

I leaned back in my chair and evaluated her. Then I glanced at Blue.

What's she thinking? I mentally asked him.

He furrowed his brow. *She's pissed at us for taking her, pissed at her mother for this whole stupid war, pissed at her husbands for backing her mother, pissed that she was left behind again—*

So, pissed.

Pretty much.

Not scared?

Resigned. She's hoping there aren't too many rats in your dungeon. She's hoping that since she didn't start the war, you'll kill her quickly.

Not hoping for a rescue?

Nope.

Any sense of calculation? Any plans?

She wants to see if she can get Harsh—her bunny ... she calls him Ed—back.

That was interesting. So little for a princess to wish for, so little calculation involved. I was surprised she wasn't thinking about her own freedom.

Prisoners become resigned to locks, Bloss, Blue told me. *Before I was sent to the army, I didn't think to run. A prison isn't just physical. A true prison is a mental cage as well.*

I turned that over in my head for a moment. Would someone who'd been a prisoner make a good ruler? A good ally?

Does she know the bunny is a man? I asked.

She suspects he's more than just a rabbit. He's too smart, she thinks. But she thinks of him as a pet ... and it's a bit sad, but her only friend.

Well, if she suspected the rabbit already, then Corinna wasn't a complete dunderhead. There was potential there.

I asked Corinna, "Your mother pretended to visit here to ask about some additional water sources, when really her intent was to capture my knights and set off explosives."

Tell me what she thinks about that, I commanded Blue.

She's mentally rolling her eyes. Her mother was always obsessed with taking more instead of managing what she had. Corinna is picturing some guys—maybe her husbands? —and thinking they're the same. She's thinking about some asshole named Firden, and how stripping him of his title would solve the resource allocation problem—

I eyed Corinna. "How'd you like to make an alliance?"

Her court face didn't hold up. Her jaw dropped. She stared at me a long moment, trying to decide if I was serious.

I stood and put my hands on the table, asserting dominance even as I kept my tone even. "My war was with your mother, and to be honest, I didn't initiate it. I have no interest in slaughtering both our populations. Both our countries have far less magic than Cheryn or Sedara, and I think that we should end the fighting so we can do what we were meant to do—take care of our countries."

Corinna tried to stay still but I noticed that she chewed the inside of her lip.

What's she thinking?

That there has to be a catch. She doesn't trust that there isn't a catch.

There is no catch. I really want her to get her giants and soldiers off my land.

Quinn chimed in as he sent an image of him setting down the frozen woman with her skirts bunched up on a settee so that her frozen neighbors got a gander at her bloomers, *Can I just say how much I hate not being able to hear her? I feel useless. This is shite.*

First off, put that woman's skirts down! And you're not like anyone else, dear. You're as unique as Donaloo.

Hey! I know that was an insult. I'm hurt. And trapped. And I can't hear anyone but you few idiots. You should feel bad for me, not insult me! Quinn sent me an image of a caged baby deer, batting its eyes plaintively.

Blue interjected, *I hate to interrupt your attempt at getting pity sex, but Corinna's suspicious, Bloss. She won't believe you or trust you if she doesn't know the catch. She'll always be waiting for the other shoe to drop. She's more like my family that way.* Blue added.

She wants me to be a bitch?

Blue gave a single nod of his head.

Finally, something I can excel at, I thought.

I gave Corinna a nasty smile. She wanted our deal to have a catch? Fine. I'd give her one. I slowly traced a nail over the woodgrain of the table. "Of course, in order to agree to a ceasefire—I will need you to cede a hundred miles along your northern border, from my land all the way to the sea. Since I'm fighting Cheryn and a sea witch, I want unfettered access to the ocean."

My demand was met with silence.

Shite. Did I ask for too much? I was improvising.

Dammit all. So much for being good at something, I chastised myself.

No, she's mentally reviewing pictures of the territory up there. She's trying to remember numbers. She's listing out the family names of those up north, who might give you a hard time, who might move south. Seems like she's taking things seriously.

I thought she was supposed to be a pushover. Quinn?

She used to talk nearly as much as I ever have. My people never had direct conversations with her because she hardly spoke. Quinn responded. *And she was very sick the past two years.*

I struggled to stay patient and keep my face neutral as I waited for Corinna's response.

Corinna cleared her throat and asked, "Can I have my rabbit, please? Edward doesn't like to be away from me."

I swallowed a laugh. "We called him Shiter here before Donaloo gifted him to you."

I gestured for Blue to hand over his rabbit-shifted brother, who immediately cuddled up to Corinna. She stroked his fur and kissed the top. "That's a horrid name for a sweet little man."

I bit down on a smile and exchanged a look with Blue.

Do I want to know what she's thinking now?

She's wondering if she can ask for anything in return.

Oh, good. After Donaloo and the flower thing, I think Quinn's kind of twisted my mind. I was expecting … other sorts of thoughts.

Quinn jumped into the conversation at that point. He couldn't resist after I mentioned him. *What were you thinking she was thinking, Dove?* He moved close to me and his grey eyes studied mine. *Was it something dirty?* he asked, giving me a naughty grin.

Hush. I'm busy negotiating a peace treaty. I turned away before I could blush. I couldn't help if the fact that Dini and Donaloo had somehow managed the deed. Or that it made me wonder about this princess.

Dove—

Quick, tell Connor to ensure when he draws up a map, that it has that hedgewitch lodge on it. I don't want anyone else getting access to that place.

Quinn left me alone to relay that message as Corinna glanced back up at me.

"You have someone take out those husbands my mother forced on me and you have a deal."

I leaned forward with a smile to shake her hand. "Done. It might take a bit. War and all."

Corinna nodded. "I've survived their attention this long."

We shook. "I'm going to leave you with Connor to draw up the paperwork. I'll have some food sent in. After you sign, you can be on your way."

Corinna's eyes narrowed. "That's really it?"

I nodded. "Unless you don't withdraw your troops. Then I'll pelt your kingdom with gargoyles until it's as pitted as teenager's face."

Corinna gave a smile. "I look forward to our alliance."

So did I. One enemy down. But I had two to go.

I marched out of the green parlor, Blue trailing behind me. Quinn met us in the hall. And instead of being naughty, as I expected after his stunt with the frozen courtier, he looked sad.

"What is it?" I reached for his hands.

He didn't respond immediately. He swallowed hard first. *There are two things. One worse than the other.*

What's the first? I asked.

I sent a spy to see if the sea-sprite's magic cost her breath. I thought, perhaps like Sedara's princes who blow the air, she might blow the waters and lose her breath. But my man reported back that she held up in battle for over an hour. So, we still don't know her price.

I nodded, disappointed. It wasn't good news. But it wasn't the worst. It didn't warrant Quinn's downtrodden face.

What's the other news? I asked.

It's Ryan, he thought.

I didn't even ask what had happened. I just started to run as I screamed in my head, *Where is he?*

We ran the entire way to the castle healer's work chamber. The man had been frozen during the attack on the castle. His stiff form had been shoved in the corner; arms raised as if he were about to enchant a bandage he held. Apparently, Declan had called up a magical healer from Marscha. The new man had laid out his black bag and tools on the worktable that lined the side of the stone room. Ryan was laid out on a large surgical table in the middle of the room, shirt off, pants cut open. His ankles and wrists were tied down by leather straps. That was the first time I could see exactly what Isla's bears had done to my love.

If I had seen it sooner, I never would have made the treaty with Corinna.

Horror, pity, and fury filled me as I walked toward Ryan, who cringed and moaned as the healer worked on the massive scar that laced his side and the top half of his leg. The scar was at least three inches thick and a dark, gruesome shade of pink. It didn't look healthy. Or fully healed. The healer was spreading a grey paste over it.

Fear trumpeted in my ear like a herald. I didn't want to know what came next. But I needed to know. I had to be able to help my Ryan any way I could. I latched onto his huge hand; my palm hardly covered three of his huge fingers. "What is it?"

Ryan cringed again, so it was Declan who answered. "The bear got him good. Connor healed him enough to save him. But the scar tissue," he shook his head. "It's too thick."

"That means?"

"Right now, it means he can't walk, Bloss."

Oh gods.

I felt like I'd been shot through with an arrow, like my insides were pierced. My breath grew shallow. And I met Ryan's eyes. I saw fear in them that matched my own. My warrior. What would he do if he couldn't walk?

How can he lead his men? How can he … my thoughts trailed off as disbelief clouded me. This couldn't be happening.

My eyes flew to the healer. "You can fix it, right?"

The man glanced up at me as he continued to apply a paste as thick as porridge. "I'm doing my best."

That wasn't good enough.

I looked at Declan. "Get three more healers, get a dozen in here—"

Declan held up a hand, "I'm trying. I've sent out—"

"Bloss," Ryan's hand squeezed mine.

I squeezed his back and turned to Quinn. I fingered the black ring on my thumb. "We could use a wish."

"No!" Ryan's voice boomed and echoed in the small room. "No wishes."

I turned to him. "But—"

Ryan glared at me. "We don't have enough wishes to heal everyone, Bloss."

"You're not everyone!"

"I won't get treated better than my men."

"I won't let you—"

Ryan cut me off, and his tone was full of fury. "It isn't your choice!"

I spun away, angry and devastated. And my eyes lit on Blue.

My newest knight was standing there, shell-shocked, still wearing the bloody, torn uniform he'd had on when he'd fought Isla's bears.

Before I knew it, poison darts shot out my mouth. "You did this," I accused him. "If you hadn't been so obsessed with your father, and abandoned your post, this wouldn't have happened!"

Blue's eyes widened and he took a step back. "I didn't mean—"

"Because of you, he's a sarding cripple!" I screamed.

Blue swallowed hard and shook his head.

I took a step toward him, my fists balled. I was pure rage in that moment. Nothing else.

Blue spun on his heel and fled.

I started to stride after him, but Declan blocked my path.

"No, Peace."

"Get out of my way," I snarled.

"I can't. You're about to do something you regret."

"What? Like execute him?" I tried to push around my scholar, but he held me firm.

"Bloss! Come here!" Ryan growled.

Declan pushed me gently toward Ryan.

I took a deep, cleansing breath and squeezed my eyes shut, trying to regain control. Tears filled my eyes and it took a second breath before I felt strong enough to turn around and face Ryan.

I walked toward him; head hung in shame. Ryan took my hand in one of his, but couldn't do more, since he was still tied to the table.

"Look at me, Dearling," he commanded.

I glanced up and the vision of him swam before my eyes. Two big fat tears spilled over onto my cheeks before I could clearly see him again.

"None of that," he murmured softly, his giant fingers stroking my palm.

"But you're hurt," I said, petulantly. "And you won't let me fix it."

"Little Dearling," he whispered. "War has a price. Just like magic."

"But—"

"But, nothing, love. If I'm not willing to pay the price, how can I ask any of my men to pay it?"

"But—"

"Anger has a price, too. You were pretty hard on Blue, just now."

"He left you. He went after his father. I knew he was obsessed. I knew it!"

"First of all, sit down."

Ryan wriggled backward so that I could hop up onto the table beside him.

Declan wisely cleared the room, though at that point, I wasn't paying attention to anyone other than Ryan. I swiped at my face and focused on him, on the strong jaw and the stern eyes that I loved.

My general squeezed my fingers and asked, "How did you know he was obsessed with his father?"

I curled into Ryan's side and sniffled as I answered. "His thoughts. Blue sent memories. I don't think he meant to send them. But he had a lot of memories of his father hurting him. A lot of thoughts of vengeance."

Ryan gave a small nod. "And did you ever talk to him about it? That you thought he might have a fixation?"

"No. I hardly know him—"

"Then aren't you to blame just as much as he is?"

I leaned back, blindsided. "What?" But his words grated on my bones. If I'd said something, Blue might have stayed put. He might have realized his father would show at some point. He might have held himself back.

Self-rutting idiot, I scolded myself.

I leaned over my giant and narrowed my eyes at him, before planting a small kiss on his lips.

"I sarding hate it when you're right."

Ryan grinned. "Now, pretend I smacked your ass and go apologize."

"Yes, sir."

CHAPTER EIGHTEEN

I honestly had no idea where in the castle Blue would go, so I asked Quinn to help me find him.

He's in the music room, Quinn's answer surprised me.

I went to the second floor, to a room where noble ladies prattled on and pretended they were talented at harpsichord or singing. When I entered, I heard the most beautiful music.

I stopped in the doorway, enchanted.

Blue sat in the corner, strumming a lute. He held the wooden instrument on his lap. The sounds coming from it were plaintive and sad.

His thoughts were just as sad as they leaked across the room. Our faces flashed in his head. And then an image of Blue walking alone in the desert, living in a tent as the wind whipped at the walls, growing old in solitude with no life—no people, no trees, no happiness around him.

Shite.

I closed the door softly behind me, but Blue heard the click and looked up. His melody died.

I met his eyes and wrung my fingers. "I came to—"

"I'm sorry. I'll go." Blue was up and halfway across the room before I'd processed what he said.

"What? No!" I grabbed onto his sleeve.

He froze, torn between wanting to wrench himself away from me and desperately hopeful thoughts. He pictured me smiling and telling him that everything would be alright. And then my face morphed into his mother's. And then he saw his mother hanging from the ceiling—

I tried to cut off that thought by pulling him into a hug. "I'm sorry, Blue." I whispered into his neck. "I lashed out at you. And I'm sorry."

His arms tentatively went around my waist. I could literally hear his panicked thoughts about where he should touch me.

I tried not to laugh as I reached back and set his hands on my lower back before pulling him into the hug again.

"The stress is no excuse," I told him. "I shouldn't have done that."

"I shouldn't have gone after him," Blue murmured into my ear. Regret flashed through his thoughts, along with the fact that I somehow smelled a bit like lavender.

"I would have done the same," I admitted. "Possibly worse. At least you have some skill as a soldier. I'd have had no chance—"

"That only makes it worse. I should have stayed."

I leaned back. "Let's agree that from now on, as your queen, everything's my fault."

Quinn popped into both our minds at that moment. *I'm telling everyone. Knights! Knights! Everything is Bloss's fault. By royal decree, anything we do is her fault. I'm off to steal all the lacy underthings of all the noblewomen in the castle and dangle them from the frozen courtiers. But just remember, that's Bloss's fault.*

Blue and I both collapsed in laughter.

"Quinn, you're a toad-spotted dunderhead!" I called aloud.

Our laughter dissolved into awkwardness as we realized we still held one another.

Blue cleared his throat and stepped back first.

The silence stretched out as we eyed one another. I'd known my other knights for years. Blue had been my friend as a bird. But I knew nothing about him as a man. I was attracted, he was attracted, but still, I felt myself at a loss.

"You play the lute," I finally pulled out the one lame fact I knew about him.

"A bit. Something to pass time in the barracks. I wasn't much of a drinker. So, I tended to sit in the corner and fiddle around with the musicians."

"Fiddle around with them?" I raised my brows.

He blushed, adorably, but leaned forward and teased, "Well, you have to practice strumming quite a bit to get the hang of it."

"O really?"

"The lute requires strong, steady fingers. You have to stroke the strings just right to get them to sing."

My breath caught at that. "Show me."

Blue winked and grabbed my hand, leading me toward his instrument. I could read the nervous excitement in his thoughts. The quick flashes as he thought of my breasts, my lips, remembered what I looked like naked in the cave.

I giggled, his own nervous thoughts affecting my own.

He sat back on his chair and crossed his legs, pulling the lute onto his lap. "Do you have a favorite tune?"

"The Maid's Foolish Wish," I replied.

Blue nodded once and tapped his lute before beginning the ballad. The melody washed over me and I smiled. But when he opened his mouth and he began to sing, my heart puddled at my feet. I melted. His voice was angelic.

"It's beautiful," I breathed, whispering so that I didn't interrupt his gorgeous song.

He smiled wider and pushed his voice just a bit more.

"She wished for riches, for a castle near the sea,

But the maid oh, the maiden, didn't wish for me.

I had a ring for her finger, a flower for her hair,

But simple happiness hadn't a prayer."

He stared at me, and he looked so heartbroken and swoon-worthy in the same moment. My cheeks heated and my heart tripped over itself, like I'd done at my very first court dance, when my dress had been hemmed too long. My breathing grew more shallow.

When he finished, I felt my claps were too paltry a reward, so I leaned down and kissed his cheek.

Then I whispered, "I haven't felt like a blushing maid since I ran from home, but you make me feel that way."

Blue grinned up at me. "Any time you'd rather feel like a blushing woman of the night instead of a blushing maid, I'm happy to help."

I giggled at his words, then even more at his thoughts as he told himself to set the lute down carefully, not to let his hands shake, not to let me see how nervous he was.

I sat down on his lap once he'd put the instrument aside. "Are you very experienced with ladies of the night?" I asked. "Because, I'm certain Quinn told you, but I once worked at a brothel."

Blue laughed. "I've been told more than you probably want me to know. And I know that you happened to work with the coins not the men," he winked.

His thoughts clearly shouted, *I wouldn't have minded if you'd worked with something else, though.* The image of me and Declan, naked on the cave floor, swam into his mind again and his cock hardened under my thighs.

I leaned forward slowly, my eyes flickering back and forth to each of his. I could see the pulse leaping in his throat as I tilted my head.

And then I pressed my lips to his.

I was gentle, softly brushing my lips over his. I pulled my head back slightly, intending to lean my neck the other way, but Blue pushed forward, and his forehead smacked mine.

I reeled back and fell off his lap. "Ow," my hand went to my forehead.

"Shite! I'm sorry!" He knelt and helped me up.

His hand went to examine my forehead.

"I'm fine." I couldn't help but chuckle. "I think we're both just nervous."

"Me more than you. I'm the one who's gonna be compared to every other man here."

I grabbed his hand and intertwined our fingers. "What about me? You come from a land where a woman could grant your every wish. How can I compete with that?"

He laughed, and the warm rich sound wrapped around me like a hug. "Somehow, you picture the women of my country as very selfless. Very few people use their wishes for others where I come from. Most wishes are like that song—made and granted for personal gain, not happiness."

That admission made me reach up on my tiptoes and lean into him once again. "Not you," I whispered. Blue had given me exactly what I wished for. Even knowing that I might hurt him, he brought my husbands back.

My lips latched onto his. This time, I didn't simply brush my lips over his. This time I pressed hard, as I devoured his mouth. I squeezed his fingers tightly as we held hands and my tongue danced with his. My other hand gradually snaked up around his neck. I grabbed his brown hair in my hands and pulled back, nipping his lips and then his neck.

A blush rose on Blue's cheeks and I couldn't help myself as I leaned up to touch it. That only seemed to make him blush harder and he ducked his head to hide it.

"What made you give away a wish so selflessly?"

He shrugged one shoulder and stared down at his boots. He took a while to answer me. "You chose mercy. And then your wish was made for love. Not power." His eyes met mine and the intensity in them nearly knocked me over. His hand covered mine on his cheek, and he slowly lowered my hand staring down and tracing the seams of my palm as if he were reading, trying to find the direction of his thoughts in my skin.

If my heart was a bell, it would have rung—like the bells that young girls wove into their hair during the planting celebrations each spring; tiny silver bells that tinkled with a sound more pure than laughter as they danced. I felt the truth of his words vibrate through every bit of me. It was exactly how I'd felt at mother's court. I been surrounded by charlatans, and schemers.

"We have a saying in my country ... when you walk through the desert, do not forget the sea." Blue glanced up at me with a shy smile. "I had forgotten the sea. Until I met you. I'd forgotten that life doesn't have to be harsh and empty. You made me remember that there's always life and goodness and beauty somewhere. Sometimes we just have to search a bit to find it."

My heart swelled and I floated up onto my knees until my face was level with his. I studied his deep brown eyes, the stripes of chocolate so warm and inviting.

His thoughts were both longing and unsure.

It made my heart pound faster as I leaned closer. I noted his sharp intake of breath as energy crackled between us. I didn't close my eyes as I let my lips touch his. It was just supposed to be a simple closed-mouth kiss, an acknowl-edgment of a truth we both shared—life at court was full of cruelty and lies. But emotion cracked like a whip, surged through me so strong that it was almost painful. And I found myself pressing into Blue, molding my body against his, taking his shoulder-length hair in my hands and pulling hard.

Once I realized what I had done, I pulled back, my hand flying to my mouth. "I'm so sorry. I didn't mean to yank your—"

Blue grinned. "I have that effect on women. They can't help themselves."

But I could see the fist-pumping, whooping dance going on in his head. It completely undermined the arrogant teasing of his words.

I smiled and smacked his shoulder.

His face grew serious for a moment, and I worried that something was wrong. "What?"

Then Blue rolled his eyes. *Ryan told Quinn to tell you that he can walk again, he's limping, but the city mage did a great job. And ... I'm supposed to tell you that you're not allowed back in their sight until you make a true knight outta me.*

My heart soared and then smacked into a window and went sliding down the windowpane. "What?" My knights were trying to coerce us into … sex? Shocked did not begin to cover the way that I felt. Horrified embarrassment was more like it.

Blue's hands covered his face. *I know. But Quinn threatened to show you—*

ANN DENTON

Quinn's voice popped into both our heads. *Presenting Blue's initiation rituals as a soldier*—a vision of naked Blue running through the barracks appeared in my head.

Blue grabbed my shoulders and kissed me. This time he pressed against me.

The vision of Blue in the barracks faded as my thoughts became clouded with lust.

He pressed me into him, yanked on my hips until I moved to straddle him.

His mouth moved to my neck and he ground up into me, as he apologized. *I'm sorry, but Quinn's gonna show you everything if I don't—*

I laughed and reached for his ragged shirt. I helped him pull it off. And for the first time, I got to trace his intricate tattoos. Tattoos that had drawn my eyes to his very cut, defined body the moment I'd seen him. My fingers swiveled over his pecs and across his nipples. He moaned in response.

"I don't want Quinn to ruin anything for you. So, I'm happy to play along." I winked.

His hands traced up my ribcage.

I wasn't certain if Blue realized his thoughts were leaking into my head. But I received every single thought he had as he pulled down my dress. My mind saw how rosy my nipples looked to him, how he felt his breath hitch, how he yearned to lean down and latch onto them, to make them stand up hard and at attention. He didn't

reach for them—though I heard his internal struggle—
the voice in his head that wanted to see all of me
won out.

"Stand up and take off your dress." His mind added, *Please,*
oh gods, please.

I heard Blue's passing guess that I'd be a soft moaner, his
hope that he could make me mewl.

Shite. His thoughts alone were such a turn on that I was
soaking even as I dropped my tattered red dress.

His eyes traveled down over my stomach, thinking about
how soft my skin was, before his gaze landed on my
mound. His hands gently pushed my thighs apart. He
stared at my opening and I heard his thoughts literally
stutter to a stop.

His breath quickened and his thoughts restarted a
moment later, but they were tinged with red, as though
colored by lust. He imagined the feel of my pussy gripping
his dick. He imagined the wet heat and the soft give of my
insides as he pushed into me. He thought I'd feel like
heated silk rubbing against his dick.

Holy sarding hell. Is this what all my knights think? I
wondered as my pussy clenched.

It was a wonder my knights didn't come before they got
inside me if this was what went through their heads.

Blue's thoughts didn't let up. He went to his knees and his
tongue lashed at me as he thought about how tight and
slick I would feel around his swollen cock. I grew wetter

ANN DENTON

than I'd ever been. My nipples begged for attention and my hands reached up to tweak them.

When I did, I soared into an orgasm that nearly made me collapse on top of Blue. If he hadn't been reading my thoughts and anticipating it, I'd have hit my head on his lute.

But he caught me and lowered me gently to the ground.

He waited while I caught my breath, grinning down at me when I panted, "Get naked. Now."

He made sure the show was worth my while, slowly yanking off his boots and lowering his trousers. Then he stood over me and stroked himself with a wink.

I grumbled, "Get down here."

His eyes traveled down my body before he got onto the hard, marble floor next to me and leaned in for a kiss. It was simple and chaste and sweet. But the thought running through his mind was of him slamming forcefully into me, his fingers digging into my thighs and spreading them wide so he could watch his cock as he pounded me and stretched me from the inside out.

I moaned and rubbed my thighs together, wanting more friction.

I tried to pull him closer to me, but he wouldn't budge. He was too busy imagining pressing my breasts together, sliding his thick dick between them and rutting into my mouth until he sprayed his cum across my body.

His lips moved to my neck and he slowly nibbled on my pulse. When he realized how rapidly my heart was beating, he pulled back and looked at me.

"Your thoughts are leaking," I told him breathlessly.

Instead of growing embarrassed, his smile widened. *Oops.*

I grinned and laughed when I realized he'd done it on purpose. "You need to get inside me. Now!"

Blue rolled on top of me and I spread my thighs so I could feel his tip at my entrance. This time, when he kissed me, he thrust his tongue into my mouth and used his thumb to swipe across my nipple. His thumb slowly circled until my peak was hardened. Then he slid down my body and captured the little knob in his mouth. He latched on and sucked hard as his fingers trailed down my ribs and across the tops of my thighs.

He placed a hand on either side of my opening and spread it wide. I felt the cool air of the room against me before his hot fingers slowly started moving my folds in opposite directions, one side up, the other down. My lips slid against one another easily. The friction took everything to another level. When the fingers of his left hand sought out my clit and gently rubbed, I was done for. I howled at the ceiling with all the wild abandon of a wolf howling at the moon. Blue didn't stop working my body, his hand grew faster and he moved his lips from one nipple to the other and exchanged his sucking for quick flicks of his tongue. His increase in intensity doubled my orgasm and instead of trailing off as usual, another orgasm exploded inside me. I went mindless with pleasure.

That's when Blue shoved inside me, pumping hard and fast. He sent me every thought he had—the sight of my breasts jiggling as he held me down and rode me, my post-orgasm face that filled him with such a sense of pride, the sight of his dick sliding in and out of me.

A thought I don't think he intended to send me slipped through, too. Right before he came, Blue thought, *I'm falling in sarding—*

He finished before he could say the 'l' word, but as he collapsed on top of me, I couldn't help but feel joy.

"Blue, you're the best animal turned husband there ever was."

He laughed.

I moaned. "I'm so blissed out right now, I don't even want to think about war—"

But fate had other plans.

Just then, colored smoke filled the room.

Blue grabbed my hand and yelled, "Run!"

CHAPTER NINETEEN

*W*e ran. But we couldn't outrun smoke.

My heart felt like a house of cards that had toppled. Pure panic pumped through my veins and kept my feet moving.

The purple hazy smoke invaded my lungs as Blue and I darted naked through the halls, shoving frozen courtiers out of our way. I started to cough, and tears streamed from my eyes as the colored smoke darted back and forth. Blue screamed in my thoughts, *Quinn! There's an attack!*

Djinn solidified all around us in the hallway and the smoke dissipated. Eight soldiers, wearing loose pants and armored black chest pieces emblazoned with a ring for Raj's house walked forward. Their arms were uncovered, heavily tattooed and muscled just like Blue. Throwing stars, knives, and scimitars glinted on their waistbands as they closed in on us.

Shite! Raj knows I'm alive, I thought, as I skidded around a corner.

That probably meant he knew the capital wasn't destroyed either. Everyone was in danger.

"Donaloo!" I screeched.

I shot a stream of peace behind me. The green light hit two of their soldiers, who stopped dead, dazed and blinking, temporarily uninterested in the fight.

We turned and ran in that direction, shoving the stunned half-djinn aside.

Blue pushed me ahead of him, so he could block any attacks from behind. He read their thoughts, grabbing my shoulders and making us both dodge left as a throwing star buzzed through the air to our right.

He shoved me down to the ground when a wish whizzed overhead, a golden jet of light that smashed into the wall and disintegrated it.

Oh shite. Thank the gods that hadn't hit us, I thought.

Though I could hear a panicked edge to his thoughts, Blue mentally said, *Remember, these are half-djinn. They'll use wishes when their commander orders it. They won't have a choice. But, whenever one of them grants a wish, he has to pay a price. It typically disables them. Makes them easy targets to kill—*

The ground beneath our feet rumbled. Sinkholes appeared behind me.

I screeched and shot forward, scrambling as stones disappeared beneath my feet.

What the hell is happening? I asked Blue. *Is that a wish?*

He didn't answer. Just shoved me forward.

Vines shot out of the holes in the floor and latched onto several of Cheryn's soldiers. The vines dragged the soldiers down out of sight, to the floor below.

Their screams rang in my ears but were cut off.

I gulped. I didn't look back. I didn't want to know why they'd stopped screaming.

One of the soldiers unsheathed a gleaming scimitar from his waist and ran up onto a wall, kicking off to avoid a sinkhole. As he ran at us, he said, "I'm disappointed, Abbas. I thought you'd be faster."

Blue ignored him even though I glanced behind at the blade.

Blue's thoughts filled with the picture of an older soldier who floated in midair behind us, legs still not materialized, next to the man wielding the sword. "Captain?" Blue asked.

I recognized the man from Blue's memories; he was the same man who'd greeted Blue the first day the prince had arrived as a soldier.

The captain shook his head. "You know the consequences." His voice was harsh.

But as the captain said that, his eyes darted sideways toward the man holding the curved sword.

Blue nodded. "I understand." But in his mind, he said, *Bloss, he's gonna create an opening for us.*

The captain gave a signal and one of the part-djinn soldiers at the back started to mutter a wish. Blue whispered rapidly, "I wish I was faster than the wind."

Another soldier in the back mouthed, "Granted," to his compatriot, but Blue had finished speaking first. Blue's wish had been uttered before the other man's. So, as the soldier who granted the wish collapsed with boils erupting on his skin, it wasn't the other djinn's wish that came true. It was Blue's.

Hell sarding yes!

He'd stolen a wish!

I wanted to fist pump. I didn't even know such a thing was possible.

But a second later, Blue scooped me up as the captain appeared to stumble into the side of the soldier wielding the scimitar, knocking them both off balance.

The building blurred as Blue rushed away with me.

Why didn't you wish for them to all disappear back to Cheryn? I asked.

They'd just wish themselves back seconds later. I needed an advantage. Speed is something I know. He ran down a stairwell so fast it appeared to be just a dip in the stone floor.

Seconds later, I saw Quinn next to us in full armor. He was running too—at full speed. It was disorienting to see Quinn clearly but the world around us was just a smear of color. My knights zigzagged through the halls.

Quinn mentally yelled at me, *Right about now would be a great time for you to wish something.*

No! I thought back at him. *If I wish something, it's gonna be thought out. I'm not gonna waste a wish.*

I saw another sparkling golden haze shoot toward us.

You sure we can afford that? Quinn asked.

We ducked around another corner and the wish magic shot past us, surrounding a frozen butler in glimmering light.

"It's not sarding fair that wish magic is so beautiful!" I complained as one of our butlers turned into a wooden puppet.

Donaloo appeared down the hall with a mirror shield in his hand. Dini was notably absent from his forehead.

He ran forward with more speed than I expected. "Traitors have betrayed my spells, let them in and cut the bells. Go!" he yelled at us—raising the shield so that a new stream of golden light reflected back at the djinn.

For once, I knew immediately what Donaloo meant. His spells should have made Raj see a broken capital; a castle destroyed by explosions. The wizard had carefully maintained those spells each day. How could Raj have seen any different? Someone had told the sultan it was all an illusion. My blood ran cold. I listened, but Donaloo was right. We were under attack, but no alarm bells sounded in my towers. No piercing toll roused the guards down in the city to come to our aid.

We'd been betrayed.

Blue hefted me higher as he ran. I watched over his shoulder as the wish magic rebounded from Donaloo's shield to hit one of the djinn soldiers. The man was encased in a gold cloud for a moment before he turned into a stumbling newborn lamb.

Three of our royal guards appeared then. They gave war cries as they ran toward the fight carrying mirrored shields just like Donaloo had.

As we went down the hall, I saw plenty of people who hadn't been lucky enough to have reflective armor. Frogs hopped, worms wriggled, two baby deer cowered behind a statue. The djinn might not be able to wish for death, but they could wish for other things. Worse things.

Did they wish for my soldiers to change consciousness when they wished for them to change their bodies? Or were the men's human minds trapped in an animal form? Would a wished worm still dry out in the sun?

How devastated would their families be if they returned home as animals?

These random questions filled my head as we rushed down the hall.

Our trio entered the Great Hall, where the rest of my knights were already engaged in battle. Blue set me down between himself and Quinn when we reached the hall, their bodies shielding me from the fight.

Quinn tried to offer me his shirt, but he was attacked from the side and had to whip around the man, using his speed to trip the half-djinn and make him fall onto his own sword.

The clash went on all around us. Hundreds of bodies were engaged in battle. Swords were flying, and a golden haze, like the aftermath of dozens of wishes, floated above everyone's heads like smoke.

The tiny purple warrior fairies that Donaloo had created for the mage's tower swooped down on the djinn, targeting one at a time. They worked en masse, covering a man's entire body, until he ended up howling and bloody, their tiny swords sticking out of his body like a hundred metal toothpicks.

Ryan and Declan stood off to the side. Ryan was using a chair to lean on, supporting himself on his good leg. But, like any true general, he couldn't stand to be left out of a fight. I had no doubt he'd threatened Declan into bringing him up here.

The djinn who tried to get near them ended up collapsing on the ground, clutching their heads in their hands and crying. Some of them unsheathed their knives and slit their own throats.

Declan must have been using his magic to drain their will to live.

Ryan shot yellow magic out across the room, toward the front doors, where more half-djinn soldiers tried to storm the castle. He blocked them with a giant wall of dirt. I watched Declan whisper to him and slowly the dirt heated, growing molten.

Behind the two of them, Connor watched our soldiers. He shot pink rays of healing magic toward our men whenever one of them fell.

My heart swelled with pride. We were fighting the djinn soldiers. And we were holding our own, even with my knights' swapped powers. They'd worked so hard, trying to learn what they could—

Ryan's molten dirt wall collapsed as a spear flew at him. He ducked, clumsily, because of his injured leg.

And suddenly, my need to get to him intensified. If it came down to running away, he couldn't do it.

I had to be with him. I couldn't watch him fall.

Pony! I screamed in my mind. Where were our gargoyles?

They're fighting outside, Quinn responded to my thoughts.

Pony came smashing through a window, tumbling down on top of a pile of soldiers. He sprang up, at attention, his tongue lolling in front of his tusks, like he was some overgrown pup, and this was a play date, not a battle.

Smash the djinn! I told him. *They're toys—chew them up.*

Pony dove into the fray and beheaded the first djinn he came upon. He spit out the head and batted at it.

My stomach churned, but I felt better having him in the mix. And he blocked part of the way toward Ryan and the others.

We tried to make our way toward the other knights, but the room was crowded, and enemies were everywhere.

I shot peace magic at two of Cheryn's soldiers who came near us. They slowed, dazed, but didn't stop. I should have shot more, but I was naked still, and I felt vulnerable. I didn't want a roomful of djinn to see the price of my magic. They might just wish I used it until I had nothing left.

I watched as one of them started to mutter a wish. Taking Blue's tactic, I whispered, "I wish I was clothed in mirrored armor."

As one of them whispered, "Granted," I felt the armor click into place over my wrists. I glanced down and saw my entire body was encased in form-fitting armor that was as shiny and reflective as a mirror. It was completely badass. But I hadn't wished for any godsdamned under-garments. The metal was right up against my skin. I took a step and could tell immediately that my nipples were about to be chafed raw.

"Sarding magic," I muttered under my breath. Apparently, wishes were quite literal.

Once they saw I was a bit safer in the armor, my two fast knights took turns rushing at djinn warriors and stealing their weapons then cutting their throats. They almost seemed to be making a game of it. Who was faster. Or so it appeared to me, anyway.

I tried to steal another wish, this time, not for myself or my nipples.

"I wish all my soldiers that have been wished into animals were human again."

But nothing happened. I must not have overlapped anyone else's wish.

Shite.

I started to uncomfortably clank over to my other knights. But the armor impeded my vision. I didn't see the djinn bastard on my right side until it was too late.

His scimitar arced down and I could tell it was well-aimed. I could tell it was going to hit my neck. I could tell I wouldn't be able to move fast enough to get away. I shot peace at him—so much that my thighs ripped open. But it was too late to slow the sword.

I love—I started to tell Quinn, to tell my knights that I loved them.

But then the floor sank into the ground and swallowed up the half-djinn. A huge vine arose out of it, thick as my entire waist. It was covered in thorns like a rose bush, but the thorns were as big as my hand and looked as sharp as any knife. The stem undulated and moved, and a red bloom popped out at the top. This bloom had beautiful, soft petals, but the center of the flower looked like a horrific set of jagged green knives. The vine writhed as it grew large enough for the flower to bump the ceiling.

Fighting paused as everyone turned for a second to watch this plant grow as big as a dragon.

Shite! My own heart leapt into my throat as I watched the beast-sized plant.

Just like a dragon, the plant struck quickly. The flower plunged down and the petals closed over the torso of the djinn closest to Quinn. The man screamed as the flower devoured him, gulping until his boots clattered to the floor. The flower's stem bulged, like a snake that had just swallowed a mouse.

My pulse pattered in my chest.

Holy sarding hell!

Shite! Blue was at my side in an instant. *What the sard is that?*

The flower turned its massive face toward us. The green knives in the center flexed in a threatening way. My hand tightened on Blue's arm.

And then the Flower squeaked, "Where's Donaloo?" in a voice that was far too innocent for the act we'd just witnessed.

Blue just pointed down the hall as I stared, aghast.

"Dini?" I asked.

The flower twirled her petals at me before diving to eat another djinn. Eating them seemed to fill her with power, because two new shoots unfurled. One cut right through a crowd of soldiers battling, her thorns slicing through armor like butter. The other shoot went toward the hallway Blue had indicated, and dipped around the corner, as if searching for Donaloo.

Djinn magic blasted against Dini's stem, but she seemed unaffected. The golden droplets simply slid off of her and puddled harmlessly on the floor.

Cheryn's soldiers realized that and started to run.

My knights made it over to me and, as Dini grew more blooms and started to dominate the battle in the front hall, we ran toward the courtyard to see if we might help there.

Outside, there was a bloodbath that matched the gory sunset. There were bodies all around. Cheryn's soldiers had scaled our walls and were jumping off of the rope they'd lowered over the side. Most of our archers had been forced to retreat up into the towers and they didn't have great angles as they shot their enchanted arrows. More often than not, the red streaks they unleashed from their bows plied the dirt instead of the djinn. Overhead, a rainbow-colored twist of smoke churned like a tornado.

Fear sliced through my stomach. Somehow, I knew that Raj was at the center of that tornado. I just knew it.

An eerie laugh echoed off the cobblestones. Goosebumps rose on my skin.

Blue accidentally shot us all his thoughts. Most prominent was the image of his father—a close up of the sultan's face as he whispered, "You fail me, and your end will be the most painful thing you could ever imagine."

Shite.

My eyes searched for Blue; he was frozen at the back of our group, still naked, staring up at the whirlwind that started to descend on the courtyard.

I stepped back to stand beside him. I shoved off one arm of my armor and let it clatter to the ground. I laced my fingers through his.

"He's coming for me," Blue said. "Get away."

I shook my head. "He's coming for all of us."

Right now would be a damned good time to use that wish! Quinn bellowed.

Wish for what? I yelled back as our hair started to whip around our heads. In the corners of the courtyard, the wind grew so fierce that soldiers were blown backward, tossed sideways; they had to grab onto pillars and posts to stay upright. But we were in the center of the whirl. It was calmer here. Calm enough that I could see a figure floating above us.

Looking straight up, I could see the evil in Raj's eyes as he descended on us.

He had a dark beard and black eyes. His hairline was receding, or it looked that way from below. Raj didn't look as though he were a thousand years old. His torso, above the blue twist of smoke that obscured his legs, was muscular. I did notice the fake ring he thought was on his finger. To me, it still appeared to be a bubble.

We had that at least.

But that was nothing when the wishes started to rain down around us.

He didn't care if he used every last wish the women in his harem had left. He'd discard them and get more. Blue accidentally sent us all Raj's thoughts.

Disgusting. Foul, evil man. Unworthy. Bile churned in my belly and anger in my mind.

Raj watched us, pointing, directing his harem to send wish magic at those around us. His harem, a group of at least thirty women, who still spun so quickly that they were blurs of color in the wind, shot golden jets down on our soldiers, who transformed into snapping crocodiles.

Raj didn't seem to care when one of his own soldiers got caught in the jaws of his wished creatures.

That was what made me paralyzed with fear. He didn't care how many men he lost. He didn't care how much this battle cost him.

He only cared that he got to punish Blue and end me.

I realized Blue had accidentally projected the sultan's thoughts again and I swallowed hard. As I stared up, I could see the hunger, the cruelty in Raj's gaze. How could I fight someone so obsessed with power and punishment? How could I win when I had two wishes left, and he had a million at his disposal?

"Never give up, the heart is greater than the mind, the more you love, the more you'll find—the truth!" Donaloo's voice streamed past me as he flew into the air, spinning and causing his own whirlwind. "Round and round we spin, what a way to go, to fight and win with a dizzy grin!" His tornado zoomed upward. The rainbow-colored twists of smoke started to scream and materialize as women. The same women that had surrounded Raj when he'd tried to destroy Marscha. His harem.

Donaloo brought them up, up, up, farther into the sky, past the orange rays and into the blue of the encroaching night. He and the harem women went so far up that they became mere pinpricks. And then I saw all of them fall. Each pinprick fell down to earth like a meteor made of shadows instead of light. I searched for Donaloo, floating up there in the sky, cackling about whatever he'd done, but I didn't hear him. I didn't see him. Until his body landed in the courtyard and splattered across the stones.

I might not have known it was him but for the jester-styled shoe that remained on one of his feet.

The sight made me dizzy. And ill. Then I thought that Raj was putting a hallucination spell on me. But he floated above us and his expression was also shocked. Everything had happened so quickly. His harem was there and then they weren't. And then they were so high in the sky—

He flew to where the air was too thin, Quinn told us all. *That's what Declan says.*

My shock slowly faded to a dull pain that glowed like an ember. It was hot and hurt, but it didn't consume me. Not yet.

Because as I stared up at Raj, I realized that Donaloo had given me a shot. Donaloo had done something selfless—surprising the sultan, who had built a life based on greed and fear. And that had given me an opening.

What had Donaloo said? The heart is greater than the mind … My memories clicked through my other conversations with him. "A buzzing mind is but dung and flies, the heart is where humanity lies." He said a simple wish would work. Blue's song started to play for some reason. The Maid's Foolish Wish. "I had a ring for her finger, a flower for her hair, but simple happiness hadn't a prayer." And it clicked.

Raj turned his face back down to us, a sneer forming on his lips.

Quinn! I need that wish! I mentally screamed.

Yes, Dove. Do it!

I started to shove a mental apology Quinn's way for what I was about to do, but Raj opened his mouth—no doubt, to make a wish that would get granted by one of his own cohorts. Panic took over. Adrenaline. I had to finish this wish before he finished his. My fingers trembled as I held Blue's hand. I whispered, "I wish Raj was happy. Truly, blissfully happy every day for the rest of his existence—" Inspiration struck, and I tacked on, "As blissful as if he were having an orgasm."

Raj's jaw dropped. His eyes rolled back in his head and a strange, nearly pained expression came over him. He moaned.

Everyone in the courtyard froze and looked up at the sultan.

The moan dragged on and his hand reached down into the blue smoke so he could touch himself.

"Uh. I don't know if I'm relieved or traumatized," Declan muttered. "I'm pretty sure that's Raj's 'O' face."

The sultan's eyes snapped open and he stared down at us for a second. Then he muttered something as his hips swiveled in the air. From the ground, I heard a djinn soldier yell, "Granted." Then Raj disappeared in a navy puff of smoke.

Around us, soldiers climbed to their feet, the whirlwind gone, the sultan gone.

To my surprise, Cheryn's soldiers tossed down their swords. All but the two or three who were next to alligators.

"I surrender," one said. "Any queen who can defeat a man with orgasms is worth dying for."

A chuckle went through the courtyard. And the chuckle grew to full on tears-streaming-down-their faces laughter as Cheryn's men all put their arms in the air and my soldiers took them into custody.

I was familiar with the giddy after-effects of surviving against the odds. But this time, the silliness didn't over-take me. Because my eyes drifted back to Donaloo. Regret filled me instead of silliness. I wished I'd been nicer to the old coot. He deserved better. He deserved to know how much I admired his magic. And his principles. Even if I couldn't stand his rhymes. But why did he go and do such a foolish thing? He was so powerful! He could have taken on that harem. Maybe even Raj. I stared at his crumpled form, full of wistful regret.

"He didn't have to die himself," I shook my head.

Behind me, a squeaky little voice said, "If he hadn't, the sultan would have only seen another soldier killing people. He wouldn't have seen a sacrifice made from love." The giant vine snaked through the courtyard. Her petals gazed down on Donaloo for a moment, before she lowered her lips and swallowed him up.

I gave a shriek. "What are you doing?"

Dini turned her petals toward me. "I'm a flower sprite. Plants eat dead things all the time. How do you think I survived down in that hole? People are just fertilizer."

A hand on my arm kept me from arguing against the undignified ending she just gave one of the most powerful and amazing men to ever live.

Connor—ever the diplomat—held me back. He pulled me into a hug as tears filled my eyes. "Come inside, Bloss Boss. We still have more to do."

That phrase cracked me open. My fear and insecurity dripped out of the hard, little shell I'd tried to build around them. Isla was dead. Raj was gone—for now. But we still had a huge monster beneath the sea to fight. I still had a frozen castle. Provinces that were occupied or half-destroyed. Avia was still gone. There was still so much. So much. And Donaloo wouldn't be here for it. I wouldn't have that annoying, idiotic wizard skipping around and telling me nonsense that actually made sense. I wouldn't have the comfort of knowing that my people would be protected, that someone far more powerful than me watched over them.

I hadn't even gotten to say goodbye.

My tears spilled over. My vision blurred and I had to swipe at my eyes numerous times.

Connor rushed me inside. Queens weren't supposed to cry in public. They weren't supposed to show emotion.

I'm the world's worst queen, I thought.

ANN DENTON

But I couldn't stop the tears that fell as we went through the decimated Great Hall, past soldiers limping and moaning in pain. I didn't try to, because pretending that I wasn't hurting almost made my pain lessen. So much of my mother's focus was on maintaining a façade that I felt sure that the pain itself started to fade. I wondered if that pretense of strength was the beginning of the end of emotions for monarchs. If they were always so focused on pretending not to feel, eventually, did their feelings just fade away?

I refused to be that monarch. I refused to pretend that idiot Donaloo meant nothing to me. I restrained myself from sobbing, but tears rained down my cheeks.

My knights took me to the rainbow salon, one that I'd always loved growing up. It had hundreds of crystal figurines in it and normally was a source of dancing rainbows.

Not this evening. This evening, the room looked like I felt. Everything inside it was shattered.

I took several deep breaths as Ryan used a blanket to swipe away some glass so we might have a path to the chairs and settees near the fireplace.

I yanked the other arm off my armor and asked Connor to help me out of the awful contraption. I'd tolerated the metal on my skin as long as I could.

Connor gently undressed me and took off his own shirt to toss it over me.

I started to shiver as the chill of night took over the castle.

That's when I looked around at my knights. Ryan had limped over to the fireplace and was struggling not to bend his injured leg as he lit a fire. Blue stalked over to help him. Declan was still talking with the nobles—probably shouting, since they'd ask questions he'd consider stupid. Connor was still rubbing my back.

My blood ran cold.

The nightmare. I'd forgotten the nightmare.

I pulled away from Connor. "Where's Quinn?"

CHAPTER TWENTY

"Ⓦhat the sarding hell happened?" I latched onto Blue's arm and gripped it hard. I was demanding and begging for answers at the same moment. "We just left him in the courtyard? Where is he?"

I felt like pulling my hair out. I ran to the window and shoved aside the drape. My eyes flashed around different parts of the courtyard, searching for him. Was he an animal now? Did he have painful boils? I'd been so focused on Donaloo's sacrifice. I was an awful wife. Not just an awful queen. Being an awful wife was worse. My heart shredded into tiny, inconsolable pieces.

What are you talking about? Blue thought. There was a bitter edge to his words. *It doesn't even look like he's paying a damn price. I can hear him just fine.*

"What do you mean you can hear him?" I asked aloud, whipping around.

He's being a complete fop-doodle. Telling me I must have been wishing wrong all my life. Blue rolled his eyes and pointed. *I mean, look at him waggling his tongue.*

I glanced about wildly, pulse pounding. "He's not here!"

Declan walked over and I rushed toward him, nearly colliding with him as I grabbed his arms. The most serious of my knights, he'd give me a straight answer. "Dec, where's Quinn?"

"Right there," he arched his brow and cocked his head as he looked at me. His expression grew serious as he stared down at me. "I thought Donaloo might have said some final spell midair to protect him." He ran a hand through his blond hair and glanced next to me. Then his eyes traveled back to mine. "Shite. I think his nightmare is that you won't see him anymore."

All my knights' eyes drifted to an empty space on the rug near me. I made my way over to it and tentatively reached out my hand. "Quinn?"

But my hand swiped through empty air. No matter how frantically I swung it, I didn't feel a thing. Panic set in.

"Bloss! Stop hitting him!"

It felt like a throwing star was lodged inside my throat as I responded, "I can't feel him."

Horror swept over me at the realization. I couldn't see, feel, or hear Quinn. It took everything I had not to collapse on the ruined glass figurines that lay shattered on the floor. Because this wasn't just his nightmare, it was mine.

How could I cope without my jester? How could I manage without the gentle man who called me his dove?

Connor saw the look on my face, and Declan must've tasted my desolation. The two of them came to either side of me and gently escorted me to the settee.

Tears trickled down my face.

"It's only temporary," Declan said gently. "Just remember that."

"Temporary?" I swallowed hard. "I've read about night-mares that last three years!" My face fell into my palms. How could I live without Quinn for that long?

My knights balanced and offset me, they helped make up for what I lacked. They made me stronger. I needed Quinn.

I choked on a sob. Connor's arms wrapped around me. He held me and rocked me as I said, "It's not fair."

But magic wasn't fair. I knew that. The price you paid for using magic as a part human overpowered any other kind of magic. And you couldn't choose your price.

I squeezed Connor hard, some of my anger at the stupid sarding world leaking out into my hug. And then I pushed him away and stood, just as a frog hopped into the salon and let out a croak.

We all turned. The frog waved an arm at Ryan. Then its beady eyes looked down the hall and back at us.

Shite. That wasn't a frog. It was one of Ryan's soldiers. And my question about whether they kept their human consciousness was answered.

Poor man.

I swallowed hard. Quinn was invisible. He wasn't lost. Not completely. And he wasn't alone inside his own head like the last nightmare. He wasn't a worm that could get stepped on at any moment. It could always be worse. My knights could see and hear him. I took a deep breath. I needed to keep my head on.

You're being selfish, Bloss, I told myself. You're being selfish when your soldiers have it much worse. Your people need a selfless queen.

I eyed the frog on the floor as I wiped my cheeks one last time.

Queens can't have meltdowns, I recited one of my mother's old lines from when I'd thrown tantrums.

I could feel. But I couldn't get swept away. We still had a castle and the aftermath of a battle to deal with. I swiped at my face once more and took a deep breath.

This was the new reality. Whether I liked it or not, we had to live with it until the wish magic was satisfied.

Sarding wish magic.

Ryan came over and kissed my cheek, "Little Dearling, why don't you take a minute? I need to go check on my men. And gather up those that have been transformed." He limped over to the doorway and told the little frog, "Follow me." And then he tromped out the door, a croaking frog hopping along behind him.

Connor stroked my hair. "I need to go back and heal whomever I can."

I nodded and pressed on my temples, fighting a headache that came on in the aftermath of my tears. "I need to get dressed. Then I'll be down to do whatever I can. Is Quinn still near me?"

Blue's thoughts were a little smug as he answered, *Yes. And he's pissed he has a nightmare and that I was right.*

Don't be an ass, I told Blue.

Aloud I said, "Can he hear me?"

Declan nodded. "He says he can see and hear you. It's his nightmare that you can't do the same."

Let me try to send you his thoughts, Blue said.

But as Blue scrunched his face, nothing came through to my mind.

Sorry, my newest knight apologized.

I tried to hide my disappointment. It wasn't his fault that magic had such a high price.

Declan said, "If Donaloo's beads couldn't counter his magical nightmare earlier, I suppose it makes sense you can't do so now."

I chewed my lip and then asked, "If he can see me and hear me, can he feel me, too?"

My knights looked at some point in midair and I struggled to see something, some wavering cloud, some bit of movement, anything. But I saw nothing. I didn't know if Quinn tried to touch me. I couldn't tell. I couldn't feel a thing. It was awful and frustrating. I felt like my hands were tied and my body was bound. It was just as bad as any torture chamber.

"Yes," Declan finally answered. "He kissed you. You didn't feel anything?"

My hand flew to my lips. But they didn't feel any different. I hadn't felt warmth or cold or tingles or pressure. I pressed my lips together in a thin line and shook my head.

Declan said, "I guess we'll have to hope this wish was small enough that the nightmare doesn't last very long."

My eyes closed and my stomach sank. I'd made a wish and asked for it to last every day of an immortal's life. That was no small wish. We all knew it.

I had no idea when I would get to see my Quinn again. My sweet half-elf.

I doubted it would be soon.

My eyes closed and I stared down at the ground. "I'm sorry." I apologized to my spy master.

Everyone grew somber. Reality sank in like the bottle-ache that made men ill after a night in their cups. An hour ago, I'd been drunk on wish magic—thinking myself so clever. Now ...

I walked back to the window and stared down at the courtyard. My eyes traveled around the devastation; the space was littered with bodies. I was surrounded by all the reasons I had never wanted to be a queen. War. Death. Watching those that I loved suffer injury, suffer nightmare situations like this ... and gods only knew what came next.

It was my own personal hell.

As that thought popped into my head, the doors to the ballrooms down the hall burst open. Noise spilled out.

Declan, Blue and I hurried to the door. Courtiers streamed down the hall, negligée dangling from their faces and their arms. They plucked it off as they stared around them in shock.

"What the sard is going on?" one asked.

"Looks like we've been attacked!" screeched another.

Declan sighed. "Quinn, toss Blue your clothes. You stay with her."

Boots and pants suddenly appeared on the floor. A shirt smacked Blue in the face. "Get dressed and come on, Blue.

Let's get out there and calm them down before a riot breaks out."

Blue tossed on Quinn's clothes quickly. Then Declan pulled my newest knight into the halls and held up his hands. "Everyone! Everyone! I need your attention!"

I gently closed the door and locked it.

I could hear Declan trying to explain the spell that froze them and the battle that had just happened over the panicked questions of dozens of people. I backed away from the door and the chaos. I crossed my fingers that Declan didn't start drinking emotions just to shut the idiots up. Because there was a mob of dunderheads out there for him to manage. With Connor off healing the wounded, poor Declan and Blue would have to suffer through.

I sighed and leaned against the locked door for a moment, trying to gather my thoughts. I didn't need courtiers finding me in only Connor's shirt, a naked Quinn beside me. We were married, but still, I had enough whispers to deal with.

"Too bad I can't hear or see you," I said softly to Quinn. But the reality was, we wouldn't have been able to do anything anyway.

I knew Declan's patience would only last so long. He would need help. I couldn't hide in here for long.

I scrubbed a hand over my face and walked carefully around the shattered figurines toward the secret passage at the far side of the room. I ran my hand along the seam and the secret door opened. Then I stepped into the dark, stone hallway. "Quinn, I hope you're following." I whispered, as I used my magic to light the path.

I didn't hear a response, and I sighed as I pulled the door shut.

This nightmare was going to take a toll on the both of us. I could feel it.

But I didn't have any more time for self-pity. Donaloo had said that someone had revealed our secrets to Raj. And I needed to help Declan. Then I needed to find out who the traitor was.

❦

The next few days were chaos. We had dead to bury, soldiers wished into animals that had to be contained, enemies to spy upon, enemies to research, and that traitor still hovering in our midst.

It was never-ending chaos. And I nearly collapsed in tears when I'd gone up to the mage's tower for a moment of peace. There, among the fairy vines that had taken over the place, I had found the entire bundle of nasty-smelling tablets. It looked like Donaloo had brewed another batch of the wakefulness potion for me and my knights. It sat there just waiting on his worktable on a plate. Next to the plate stood the little purple love potion that Cerena had carried on our journey. I hadn't even realized we still had it. I'd forgotten all about it. But I took a bit of leather string and tied the glass vial up into a makeshift necklace. Donaloo had clearly left it out for me. And if he thought it was important then, ultimately, I believed him.

Faith in his crazy sayings, in his belief in happy endings, were all that I had left of him.

I bowed my head and fought tears. "Quinn, are you there?" I stifled a sob with a laugh. "Because I was just thinking that Donaloo turned down this room, this job, because he didn't want to get blown up. How ironic—"

The sobs pulled me under. And it was a few minutes until I surfaced. When I did, I rubbed my face free of tears, ate a tablet, and marched my ass downstairs. I wouldn't do Donaloo any good hiding out in the mage's tower. I went out to the courtyard and found Dini.

Since she'd grown so big, she'd chosen to stay outside. She had been helping a bit with the reconstruction, closing up sinkholes, somehow grabbing boulders from underneath the ground and yanking them upward so that our stone masons could use them to repair any holes in the walls.

When I approached, her oversized red petals turned my way. Her razor-sharp teeth glinted in the sunlight, and I had to repress shivers at the vision.

"I think I need to move somewhere else." She shook her leaves.

I started. "Leave?" That was not what I was expecting to hear.

Her flower face turned toward the east. "I can taste the ocean breeze. She's coming for you." Dini shook her petals sadly. "I can withstand many things. But saltwater …"

I nodded. Yet another of my strongest magical defenders was leaving. And I couldn't ask her to stay. "Of course. Please, if I can do anything to help you …"

I fought the shiver that crawled up my spine and whispered in my ear, "You can't win without their power." That shadow of doubt tried to pull my thoughts toward darkness.

I shoved it down. I would find a way. I had to.

Dini turned her flower face down to me. "I'll need someone you trust to take me inland. I'm not leaving completely. I'll do what I can to help Evaness. Perhaps you could plant me back at the hut where we met? It's part of Evaness now, isn't it?"

I nodded.

"At the very least I can help ensure those …" she lowered her tone to a whisper, "amulets don't fall into the wrong hands."

I nodded. "As you wish. And thank you, for all your help, Dini."

Dini shrunk down before my eyes. "You'll remember to help Posey?" she squeaked, once she'd regained the tiny, single bloom form that I'd first met her in.

I nodded. "We're trying to settle a few things here, and then yes. We'll need to get Gitmore's approval to use the undead army to go under the sea. We'll need them to be able to attack Mayi. I don't see another way. The surface of the water is too vulnerable. We'll have to go where she doesn't expect us to go. So I should meet your daughter. I hope."

Dini popped out a second bloom. "If you see her, please give her this." Her leaves pointed toward the bloom.

I hesitated. "I don't want to hurt you."

She giggled. "I'll be fine."

I gently broke the tiny bloom off and tucked it into my coin purse. "Thank you, Dini."

Dini nodded. "I won't say goodbye, since I'll see you soon, hopefully with a few soldiers." She changed the subject, "Any luck finding out that Mayi's magical price?" Dini asked. "My daughter never used her magic. At least not when she was growing up. Used to want to embrace her human side. Donaloo said the price wasn't worth it."

I tilted my head. "That surprises me."

Dini crossed her leaves. "Just because he used it, doesn't mean he loved it. He always wanted to do good. And he paid many a price himself." Her squeak grew quiet. "Sorry. Memories. Mayi's price?"

I shook my head. "Blue tells me that Quinn sent another soldier to see if she had to pay in heat for what she used in water, but the man reported the water around her was cold before she—before we lost him."

I sighed. Quinn still hadn't reappeared. And I missed him horribly. The other men joked, and Blue did his best to pass on Quinn's thoughts. But it wasn't the same. Without him in my head, sending his quirky and naughty references to lighten the mood, everything felt strained and heavy.

Instead of asking one of the gardeners to tend to Dini, I asked Jace to help her get resettled. Since she was talkative, I figured he'd handle her better than a gardener who was used to trimming and tweezing plants as he fancied.

The beast master had smiled and said, "It'd be an honor." And he'd taken to Dini like he took to baby horses. I wasn't shocked at all to find her riding on his arm later that day, as he loaded up a cart full of dung and a shovel, then set off to rebury the pretty plant.

I'd waved them off but hadn't been able to linger. With Dini's statement about the threat of seawater, I set Connor to evacuating the castle and the districts of Marscha closest to the sea. We stripped the castle of everything but the absolute necessities. The library and mage's tower were packed up, the contents moved to Fer's province in the forest for safe keeping. All but the essential employees were told to relocate to the summer palace in Kycee's province. My home became but a shell.

I tried to convince the fairies that Donaloo had brought to the mage's tower to relocate, but they were stubborn creatures and refused to leave their vines, no matter how I pleaded. I gave up when one of the purple fairies stabbed me with her sword.

"Go fight for us instead of telling us to run!" she'd screeched.

And so, I'd left, to find Connor to heal my hand and the rest of my knights to help me come up with a battle plan.

The djinn still attacked from the north. Even with the sultan supposedly out of commission, his generals were war hungry. So, Ryan decided to barter a deal with the soldiers we captured. He gathered them in one of the ballrooms, still handcuffed. He fed them first, insisted—over Jorad's protests—that a hungry man couldn't listen to reason, let alone make a decision.

And so, they'd been marched into one of our ballrooms, a room full of marble columns and mirrored walls. It was one of the few rooms in the palace that hadn't been ruined by battle, possibly because it had been stuffed full of courtiers, possibly because of dumb luck. My hand had traced down a tapestry, one of a dragon protecting a maiden from a knight who'd come to steal her, as I watched Cheryn's soldiers ignore their cuffs while they ate their soup and tore their trenchers to devour the sopping bread. The thick smell of stew filled the air and mixed with the scent of melted metal floating in from the open balcony doors. A forge had been set up behind the castle, the blacksmith from Marscha temporarily relocated here to help with repairs and with weapon-making.

The dual scents contrasted as sharply as filthy prisoners in a ballroom.

But that was life now. War was full of unlikely combinations. War made a mockery of everything normal, until chaos became the new normal, and people settled in with lowered expectations. I remembered how it was when I was young. Mother's council meetings with the duchesses had been in tents, in huts—hurried, rushed conversations. Taxes had consisted of deliveries of bread for the soldiers, leather for their boots. Farmers were hesitant to plant crops that would be burned or trampled, and food shortages had been horrid.

I vowed not to let that happen again. I didn't want another Fire War. I didn't want all seven kingdoms swept up in years of fighting. I was doing my best to end it.

Our tentative peace with Rasle had been the first step. And while I had no doubts that Raj wasn't truly defeated, this was the next step.

Converting some of his soldiers.

After most of the men had been served seconds, Ryan and Blue stepped over to the musician's platform while the rest of the knights and I stood to the side.

Declan smacked his lips next to me. A funny look crossed over his face. "I'll be right back."

I simply nodded and turned to face Ryan. Despite the cane he was using, my half-giant radiated confidence and strength. He eyed the prisoners, waiting until they were quiet, and every eye fell on him.

My heart couldn't help but swell with pride at the way he took command.

"We brought you here for a reason. Those of you that choose to give us information on the plans of Cheryn, attacks, formations, etcetera, will be compensated and receive citizenship. You'll have the official protection of Evaness. Those of you who agree to give up a wish to restore some of our soldiers to human form will receive both citizenship and a plot of land."

"How do we know we can trust you?" one of the half-djinn had asked.

Blue held up a hand. "Evaness is different. They work things out with magically-binding contracts here."

That seemed to be an explanation the djinn could understand. It made me sad to know that they didn't trust honor. But, a secret part of me was glad for the magically binding contracts as well. Because included in the contract was fealty to Evaness … and a consequence not too different from my own engagement contract. If they betrayed the country, they'd die. I supposed, I wasn't much better than them, since the contracts made me feel more secure as well.

The new hedgewitch, Markle, whom we brought up from Kycee's province, wasn't as keen on explosions as Wyle had been. "Too messy," she'd shaken her head. I'd agreed, so the new language in the contracts stated simply that violators would fall over dead rather than explode.

Ryan unfurled a magical decree and passed it around so that those soldiers who could read could tell the others what it said.

I waited impatiently—my mind listing off the thousand other items that needed doing. I watched as Jorad had the recently unfrozen kitchen staff clear the food from the room.

One of the prisoners asked, "And where is this land?"

Connor responded, "Lady Agatha's province has a number of homesteads—"

Just then Jorad squealed. The manservant fell to his knees, knocking over a tureen of soup and writhing on the ground.

My eyes widened. I glanced around. Had one of Cheryn's soldier's attacked?

But then I saw Declan's hand extended, saw the fury on my knight's face.

I hurried across the room as Jorad grabbed a knife. I latched onto the manservant's wrist; and yanked it away from his throat. Ryan was only a step behind, and he lifted Jorad bodily by his collar, so that the man hung in midair like a baby kitten.

The soldiers of Cheryn watched with wide eyes, waiting to see what we'd do next.

I turned to Declan.

"He tasted of rye bread. Just as my mother did before she tried to take me." Declan's face was the darkest I'd ever seen it. Even worse than after he'd met his mother. Because this time, his features were twisted in rage.

I stared at Jorad as Declan's words sank in.

"Blue, his thoughts?" I asked, in a dull, neutral queen-like tone.

Blue sent me flashing images of Willard, Agatha, a stream of curses that shamed me for giving their lands away. And then, most interestingly, a quick flash of Raj in a soldier's tent.

Jorad tensed when that image came to his mind. He knew what Quinn could do, and how my knights had switched powers. Immediately, he started to shuffle his thoughts to the prisoners in front of us, to the menu for the evening.

My heart constricted. Jorad and I had always been at loggerheads. But I'd never thought he'd betray the people of Evaness. He was propriety and—I'd thought—rule-following incarnate. Things that didn't mesh well with my personality. But I'd thought at the heart of it all, we'd both been staunchly loyal to Evaness. I was wrong.

"You went to Raj." I shook my head as if I was merely disappointed, and not as if I were hurt. Though I was.

Blue projected more thoughts, this time, unrestricted thoughts—glances of me colored by furious words. Even a flash of Willard trying to blame me for his own choices.

And I realized that's where the hatred began. It was rooted in the moment Jorad's lover had betrayed him, broken his trust and blamed me for it.

It didn't seem to matter how much right I did. Being accused of one wrongdoing, something I hadn't even done, was all that mattered. Even the most loyal people could be turned by a lie.

Was it hopeless? Was it always this way for a Queen?

Blue stepped closer to me. *No, Bloss. It isn't. For every one of him, there is someone like me.*

It doesn't feel like it.

My brain ticked away. No wonder Isla had such an easy time planting explosives here. No wonder Raj had easily been able to take Agatha's province. Jorad, no doubt, knew that province like the back of his hand. And then another more recent memory clicked into perspective. I hadn't eaten recently. I'd used Donaloo's tablets since before his death. But the one time I had eaten back at the palace, Jorad had served me. And I'd gotten sick.

"Did you try to poison me?" I tilted my head and studied Jorad.

His face grew red. And then, in a very uncharacteristic move, he spat on my face.

All around us, whispers went up amongst Cheryn's guards, as I wiped my cheek. They watched every move, wondering what I'd do next.

I kept my eyes on Jorad, but asked Blue, *What would the sultan do to punish him?*

Make him gut himself, slowly. Or put him in a cage and wish leprosy upon him, then set him out at the gates so travelers can see him.

I looked to Ryan. "I hereby accuse Jorad of treason. Cut his throat. End it quickly."

I turned back to Jorad. "Your years of service have earned you a clean death. Your betrayal—I hope it earns you a godsawful afterlife."

Ryan slit Jorad's throat deep, severing the artery. And as the ballroom floor grew soaked in red, and a glugging noise filled the room with Jorad's final moments, a number of Cheryn's soldiers lined up, quietly, to sign a contract with Evaness.

I was a little surprised that an execution had that effect on them.

Blue? I asked for an explanation with my thoughts.

People don't fear death so much as they fear evil. And you've just shown them you aren't evil.

CHAPTER TWENTY-ONE

*E*vil or not, I couldn't stop the attacks from the djinn, or the giant waves that battered our docks the next day.

Our country was a wreck. I was a wreck. I was an emotional mess because I still couldn't see or hear Quinn. I carried heaping loads of shame on my back because every attack that hit us felt like it might have been prevented. Or I might have known how to respond better … if I'd never run away.

Sirens came ashore, singing to the dockworkers in Marscha. We sent gargoyles to run them off, but I heard thirty civilians had walked themselves into the water and drowned.

The guilt of that gnawed on my bones.

My knights and I issued orders and divided responsibilities. We did all we could to help alert the people and levy the shores. But we couldn't stop the attacks. Not without help. We left Connor's mother in charge as we mounted gargoyles and flew to see if we might convince Gitmore to ally with us.

If all else failed, at least my husband's family would rule Evaness with a fair hand.

I dressed for a formal court appearance once again, this time Gennifer was unfrozen and could actually plait my hair. But it seemed her freezing experience hadn't left her much more talkative than she'd been before. If anything, she seemed to have withdrawn further.

She helped me into a bright orange gown, this time, the burning rose of Evaness was embroidered in a tiny, repeating red, orange, and black pattern of flowers on the skirt. She helped me into my black traveling coat. I grabbed my coin purse and stuck it onto my waist as she set a tiara with onyx stones on my head. Inside was the flower I'd promised to give to Posey. Surprisingly, it had yet to wilt.

Gennifer hesitated, looking me over one last time. "Your necklace, Your Majesty," she said hesitantly.

My hand flew to my neck, where the love potion sat. "This will do." It was all of Donaloo and Cerena that I had left. I wasn't about to leave it. I needed them with me. I touched it gently and nodded to Gennifer. "Thank you."

"Um … Your Majesty?" Gennifer asked as I turned to leave.

"Yes?" I turned back around.

Gennifer turned nearly puce as she whispered. "If you ever … um … require an audience again … I'm courting a man from the laundry. He'd love to –" She couldn't finish. My poor, shy maid, couldn't finish her offer.

I gave her a grin. "We'll call you first."

She bobbed a curtsey and I had to tamp down a laugh so that I didn't insult the poor, sweet thing. Connor and I had definitely traumatized her.

Then I left the Queen's chambers, my amusement melting as my mind turned to the task ahead. I left Gennifer and a few staff to pack up what was left so that they could move to the safety of another province.

I swallowed hard as I took a saddled Pony from Jace. My gargoyle gave me a lopsided smile as I climbed onto his back and stared at my castle.

The sea crashed violently against some buildings in Marscha. It had invaded the streets nearest the ocean two days past and was slowly creeping forward. Other than the violent smack of water against stone, the capital and my castle were empty and quiet. With the damage from recent battles and the tangle of flowering vines growing on the mage's tower, my home looked like an abandoned castle from a kingdom fallen long ago. Most the people had already left. Only a few like Gennifer remained. Most of our gargoyles had been sent north to fight the djinn. Only five remained for us. Each of my knights and I clambered onto our gargoyles.

I looked at Declan. "Is Quinn on?"

I still couldn't see or feel my knight. I didn't know if it made him feel bound, to have to stay with me at all times. But knowing he was there, even if I couldn't see or feel him yet, made me feel better.

Declan nodded. "He's good."

I yanked Pony's reins and rose into the sky. I didn't look back at my castle. There was no point. I had to look forward. It was the only way to keep all of Evaness from falling victim to the same fate as those battered towers.

I soared into the sky, my eyes and hopes directed toward Gitmore.

๕๑

We descended on the castle, which looked like something from a tapestry or some illustrated tome. It didn't look real. Nestled in the midst of some jagged mountain peaks, the castle was well-protected and nearly as large as the mountains themselves. The castle was made of pristine white stone. Green stained-glass created geometric patterns in the archway above the main entrance, above the windows, on the many towers. Metallic blue domes capped the towers and to the right, a waterfall spilled through arches underneath a bridge that led toward the entrance. The effect was stunning.

I found myself feeling a little intimidated as our gargoyles descended to the bridge.

But my sense of trepidation only increased when two guards blocked our path.

"Who goes there?"

Connor took the lead. "Queen Bloss of Evaness is here to meet with her Majesty, Queen Shenna."

One of the guards nodded to the other, and the younger man trotted off to verify Connor's statement.

We waited. And waited. And waited. My anxiety grew. I kept my face calm and confident, but I mentally asked Blue, *Can you read any thoughts beyond this guard's? What are they doing in the castle? Can you tell?*

It seems like this is pretty much their standard intimidation technique. It also looks like they typically have the waterfall overflow the bridge once we pass, making visitors feel cut off. They're discussing that in the guard tower right now.

Lovely. Good thing we have gargoyles.

They'll ask us to leave those behind.

My stomach sank. *What do you think our chances are? Shite. We need this. I need this.*

This is just another head game. Don't let her win before we even see her.

I took a deep breath. He was right. I gave myself the pep talk that my mother used to give me, one I used to roll my eyes over. She used to say it when I'd lost a battle and typically wanted to toss her war map with all its little figurines across the room. "Perseverance wins the day.

Not magic. Not strength. The ability to endure agony and keep fighting. That's what separates the wheat from the chaff. It's the difference between the strong and weak. Suffering is inevitable. But some people let it destroy them. Others use it to become more. You have to become more, Bloss."

I am more, I chanted to myself.

We waited for more than an hour, when finally, and entourage seem to approach. Queen Shenna set atop a liter carried by four nude fairy men.

My eyes immediately tried to focus upward, on the queen and her white gown. Her blue hair was streaked with silver and her eyes were the large, luminescent orange many part-fae had. She herself didn't have wings. I had to struggle to keep my eyes on her face because her nipples were clearly visible through her gown. The men who carried her litter were insanely attractive, young and oiled so their muscles gleamed. Their wings were folded against their backs, but I had no doubt they could take flight in an instant if a threat arose.

As I looked square into her eyes, I gave a small smile. She was clever, this doxy. It was quite a unique way to intimidate her more prudish visitors. Instead of a show of strength, she put on a blatant show of sexuality. There were no weapons on her or her fairy men, she showed an utter disregard for any threat we might pose. That in itself felt dismissive.

But I caught a flicker of movement in the sky behind her. It made me certain she had archers flying somewhere.

Perhaps I needed to take a leaf out of her book.

Blue interjected. *I told the men your thoughts. Quinn's the only one who's in favor of nudism at the castle.*

I fought a laugh. *Of course, he is.*

We watched the young men lower the Queen and help her alight from the litter. Her dress had slits up either side, that revealed a great deal of skin as she stood. Two of the men prostrated themselves before her and began kissing their way up her ankles, past her knees, toward her thighs. The other two started their kisses at her wrists and worked inward.

Shenna merely watched me as they kissed her.

This is sarding awkward, I thought.

Be careful, Dove.

Shock buzzed through me. Quinn's voice in my head nearly made me fall over. I felt a hand on my waist and my hand automatically went down to cover it. I could feel him!

Holy sarding hell.

You have the world's worst timing! I thought, as I stroked the back of his hand.

Are you joking? I came back just in time for an orgy, he laughed in my mind.

I turned to look up at him. His hands were on my waist, and though he laughed, his eyes were full of tears.

My chest tightened and my eyes drank in the sight of him hungrily. For the first time in nearly a week, I could see him. His pointed ears, his dark hair, his naughty grin. I pressed my lips together. *That wish cost too much.*

But he gave me a slight head shake. *Let's think of other things.*

He was right. We had an audience. I had to stay focused.

I turned my head back to Shenna, but thought, *I love you.*

I love you, too, but be aware. I recognize one of them. He was originally from Lored. He's another mind-speaker.

Should I say hello? Maybe tell him we've got some open positions in Evaness? I pictured myself opening my legs like Shenna was, winking.

Quinn pictured hitting me over the head with a rotten fish.

One of the fairy men kissing Shenna's thighs grinned.

Calm down, I was only joking, I told Quinn. *But I found you,* I told fairy man, with a mental image of myself putting my hands on my hips and shaking my head at him.

The fairy only grinned wider. I assumed that meant he heard me.

I took a deep breath and carefully thought.

Well, Shenna's more attractive than I would've thought, given mother's reports about her. And clearly strategic.

I maintained eye contact with her as the mind-speaker dove under her skirt, his intent clear.

Does she do this to all visitors? I asked as I held eye contact with her. It felt a bit like the staring contests I'd had as a child.

She hasn't had visitors since the last Fire War, Quinn replied. *Connor doesn't know of any.*

I glanced over to see why Blue hadn't joined in our mental conversation.

Blue's eyes were not focused on Shenna's face. He accidentally projected an image of Shenna's nipples, wondering how hard they were now.

Excuse me! I gave him a mental smack, though I could hardly blame him. I couldn't say every one of my thoughts was completely innocent and unaffected.

Blue immediately started thinking of military maneuvers. *Fire attacks. Force concentration, Reconnaissance.* His thoughts cleared and he mentally said, *I know Cheryn did not send an entourage here.*

Queen Shenna finally spoke. Her deep brown eyes bore into mine. And she acted like she did not feel the two men suckling on her breasts, or the nude man I could hear lapping at her.

"How times have changed. Evaness has come seeking alliance."

I nodded, eyes locked on her face as the final man in her foursome stuck his head underneath the back of her skirt and started noisily slurping.

Shenna raised a brow. "An alliance is such an intimate act, don't you think?"

Her hand slid down to caress the shoulders of the fairy who lapped at her most tender parts.

"Indeed."

I decided terse responses would be best. My discomfort would be less likely to slip through.

Dammit. The mind speaker. He'd have heard that.

Oh well, I supposed it was the truth. I was uncomfortable, but it was better than Sedara.

I reverted to the speech that Connor had prepared for me. "We come with an offer of grain and magic."

"I will not entertain any offers, until I've been entertained myself," Shenna replied as her hips began to undulate.

I had worked in a bawd house. I was no stranger to public copulation. But on a bridge? In front of the castle? By the Queen? During a visit from foreign royals?

Everything I'd learned about royalty was about restraint. Control. But as I watched a queen more than twice my age dissolve into orgasm as she stood in front of me, I wondered, was everything I had been taught wrong? Or was this Queen … I cut off the thought and stared up at the clouds for a moment. I thought I saw two quick blue blurs cross a cloud.

Two archers, at least, I thought as in front of me, the Queen pressed her fairy men into giving her two more orgasms before she was sated.

On the last one, she howled and bucked against the fairy mouthing her clit.

I hope my orgasm face is a bit more attractive, I thought, before I could stop myself.

By the time she was finished, I began to doubt whether the show had been all for intimidation. I began to wonder if Queen Shenna didn't have a bit of an affinity for an audience.

Oh, she does, a voice I'd never heard before rasped in my mind. Then the thought of peach nectar, and a hand swiping at a man's chin flickered behind my eyes. A woman's dripping cunt popped into my head—

Hello, mind talker, I said. *Fewer details next time, if you don't mind.*

I heard him chuckle in my head.

"Your Majesty," I ducked my head respectfully at Shenna, hoping we could finally get to the reason for our visit.

Her eyes cut toward my knights' cocks after she was finished. She smiled as if she was pleased with what she saw.

An animal-like sense of territoriality arose in me. I had to suppress a snarling word or two. But I couldn't help myself, I stepped forward, doing my best to block her view.

My sweet tone contrasted my possessive gesture. "Queen Shenna, thank you for sharing that intimacy with us. After so many years as strangers, I'm so happy to renew the bond between our countries." I hoped that's what that sarding was. Otherwise … I cut off the thought as the four fairies emerged from their tasks and lined up beside the queen.

Shenna swiped a hand lazily through the air. "Oh no. You mistake me. If you want something as intimate as an alliance with me, other *intimacies* are required."

I tried to keep my face neutral as my mind reeled in shock.

Is she saying what I think she's saying? I asked Blue.

Yes.

I'd been less blindsided by Jorad's betrayal. I forgot to breathe for a moment as I took in what Shenna wanted from us. A show, like the one she'd put on.

Blue's response had been so curt that I turned my head to look at him. He swallowed hard. I glanced down and saw that he had a raging hard on.

You like the idea of this? I asked. To me, this request went beyond the pale. It was so far afield that it felt like a trick.

Actually, I don't. Strategically, she could have archers take us out while we did that. It's one thing for her to be that vulnerable in the open in her own country. It's another thing to ask us to do so. The idea of taking you in public does make me hot but using sex as a tool and a weapon ... it reminds me of my father.

What Blue said resonated with me. His words echoed in my heart; the way a choir's song echoed off the stones of the Great Hall. Goosebumps formed on my arms as I decided on my next move.

She wanted intimacy. Intimacy. Thoughts rolled through my mind.

I curtsied to Shenna, a rare sign of respect and almost fealty when given from one queen to another. "Your Majesty, I'm honored that you trusted us when you are at your most vulnerable. I, too, am at my most vulnerable in this moment. Floodwaters from the sea are ravaging my castle as we speak. The djinn have stolen an entire province from me. And while I understand and appreciate your request that I be vulnerable and open as well, I think that honesty—particularly among rulers—is as vulnerable as one can get. To be honest with you, I'm scared. My family is all dead or stolen. War broke out the very day I was crowned. I'm petrified that the legacy that my foremothers gave me will be destroyed. I'm scared that the families of my husbands will be murdered in their beds. I can't sleep because I see bodies—those of the courtiers and soldiers who were killed in my own courtyard—when I close my eyes."

Shenna gazed down on me. And I thought I'd gambled wrong. She raised her arm and my heart jumped into my throat. I couldn't breathe, certain she was about to signal her archers. But then she reached for my hand and closed her own around it. "Go on, child."

And I felt the calculation and cunning slip away from her facade.

I took a deep breath and continued, "The sea witch, Mayi–I've sent spies to find out her weaknesses, to no avail. She has the power to create whirlpools that suck down ships, tsunamis that threaten even Sedara. She took my sister already and thought she'd killed me. I don't believe she'll stop until she has. I'm about to go into battle with a creature far more magically powerful than myself. And I have no weapon with which I might defeat her. The only chance I have would come from your undead army. If you would allow some of them to accompany me, I *might* be able to survive."

That's pouring it on a bit thick, Quinn thought. *We're here. And we all have magic again. Not to mention these weapons.* He flexed his biceps in his mind.

I barely avoided rolling my eyes. *None of us can take down ships.*

Faith, Dove. Donaloo wouldn't have told us to seek out the undead army if he hadn't thought it would work.

I took a deep breath and tore my mind away from his. I needed to focus.

Shenna watched me steadily. Then she asked, "And?"

"And what?"

"You could move inland. You could abandon your ports and trade only over land. You could close your borders. You could deal only with Raj. Why face this witch when you know she'll likely kill you?"

Those were all excellent questions. Valid points. I thought long and hard before I responded. "Because I've learned that death isn't the worst thing out there. If I were to curl inland, I'd be letting her chain me. Slavery is worse than death."

"And why not fight her from the air? Why not tempt her into coming to you?"

The truth was hard to hear. It was painful. These were strategies we'd discussed, during the grey hours between midnight and dawn. Strategies I'd turned down, because all of them left Avia trapped in an underwater cave, surrounded by sea ghosts.

I bit my lip as I looked at Shenna. I was certain she already knew the truth from her mind-speaker. Otherwise, I might have attempted a pretty lie. "She has my sister."

Shenna's understanding look turned cold. "Love. Love is a lie. It's a tale told to children. Only grown fools believe it."

She withdrew her hand from mine. "You may ask the army yourself. I formed them after that sea bitch tried to take my brother's life."

"What?"

Shenna raised her brows at me. "A year or two before your mother killed him, that Mayi seduced him. After his engagement was announced, I found the sea witch carving open his chest. She cracked it like a clam shell."

I reeled back in horror. I knew the part-sprite was heartless. But that? That was monstrous.

Shenna nodded. And she accidentally responded to my thoughts. "Yes. Monstrous. I hate the sea witch nearly as much as you. The undead army is free to go with you if they choose."

Shenna climbed back into her litter without another word. She clapped her hands twice and had her fairy men lift her up. They turned and marched away, the queen not sparing us a second glance.

I swallowed hard. I was half-relieved and half-annoyed at the outcome. But at least we had her leave to ask the undead instead of an outright refusal. "Well, that could have gone worse."

Declan bit his thumb at Shenna's back. "It could have gone a shiteload better. The undead army is known to kill anyone who approaches without an escort from Shenna's fairies."

I took a deep breath and climbed back onto Pony. "Well, if they kill us, we can just head underwater ourselves, I suppose."

Quinn climbed on behind me and snuggled up to me.

Don't worry, Dove. We'll find a way to survive. And if we don't, I'll still love you if you end up undead. He sent me a horrific image of me stumbling around as a desiccated corpse. Suddenly my arm popped off and rolled away. Imaginary undead Quinn winked at me and picked it up. 'Mind if I borrow this?' he asked. Then he shoved the severed hand down his pants with a look of bliss.

Everyone's faces contorted in horror then laughter— apparently, Quinn had sent the thought to the entire group.

"You're awful," I shook my head even as I reached backward and hugged his neck. He kissed the top of my head.

I was grateful for the moment of levity.

But as the laughter trailed off, my mind whirled: What could possibly convince an undead army to help us?

CHAPTER TWENTY-TWO

 e rode through the sky toward the desert. Quinn's arms wrapped around my waist, and I reveled in the luxury of his touch. It was something I never wanted to take for granted again. I kept my hand over his and I stroked his skin, just reassuring myself that he was still here. Pony kept our pace smooth and even, despite the storm clouds gathering in the distance.

Declan was the first to bring up the display we'd just witnessed. "Did anyone else find that little orgasm display completely awkward?"

Connor shrugged and called out, "Personally, I thought it was hot. Might be something we should recreate sometime."

Ryan shook his head. "Forcing us to watch three orgasms was a bit much."

Blue laughed and added, "She only went to three because Declan told me she faked the first one. I called out her mind speaker on it. When she heard that, she forced them to give her two real ones."

I nearly fell off Pony, I laughed so hard. "That's what that was? Sarding hell, why didn't you tell me? It was the most uncomfortable experience of my life!"

"Because your face, the tiny twitches you couldn't control, your attempts to control your thoughts—it's a moment I'll treasure forever." Blue held his hands up to his heart, mocking me.

"If I could throw something at you right now, I would," I said.

You have your coin purse, Quinn reminded me.

I rolled my eyes and shook my head. "I've left the palace without coins before—when I was an eighteen-year-old hothead. I don't have time to work my way across this country. Now, I need you cabbage heads to be silent so I can think."

I turned my mind to the undead army. Donaloo had seemed so certain I could help them. But would they help me? Would they know what we could do to stop Mayi?

We might need to wish for their help, Quinn thought.

No! Absolutely not. I just got you back. That wish was even worse than the last one.

We can survive whatever comes, Dove.

I don't want to survive whatever comes, I thought stubbornly.

Well then you need to figure out another solution.

Shut your mind so I can, I snapped.

Quinn laughed. He sent me a mental image of himself stitching his brain closed.

I only had about an hour to think. But by the time Connor pointed at the ant-like figures marching in the distance, I had a plan. I hoped it would work.

As we descended, I told Blue and Quinn, look for Posey. I had to send them both mental images of Donaloo and Dini's daughter—and then explain my meeting with the wizard, before they grasped what I meant.

"You mean he did get it on with a flower?" Declan asked.

I rolled my eyes. "I thought we went over all of this when we started discussing the sea sprite.

"Must've left out that very important detail —a detail that allows me to win a bet with these knob-noggins." Declan crowed. "You lot are gonna have to organize the new library per my exact instructions."

Quinn leaned around me to give Declan the obscene fig-hand gesture.

I pushed Quinn back as I rolled my eyes and said, "Can we please save this for after we survive a war with the entire ocean?"

Ryan scoffed. "I can handle a few fish, Dearling."

ANN DENTON

Declan teased, "I thought you only liked to eat fish, not catch them."

Even Connor joined in the banter. "He loves the taste of Bloss's—"

"Oh! Hello there. Lady in your presence," I tried to remind my hare-brained husbands.

"Pretty certain you're glad we all like the taste of trout," Blue retorted.

"Bloss certainly wiggles that tail of hers like a fish," Ryan added.

I know I have her hooked, Quinn said to all of us as he wrapped his arms around me.

Ugh.

They were insufferable. But as this was the last bit of banter they might ever get, I simply rolled my eyes and let them top one another's cleverness with fish pun after pun.

I tried to close my ears as I steered Pony into a descent toward the undead. They marched along the same stretch of desert I'd seen in the scrying stone. The beach crashed into the shore only footsteps from where they trailed across the sand, patrolling the border of Gitmore.

I dismounted, the legion stretching out in front of me for at least a mile.

My knights hovered above me, and I held up a hand. "Wait there," I commanded, even as the undead archers nocked their arrows and took aim.

338

I held up my hands in a gesture of goodwill as I took a solitary step toward the undead general. I didn't wait for him to approach, worried he'd draw his sword and ask questions later, after turning me into an undead soldier.

The general stood at the head of the formation, a feather in his cap. His eyes were still in their sockets, but his grey-green skin was weathered, and a loose flap of skin on his cheek (that had been sliced open at some point so that the muscles of his mouth were exposed) gently smacked against his jaw in the wind. Surprisingly, the undead didn't smell. Thank goodness. Or I might have ruined my introduction by puking on the general's boots.

I nodded toward him. "Good afternoon, General." I realized Shenna hadn't given me a name. Dammit. I raised my head to look him in the eyes. "Queen Shenna has given me leave to speak to you. And as a gesture of goodwill I offer you peace magic." I shot green peace magic at the general just as an arrow sliced through my shoulder.

Holy sarding shite!

A burn like I'd never felt before ripped through my arm as the arrow pierced my muscles.

Dove! Quinn mentally yelled.

Bloss! Blue's mind-voice cracked like a boy's.

I'm fine, my thoughts back to them were shaky. *But if this is an arrow, I have no desire to feel a sword wound. It feels like a sarding ax chopped me open.*

I refused to look down at the arrow that protruded from my shoulder, though the shaft stuck out in the corner of my vision.

I shot another jet of peace at the general and another arrow flew toward me. This time, Pony blocked it with his wing.

The general held up a hand to stop his archers.

He took a step forward, his black and white, undead eyes blinking. "What is this magic?"

I sopped up some of the blood on my wrists with my sleeves. "Peace magic."

"I feel it. I have lived so long, and seen so much, that most things do not affect me. But this magic …. It feels … good." The general took another step toward me.

"Would you like more peace, sir?" I asked him.

He nodded, and my palms lit again with green light. "May I?" I gestured toward his chest.

The general stared at me for a long moment, then nodded. I pressed my hand gently against his jacket. Green peace magic soaked into him and surrounded him. Behind him, the other undead shuffled and muttered but he held up a hand to silence them.

"I am Enderson," the general said.

"I am Bloss, Queen of Evaness," I replied.

"And Bloss of Evaness, what is it you seek?"

"I want to end Mayi, the witch of the sea. And I want to recover my sister from her underwater prison."

Enderson's eyes gazed steadily at me as I let my peace magic fade. He took a step back and gestured toward my hands. "What do you offer my people if they fight for you?"

"Peace."

Enderson glanced down at my wrists and shook his head. "Your magic makes you weak. You cannot offer it to all of my soldiers."

I nodded. "That's true."

Ryan called out from above. "I can learn to do what Declan did—"

But I held up a hand to stop him. I stared up at the general. "I heard a sad story. That many of you were tricked into joining this army. How many of your soldiers would rather have eternal peace?"

The general studied me for a long moment. "You have no such magic. Only the most powerful magic can put us to rest. A wizard once tried to end us and failed."

For some reason, in that moment, I knew he spoke of Donaloo. My hand went to the little potion on my neck and clutched at it, feeling connected, even though he was gone. "I'm sorry he failed. I'm fairly certain he was sorry, too."

ANN DENTON

I pulled out my coin purse and took out the single red flower that Dini had given me. I handed it to the general. "One of your captains is named Posey. Her mother is a flower sprite. And she's currently guarding a cache of death amulets for me. If you and your soldiers help, I promise to take you there. And any of your soldiers who want eternal peace shall find it."

General Enderson raised a hand and had one of his lackeys march down the line to find Posey. When she came toward us, I couldn't help the small smile that crossed my face. Though she resembled her mother, there was a skip to her step that was distinctly Donaloo's.

Enderson handed her the flower and Posey clutched at it. He whispered softly to her. She glanced at me and nodded.

Enderson clomped forward. "I have a hedgewitch here. If she scries these amulets, then we will help you."

I nodded, my heart leaping in my throat. It took all my years of castle-imposed self-restraint not to whoop like a banshee. Instead, I stood calmly, while my claim was confirmed.

Connor descended and pulled the arrow out of my shoulder, healing me as we waited for the hedgewitch to scry the truth. As soon as she nodded, whispers spread down the line of the undead faster than the wind. A torrent of words whipped around the army.

Captain Enderson gave me a full smile, revealing several teeth had fallen out of his rotting gums. "Queen Bloss, it appears we are yours to command."

*T*he undead could march under the sea, they'd magicked their troops, so they didn't float on the water. They could move through it as easily as the air. So could our gargoyles. We couldn't. They had spent years preparing for undersea warfare. We hadn't.

They had harpoons and spears to use against the magical sea creatures. Half of them had ripped off their own ears to become impervious to the sirens' songs. The other half did so as we watched.

I had to turn away. The sight made my stomach churn as ears were tossed to the ground like peanut shells and seagulls swooped down en masse to snap them up.

General Enderson and his captains spoke excitedly, over one another. They'd only been allowed to protect Gitmore, never to full on attack the sea. But they'd sent out scouts and prepared for attacks. Practiced. They knew exactly where Mayi was located. And they knew about a concentration of sea-ghosts as well.

So, we had a direction.

But then we had to determine how exactly my knights and I could join the undead underwater.

Our solution made my stomach cramp with fear.

My hands trembled as we walked into the sea. I watched the waves part in front of us, not touching us, swishing and splashing as Ryan leaned on his cane and multiplied the air, reducing the water in front of us. The air cut a path through the waves. They were held back by walls of air, but I could see the currents wavering on either side of us.

"Sard it all, Ry, are you sure about this?" Connor asked as we took another few steps forward. The rocky ocean floor dipped beneath our feet. We reached the edge of the continental shelf. We were about to walk down a ridge into the middle of the sea. The walls of water on either side of us grew hundreds of feet high as that ridge descended. If Ryan lost his concentration, we'd all drown.

"Shut it," Ryan growled.

"He needs to focus," Declan pushed Connor lightly. "Be quiet. You have no idea how hard it is to be specific with this magic."

Quinn hopped down a boulder and reached a hand back to help me climb down in my idiotic dress. Perfect for meeting with foreign queens, it was constantly getting hung up on the coral. *He could just switch out the whole ocean for air.*

"And what, condemn a whole kingdom to die?" Declan scoffed. "Great plan."

"I'm with Dec," Blue joined in the argument. "Besides, think of the smell of all those dead fish."

I took a deep breath, to gather my temper. We were all on edge. "One step at a time," I told my knights. "First step, calm the hell down."

I blasted all of them with a little surge of peace. "Now focus." I wasn't certain if my power or my order did the trick, but they all grew quiet as we made our way down the steep ridge that was the continental rise. The water grew around us; first it became a tall blue wall, then a blue tower, then a black sky pierced only by the thin column of air and light that stretched directly above us.

I stared up in awe, heart pounding as the delicacy of our situation—the precarious line we walked—manifested before my eyes.

Ryan changed tactics. Instead of an entire path, he reduced water and multiplied air in a rotating pillar that kept pace with us. It moved as we did, swirling air funneling all the way to the ocean's surface.

Declan talked him through every step of the way and insisted that the column was safer than just forming a bubble within the water around us. Dec's nerves meant he spouted out calculations about how this was safer. I didn't listen, my eyes and ears were alert for attack. But the gist of it was that if Ryan lost control, my giant would try to at least focus above us, letting the water flood below our feet and the pressure propel us upward through the column and spray us out the top, much like a whale's blow hole.

Whatever their strategy, the glimpse at life under the water was fascinating. If we were going to die, it would be surrounded by beauty. (I ignored the undead that tromped thirty feet away through the water. I could hardly see them. And so they didn't ruin the view.)

The water swirled around us like liquid wind. It made little rushing and rustling noises. We walked carefully, avoiding purple crabs that scuttled out of our air pocket, picking our way around bright peach clusters of stinging coral, and traipsing through the vast deserted nothingness that stretched as far as the eye could see (which was mere feet through the water). We walked by a broken ship-wreck and Declan trailed his finger along the rotted planks before he turned to me, a look of wonder in his bright blue eyes.

"Think of how many questions could be answered if we could only study these ships."

My chest tightened. The scholar in him couldn't help but be excited. He was so adorably himself. And moments like this drew me to him. I stepped closer and latched hands with his. "Let's end this war, then maybe Ryan can—"

"Bullshite," Ryan called out, from where he was heaving, sweat dripping freely down his forehead as he placed his cane and took another slow step forward, concentrating on moving water taller than ten stacked castles. "I am not doing this again."

"Fair enough," I kissed Declan's hand and went back to put an arm around my giant's waist. He didn't necessarily need me, but I wanted to be with him. And I shot him a bit of peace as we moved.

I heard a moan go through the water. And our column wavered.

I saw the undead troops duck in slow motion, the water impeding their movements. Our gargoyles simply stopped walking and sat, little clouds of sea dirt swirling around their feet.

"Something's coming!" I shouted.

Just then, a school of silver fish swam right into our column of air. Fish after slimy fish smacked me in the face. As soon as they hit our air pocket, they flopped onto the ground. Declan tripped on a few and went sprawling, his face plunging into the water. Blue yanked him back and Declan sputtered and coughed, his face cherry red.

"Quick, quick, chequered retreat!" Ryan urged us backward in a diagonal, away from the massive swarm of fish.

We stumbled backward, holding onto one another and ducking, as if that would somehow help protect us from fish that went from swimming one moment to falling through our tunnel of air the next. The fish fell like rain, splattering us.

"Well, this bodes well for our battle plan," Blue snarked.

"Shut. Your. Mouth." Declan spat, still clearing his lungs.

Quinn sent an instant reply of Declan tripping and falling on the fish. He looped the image in his mind, until we all laughed.

"Ryan, you kept the column of air. Great work," Connor said over the spat that was erupting.

I grabbed my giant knight's arm proudly. "You did. Even while leading us to retreat. Great work, Ry."

Ryan nodded briskly. "Quinn's right though. We can't fight swarms of fish. Next time we go past, see if you can blast them with peace or something."

"On it."

Blue took it upon himself to point out fish for me. I blasted them as we walked, lighting their silver bodies up with a green glow. Their eyes grew wide and they stopped swimming, just floated upward, blinking.

Blue high-fived me. "Fish down. I repeat. Fish down."

A low rock wall and a glowing glass castle appeared in the distance; it sparkled with different colors, as enticing as fairy lights. As we drew closer, it seemed like the water around us grew even darker, more shadowed. The air in our column grew colder. Goosebumps rose on my arms and I flexed my fingers to keep them from growing stiff.

A shark burst into our air pocket with no warning, all rows of teeth snapping at my face. Blue yanked me to the floor as the knights ducked. All but Ryan, who kept his eyes on the shark and blasted it with yellow light. A second later, a bird flapped in its place, opening and shutting its beak, flapping its wings and squawking, getting used to this new body.

"That poor shark," Blue stared up, watching the bird fly up our column until it disappeared into the sky. "It stinks to be a bird."

After that, Connor went over and encased Ryan in pink light. My giant looked ready to fall over from exhaustion.

I pushed a little peace magic into him, hoping that between Connor's healing and my peace, he might feel a bit better.

I had just wiped my bloody wrists onto my skirts when everything went to hell.

"Sarding figures," Declan kicked a crab out of his way. "Two seconds with my powers and you're already better at controlling them than me. Two things at once, Ry? Really?" he shook his head.

"That was a strange way to compliment him," I peered at Declan, to see if he was feeling alright.

He avoided my gaze. He didn't apologize to Ryan, just shuffled along.

Ryan just shook his head at me, mouthing, "Stress."

I didn't push it. We were all stressed. And if we were feeling it, that meant Declan was drinking in our emotions, feeling them twice as much.

I questioned dragging my knights into this for the millionth time. Had I made a mistake? Was this just a selfish choice? Was Queen Shenna right? Should I have closed up Evaness' borders and simply retreated from the sea?

My heart grew cold at the thought. I couldn't stand to abandon Avia. Blood or not ... she was family.

We kept walking.

As I worked, Quinn tried to coach Blue on sending out illusions. Declan became their guinea pig.

Several times he stopped so quickly I ran into his back. "Damn snakes again! Cut that out."

"Are you okay, Dec? Are they sending you too much?"

Declan just clenched his jaw and shook his head.

I turned to Blue and thought, *You'd better go easy on him.*

I have to practice, Blue's inner voice snapped—sending his thoughts to all of us and making me cringe. *Don't coddle him. He's a sarding man, for gods-sakes.*

"I'm not coddling—"

"You've always coddled Declan!" The vitriol in Connor's voice brought me to a dead halt.

"What the sard?" I turned to stare at Connor. He was the peacemaker among us. Sweat beaded on his brow. The magic rage was taxing him.

Connor spoke so everyone could hear. "You've always had a soft spot for him. Whenever a tutor railed on him, you always got so mad."

"So what? Our tutors were curdled shites."

"He's jealous," Declan cut in, drawing me to his side. "Jealousy tastes like cabbage. An edge of sweet, but mostly slimy and disgusting. Like everything else about Connor."

You're jealous? Quinn scoffed. You got Bloss your whole sarding life! And then, I barely get her, and this asshole joins in—he gestured at Blue.

"Guys!" Ryan bellowed.

The guys didn't listen.

"Maybe you aren't her favorite anymore," Declan taunted Connor

He had his turn, Quinn bellowed in our heads. *Now it's mine!*

Blue jumped into the fray, "At least she doesn't think of you half the time as a sarding pet!" He spit out the words like they were sour.

"Shut the sarding hell up!" Ryan's yell finally got everyone's attention.

I sighed in relief. I had no idea what was wrong with the guys. Thank goodness Ryan still had his—

"She's mine!" Ryan yanked me out of Quinn's grip and lifted me. His concentration on our air column slipped and the wall of water closed in, forcing everyone to stand shoulder to shoulder.

"You selfish prick! I always knew you'd try to steal her for yourself!" Declan yanked on my foot, trying to pull me away from Ryan.

Quinn grabbed my dress and yanked, trying to get me away from Ryan. But all he did was tear my sleeve.

"I haven't even gotten a chance—" Blue punched Quinn in the face.

They'd gone mad. Angry. Like some kind of spell…

Shite!

"Stop! Stop it all of you!" I shot out a burst of peace, stunning all of them. I struggled down from Ryan's arms, ignoring the gashes in my arms. The peace made them complacent. But who knew how long it would last? What was happening? What kind of spell was this? I went from knight to knight, standing on tip-toe so I could stroke their cheeks. We couldn't go into battle like this. Not jealous. Not divided. "We're a family," I whispered. "You all are like brothers."

"Not me," Blue muttered.

I grabbed his hand and shot another bolt of peace into him, until I saw his eyes relax.

Then, with my men temporarily pacified, my eyes scanned the dark water. My skin tingled. I felt certain someone was watching us. But where were they?

In the distance, I saw figures. And I thought I heard a faint sound. A song.

Shite. We hadn't put wax or cloth in our ears.

Idiot, Bloss! I raged at myself.

I turned to General Enderson and screamed, "Sirens!"

CHAPTER TWENTY-THREE

*B*ut the undead had ripped off their ears.
General Enderson didn't turn toward me until
I shot a wavering jet of green peace power at him. Even
then, I think he might only have turned because of the
light.

"Sirens!" I yelled again.

I ended up reverting to jumping frantically and pointing.
That did the trick. The general sent a line of soldiers
marching after the sirens, who fled.

They'd better run, I thought bitterly. Those awful creatures almost made my knights attack one another.

I watched with satisfaction as the troops calmly followed
their prey, even after the sirens had disappeared from
sight. The undead army didn't stop when the sirens
retreated. They kept marching, until they too faded into
the black abyss of the ocean. It didn't matter if it took ten
days or ten years, those sirens would be hunted down.

I felt a bit of bittersweet satisfaction over that.

Once the sirens were gone, my knights settled down, confusion etching their faces.

"They must be able to put you under their siren's spell even from a distance."

"I've read that sounds underwater are different," Declan said. "There's a mer-written text on it."

"Why didn't it affect you?" Connor stared at me.

I shrugged. "Based on what happened, it looked like they targeted you with the song, not me."

We didn't have a chance to discuss it further, because just then, a contingent of mermen riding sharks appeared. The mermen each held a monster's dorsal fin in one hand and glowing orange tridents in the other. They wore chest plates of glowing green armor, and clear helmets that looked like crystal.

The first one of them to arrive was the largest, easily twice Ryan's size. And the smile he gave us was as sharp as the blade in his hands.

I reached back and wrapped my fingers around the closest knight.

It's okay, Bloss, Blue tried to reassure me.

I squeezed his hand. The giant merman speared three of the undead with one throw. Their bodies glowed orange as the sea magic sizzled through them. Their faces turned black and charred. When the merman swam forward and yanked his trident back, those three undead soldiers dissipated into swirling black flecks that settled on the sea floor. His trident had a disintegration spell in it.

That sight made me seize up. It made me wish we'd brought the death amulets with us. We'd only lucked out defeating the giants. How could we fight monstrous magical people in water? I hadn't thought this through.

The adrenaline pumping through my veins shouted my thoughts to Blue and Quinn. *I shouldn't have brought you. This is a death trap.*

Blue was quick to protest. *Nowhere I'd rather be.*

Quinn didn't respond. And I felt a quick brush at my side. Suddenly, the water in front of our column wavered. And the undead were shoved aside as a current rushed past them.

The giant merman's trident yanked backward and then shoved up—right through his jaw into his face. One of the spears poked out through his eye. He floated down in the water.

I hardly had time to process what I was seeing. I had to blink to be certain it was real through the waves, because the currents were making everything a bit of a blur.

Suddenly, a spray of water burst through Ryan's column of air, soaking my face and the front of my dress in freezing wet droplets. Quinn stood before me, sodden, panting, victorious. He held a wicked-looking dagger he'd stolen off the merman in his hands. He tucked it into his belt.

He gave me a wink. *What was that you said about death trap?*

My knights cheered. "Sarding yes!"

They punched the air. They smacked Quinn on the back. Even I couldn't help how my heart did a little dance.

But what came out of my mouth was, "You could have drowned!"

Quinn turned to Blue but projected his thought to all of us. *This speed shite isn't half bad.*

Posey stuck her head into our column of air, her purple petals damp and drooping from the water. "The general asks that you all stand back. He doesn't want you to interfere again."

"Interfere?" Declan pointed. "Did you see that? He took down a *beast*!"

"Yes, I did see." Posey didn't sound impressed. "Now we have to spend time converting him to an undead, which will slow us down. We prefer permanent injury over death. Or complete disintegration," Posey said dryly as she stepped all the way into our column. "Now, I've been assigned to prevent you all from 'helping' again. Move this way, please. "She pointed off to the left away from the battle and sighed.

My knights protested but when the back of Posey's head grew teeth like Dini's, they closed their mouths and started moving. None of us had forgotten the number of soldiers that Dini had swallowed whole.

Posey leaned over to me and smiled. "No man wants to go down in history as being killed by a flower. The men I've taken out who've become undead, they get a bit of a rash from the others. Apparently, it's better to be taken out by a bear in the woods. Much more manly ending."

I laughed, slightly giddy. "Yes. Well, you know, I do have a disembowelment preference list."

She rolled her eyes and her teeth clenched like she was smiling. With her lips rotted off, it was hard to tell.

As she ushered us backward, another group of sharks circled around the flank of the undead and tried to come after us.

Pony, attack! I mentally yelled. Our little group of gargoyles leapt up—or tried to at least. But they couldn't float in the water. Instead, they extended their wings to knock the sharks back.

They ended up surrounding our column of air and doing just that. In between wing shots, I tried to shoot jets of peace at the sharks. I didn't have much luck. Connor ended up having to heal me, since I seemed to do more damage to my wrists than the sea creatures.

The undead army filled in the spaces around us, leaving a wide circle for us in the middle, in case Ryan needed to

ANN DENTON

move our column of air to avoid anything. They set up slowly and calmly, as if they knew exactly what to do, though I suspected slowly was the only speed for the undead.

General Enderson had them build human pyramids, stacking soldiers on top of one another until they'd made a barricade of bodies around us. They launched spears from behind the barricade. Several undead hedgewitches created bright red, boiling jets of water and shot them at the sharks, who turned tail. I watched several of the mermen collapse in pain as burns blossomed on their skin.

Another group of part fae undead used their wings like fins to propel themselves through the water. The fae absorbed the magical blasts that the mermen tried to send through their tridents. The undead fae repurposed the magic in the way only fae can—creating nature. They made jellyfish appear right on top of the mermen, stinging them until they howled.

Posey sat down on the ground and began to draw in the dirt. "Ugh. This is beyond boring."

I knelt next to her. I had rather the opposite opinion. "We're well protected here and very unable to help, since we're surrounded by undead. Don't you want to join the fight?"

"Can't. I'm not allowed to join in magical fights," she made a horrific gargling sound in her throat. It took me a moment to realize it might be the undead, lipless version of blowing a raspberry.

"Why can't you fight with magic?"

Posey shook her head as her hand smoothed over the scribbles she'd made on the ocean floor. "It would be too dangerous for me to use magic."

"I don't understand," I sat next to her.

Declan joined us.

"My mother isn't human. Her race isn't even close to human. In order to access her powers, I have to give up my humanity."

I let the meaning of her words sink into me. "You have to lose your humanity." Something about that phrase reminded me of Donaloo. Something, but I wasn't quite sure what. That memory hovered just out of reach. "What's that mean, exactly?"

Posey gave me her standard flat look. "It means that I stopped caring about anyone or anything around me. I didn't even care who I killed after I ripped out the piece of myself that makes me compassionate."

The memory smacked me across the face. Compassion. Love. Donaloo had said, "A buzzing brain is but dung and flies, the heart is where humanity lies."

My own heart pounded in my chest and my fist rose automatically to cover it. "Your heart," I said just as Posey said —

"I have to rip my heart from my chest. Then I can access my powers."

Part of my mind was a wise old woman, sitting calmly in her chair by the fire as she processed this knowledge. The other half of me was a child who'd seen her first execution. That half of me was sick and disgusted; that part was traumatized shaking and unable to contain it. Posey would have to rip out her own heart? If that was what a half-flower sprite had to do, what would a part sea sprite have to do?

"How similar are sea sprites and flower sprites?"

Posey shook her head, her purple petals waving back and forth. "I'm not sure."

I turned to Declan. My scholar knew exactly what I was thinking.

Declan spoke slowly, thinking aloud. "If you have to take your heart outside your body to access your magic, does that mean you can live without your heart? For how long? If someone took your heart would it destroy you? Does it still function? Or is it merely an extraneous body part? Like an extra limb?"

Posey's petals fluttered and, for a moment, I was reminded of Dini. "My heart must remain alive. In order for me to access my magic it has to be safe and protected. And like any heart, it still needs blood to live and function. If I were to access my powers and lose my heart, I'd want to find a trustworthy host."

I stared up at Declan. "Didn't Queen Shenna say she found the sea sprite ripping open her brother's chest?"

He nodded. "She said he was a sailor before he met your mother."

I started to rock on the ocean floor, scared and horrified. But I nodded. We were on the right track then. Sea sprites and flower sprites couldn't be that different.

Ryan ducked as a shark careened through our air tunnel. It might have crushed us if the undead hadn't sent a harpoon on a rope flying at us. The spear gutted the fish, raining down blood on our heads as an entire line of troops dragged the jagged-toothed monster back into the water.

I stared at my knights for a moment. And then I looked back at Posey.

As much as I feared her answers, I had to know. We couldn't stay down here much longer. Unlike the undead, we weren't trained to battle underwater.

I took a deep, shuddering breath before I asked my final question. "What happens if you and your heart's host are separated?"

Posey shrugged, nonplussed, unaware of how all of us breathlessly awaited her answer. "Well, now, there's the rub, isn't it? You have to find a trustworthy host. The irony of this shite price is that you can't have your heart, but it can't be too far away, either."

"Why?"

"Why does magic have any price at all?" Posey shrugged.

"But what happens if the host is too far away?"

"Did you rip your ears off, too?" she asked. "You can't use your magic."

I felt like I'd been swept away by one of the undertows. I felt like I was the seawall around Sedara, battered by the tsunami and cracking in half. I was horrified.

I turned to Declan. "What if you'd tried to give your heart to a prince, but found out he was an unworthy host?" I whispered.

Declan pressed his lips together and his eyes filled with tears as he said, "Then you'd search for another host, one who could never betray you."

The awful truth pulled me down like an anchor.

Declan and I clasped hands.

"Excuse me," Blue interjected. "I can see you all are having a moment. But care to clue us newbies in?"

Declan and I stood, still facing one another.

"Who's the one person in the world that will never betray you?" I asked. "Whose loyalty is utter, complete, undisputed?"

"No one," Blue said. "In my house, not a single, sarding person."

I turned and looked at Blue as tears blurred my vision. "Your child."

Shocked silence met my answer.

"The sea witch was controlled because my mother stole Avia. And Avia has the sea witch's heart."

CHAPTER TWENTY-FOUR

The undead slowly lead us toward the castle, fighting the entire way. They cut down sirens, mermen and mermaids, jellyfish, and so many sharks that I thought the sea might be empty of that predator. The castle gleamed in the distance, a bright peridot green. It was shaped like a conch shell and appeared to be made of green sea glass. I didn't know where the glow came from —sea creatures or some sort of waterproof torches. But the dancing light was beautiful, entrancing. It drew your eye and made you want to draw near.

The beauty of the castle was a trap. Because inside lived the monster that destroyed without care or conscience.

The undead army shuffled steadily forward. I saw Mayi on the balcony, her white hair whipping in the current. Her shimmering wings glowed green in the light from the castle. Seeing her there in the open was so tempting. But she wasn't my real target anymore.

If I could get my sister away from her, I could stop her. I could save Avia and end this, all in one swoop.

My eyes searched the murky depths. There was an underwater mountain just behind the castle. There. Avia had to be there. She was in a cave when Donaloo scried her. And she couldn't be kept far from Mayi. She had to be there.

Emotion bubbled in my stomach. I wasn't sure if it was fear or anticipation. Probably some combination of both.

I pointed at it and told Posey, "If what you say is true, my sister will be there."

My knights and the part-flower sprite all turned to study the mountain.

Posey nodded. "We'll need a hedgewitch." She waded off through the water before I could ask what she meant.

The undead still kept our group tight in the middle of their ranks as they fought. And they did a great job of warding off most attacks. The biggest threats that made it past them were the cold currents that pressed against Ryan's power and forced him to use all his willpower to keep his column of air from collapsing. We were half a mile closer to the castle when Posey returned, an undead woman missing her two front teeth tromping along behind her.

"This is Lizza." Posey's vine fingers unfurled to point at the woman.

Lizza was short and a bit hunch-backed, her hair stringy. There was one bald patch on the top right. At first, I thought the hair had simply fallen out in that spot, but she gave a small bow and I realized the skin had fallen off there too. There was only skull left. Lizza entered Ryan's air column. And without another word she began muttering a spell sprinkling salt onto the ground from one of the many pouches at her waist.

I'd hardly had time to process the fact that her salt was dry, not soaked mush, when she pulled open another pouch from the many strung about her waist.

Lizza yanked out a wedge of green, moldy cheese. "Each of you take a bite," she commanded imperiously. Her voice had a low rattle, almost as low as a man's.

My eyes flitted to Posey. They asked, what the hell?

Posey tapped Lizza. "The living often want an explanation."

Lizza's eyes widened. "Oh. Yes, I forgot. This spell will help make you invisible to enemies. It's what our scouts are using. I'm also adding a bit of a spell to let you all breathe underwater and give this poor fellow a break," she gestured at Ryan. "Bite the cheese and pass."

Declan took the first bite. From the way his eyes nearly popped out of his head, I could tell it was awful.

I gagged when it was my turn. Blue spit his out and had to take a second bite as Lizza scolded him for wasting her magic.

"Never thought I'd say this, but I miss Donaloo's tablets," Connor whispered.

Lizza pulled out a cinnamon stick and chanted as she waved it at each of us.

Posey turned to us. "Lizza was undead before the army even started. She's been an undead for nearly five centuries. Isn't she in great shape?" Posey smacked Lizza on the back. "She uses her powers to stop her decomposition."

Blue's thoughts suddenly projected to all of us. *Oh my gods. That decomposition is a full body thing, isn't it?* The image of a rotted penis suddenly appeared in all our minds.

Quinn mentally shouted, *Undead army is not an option! I repeat, not an option, do* not *die.*

I nearly choked on laughter.

Lizza waved her stick one more time and it caught on fire. She extinguished the flame with her fingers and said, "Ok. You can step on into the water. The invisibility spell only lasts about an hour. The breathing is permanent. It will allow you to breathe in air or water from now on, because I don't have time to be coming back here every few days or years to fix it."

Years. Shite. I didn't want to need this for years. I swallowed.

One by one, we abandoned the column of air. I was nervous to walk into the water, but when I stuck my hand into it, it felt the same as Ryan's column. I took a step forward, immersing part of my body. But I couldn't feel a difference. It felt like I had stepped outside on a cool day. I pushed my head into the waves. While my hair did float around me, everything else felt the same. I stared down at my hands in the murky ocean light. I waved them. They moved naturally.

I opened my mouth and said, "This is amazing!"

Ryan sighed in relief as he let the water collapse. "Why the sarding hell didn't we do that ages ago?"

Lizza stared up at him. "I was busy creating spells for soldiers who actually know how to fight in water," she said dryly. "Besides, every man could use a bit of work on his stamina."

With that, Lizza turned and disappeared back into the crowd of undead soldiers.

I turned to Posey. "If she decides eternal rest isn't for her … I'd love to have her as a castle mage."

My knights narrowed their eyes at me. I shrugged. "First off, this magic is amazing. Secondly, and very importantly, she can't die. I mean, not unless the amulets work and she wants to."

Connor sighed, bubbles escaping from his lips. "Good point, Bloss Boss. But we need to make it back to the castle first."

I nodded. "Well, we're invisible now. So, let's go steal a princess!"

&

he cave entrance we found was high on the mountain, much closer to the surface than I expected. I should have thought of that, considering that when Donaloo had scried my sister, light had filtered down into her cave. It didn't matter now, but it had taken us hours to find the entrance while the battle raged on by the castle. Mayi raised shipwrecks and brought them hurtling through the water to smash into the undead. But the army just rose up, limbless, headless, legless, and continued to attack.

Her howl of frustration echoed off the mountain. It was music to my ears.

As we slipped into the cave entrance, I took one last look backward. The undead army was scaling the walls of the castle with any soldiers who still had arms. Mayi shot arrows and spears of ice through them, her wings fluttering as she flew through the waves. But ice didn't stop them. They kept pressing forward with ice shards protruding from their chests.

I left the battle, disappearing into a long, dark cavern. I blinked, but the darkness was so complete that my eyes couldn't adjust. I lit the path with my peace magic. Connor and Declan walked in front of me. Posey walked just behind me; her 'supervisory' duties apparently didn't end until the enemy was defeated. Behind her, Blue and Quinn set their ears to the rough rock walls, searching for thoughts. Ryan guarded the rear, a thick timber from a shipwreck in his hands.

Left, Blue told us. *I hear thoughts to the left.*

We took the first turn in the cavern that led left and the water grew colder around us.

"Do you feel that?" I asked Posey, as shivers started to wrack my body.

She shrugged. "Mildly. Most of my nerve endings have been injured over the years."

I turned my head and my hair swirled around my face. I had to bat it away as it floated in front of my eyes. "Ryan. Can you reduce cold and multiply heat?"

Next to me, Posey added, "How about reduce darkness and multiply sunlight? The sea ghosts are sensitive to sunlight."

Ryan nodded but his face was haggard. He looked exhausted as he dragged his injured leg without a cane. But, ever the warrior, he wouldn't stop. Wouldn't quit. He moved the timber to one huge hand and lifted the other to blast the cave with sunlight.

As the passage lit up around us, I heard the shrieks of ashrays. Their glowing eyes popped open as they abandoned the nooks and crevices in the cave wall around us and fled down the passage.

"Shite! They might as well be trumpeting our arrival!" Blue cursed.

"Declan, can you try to suck out some of their panic?" I said as I shot peace at the jelly-like creatures.

But it was too late. Ten merguards swam through an archway on the far side of the cave. Their blue tails straightened in alarm when they saw us.

Shite! Lizza's invisibility spell must have worn off! Blue stated the obvious.

The mermen's tridents lit up with orange magic. And then they attacked.

I redirected my peace magic from the ashrays to the mermen, but only managed to make two of them look relaxed and dopey. Declan soon had one cowering in the corner, shaking and holding his head as happiness drained out of him. Blue and Quinn ran among the rest, using their speed to take quick swipes at the half-fish. Posey unsheathed her sword and calmly walked forward, ignoring a merman whose trident dug into her side. She simply kept walking into the weapon until she was close enough to take off the merman's head.

The battle space was confined. The fighting was quick. It felt like I had hardly blinked before Connor cried out. A trident was lodged in his chest, just above his heart.

I tried to rush forward, but Ryan held me back. He launched his boat timber at the merman who'd stabbed Connor. And then he changed his magic. With a burst of yellow light, Ryan swapped all the water in the cave for air.

The merman fell to the cave floor, gasping. My knights and Posey made quick work of them as I rushed over to my best friend.

I was so scared I could hardly see. Blackness danced on the edge of my vision. He had to be okay. He had to. I had never lived in a world without Connor. Even my early memories were full of him. He was a constant in my life. Even when I'd run, I'd talked to him in my head, in my letters. I needed Connor.

I knelt and put my hand on his unruly mop of brown curls. He gave me a weak smile.

He already had his hand to his own shoulder and was using pink magic to heal himself. He took a shaky breath and said, "Pull that sarding thing out, Bloss!"

"But—"

Ryan reached around me and yanked the trident out in a single pull.

Connor screamed in pain and smashed his fist into the ground.

I smacked Ryan's leg.

"Hey, he couldn't heal himself with that thing in there," Ryan protested.

Connor simply put both hands to his chest and then let his head sink to the floor. His eyes rolled back in his head and his hands lit up with bright pink light. "Go on," he murmured. "I'm gonna be here for a while."

I leaned over him, checking his pulse. "Are you sure you're gonna be alright?"

Connor nodded weakly. "Go. Get Avia."

Declan and Blue offered to stay with him and keep him safe.

I pointed a warning finger at them. "You call us back here if anything starts to happen."

Blue's thoughts accidentally projected. *She looks like a hot tutor right now.*

I narrowed my eyes at him. *Focus.*

Sorry. Random thought.

Keep him safe.

Yes ma'am.

Ryan, Quinn, Posey, and I ran down the passage the mermen had emerged from, assuming they'd been guarding Avia. But the cavern twisted and turned and looped. There were so many offshoots it was a maze. We had to have Quinn speed ahead in order to figure out the right path. Even so, we took the wrong passage a few times and had to backtrack.

The entire time, my heart pounded. My body was on high alert for more ashrays, more mer creatures. But Ryan's blast had cleared the caves of water, and that might have made all the difference.

When we finally came to the cave I'd seen in the scrying stone, a large cavern with a circular hole at the top which let in a ray of sunshine, we found my sister.

My heart glowed the brightest white; it felt like it was lit directly by the moonlight outside. My face hurt instantly as a barrage of tears threatened to overtake me. I had to use every ounce of willpower to shove them down.

Avia was on the floor, her legs splayed out, and cheek in the dirt. Her beta-fish-like wings spread on her back limply. The orange and purple coloring on them formed a limp little rainbow as the wings wilted on the floor. Avia's scales glittered on the outside of her arms, but they were the only part of her that looked healthy at all. In fact, it looked like she was gasping for air.

"Ryan, she needs water!"

Shite! Shite!

I rushed forward scolding myself: Why didn't you think of that earlier, Bloss?

Ryan quickly multiplied a little pool of water around Avia. I splashed through it and grabbed onto her hand. It was a minute before she opened her eyes. When she did, she blinked slowly, as if she wasn't quite sure what she saw.

My hands cupped her cheeks. "Avia?" I asked gently.

"Bloss?" her eyes, now the most amazing lavender color, filled with tears. "Is it really you?"

I pushed back the golden locks that were now her hair, the brunette color they'd been enchanted with long gone. I nodded and pulled her into a hug, so relieved I'd finally found her. So relieved and happy she was alive. I felt whole again for a moment.

But my sister didn't hug me back.

Avia whispered, "Prove it."

My heart crashed like a star ploughing into the dirt, light extinguished.

If she was saying something like that, I couldn't begin to imagine what Mayi put her through.

I glanced up at Ryan and Quinn, who waited at the entrance of the cave, guarding us and giving us space. Ryan gave me an encouraging nod.

I racked my brain for a memory that only Avia would know.

"When you were eight, I tried to convince you that you were actually from Lored. I tried to get you to leave with their royal party at the end of a visit. Remember?" my voice cracked.

Avia gave a shaky laugh. "You let me get into their carriage! I think you might have let me go if Connor hadn't stopped you."

I shrugged. "Not far. I would have said something by the time you'd gone over the drawbridge."

Avia smacked me, her eyes a mix of laughter and tears. "Another. Prove it again."

I took a moment to think and then said softly, "When you were twelve, you remember how you invited several of the courtiers' daughters to your chambers for a round of games?"

Avia nodded. "And one of those nasty girls dipped every one of my tiaras in ink. I ended up with a black line across my forehead the next day—the day we went outdoors for an archery tournament against the boys."

I cleared my throat. "The nasty girl might have been me."

Her jaw dropped. And tears did start then as my little sister hit me repeatedly. "You. Did. Not."

I shrugged apologetically. It was the best I could do. "I always told you that you'd be the better queen."

She gave a bitter laugh. "Well, now I believe it."

We both dissolved then, into a fierce hug—heavy with unspoken words, apologies and love. It felt like sunshine flooded my body. And for a moment, I was content. But we were still in danger. We'd found my sister, but we hadn't rescued her.

"We need to get out of here," I told Avia, pulling back to look at her.

Avia shook her head. "I can't live out of the water right now. She transformed me into this monster!"

I stared at my sister, who was staring at the shining scales on her arms with disgust. Horror crept into my heart. A dark shadow fell over me. I realized … Mayi hadn't told Avia.

Avia had no idea this was her true form. She had no idea Mayi was her mother.

"Sit down," I said, stomach churning.

I didn't want to do this. I didn't want this burden to fall on me. But I was her older sister. I was supposed to protect her and tell her the truth and keep her from all the bad things in the world. I failed. I constantly failed. But I loved her too much to let her keep believing a lie.

I told my sister everything about Mayi, mother, and the heart. I didn't leave anything out.

When I was done, Avia looked as if she'd been hit by a runaway carriage. She stared at me for a long minute, not blinking, not saying a word.

I waited. I tried to wait patiently, knowing that if my entire existence had been turned upside down, that I'd need time to adjust.

Avia's eyes were dull as she stared at me.

I searched her expression for any sign of what she was thinking, feeling, but I couldn't tell. Her face remained flat.

Finally, her eyes traveled over me, as if she were coming out of a trance and seeing me for the first time. She leaned forward and gave me a hug. "Thank you," she whispered.

She turned and her eyes went to Ryan and Quinn. She nodded and floated toward them. She tentatively bowed her head toward Posey, always polite, even when faced with a living corpse. "Thank you for helping my sister."

Posey nodded in response.

Then Avia held her hands out toward my men, waiting for a hug. Ryan stepped forward first. He was careful not to touch her wings as he wrapped his arms gently around her waist and lifted her up.

Quinn was less restrained. He hugged her hard, picking her up and swinging her around. When he set her down, she looked at the jagged dagger he'd won. "Is that one of theirs?" she asked.

He nodded. He pulled out the blade and handed it toward her.

Tell her how I got it, Dov—

Quinn's thought was cut off as Avia plunged the dagger right into her own chest.

It felt like she'd stabbed me instead. Disbelief shackled me. Hopelessness grabbed her whip, ready to strip me of all the happiness that had just been within my grasp. Despair whispered in my ear.

What the sard?! Why?

I had to shove back all emotion as I ran forward, splashing through the pool as my sister collapsed in the water.

Quinn went to yank back the blade, but Ryan stopped him. "It'll make the bleeding worse."

"No!" I scooped up my sister, my hands sliding on her wet wings as I pulled her up and cradled her on top of the water. She looked so small, so young. Helpless. I caressed her face as I held her close. "What did you do?" I scolded.

"You said … she put her heart … in me," Avia closed her eyes and whimpered.

"Yes, but why'd you go and stab yourself?" I demanded, my voice gruff with panic and fury.

"It hurts," she sounded surprised.

"No shite!"

I looked up at Quinn. "Get Blue and Connor down here now!"

Avia looked up at me confused. "But Ryan's here. He can heal me. Right?"

Agony and irony shot through me. I'd told my sister her story. But I hadn't mentioned ours. She had no idea my knights' powers were swapped. She had no idea. My knees nearly buckled.

Ryan splashed toward us and his big arms enveloped Avia and me.

"Sweetie," he looked down at Avia with pity. "Connor has my powers now."

"What?" her face grew pale. Her lavender eyes grew panicked as they met mine. "What?"

I shot a tiny thread of peace through her. I didn't want her heart pumping faster. I didn't want her losing blood any faster. It already coated her stomach. It already had turned the water around us a sickly-sweet pink.

"A wish swapped their powers," I explained as briefly as I could. "Sweetheart, Ryan can't heal you."

Avia's eyes swept down toward the knife. "I — I didn't think ..." her hand latched onto mine. Tears marred her beautiful inhuman eyes. "You mean ... I'm gonna die?"

Quinn, where the sard is Connor?! I roared

He's coming!!! Declan and Blue are carrying him. He's not healed yet, Quinn said back, tersely. *I'm trying to help Blue navigate the caverns.*

Shite. Shite.

Sarding gods in hell.

I stared down at Avia and shook my head. I clenched my teeth to release some of the tension in my body. Then I said, as softly as I could manage, "You're not gonna die. Connor's almost here."

A tiny smile crossed her lips. "You know I can tell when you lie, Bloss. You're my ... sister. Or—"

"Yes, I'm your sister dammit." I wanted to crush her in a hug and tell her I didn't care about blood. I cared about her. But that stupid jagged knife still stuck out of her chest.

I glanced over at Posey, who was watching this whole scene stoically.

"Maybe she stabbed Mayi's heart?" I asked, hopefully, wishfully thinking that somehow, magically, maybe all this blood belonged to the sea witch.

Posey shook her head.

Time slowed as I stared down at Avia. My soul dissolved into a fine mist; it existed, but barely. It hung in the air, a collection of tiny tears just waiting for the sunlight to pierce it, destroy it. How could a world exist where Avia's pure soul was tied to someone so evil? How could the gods allow her to fall? My heart throbbed painfully as she gasped in pain.

She weakly gripped my hand. Her own felt clammy. "It's okay, Bloss."

"No, it's not."

"You said her heart needs my blood, right? When I'm gone, so is she."

No. No. No, no, no.

Even on the brink of death, she shone like a lighthouse. She saw the sarding good in everything.

I clenched my jaw.

"It's a good ending for me," she whispered. "I'm the peace-keeper in our family, remember?"

Avia had always been the water that doused the flames between mother and myself.

"I feel dizzy. Is that a new necklace? It's horrible," Avia tried to keep the tone light. Conversational. Even as her eyelids fluttered closed.

Shite. I felt like collapsing, but I didn't want to let her go.

"Let me hold her a bit," Ryan said softly. "You can hug her while I keep her in the water."

His arms surrounded me and gently lifted Avia. As he pulled her up, her limp hand swiped at my neck, and the leather strap pulled tight against my windpipe.

I yanked the necklace off and stared down at it.

Why the sard had Donaloo given me a love potion? Why not a healing potion? I squeezed my eyes shut and tried to think.

The old bastard was all about love. Thought it was the strongest magic.

Cerena's wrinkled face popped into my head. She fingered the vial in my memory. "He said it strengthens hearts."

I uncapped the vial and shoved it toward Avia's face. "Drink this, now!"

I didn't give a shite if it strengthened Mayi's heart too. I just needed it to strengthen Avia's heart long enough for Connor—

Avia gulped down the purple vial.

My eyes scanned her face, her body. My heart pounded as I searched for some sign that the potion had worked.

I wasn't certain if it was wishful thinking, but her color looked a bit better.

Are they almost here? I asked Quinn.

Quinn didn't get to respond before Avia shuddered in my arms and Ryan fell down beside me. I blinked, confused.

But then I looked up to see Mayi rising out of the water, another ice spear in her hands.

She launched the spear at my chest.

Quinn and Posey were in front of me in the blink of an eye.

Posey stepped in front and took the spear to her chest. She blinked at Mayi, "That all you got?"

The sea witch let out a howl of fury.

I could hardly focus on her. My eyes were on Ryan and Avia, who were sinking in the rapidly rising water. The ice spear that pierced Ryan was in his upper back. It hadn't gone all the way through. But Avia had a little bit of ice protruding from her stomach. With all the blood, it almost looked like a glittering ruby set in the middle of her dress.

Shock spread over me like a thick quilt, insulating me from reality.

Quinn grabbed my hand and yanked me around to face him.

Bloss. Wish! Now!

I blinked. It took a moment for his words to filter into my brain. Even then, it took seconds for me to think of something.

Words tumbled from my lips. "I wish I had the sea witch's heart in my hand."

And then it was there.

It looked almost like a human heart, but for the fact that it was a robin's egg blue. It pulsed once in my hand, and blood gushed out of the arteries that had been connected to Avia. Blood gushed over my hand, coating it a deep red.

I held the source of her power up, ensuring Mayi could see as I dug my nails into her heart and crushed it in my hands. I watched as she collapsed, writhing. When Posey reached back and handed me a small knife, I stuck it through the witch's heart and carved out a section.

Mayi splashed face first into the water. I cut again and again. Manic, single-minded fury drove me. I had tunnel vision. Bile rose in my throat as I sliced apart the witch's heart until it was in pieces no bigger than my fingers.

It was over. Mayi was gone.

She'd never hunt down ships again.

She'd never attack anyone else again.

Avia was free.

As if I were coming out of a daze, I looked over at my sister and husband. Ryan was hunched over Avia, his breathing ragged. Avia's face was as pale as death.

Sarding shite, I realized. I wished the wrong thing.

I rocked where I stood, already grieving as I watched two people I loved about to die.

I realized that if Ryan went, my other knights would die, too. The bonding spell would take them.

Posey put a hand on my shoulder and said, "I'll get them. I'll be right back."

Then she ran from the cave, splashing through the thigh-high water.

I stared at the knife in my hand. I studied it.

I held it to my wrist experimentally. If Ryan and my knights died, did I even want to live?

A hand latched onto mine and yanked the knife away.

I looked up and scrambled backward.

Had Mayi brought reinforcements?

Shite!

I had no other weapon. I extended my hands and blasted the stranger with peace until he stumbled backward, out of the water, to sit on a small section of rock near the entrance.

My wrists ached and the smell of my blood mixed with Avia's and Ryan's.

I waded toward the stranger, arms extended, in case I needed to strike again.

A man with black hair, pointed ears, and bright grey eyes stared at me. He raised his hands in surrender, but said nothing when I screeched, "Who the sard are you?"

CHAPTER TWENTY-FIVE

*B*efore I could blast him again, the stranger stood and ran. He ran so fast that he became a blur and disappeared out of the passage that led to the cave.

Shite!

Was he going to warn others? Was he going to get reinforcements? Would the sea people still fight us if they knew the witch was dead? I couldn't follow him, I'd never catch him anyway, and I'd leave Avia and Ryan even more vulnerable. My heart pounded as I thought of possibilities and waded through the murky water searching for the knife he'd thrown. I needed a weapon.

A sound echoed off the rocks behind me and I whirled, spraying dusky red water everywhere. I had to tell my heart to calm down, because it wasn't an enemy. Posey arrived back, her purple petals drooping as she supported Connor under his good shoulder. His curls were plastered to his forehead and sweat beaded on his brow. His eyes even had that droop of illness to them. She pulled him down the narrow walkway toward the water as she said, "I sent Blue to get Lizza."

"Did you see someone in the tunnel?" I asked, eyes darting behind her.

"No."

Declan leaned around her; blue eyes concerned. "There's someone else here?"

"Declan, I need you to guard us," I spat out, as soon as I saw my scholar. "A man followed the sea witch in here. He was spying on us."

Declan's brow furrowed. "A human?"

"He looked human. Wait. No. He had pointed ears. Part-elf maybe? But he had speed like Blue."

"No one has speed like Blue." My blond knight shook his head, his hair falling over his forehead. He took a stronger stance as he turned to guard the entryway of the cavern.

I hurried forward to help Posey bring Connor over. He looked too weak himself to be able to do much. Every step we took, he gritted his teeth in pain.

I helped set him gently on his feet in the water next to Ryan, who crouched protectively over Avia. The ice shards that had stabbed them were starting to melt, letting even more blood flow from their wounds. They were both also wracked with shivers from the cold.

Connor studied the two of them. "Shite. This is bad. This is worse than I've ever healed." That was before he saw the knife in Avia's chest. When he did, he took a step backward, and might have stumbled if we hadn't caught him.

"Can you blast us?" Ryan's voice was breathier—weaker—than I'd ever heard it. His gaze was dull as he stared at Connor.

Panic surged through me and my eyes flew to my best friend. For the millionth time, I cursed my sarding magic. Why couldn't I have gotten healing? Or something useful? Shite! The seconds seemed to crawl on as Connor's eyes studied the wounds.

Connor swallowed hard and nodded at Ryan. "Guess a blast won't hurt." Then he extended his hands, blowing out a shaky breath. Pink magic streamed from his fingertips and covered Ryan and Avia. But Connor's healing magic didn't have its normal luminescence. It was pale and weak. He was clearly exhausted. I saw him squeeze his eyes shut and push harder.

He wouldn't be able to heal them like this. No one would make it if they kept going like this. We had to do something. I had to do something. I pressed my hand into Connor's back and blasted him with peace. I yelled out, "Dec, take their exhaustion!"

"I won't be able to defend us."

"If you don't, there won't be an *us* left to defend," I yelled back.

I sent another blast of peace through Connor, trying to light up his spine. My thighs ripped apart and I nearly collapsed from the pain. But I kept the magic pulsing through him. And the pink light seemed to grow brighter.

When I heard Declan howl behind me, I knew he hadn't just taken their exhaustion. He'd tried to take their pain, too. I looked over to see him latch onto the rough rock wall in front of him as he screamed. His back arched and his lips twisted in pain.

The pink light grew brighter around me.

I looked back at my sister. Avia looked peaceful; Ryan's gaze on Connor was steady and Connor was pouring light into both of them, one hand extended toward each person.

"It's working," I yelled. "Keep going!"

Ryan started instructing Connor in what to do, how to weave his magic to heal them best as Declan sobbed in the background. Those sobs tore at my heart. And once I felt like Connor was stronger, I turned one hand and sent another blast of peace toward Declan. His screams softened to whimpers of pain.

"Come on, come on," I chanted under my breath. Every bone in my body ached but I shoved it aside as Connor worked.

The minutes passed in tense silence, the only sounds the small ripples of water when we moved or Declan's breathless pants.

When Ryan stood and clapped Connor on the back, I expected to feel relief. Joy. But my eyes simply turned to Avia. We weren't done yet.

My sister's golden tresses were stained with blood. Her wings were still limp in the water. Even her scales had lost their luster. I moved closer to her, now that Ryan wasn't clutching her so protectively. My hand stroked her cheek.

"It's okay to let me go, Bloss," she whispered. "It's okay."

My heart plummeted, like it had been shot from the sky, pierced by an arrow. I fought against that feeling, fought against reality and gravity and the certainty of death. It couldn't be true. It couldn't happen. Not to my little sister. Not before me. "Connor—"

"I'm trying, Bloss!" he snarled, the anger that was his price made his hands clench into fists, even though his own body was too hurt and weak right now to lash out.

But I saw Avia's breath grow more shallow, even as my best friend shoved all his pink magic into her skin. Her eyes fluttered. I grabbed her hand, needing to hold her, needing to touch her, to be with her—

A raspy voice echoed through the cavern. "What the sard is going on? You're trying to heal someone in a pit of blood?" Lizza *tsk*ed as she turned to Posey. "I swear, sometimes the living have no sense at all."

Then the undead hedgewitch whispered some words, took a bite of moldy-looking bread from her pouch, and waved her arms. Avia floated up out of the water, droplets

ANN DENTON

falling from her hair and dress as she levitated in midair. Lizza waved her hand and my sister floated over to her.

She looked at the knife in Avia's chest, and the ice spear poking out of her back. Then over at us. "It'd be easiest if I could make her undead."

I shook my head.

Lizza sighed, scratching at her exposed bit of skull. "Thought you might say that. Come on then, we've taken the castle. Let's get her in there."

❧

*L*izza put another spell on Avia, freezing my sister, preventing any further injury or blood loss until we had her settled into a bedroom. Instead of taking us up through the mountain, she marched down, toward the opposite side of the cavern and led us into the castle via a passageway there. I had to assume that it was the same passage that Mayi had used to find us.

We tromped right through the great hall, mermaids stopping dead at the sight of us. Their rainbow-colored tails glimmered in the light of floating orbs of glass that served as sea lanterns. Each woman had hair that matched their tails. Their breasts were unbound and uncovered, and their plush mouths were open in shock as they watched us. Their eyes all flew to Avia and they watched as Lizza levitated my sister's body up the blue glass staircase and we followed. General Enderson tromped through the room and scattered them, saying, "Don't you all have work to do? Or should I toss you in the dungeons too?"

Lizza brought my sister right to the queen's chambers. I tried not to focus on the fact that this had once been Mayi's room. I tried to think only about Avia. Lizza set her on a canopied bed hung with seaweed that dominated the room. Glowing lights in round glass lanterns floated throughout the space, gently bumping into the walls with a clink and then floating back toward the middle of the room. While the walls were made of glass, they were opaque green inside the palace rooms instead of translucent as the outer walls appeared. Avia had privacy.

Lizza got Avia settled onto the round mattress, turning my sister on her side so the undead woman could see both wounds. The hedgewitch examined them for a moment and then she turned to my knights. "Get out."

Ryan, Connor, and Declan protested furiously. Blue was still off chasing the stranger.

"We can help."

Lizza gave them a sharp look. "No. I'm going to heal the princess. And then I need to discuss some matters that might be sensitive for Avia … female matters."

Declan's eyes went wide, and he looked at me. Ryan and Connor were already avoiding eye contact. "You'll be okay?"

I nodded. So long as Avia would be okay. Lizza seemed confident as she pulled a decapitated lizard out of one of her pouches.

I closed my eyes and hoped fiercely that she didn't try to make Avia eat it. But, in all honesty, I'd do whatever it took. If I needed to hold Avia's jaw open and force that lizard down so that she'd survive, that's what I'd do.

My knights left, muttering about speaking to the general, the captured Mer soldiers, and the castle servants.

I went to sit next to Avia as Lizza prepared her tools. "Anything I can do?" I asked as I stroked my sister's hair. Still frozen, Avia didn't respond.

"Take the knife out," Lizza ordered.

I nearly wished she'd asked me to force feed my sister the lizard instead. My heart leapt into my mouth as I wrapped my fingers around the dagger's handle. No sight in my life had seemed more wrong. But I shut down my thoughts and yanked.

As soon as I did, Lizza clapped her hands. A bright purple light sizzled around Avia and she sat up, gasping. My sister blinked and then reached for my hand. I let the knife clatter to the floor as I hugged Avia to me as hard as I could. I wanted to fuse our bones together, make it so no one could ever take her again. I crushed her into my shoulder as she sobbed.

"Am I healed?" she whispered.

I realized I didn't know. I might not have been supposed to hug her at all. I might have been interrupting a second part of the spell. I turned to look at Lizza. "Is that it?"

Lizza was stuffing the decapitated lizard into her own mouth. She gave me a smile as she crunched one of the bones and slurped the tail into her mouth. "For this bit, yes." She chewed a little more and then swallowed. Then she walked closer. Her weathered face was serious as she said, "But Avia has done serious injury to her body. You shouldn't go around stabbing yourself, child."

Avia blushed and I hugged her to me once more. My elder sister instincts kicked in. "She thought Ryan could heal her."

Lizza rolled her black, undead eyes. One of them got stuck as she rolled, and she had to use her finger to shove it back into place. A horrid squelching sound accompanied that task. "Never expect a man to save you."

Avia squeezed my hand as we watched Lizza right her eye. I knew exactly what she meant. She was gagging inside— just like me.

It only got worse when Lizza dug into her pouch for another lizard. This time she handed it to me. "It'll strengthen you. You've lost a lot of blood."

My body instantly recoiled. I pressed my lips together. "I think I'll—"

Lizza waggled her fingers and made me freeze. Then she stuffed the lizard into my mouth. "Chew," she commanded.

My teeth moved on her command. I tried to make my mind fly to another place as I chewed and swallowed the disgusting, crunchy, textured thing.

Avia merely giggled at my discomfort. But when the tables turned and she had to eat her own headless reptile, I stuck my tongue out at her.

When we'd all been thoroughly traumatized, I searched the room only to find there wasn't a water jug so we could wash away the taste of lizard guts. Perhaps the mer creatures didn't drink water since they breathed it all day. I sat back down on the bed and said to Lizza, "You sent my knights away because you said we needed to discuss feminine issues."

"Well, now here's the issue," the undead hedgewitch plopped herself down on the mattress and looked at Avia. "You've damaged all the bits around your heart, Princess. They aren't going to hold up very long."

My hand reached for Avia's and tightened around her fingers.

No. No. We hadn't come this far and done this much for me to lose her. My breath grew shallow. "Isn't there anything we can do?"

"Of course, there is. It's why I sent those fools of yours away. The good news, Princess, is you can live without a heart in your body. The bad news is, you need to find a host trustworthy enough to keep it."

I stood immediately. "I'll do it."

But silence met my declaration. Both Avia and Lizza just stared at me. I glanced back and forth between them. "What? I'm perfect."

Lizza said, "You have a kingdom to run—"

Avia pulled her hand from mine and said,

"I don't *want* to become a heartless monster—"

I sank back onto the bed. I felt like smacking something, or someone. I wrang my hands instead. "There has to be a solution."

Lizza cleared her throat. "I can help with the monster bit. I've got some experimental spells I always wanted to try on Posey, but the stubborn old bloom has never given in—"

Avia looked up at her, bright lavender eyes unblinking as she studied the undead healer. "If I leave my heart in my chest …"

"You'll end up in the ground or like me," Lizza shot back instantly.

I tried to keep a neutral face, not to let my horror at that possible outcome flood my features. But everything inside me cringed. The thought of Avia becoming undead pinched some nerve inside me. It felt wrong.

I glanced over at my sister, who was handling the news with more grace than I would have.

"Then I don't have much choice," Avia responded. "I'll have to find someone to …" her hand went to her chest.

I nodded. "Well, let's get back to Evaness and we'll figure it out."

Lizza laughed, the scratchy sound echoing in the green glass room. "She can't leave the sea!"

I looked around. The castle … it was a castle. But it was a stranger's castle. That witch's castle. The woman who'd kidnapped her. It wasn't home.

"She can't leave the sea, ever?"

Lizza shook her head. "Unless she has a powerful enchantment."

"Disguise spell won't work?"

"Disguise spells don't change what you breathe," Lizza retorted.

Avia looked stunned. "I have to stay like this?"

Lizza rolled her eyes. "I have to stay the most beautiful and powerful being under the sea? Try again. You won't get any pity from me, Princess. You're a queen down here now, you realize. With Mayi gone …"

Avia and I exchanged shocked glances. I'd known that the mer creatures considered themselves their own kingdom. I hadn't realized they considered Mayi their queen.

"Now, why don't you two sleep on things? We can talk about destiny in the morning." She walked toward the door as she spoke.

I gathered Avia into a hug. Her eyes welled up. This was too much. I wished I had a shield and a freezing spell and a magical genius who could take all of this away from Avia and put it onto me instead.

My sister was only eighteen. She didn't deserve this. Didn't need this. Couldn't handle this.

Sarding hell. I hugged her closer. I'd never felt more powerless. I opened my mouth and turned toward the undead hedgewitch, about to demand that she spend the night brainstorming solutions with me so that we could spare Avia.

But Lizza grabbed a bit of dirt from one of her pouches and tossed it toward us. Avia fell backward, eyes closed, sleep upon us both before I could say another word.

The next morning, everyone was feeling better and we gathered in the royal sitting room for breakfast, just outside Avia's bedroom. Apparently, Lizza had found my knights and given them the same enchanted dirt sleep. Only, she'd let them fall over on Avia's floor instead of having them climb into a bed somewhere first.

General Enderson joined us for breakfast, reporting that the castle was secure, the mer creatures seemed to accept Avia's rule, that the gargoyles were running amok out front, stomping all over the place as siren men tossed sea stars for them to catch.

"I've also gathered up those who wish to get that peace you offered," the general said after he slurped up some cooked seaweed. "The others will head home today. Except for Posey, of course." Enderson nodded toward Avia. "Got a half-flower sprite in the ranks. She'd like to stay and help for a bit, she says. Says there's a bit of half-sprite stuff that you need to know."

Avia's eyebrows lifted, but unlike me, she didn't blurt out the first thing that came into her head. She smiled. "That sounds wonderful."

Wonderful? What the sarding hell? I leaned forward to talk to her but then an entire group of people walked in. Blue arrived. Posey entered. Two giggling mermaids with pink tails served us a breakfast of clams on a table made out of the side of a shipwreck.

Blue came over and gave me a kiss on the forehead. Then pulled out a chair carved out of orange sea sponge and sat, saying, "Couldn't find your spy." He shoved aside a candelabra that somehow magically danced with flames as he grabbed a platter of clams and dragged it closer to himself. He ate ravenously.

My other knights immediately pelted me with questions. We hadn't discussed the stranger in the aftermath of everything.

I set down my clam gently and thought, ignoring their words as Blue projected my request yesterday to the rest of them.

My mind felt heavy as I tried to think about it. Everything had happened so fast. Had I really seen someone? Or had I just imagined it? I tried to remember the man from yesterday, to pull up his image in my head. But I couldn't. I sighed and set my hand on Blue's. "I'm sorry. I think … maybe I …"

He put his hand over mine and leaned in. He kissed my cheek. "Don't worry, Bloss. We were all at our wit's end yesterday."

When I turned back to the conversation at the table, Avia and Declan were having a heated debate.

"I will not use you or any of the knights. You all belong with Bloss. Besides, I'm eighteen. I'm not a child." Avia glared at him.

"I'm not saying—"

Avia interrupted Declan and turned to me. "Weren't you always saying I'd make a great queen?"

I hesitated, but seeing the fury color her cheeks, I quickly tried to appease her. "Well, yes."

"Well, welcome to my realm." She lifted her hands. "I'm stuck here—due to a shite need to breathe water—so I've decided, may as well rule the place."

We all erupted into laughter.

But Avia stood. "I'm serious. I thought over what Lizza said. This is my birthright. I might not have known it before, but now I do." Her wings fanned out behind her, gorgeous and translucent, with just streaks of orange and purple. Her scales glinted in the glowing lights. In that moment, she looked more than royal. She looked magical.

But she was my little sister. She hadn't known until last night that she had any power at all. She hadn't trained all her life. She had no idea what she was getting into.

"Avia," I told her, "Trust me, you don't want to be queen."

My little sister narrowed her eyes. "Don't tell me what to do, Bloss. If I want to be queen, I'll be queen."

And with that, my sister turned and fluttered her wings through the door, which she slammed shut behind her.

Declan cocked his head and looked at me over his bowl of crab legs. "Was that a teenage temper tantrum or was she serious?"

I stared at the slammed door. "I don't know."

❧

*A*via somehow convinced the guards to kick us out the following day. I don't know how she got them wrapped around her winged fins so quickly. But she watched as they escorted us to the door. Posey and Lizza stood beside her, supporting her as she gave us the boot.

"Thank you kindly for visiting. But I have a kingdom to get in order. As do you."

"We rescued you!" I protested, as the short dress the sea creatures had lent me floated up around my thighs. I shoved the lacy mess back down, irritated that I looked like I was in my underthings, irritated that my younger sister was trying to get rid of me.

"Yes, thank you. That rescue will be considered in the terms of our alliance."

"Alliance?" She had to be kidding. I turned to exchange a 'what-the-sard' look with Connor.

"That look will also be noted," my sister said dryly.

Behind her, Lizza and Posey cracked up.

"What is going on? Did you put some kind of spell on her?" I asked Lizza. Undead or not, I'd rend her limb from limb if she had meddled with Avia's mind.

Lizza shot me a bland glance. "We simply told her we'd lend her our support for a bit."

"And, suddenly, she thinks this makes her a queen?"

"Her heritage makes her a queen," Posey countered. "Her mother ruled before her."

I couldn't help it. My hand smacked over my eyes. "Donaloo would sarding love this," I muttered, as frustration boiled in my belly.

"Fine. Be a queen." I snapped. She wanted to make a foolish decision? So be it. Ugh. I wanted to smack her.

"I don't need your permission."

I bit down on my temper long enough to ask an important question. Something my sister had clearly forgotten.

Her heart. "What about that other—thing? The feminine matter?" I asked, my eyes flashing meaningfully toward Lizza.

"That other thing is now a confidential matter of national security," Avia trotted out big words. Posey patted my sister on the back, and I had no question about who'd fed her those lines.

"Don't do this," I whispered. "Avia, I'm just here to help."

Avia descended the stairs. She looked up at me, shorter in her new form. "I know. But you have a kingdom to run. You have your own life to live. And I've spent weeks in a stupid cave, making countless wishes and plans and promises for what I'd do with my life if I only got the chance. I have the chance. You gave it to me. I'll be forever grateful for it. But I can't waste it. And I need to start now. The *thing* doesn't give me a lot of time."

Then she'd hugged me. And my sister had whispered, "I'll see you again," before she leaned back. Something zoomed in front of my face, and suddenly my vision went black.

I screamed. The air in front of me tasted foul. Awful. Horrid. Had my own sister poisoned me?

But Avia laughed.

And then my knights started to laugh.

The black cloud cleared, and I saw a squid hovering next to Avia. Its nasty tentacles fluttered in the current. "That," she smiled smugly at me, "is for the ink you put on my tiara."

And my sister then sent me off with a face covered in squid ink.

Ungrateful chit.

CHAPTER TWENTY-SIX

I scrubbed my face clean with seawater as we marched away from the ocean palace. I should've been ecstatic. I should have been over the moon. Against all the odds, we'd beaten the sea witch. We ended a war that had threatened to sweep up every kingdom in Kenmare. Against all the odds, we rescued Avia. My sister was alive and well, though Declan and I agreed that she needed supervision.

I left Pony behind with instructions to guard her. Even crazy, Avia was my sister.

Right as we emerged from the water, on the shores I'd negotiated away from Rasle, a merman popped his handsome head out of the water. He pushed back his blond curls and said, "I have a message from Queen Avia. Once the queen has fully recovered, she will send Lizza to you. The witch has told her about your 'castle mage problem.'"

"I don't have a castle mage problem!" I'd groused, but he'd already dived back under the waves. I rolled my eyes. "None of them were my fault," I muttered, turning to Connor.

My best friend stroked my arm and said, "I know, Bloss Boss."

After that, I mounted up behind Connor on his gargoyle and my knights and I rode in silence. We rode on the ground, so that we could keep pace with the undead army. Slow, slow pace. But we were no longer headed to battle, so I should have been able to calm down.

I couldn't. Something agitated me, and I couldn't tell what.

Ryan flew off at one point, to check on the status of things with his soldiers. He came back three hours later, happy to report that Raj's generals appeared to have dissolved into in-fighting, struggling to take his place.

"That's made it easy for our troops to clear them out of Agatha's province. I've also heard most of Sedara's ships are gone. It'll take them years to rebuild, even with the elvish magic. So, they're no longer masters of the sea. Looks like Isla and Raj and that sea witch got what they wanted in the end. Only we get to enjoy it."

I'd nodded and smiled. Our enemies were gone. Threatening allies were weaker than they'd been before. Everything in the world was going my way. Yet, even after hours of riding, I felt like something was missing. I felt like something was off. I couldn't put my finger on it.

I wrapped my arms around Connor's waist as I wondered what it could be. My best friend slid his hand over mine but couldn't lace our fingers together like he normally did. The damage to his shoulder had been so intense that even though he'd worked with Ryan multiple times on healing it—even though Lizza had tried to heal it—his arm was still not fully functional. He could only lift his left arm halfway, and he could no longer curl his hand into a full fist. My best friend never said anything, but when I asked Declan how he was feeling, my scholar had responded, "He tastes like exhaustion. Like porridge."

"Why does exhaustion taste like porridge?" I asked.

My scholar ran his hands through his blond hair and sighed. "Why does sarcasm taste like salt? I'm not sure, Peace."

Declan had exhaustion written over his face as well. All my knights did. So, I ended our conversation as my eyes scanned the horizon, searching for the hedgewitch lodge that was our destination.

We landed and dismounted

My eyes squinted. I rubbed them. I squinted again into the distance. I thought I saw something streak through the tall dead grass.

I turned to Blue, who rode a gargoyle on my right. "Did you see that?" Blue stared as I pointed and said, "It looks like the grass moved."

Blue's eyes narrowed. *I hear thoughts. I'll be right back.* He was off like a shot, using his super speed.

Ryan steered his gargoyles to walk next to mine. "What's he doing?"

I shrugged. "I thought I saw something in the grass over there."

Ryan squinted. "Probably a deer or something."

"You're right. I'm probably just paranoid after all the fighting we've done."

But when the air rustled around our feet and Blue appeared in front of me, his hand gripping the collar of a ragged looking man, I couldn't help my intake of breath. My instincts had been right.

I stared down at the man, and his grey eyes pleaded with me as he met my gaze head on. Something flashed in my mind. Some sense of déjà vu. Familiarity. But it was gone as quickly as it had come.

"Who are you and what are you doing out here?" I questioned. My tone came out more harshly than I intended. I was on edge. This bit of land was mostly abandoned. Corinna had agreed to clear it of Rasle's residents. And I didn't want anyone knowing about or going near those amulets.

I eyed the young man suspiciously. His ripped leather pants and the decorative cuffs on his torn white shirt hinted that he came from money. His leather boots screamed it, though they were also discolored and ragged. What had happened? Had the war displaced him? Whose side was he on? Even with the treaty, I didn't fully trust Rasle.

The man ran a hand through his thick black hair. He turned to Blue, rather than answer me. That angered me. He was dismissing me? I had to tamp down on my inner tavern wench, who wanted to kick him in the jaw.

Blue held up a hand toward me as he watched the stranger.

What the hell is going on? I thought at Blue.

He says he's been displaced by the war. He's looking for work. He was born mute, but when he saw our big army, he thought he might be able to find something here.

You believe him?

His mental pictures are pretty clear. A couple djinn attacking a cottage. Nothing too elaborate. Looks like maybe his farm was in Agatha's province.

"Where is he from?"

A picture of a small cottage, of a woman and her husbands, projected from Blue's mind to my own. Cross-stitched above the mantel place was a little cloth embroidered with the burning rose of Evaness.

My suspicion turned to pity. It was my fault this man was without a home. It was my fault he was out of work, without a farm, with winter coming on. I gave him a single nod. "I could use someone to carry messages for me."

Blue responded eagerly. *He's fast. He has speed powers similar to mine. That would be perfect.*

I thought no one had speed powers like you.

Blue shrugged.

I reached into a tiny pouch that Lizza had given me. I cringed as I pulled out one of her headless lizards. They were awful, but restorative. They nearly made Donaloo's old tablets seem like a dream. I handed it to the black-haired man. "I don't have food right now, but this will give you energy, restore any injuries you might have."

The man nodded and took it, swallowing it immediately.

He's very trusting, I told Blue.

He's incredibly eager. Hopeful.

I gave the man a tight smile, which he returned with tears in his eyes. I jerked my head. "You can walk at the back. I'll summon you when I need you."

The black-haired man put his hand over his heart and bowed deeply.

Blue projected his thoughts.

Gratitude and sadness filled the man's mind as he thought, *Thank you, Dove—Your Majesty.*

How odd, he called me Dove.

Blue squinted after him. *That was a bit off.*

The man slowly walked to the back, looking over his shoulder several times at me. For some reason, I watched him the entire way.

Declan's tone snapped me out of my reverie. "I don't trust him. You should've felt the way he was longing for you."

Ryan leaned over and scooped me off the ground. He settled me onto his gargoyle in front of him and held me tight. "He'd have to go through me first," my giant threatened.

"He could potentially just be longing for his family, and that feeling just happened to manifest when he saw our family intact," Connor—always the peacemaker—tried to rationalize the stranger's emotions.

"Whatever he feels doesn't matter. I already have five— four husbands," I said.

My knights laughed at my slip of the tongue.

"Are you getting greedy, Little Dearling?" Ryan asked. "The five—four of us aren't enough for you?"

Declan smacked his knee and laughed. "You did it too!"

Ryan shook his head. "Maybe we're all still a bit tired."

We all nodded. It was true.

Blue was quiet. That was unusual. He usually jumped at a chance to join into the banter. When he finally did speak, he said, "This seems absolutely ridiculous. I've never felt this way in my entire life. You know how I grew up. But I feel like we should trust that man." He glanced back at the undead soldiers behind us. The black-haired man had disappeared among their ranks.

"Connor once told me that he'd trust Donaloo until the man proved him wrong. We should probably apply that same outlook here. We're going to have to hire a lot of new people to restore the kingdom. It's going to require a lot of trust," I said.

My knights nodded, and Ryan squeezed my hips. "I can't believe you once thought that you'd be a terrible queen."

Our talk turned to restoring the kingdom, to the division of responsibilities, to Ryan and Declan's need to work quickly to ensure that we had enough food for this winter.

That monotonous conversation brought out Blue's snark. "While you knights focus on that, I'm gonna focus on the long-term future of our kingdom."

"Oh really?" Connor asked running a hand through his messy curls. "And how are you gonna do that?"

"I'll take care of the heir-making."

Blue winked at me as a playful argument broke out amongst the rest of my knights.

"No, we need the smartest daughter, so clearly, I'm the best candidate," Declan said.

"We need a girl who's strong, I should be the one to focus on that," Ryan said.

"I just want to give Bloss an endless string of orgasms," Connor countered.

At that, all the knights pelted him with whatever they had on hand. Coins, the bags of clams Avia had sent us with. "You ass-kissing scalawag!"

I laughed. Long and hard.

This was why we'd fought. For moments like this. Moments of light and silliness and hope for the future.

The undead had fought for the opposite reason. For an end to the future.

We arrived at the old hedgewitch lodge near sunset. The place had been overgrown by Dini's thorns. I'd arrived and spoken with the oversized flower as she'd shrunk down to a single bloom. She'd been happy to hear Posey had found a temporary new calling, helping my sister.

"You let her know, I'll be here, guarding this place, whenever she's ready," Dini squeaked.

I nodded.

Then I turned and shook hands with General Enderson. "Thank you, General. For all your help."

On my signal, Ryan reduced the house to rubble, and we all worked to move it aside until we found the trapdoor. I'd pulled it open and called the General over.

Enderson had nodded once at me, the flap in his cheek smacking against his face. And then he'd descended down the ladder.

He was the first to disappear in a cloud of dust. Hundreds followed him; the dust pile grew so that it filled the hidden room. Ryan had to reduce the dust several times so that everyone could touch them.

We watched silently as the sun set and night stretched out, until the undead army was gone and my knights, my new messenger, and myself were the only ones left.

Ryan limped over and pulled the trap door closed.

"Think that Queen Orgasm will hate us for this?"

I shrugged. "We can always wrap an amulet in a pretty box and try to gift it to her."

Everyone laughed at that as Dini regrew her thorns and encircled the secret room in the ground.

Then we mounted up, Blue allowing the messenger to ride in front of him.

And we headed home.

We flew through the night, under a magical canopy of stars.

We landed in front of the castle just as the first streak of dawn broke through the shivering blackness of the night sky.

I turned to my knights with a smile, happy to be home.

But my eyes caught the messenger's gaze. And something in their liquid grey depths called to me.

I cried out as memories poured back into my head, like they'd been bottled up and suspended just outside my body.

A cat and a bobcat streaking through the woods, a heated kiss under the portcullis, teasing thoughts, hands, lips. Wishes and nightmares.

"Quinn!"

I ran toward him, tears streaking down my cheeks as I yanked him hard into a hug.

And as his arms wrapped around my waist, my silent knight spoke the first words I'd ever heard from him. "I love you, Dove."

CHAPTER TWENTY-SEVEN

I let each of my knights give Quinn a single hug. I let them apologize for forgetting him— though we all knew we had no control over that—and exclaim over him.

And then I dragged him bodily into the castle, ignoring the courtiers who gasped at my short, lacy dress and exposed legs, ignoring the maids and the servants who clapped and cheered upon our return.

I dragged him straight to my chambers. Gennifer was there, pouring a bath.

She turned, startled. "Your Majesty, the scouts said they spotted you. Or what they thought was you, so I—"

I pointed silently toward the door. And she bobbed her head and scurried out, shutting it behind her.

I attacked Quinn. My lips kissed every inch of his face. I stroked his pointed ears in the way I knew he loved. I kissed down his neck. "I'm so, so sorry."

Don't be. I'd do anything for you, Dove, Quinn's face grew somber as he put a hand on either cheek and pulled me back so his eyes could drink me in. *I'm only sorry I don't have more wishes to give you.*

I don't want more wishes. Not ever!

Quinn gave a sad, half-shrug. *Well, now I'm practically human. I can't give you cottages in the woods anymore.* He pictured the time we'd made love in the Cerulean Forest, and he'd created my dream out of mere thoughts.

My hand traced his jaw. *Do you actually think I care about that? I care about you. Quinn, what you've been through ... I can't even imagine. Knowing we didn't remember you. Not knowing how long the sarding nightmare would last. But know that I love you. From the second you leaned in against me under the portcullis, as our disguise spells faded away. I loved your snarky, arrogant face even then.*

Quinn leaned down so that our foreheads touched. *I loved you long before that, you know.*

I know. Part of me wishes that you'd approached me that day you realized it was me in the market. We could've had a naughty little affair.

I felt his smile against my lips as he gave me a gentle kiss. *What was I thinking? How dare I respect your independence.*

Obviously, you weren't thinking clearly enough. Perhaps I need a new spy master. If I'm the only one who can come up with a plan to have a torrid affair—that seems pretty basic to me.

We could still have one, Dove. Use a secret passage and sneak down to my office. He smacked my ass.

You mean the torture chamber? I shuddered. *I'd rather take a bath.*

He laughed and stripped off his shirt. I paused to admire him, tracing the ship tattooed across his abdominals. *We can try the torture chamber if you're feeling kinky. But I do have an office elsewhere.*

I've never seen you use it.

That's because it's proven more effective to question people while they dangle from a chain. His hand slid around to my hip and he yanked on the short dress I wore. *Damn. I think you should only dress in clothes from Avia's kingdom from now on. You'd look amazing if I had you dangle from a chain.* His fingers dragged the skirt up inch by inch until I was exposed to him. His fingers traced the inside of my hips as he thought, *Maybe I should question you that way, huh? Would you like that? To be chained up while I do whatever I want to you?*

An excited shiver ran down my spine. I bit my lip as I stared up into Quinn's sparkling grey eyes.

If you want to chain me up, I replied putting a little sass into my mental tone, *you'll have to catch me first.*

Then I shoved Quinn as hard as I could and bolted for the bathing room. I yanked open the door and tried to slam it closed behind me.

I turned, smirking, only to see Quinn right in front of me, already in front of the tub.

I'm faster than you, Dove.

Shite, I cursed, but my heart beat out an excited little pitter patter.

Quinn's fingers dug into my hips and yanked me forward.

I grew as breathless as I was aroused.

Quinn ground himself against me. My tiny skirt bunched around my waist and his fingers traveled over my ass, cupping the cheeks. He dipped his lips to kiss my neck and I felt the full length of him press against my core through his pants. Heat flooded me there. And an aching need filled me.

You're mine now! Quinn added a ridiculous villainous laugh to his thoughts and then an image of a man in a cloak with a shadowed face tapping his evil fingers together in delight.

It set me giggling. I reached my hand up toward his neck and ran my fingers through his hair.

"I love everything about you," I whispered. "I love your humor, and your silliness. And your darkness, too."

Quinn yanked my hands down and used his own hands to cuff mine behind my back. *It's no use trying to seduce me, Your Majesty. I won't play your game!*

"Why sir," I said coyly, "I have no idea what you're talking about."

Mentally, I laughed. *I thought we were having a torrid affair!*

We're playing all the games—affair, torture ... the usual. Quinn winked. *Now that I've thought about tying you up, I need to see it.*

Quinn frog marched me toward a torch that flickered on the wall, lighting the steaming bath. Once we were in the circle of torchlight, he pressed my face gently against the wall. He held on to my wrists with one hand and used the other to unlace my gown from the front, dragging his fingers over my chest as my breasts spilled out.

Shite. He bent and sucked one of my nipples into his mouth, rolling the bud with his tongue. Then he released it and yanked at the lace, pulling it out of the dress completely.

He made quick work of tying my hands together and looping the tie over the wall sconce, effectively imprisoning me.

Then he snapped to attention, pacing back and forth, putting his hands behind his back and adopting a stern face. Only his dancing grey eyes gave him away. They sparkled with mischief.

You have no idea what I'm talking about, huh?

No. I turned my head to the side, in mock protest, a defiant prisoner.

He leaned into me. *Look at me when I'm questioning you.*

I met his gaze and an evil smile crossed his face as he let his hands come forward to cup my breasts. *Still don't remember what you're accused of?*

He tugged my nipples, sending a burst of heat right through me.

"No," I breathed, arching my back, willing him to do more.

You lie, Quinn roared in my mind as he used his nose to trace down my neck.

My pulse pounded so hard that I became light-headed. Trussed up against a cold stone wall, sopping wet with warm water, my breasts and pussy exposed—it was the perfect combination. My body ached with need.

One of his hands dropped to my folds and he stroked me for a sweet, blissful second before turning away.

"No, wait!" I whimpered.

Quinn didn't listen. He went to the tub and bent over it. When he came back, he had a pitcher of steaming water.

Tell me what I want to know!

I don't know what you want to know!

He poured the hot water all over me, drenching me from head to toe. Then Quinn leaned in.

I suppose defiling the knights Declan and Ryan doesn't ring any bells?

I started. That was real—what he mentioned.

He shot me an image of Declan and Ryan both panting as they worked my body.

"You know about that?"

Watched the entire thing in your head.

My face flushed as he leaned closer. He grabbed my jaw with one hand and threw the pitcher to the side. It bounced off the wall with a metallic clang as Quinn roared, *All a knight has is his virtue!*

I started to laugh.

Quinn even bit down on a smile. But he was quick to resume our role-play. He held my jaw still as his other hand reached back down to my folds. And then he gave an evil grin as he used his speed magic.

My laughter became a moan, became panting, became begging.

I stared down at the hand blurring beneath me. The sensation was more intense than anything I'd ever felt before. "Quinn, please!"

Please what?

Please let me come. And then make love to me.

It seemed impossible, but his fingers went even faster. And then one slipped inside me as the others buzzed on top. My entire pelvis seemed to buzz with sexual tension. Quinn let go of my jaw and dropped his mouth to my nipple. He tongued it and then bit gently.

Stars. Shocking killer rainbows. My first bottle of Flight. Nothing compared to this.

I screamed, writhing against his hand as he kept going. He didn't let up. He let his other hand sneak around back and buzz against my ass as he forced me to climax again.

I wrenched on the sconce so hard that I accidentally knocked the torch off the wall.

Quinn had to jump to avoid it.

He started to laugh.

So did I.

"That was epic, darling," I told him.

He leaned in and kissed my lips softly.

"Good," he whispered.

The new sound of his voice sent a thrill through me. I loved hearing it.

Quinn reached up and untied my sore wrists. He lifted me up and stepped over the flickering torch. He stripped us down.

And then my Quinn set me in the tub.

He dropped me in and slid on top of me. He grabbed a sponge and ran it over my breasts. My skin came alive at the rough touch. After he'd cleaned me, I cleaned him, paying special attention to his chest. When I'd finished cleaning his body, my naughty knight thought, *There's one more spot you could work on.* He climbed out of the water, skin gleaming, his dick throbbing in the torchlight.

And I went down on him as he stood by the bath.

I lavished kisses and licks on his dick, sucked the head into my mouth. I used the oil by the tub to lube up a finger and stick it into his ass as I worked him.

That brought a surprised and pleasured moan from his lips.

I sawed in and out of him as I pumped his length in my hand.

He started to rut my mouth but cut himself off. He pulled away and then grabbed my hand to help me up. He turned me and leaned me over the side of the tub, kissing my shoulder as he placed my hands on the rim.

"Hold on, Dove. I'm going to ride you."

And then Quinn pushed the mushroom tip of his dick into me. The second it slid over my g-spot, I erupted. My eyes closed and yellow streaks flitted through my vision, dancing as my nerve endings sparked with pleasure.

Quinn grabbed my hips and used his speed to ride me. He pushed so hard and fast that it felt like his fingers vibrating against me all over again. It was merely a minute before my legs were quivering, arms shaking as they braced us both against the speed of his strokes. "Quinn!" I cried. "Quinn!"

"Come, Dove!" Quinn yelled. "Come!"

And I did.

So did he, roaring aloud for the first time. And it was the most beautiful sound in the world.

He laughed when his orgasm was over. *I can't believe you thought that. Me roaring is more beautiful than me talking?*

I shrugged. "Talking is just another outlet for you to be a smartass, so yes."

He spanked me and thought, *Let's go Dove. We have a kingdom to terrorize.*

"Terrorize? You mean rule."

He shook his head. *I'm pretty sure that all the courtiers have fled back to their estates by now and are cowering.*

"What? Why?"

Because I told Ryan all the naughty thoughts they had about you in that scrap of a dress, Quinn winked.

I facepalmed. "This is why you don't need to talk."

"I disagree," he said aloud. "I think those dimwits need to hear what I have to say."

"I'm going to make Connor give you court lessons," I threatened, as I struggled into a purple gown.

"Don't need them!" Quinn yelled as he threw open the door to the hall. He saluted the two guards who stood outside my chamber. "Hello, gentlemen," Quinn nodded politely.

Then my spy master walked down the hall buck naked.

CHAPTER TWENTY-EIGHT

The rest of that day was filled with one administrative disaster after the next. Connor's family reported every detail of everything that had gone on during our time away. And while all our spies said that Sedara still believed Rasle was responsible for the attack we'd secretly led, Connor wanted to go over twelve different potential countermeasures we could take.

I didn't get a chance to do what I truly wanted to do, and I lacked a manservant to do it for me.

But I woke early the next morning to see the gods had painted the sky with brilliant swathes of pink. The heavens were bright, colorful, expectant. As if they knew this new day were important. I decided that other items could be put off. I had something more important that needed to happen.

I went down to the stables and had Jace round up messengers. I sent them out on gargoyles as the sun rose, so they'd be quick and efficient.

I told my knights to dress for my first royal decree.

Connor wanted to go over it with me, but I refused.

"This announcement is the end of the war," I said, as I stepped into the bath Gennifer made me. "It needs to be from the heart."

He'd pursed his lips and furrowed his brow, but little, hesitant Gennifer had plucked some courage out of the air and shooed him away.

"Thank you," I smiled at her.

"Of course, Your Majesty," she gave me an awkward bow.

"While I don't want to practice with him, can I practice on you?" I asked.

Gennifer blushed a deep red and gave me a genuine smile. "I'd be honored."

When I was finished, she had tears in her eyes and said, "If I might make a slight suggestion?"

I nodded.

"Words mean one thing. Laws mean another."

And then my maid slipped out of the room, giving me time to think, not realizing the explosive force of her feedback.

The sky had brightened to a smiling mid-morning by the time my knights and I were dressed in our finest.

I wore a black gown to mourn the sacrifices of my people, but the bodice was embroidered with a large, flaming rose. I wore my largest, most ostentatious crown. It made me feel more authoritative. And if I was going to be changing the laws, I needed all the authority I could get.

When a sufficient crowd had gathered below, as well as scribes to write down what was said, and messengers were on standby, ready to deliver my speech to the provinces as soon as the ink dried, we made our way to the balcony.

My knights lined up on either side of me, also dressed in black, also wearing the burning rose of Evaness over their hearts. They all looked so handsome that my heart ached.

I stepped onto the platform that would allow the crowd to see me better from below and signaled the herald.

The trumpet blast nearly made me deaf.

Sarding hell, why do we use those things? I asked as I fake-smiled and clenched my hands because I couldn't cover my ears.

My ears were still ringing when the man finished.

"People of Evaness, I come to you today with a heart full of sorrow for those we have lost. This war has brutalized our country. But we are strong. We will recover. I have seen so many inspiring shows of strength these past few days. And that strength isn't physical, it's mental. It's the ability to endure. My mother always used to tell me about that. Perseverance. I didn't use to understand it. Now, I do. I'm in awe of you. You held yourselves together in the face of evil. You kept faith when the fight seemed like one we could never win. Yet, here we are. Victorious."

I paused as a cheer swept through the crowd. A fierce, hungry, rageful and triumphant battle cry.

The crowd's emotions were as hot and fierce as a fire. And they burned within me as well.

I waited until silence had resumed.

"Some of you might not know the things I'm going to share with you today. But I have discovered that honesty is important. Honor is important. And rare. Particularly among those of us who wear these silly things," I gestured at my crown, earning a laugh from the crowd.

I gave them a smile. And then my eyes drifted over my knights once more. They stood smiling, polite, completely unaware of what I was about to do.

My heart swelled so large I thought it would burst through my chest.

"You may not know that Queen Diamoni, our Declan's mother, tried to steal him back when we went to work out treaty terms."

A gasp went up through the crowd and Declan's eyes flew to mine. I turned and kept my gaze steadily on his light blue eyes. I watched my blond scholar's face grow pink as I continued. "You may not know that she tried to use him as a weapon when the sea witch attacked her gates."

Mutters started in the crowd. But I had only begun. "Despite this betrayal by his own mother, our Declan showed true loyalty to Evaness. He was essential in capturing Queen Isla. Without him, we wouldn't have formed a treaty with Rasle."

I turned to Blue. His eyes were dark, and his mouth set in a steady line.

Go ahead, he mentally told me.

I looked back at the crowd. "You may not know that King Raj tortured his oldest son for many years, turned him into a bluebird, and sent him here as part of a plot to murder me. Despite all of that, Abbas, whom I've come to call Blue out of fondness for that little bird, has proven himself loyal. He has sacrificed himself in so many ways. Most recently, he helped read thoughts, so I didn't blunder my way through negotiations with Gitmore. He helped secure the undead army that fought the sea witch."

Applause erupted and I paused again.

I turned to Connor. He chewed his lip thoughtfully as he stared at me, giving me a knowing shake of the head. He whispered, "Now I know why you didn't want to practice with me."

I ignored him and turned back to the crowd. "Connor has used healing magic to save the lives of countless soldiers. He helped save Ryan midair. He saved Princess Avia from what was certain death. And those are his dramatic contributions. But he's also been our diplomat. He's reached out to Macedon and Lored. He's the one who got the Queen of Gitmore to agree to a meeting. Without his many skills, I can assure you, we wouldn't be here today. He works tirelessly, often in the background, to ensure Evaness has the best possible existence."

Applause took over once again.

I turned to Ryan. My dark giant stared down at me, the smallest of smiles on his face. His eyes were full of love and promises of future spankings if I sold him out like the other three. I simply smiled back up at him and then turned to the crowd as my arm swung to point at him.

"We all have always known Ryan is an amazing soldier. A local man who rose through the ranks. But his dedication to all of you, his refusal to quit, is beyond anything I've ever seen. Did you know he used his magic under the sea? He's the only reason we survived under the ocean. He fought against all that water for nearly a day. Because of him, we were able to rescue Princess Avia. His strength is indescribable. But his loyalty to all of you is even more so. Ryan was injured in battle, and when we offered to use rare magic to save him, he refused. This man refused to be treated any better than a soldier. He wouldn't let himself be treated better than any of your sons."

A roar ran through the crowd.

I waited until it had died off. Then I said, "I know that among you, Quinn has a reputation as eerie. I don't know that an effective spy master can be much different. But let me tell you, this man has suffered, more than I can even describe. He was given wish powers. Every single one of his three wishes went to protect this country. Every single one of those wishes cost a living nightmare."

The intake of breath was audible. The crowd knew exactly what I meant. Of course, rumors had been circulating for days. So, some version of the story had gone around.

I continued, speaking over the whispers, "The worst of these nightmares was that he was forgotten. I didn't recognize him. My knights didn't recognize him. No one knew him. In my mind, there can be no worse fate. To do so much yet fade into the ether without anyone remembering your name. That's why ..."

I paused and took a deep, bracing breath. My chest was weighed down by the intensity of what I was about to say. Nervous excitement ran underneath my skin as I announced, "That's why I have decided that today is the end of the knights of Evaness. I will no longer allow these men who have sacrificed so much, and given so much, to be considered less than me. By royal decree, I officially revoke the Hierarchical Law Seventeen, which states the Queen's husbands are to be called knights. Instead, I present to you, the five kings of Evaness."

꩜

Kings, Dove? Quinn shook his head as he walked to the window and looked up at the moon. His serious gaze contrasted the thoughts he sent to all of us. *I don't know if Connor can handle that.*

Quinn sent us all an image of Connor gnawing on the jewels of his crown like a squirrel gnawed on acorns.

"I'm fine. It's Declan you need to worry about," Connor retorted as he kicked off his boots in my chamber and strolled over to get a bowl of grapes.

"Me? Why me?"

Ryan laughed as he sat in his chair by the fire. "Because you're the one who's most likely to go about making ridiculous laws, like telling people to stop dumping their piss pots in the street."

"Well, that's just common sense," Declan retorted. "It should have been a law years ago."

Ryan rolled his eyes.

Blue asked, "What the hell else are they supposed to do with them?"

Declan sighed. "We need a collection system. It's been on the back of my to-do list for years, but maybe now—"

"No. You have more important things to deal with than shite," Connor grumbled. "We have a winter to get through."

Declan rolled his eyes. "Ryan's got it covered. We worked on grain yesterday."

I laughed as I stood in my robe. Gennifer slunk off away from the bench I'd been sitting on, having finally managed to undo all of the tiny pins in my hair. I sighed with pleasure as I walked over and sank onto Ryan's lap.

His hands immediately started to stroke my hips through the fabric, as if he couldn't help caressing me.

"Well, who knows, Declan? Maybe we will have time to get to that," I yawned. "I mean, we finally might be able to get back to some sort of normal."

"Normal?" Connor laughed. "Raj's territory has dissolved into civil war to see who'll take his place. Sedara's navy is pretty much destroyed, so the most powerful country in the seven kingdoms is suddenly hampered. No idea how that will affect trade, by the way. We were told we could use Gitmore's undead army but not that we could kill them off—"

"For all that Shenna knows, they could have died in battle," I protested, snuggling into Ryan's chest. His chest was so warm and inviting. And while it wasn't soft, it was comfortable. And it felt so good to feel safe enough to sleep again.

"She knows," Connor rolled his eyes and flicked a grape at me.

I shrugged. "Well, what can she do about it? They're gone."

Connor sighed. "I don't know. I'm hoping she's too distracted with her fairy men to think much of it."

Blue went over to the bearskin rug by the fire and plopped down. He stretched out on his back as he said, "Connor, you worry too much."

"It's my job to wonder what those other countries are doing," Connor protested.

I waved my hand. "Dini said she'd grow along the border with Raj. So, we should be protected there."

Declan said, "Ryan can always try to multiply some jewels to compensate Queen Orgasm for her undead."

Quinn sent us all an image of the queen of Gitmore. But instead of fairies suckling her tits, the undead gnawed at her. Their horrid, throaty sounds mingled with her very fake orgasmic moans. Everyone dissolved in laughter.

I shook on Ryan's lap until tears formed in my eyes. "That name still gets me every time!"

Declan said, "Well, she was."

"Best joke you've ever made, Dec," Ryan said as he wiped his eyes.

"Maybe I should stop being a knight and become a jester—"

I cut Declan off. "King."

"Yes, well that's gonna take some getting used to," Connor said. "I'm going to have to get new wax seals made."

Quinn made his way over to us and sat down on the rug next to Blue. *I call the biggest crown!*

Ryan protested, "Obviously, I should have the biggest crown."

Blue held up a hand, "Guys, guys. It's not the size of the crown, it's what you do with it."

Connor pelted him with grapes.

Declan said, "Well then, you get the smallest crown."

I laughed so hard I choked on my own spit. Ryan had to thump me on the back to stop me from choking.

That's why it took a minute to hear someone knocking at my door.

Connor walked over and answered it.

Lizza stood in the hall, several vials in her hand. "I rode that godsawful gargoyle all the way here. I came with a restorative potion," the undead castle mage said, tromping in. Her bare bit of skull gleamed in the moonlight that streamed through my window. "It will help you sleep without dreams tonight and help restore the body."

Just thinking about sleep made me want to yawn again. I felt like I hadn't slept in weeks. With Donaloo's wakefulness potion, I probably hadn't.

We each took a vial and thanked Lizza.

"Don't drink it until you're comfortable. It'll knock you right out," she warned, raising a gnarled finger without a fingernail.

She waited as we all climbed into my bed. My kings distributed pillows and shoved around blankets so they could each touch a bit of me as we slept.

I looked over at the undead woman. Though she looked frightful and scared half my guards to death, she had a good soul. "Thank you so much, Lizza. We desperately need this."

"Oh, I know," she laughed, and her damaged vocal cords turned that laugh into a haunting wheeze. "Don't worry. I'm here to take care of you all. I'm already brewing up a fertility potion for next week."

She said that last bit as most of my kings downed their potions. But every eye turned to stare at her.

She gave a shrug. "What? You need heirs."

Her announcement was like a lightning bolt. Shocking. Beautiful. A little scary.

My eyes traveled to my husbands. We'd joked about this. But were they ready for that? We'd hardly been married—

Quinn spoke out loud, startling everyone when he said, "Dibs."

Connor gave a yawning protest as he snuggled into my back. "No way, I call dibs."

"Nope," said Blue. "I've gotten the least opportunities, so out of fairness, I get to go first. And maybe second, too."

Declan turned to Ryan and said, "Halvsies?"

Ryan nodded to Declan as he tilted a vial to my lips. "Drink, Bloss."

And I did. As I drifted off to sleep, I couldn't help but be excited for everything that was to come.

Because my kings and I had proven we could take on the world.

And win.

EPILOGUE

I struggled to wipe the idiotic smirk off my face as I stumbled into the hidden cottage. It was disguised by sand dunes to look like nothing more than the desert. It was where I kept people I didn't want found.

"You look so happy. It's good to see you looking so well," the stupid young bitch smiled as she opened the door for me and bowed, her dark ponytail dipping low. Her breasts dipped out of her low top, distracting me.

I looked away and ground down on a smile. "Make it stop. I don't want to be happy."

The teenage beauty looked up at me. She wasn't the first to be shocked by my demand. She was the first to keep her neck after her slight hesitation. Because if she failed me, my aching balls would make her pay the price with her mouth. And a severed head didn't provide nearly as good suction as an attached one did.

My hips pumped the air at the thought. I almost lost track of my goal. "The sarding bitch wished for me to be orgasmicly happy *all the time*."

For some sarding reason, that magic forced me to crave orgasms. I reached them randomly, sporadically. I was constantly in a state of near oblivion. I had to fight for every ounce of concentration I had.

Everything made me want to erupt. My hands reached for her breasts of their own accord and I squeezed. The plumpness alone nearly made me lose my head.

I backed away; a thousand years of self-control my only weapon against this sarding ridiculous emotion.

I closed my eyes and my secret, youngest concubine giggled and clapped her hands over her mouth. I hadn't had her long enough yet for her to be truly scared of me.

"That sounds amazing! But you want to get rid of it? I can't completely get rid of another wish. You can't go back to what you once had you know."

The stupid teenager recited one of the oldest known rules of wish magic.

"I know."

"Can you tell me exactly what the wish said?" She asked, tilting her head in a way that made me want to slam it down onto the marble floor.

I restrained myself. I'd already killed three idiot advisors before the rebellion had erupted. I needed this problem fixed. My country was going to shite. "She wished that I'd be happy every day for the rest of my life. As happy as if I were having an orgasm—" Seed shot from my cock even as I said the word. My head tilted back.

But I'd had so many orgasms lately that they'd ceased to be enjoyable. They'd become a burden. A menace. A dangerous moment when someone might attack. Because that sarding bitch had turned me into a joke.

Even the teen whelp in front of me wasn't scared like she should be.

Her khol-lined eyes narrowed. "What do I get if I help you?"

My smile stretched wide. "Your life."

She sniffed. "That's not enough. I wish that once I snap my fingers, you'll never be able to see me or find me or anyone I love ever again. I wish you wouldn't remember me or think of me ever again."

I hated granting wishes. Wishes were for plebeians. As Sultan I was owed payment, I didn't make it.

But I could hardly see straight, much less think. That stupid little bitch from Evaness. She'd get what was coming to her. "Fine. Granted." I spit out. I couldn't even be unhappy about doing it. The sarding wish! My mind was constantly at war with my body. My body was thrilled, content. I was *not*.

My concubine smiled. It was a smile so similar to my usual face—calculating and predatory—that briefly I wondered what her name was. But then I dismissed it as unimportant.

The stupid harlot giggled. "That wish was brilliant. She didn't attack you in the slightest. But she defeated you all the same."

"Yes," I yanked on the girl's ponytail, wrenching her face back. I pulled my hard shaft from my pants and pushed it toward her mouth. "Now say something useful. Or suck me off." My dick throbbed painfully. Even though I'd just come in my pants, I needed to come again. I felt it building, and a stupid, open-mouthed expression formed on my face.

She yanked out of my grip and danced away. "What is the point of that? You already feel like you're having an orgasm!"

I growled, ready to grab her and force her to my will.

But then the girl said, "I've got it! She said every day but not every minute of every day!" She danced over to the window, delighted with herself.

I wanted to kill my advisors all over again. How had they missed that? They deserved worse deaths than they'd gotten.

"Now wish," I commanded.

That arrogant concubine opened her mouth and shook her head. "That was not our deal." She hopped onto the windowsill and snapped. She disappeared. I assumed she jumped from the window and ran.

I didn't bother to follow. I wouldn't be able to see her.

I started to march down the hall, to grab a random soldier in this place to grant my wish. But then I felt a yank around my navel. And I dissolved into navy blue smoke.

I reappeared underwater, sputtering until a ditzy voice in front of me said, "Oh, look a djinni! I must have found a djinni's ring!"

I stared bleakly through the water, pointing at my neck in an 'I'm choking' way.

"I don't think he can breathe."

"Shite! Do I have to wish for that? Will that waste one of my wishes?"

I reached forward through the bleary water, toward the girl's bright colored hair. One had purple hair and the other turquoise. I looked at their hands. Who had the ring? I was going to pop her head off her neck—

"I wish you could live underwater!" she grumbled.

Instantly, I could breathe and see a bit better. We were in the ocean, in the midst of what looked like sea trash. Two sirens stood in front of me, buckets on their arms filled with all sorts of random human paraphernalia. Their breasts bobbed in the current. They looked young.

I bowed, averting my eyes. If one of these sauce-boxes had my ring, I didn't want them to know who I was.

"Ohh, what can we wish for?" One of them hopped in the water, causing my aching balls to pulse. I tried to hide as I came just a little in my pants.

These idiotic mer creatures didn't know the first rule of wishing, did they? I let my smile grow bigger. Half of it became real as I realized they didn't know their first wish should always be, "I wish you wouldn't kill me."

I tried to look kind and thoughtful, like a stupid man might. I tried to imitate the faces of some of my advisors as I smiled at the girl.

"Wish I was a siren," I said. "So that I can please you."

"Please us how?" the one with turquoise hair asked.

"Giandi, you know how," the one with purple hair giggled. "Ohh, if we wished he was a siren, maybe he could enter that new competition the queen's having!"

Giandi clapped her stupid hands as I fought the urge to shove my face into the pussy that was covered only by the tiniest wisp of cloth.

"I wish you were a siren!" she giggled.

"Granted," I said. Immediately, though I had been able to breathe before, I felt much more at home in the water. Scales grew on the outsides of my arms. My pecs grew to ridiculous proportions and my hair turned into a blond mop that wavered on my head.

"Competition?" I asked, after I studied my new body. It was ridiculous—completely sexual—the opposite of what I wanted.

But, getting the bubble-breathing spoonys to wish it had let me realize that Giandi wore my ring on her thumb. The black band glittered there in the weak, ocean-filtered sunlight.

"Yes. She's seeking loyal and trustworthy males—maybe we should make him a sea serpent shifter!"

"Oh! And he can enter the competition and become friends with Queen Avia—"

"Avia?" I asked, clenching my fists as an idiotic smile spread across my face. "I thought your queen was Mayi."

The purple-haired one giggled. "Have you been living under a rock? Queen Bloss killed her nearly a week ago. Avia is Bloss's sister, but also Mayi's daughter, and she's completely and totally—"

"Amazing!" they said in unison, like a group of godawful play actors I'd had executed once.

Giandi turned to her purple-haired friend. "Maybe I should just wish to be friends directly with Avia."

"That's a great wish," I stated. "But I'm having a little problem," I gestured down at my hard dick.

The girls both looked at it and giggled. "Yes, we can have that effect on men."

"Can you wish it would go away?"

Giandi cocked her head. "You don't want—"

"I'm celibate," I lied.

Both girls made a face at that. "Why?"

"Please, can you just—" It had been so long since I'd pleaded. So long since I'd even asked for something, really. I wasn't sure my tone was right. I cleared my throat and tried again. "Please. It's important to me. Can you wish I could only orgasm once a day? It's horribly embarrassing."

Giandi stuck a hand on her hip. "I feel like you're trying to make me waste all my wishes."

"No, I'm not. I swear—"

"He is! He's trying to trick you!" the purple-haired cuntmouth said.

"You have unlimited wishes," I gritted.

"Prove it."

"Make four wishes in a row. I'll grant them all."

The stupid, plush-faced poppet stood there and thought, as if wishing were hard. "I wish I was the most beautiful siren in the sea."

"Granted."

I hardly noticed her face change, but her friend groaned. "Not fair!"

Giandi grinned. "I wish I had my own palace made out of mother of pearl."

"Granted."

The stupid bitch actually gasped when a mother of pearl palace appeared in front of us, resting on top of this trash pile.

"Oh!" her hand flew to her chest and her nipples distracted me again. I tried not to stroke myself and grimaced instead.

"More," I gestured toward my dick. "Please, more. It hurts."

"I wish I had a treasure chest full of sand dollars," the unimaginative wench thought.

"Granted."

The chest nearly crushed her idiotic toes when it appeared.

"Hey, make a wish for me!"

"I wish Laranda's hair changed colors!" Giandi giggled.

"Granted."

The purple-haired girl gasped as her hair flickered through all the colors of the rainbow.

"Now, please," I begged, smiling desperately, even as I palmed my dick through my pants. "Wish it away."

Giandi rolled her eyes. "What a waste. I wish you could only orgasm once a day, had a low sex drive, all that."

Immediately, the pain in my cock subsided. But the happiness didn't. A stupid grin still stretched across my face. But I could deal with happiness. It was a mere annoyance. I couldn't deal with the mind-numbing torture of constant, orgasmic happiness.

Giandi turned to Laranda. "What should I wish for next?"

But I reached out and snapped Giandi's neck. I yanked my ring off the dead twat's finger and slipped it onto my own. Her friend swam away, but it didn't matter.

I was myself again. Or close enough. The smile actually felt sincere as I thought about the evil things I'd do to reap revenge. I wouldn't stop until I'd destroyed everything that fucking shite Bloss loved.

Starting with her little sister.

DEPTHS: TANGLED CROWNS BOOK 4

Depths - Tangled Crowns Book 4

Now Available at Amazon.com

AFTERWORD

Thank you so much for reading about Bloss and her knights! I hope you love their magical adventures as much as I do.

Thank you from the bottom of my heart for supporting my dream of constructing beautiful worlds with words. If you liked this book, please leave an Amazon review. It's how indie authors like myself make it into the algorithms at Amazon so other readers can find us. Plus, your reviews keep me motivated.

XOXO!

There's info about more books, my newsletter, and my facebook group on the following pages. I might be able to be persuaded to write some scenes from the kings' point of view. But, you have to hit me up and make a wish in order for me to grant it! So … stalk me!

ACKNOWLEDGMENTS

A huge thanks to Rob, Rachel, Thais, and Kaydence. Thanks to my cover designer, Carol Marquess at Marquess Designs, and my amazing ARC readers.

And a massive hug to all my readers. This series is close to my heart and I'm eternally grateful to you for picking it up. There isn't a day that goes by that I'm not awed and grateful that you choose to read my stories. Thank you for your endless support.

CONNECT AND GET SNEAK PEEKS

Do you want to read exclusive point of views from different characters, make predictions and claim your book boyfriends with other readers, see my inspiration for these books, and hang with fellow romance lovers? Then join my Facebook Reader Group! I promise you'll love it!

Join Ann Denton's Reader Group

Facebook.com/groups/AnnDentonReaderGroup

ABOUT ME

I have two of the world's cutest children, a crazy dog, and an amazing husband that I drive somewhat insane as I stop in the middle of the hallway, halfway through putting laundry away, picturing a scene.